A Passion
Most Pure

A PASSION MOST PURE

JULIE LESSMAN

Revell
Grand Rapids, Michigan

© 2008 by Julie Lessman

Published by Revell
a division of Baker Publishing Group
P.O. Box 6287, Grand Rapids, MI 49516-6287
www.revellbooks.com

Second printing, January 2008

Printed in the United States of America

Library of Congress Cataloging-in-Publication Data
Lessman, Julie, 1950–
    A passion most pure / Julie Lessman.
        p.   cm. — (The Daughters of Boston ; 1)
    ISBN 978-0-8007-3211-0 (pbk.)
    1. Irish American families—Fiction. 2. Daughters—Fiction. 3. Boston
(Mass.)—Fiction. 4. United States—History—1913–1921—Fiction.
I. Title.
PS3612.E8189P37 2008
813′.6—dc22   2007034664

To the man who pleases him, God gives wisdom, knowledge and happiness, but to the sinner he gives the task of gathering and storing up wealth to hand it over to the one who pleases God. This too is meaningless, a chasing after the wind.

Ecclesiastes 2:26 NIV

1

Sisters are overrated, she decided. Not all of them, of course, only the beautiful ones who never let you forget it. Faith O'Connor stood on tiptoe behind the side porch, squinting through her mother's prized lilac bush. The sound of summer locusts vibrated in her ears as she gasped, inches from where her sister, Charity, stood in the arms of—

"Collin, someone might hear us," Charity whispered.

"Not if we don't talk," Collin said. His index finger stroked the cleft of her sister's chin.

Faith's body went numb. The locusts crescendoed to a frenzy in her brain. She wanted to sink into the fresh-mown lawn, but her feet rooted to the ground as firmly as the bush that hid her from view.

Three years had done nothing to diminish his effect on her. He was grinning, studying her sister through heavy lids, obviously relaxed as he leaned against the wall of their wraparound porch. His serge morning coat was draped casually over the railing. The rolled sleeves of his starched white shirt displayed muscled arms snug around Charity's waist. Faith knew all too well that his clear, gray eyes held a maddening twinkle, and she heard the low rumble of his laughter when he pulled her sister close.

"Collin, nooooo . . ." Charity's voice seemed to ripple with pleasure as her finger traced a suspender cinched to his pinstriped trousers.

"Charity, yes," he whispered, closing his eyes as he bent to kiss her.

Faith stopped breathing while his lips wandered the nape of her sister's neck.

Charity attempted a token struggle before appearing to melt against his broad chest. She closed her eyes and lifted her mouth to his, her head dropping back with the ease of oiled hinges.

Without warning, Collin straightened. A strand from his slicked-back hair tumbled across his forehead while he held her sister at arm's length. His expression was stern, but there was mischief in his eyes. "You know, Charity, your ploy doesn't work." His brows lifted in reprimand, making him appear far older than his twenty-one years. He adjusted the wide, pleated collar of her pink gabardine blouse. "You're a beautiful girl, Charity O'Connor. And I'm quite sure your doe-eyed teasing is most effective with the schoolboys that buzz around." His fingers gently tugged at a strand of her honey-colored hair before tucking it behind her ear. "But not with me." He lifted her chin to look up at him. The corners of his lips twitched. "I suggest you save your protest for them and this for me . . ."

His dimples deepened when his lips eased into that dangerous smile that always made Faith go weak in the knees. In one fluid turn, he backed her sister against the wall, hands firm on her shoulders as his mouth took hers. Then, in a flutter of Faith's heart, he released her.

On cue, Charity produced a perfect pout, stamping her foot so hard it caused her black hobble skirt to flair at her ankles. Collin laughed out loud. He kissed her on the nose, grabbed his coat, and started down the steps.

"Collin McGuire, you are so arrogant!" Charity hissed through clenched teeth.

"And you, Charity O'Connor, are so vain—a perfect match, wouldn't you say?" He headed for the gate, whistling. Charity stormed inside and slammed the door. Collin chuckled and strolled toward the sidewalk.

Faith crept to the lilac hedge at the front of the house and peeked through its foliage. A stray ball from a rowdy game of kick ball rolled into the street. Collin darted after it just as a black Model T puttered by, blaring its horn. He jumped from its path, palming the ball with one hand. In a blink of an eye, he was swarmed by little boys, their laughter pealing through the air as Collin wrestled with one after another.

All at once he turned and loped to a massive oak where tiny, towheaded Theodore Schmidt sat propped against the gnarled tree, crutches by his side. Raucous cheers pierced the air when Collin tossed his coat on the ground and bent to carefully hoist Theo astride his broad shoulders. The little boy squealed with delight. A grin split Collin's handsome face. He gripped Theo's frail legs against his chest and sauntered toward home plate. Scrubbing his palms on Theo's faded, brown knickers, Collin dug his heels in the dirt and positioned himself. The pitcher grinned and rolled the ball. The air was thick with silence. Even the locusts seemed to hush as the ball wheeled in slow motion. Faith held her breath.

Collin's first kick sailed the ball five houses away. Champion and child went flying, the back tail of Theo's white shirt flapping in the breeze as Collin rounded the bases. They crossed home plate to a roar of cheers and whistles and all colors of beanies fluttering in the air like confetti.

Theo's scrawny arms flapped about, his tiny face as flushed as Collin's when the two finally huffed to a stop.

Faith exhaled. *Everybody's hero, then and now.*

Collin set the child back against the tree. He squatted to speak to him briefly before tousling his hair. Rising, he snatched his coat from the ground and slung it over his shoulder. The boys groaned and begged him to stay, but Collin only waved and continued down the street, finally disappearing from view.

Faith pressed a shaky palm to her stomach. She closed her eyes and leaned against the porch trellis. *A perfectly wonderful Saturday gone to the dogs!* All she had wanted when she slipped out the back door was to escape to her favorite hideaway in the park. To write poetry and prayers to her heart's content in the warm September sun. But no! Once again, her sister had to get in the way. Faith opened her eyes and kicked at a hickory nut, sending it pinging off her mother's copper watering can.

It was bad enough Charity attracted the attention of every male within a ten-mile radius. Did she also have to be the younger sister? It was nothing short of humiliating! Faith plunked her hands on her hips and looked up. *Really, Lord, she's sixteen to my eighteen and fends off men like a mare swishing flies. Is that really necessary?* She waved her hand, palm up, toward the infamous porch. *And now this? Now him?*

Faith jerked her blanket from the ground and slapped it over her shoulder. She thrashed through the bushes to retrieve her journal and prayer book, then glanced at the side porch to scowl at the very spot he held her sister only moments before. The impact hit and tears pricked her eyes. She swatted at something caught in her hair. A twig with a heart-shaped leaf plummeted to the ground in perfect synchronization with her mood.

Her sister had it all—beauty, beaus, and now the affections

of Collin McGuire. Where was the justice? In Faith's world of daydreams, she had seen him first, smitten on the very day Margaret Mary O'Leary had shoved her against the school-yard fence. Helplessly she had hung, the crippled runt of the fifth-grade class, pinned by bulbous arms for the crime of refusing to turn over her mother's fresh-baked pumpkin bread.

"Drop her, Margaret Mary," the young Collin had said with authority.

The pudgy hands released their grip. "Cripple!" Margaret Mary's hateful slur had hissed in Faith's ears as she plopped to the ground, the steel braces on her thin legs clanking as she fell. The girl's sneer dissolved into a smile when she gazed up at Collin, her ample cheeks puffing into small pink balloons. "Sorry!" she said in a shy voice. With a duck of her head, she wobbled off, leaving Faith in a heap. Bits of bread, now dusted with dirt, clumped through Faith's fingers as she stared up in awe. It had been the first time he had ever really spoken to her. Never again would her little-girl heart beat the same. He was tall and fluid with confidence, with an easy smile—Robin Hood, defending the weak.

"Did she hurt you?" he had asked, extending his arm.

The gentleness in his eyes stilled her. She shook her head and opened her hand to reveal a mangled piece of bread. Without thinking, she tried to blow off the dirt but misted it with saliva instead. "I don't suppose you want some?"

The grin would be branded in her brain forever.

"That's okay, Little Bit," he said with a sparkle in his eye. "I'll just help myself to some of Margaret Mary's."

Faith's mind jolted back to the present. She blinked at the lonely porch and sniffed. Jutting her chin in the air, she flipped a russet strand of hair from her eyes. "I refuse to entertain notions of Collin McGuire," she vowed. Her lips pressed into a tight line. *It's just a crying shame Mother hadn't found them first!*

As if shocked at her thought, the sun crept behind a billow of clouds, washing her in cool shadows. She crossed her arms and glowered at the sky. "Yes, I know, I'm supposed to be taking every thought captive. But it's not all that easy, you know."

A curl from her halfhearted chignon fluttered into her face. She reached to yank the comb from her hair, then shook her head until the wild mane tumbled down her back. Hiking her brown gingham skirt to her knees, she ignored the curious stares of children and raced down Donovan Street.

She was almost oblivious to the faint limp in her stride, the only mark of her childhood bout with polio. Some of the children still laughed at the halting way she walked and ran, but Faith didn't care. If anything, it only made her chin lift higher and her smile brighter. That slight hitch in her gait—that precious, wonderful gimp—was daily proof she had escaped paralysis or worse. She needed no reminding that countless children had perished in the Massachusetts polio epidemic of 1907, her own twin sister among them. She shuddered at the memory while her pace slowed. God had heard the prayers of her parents—or at least half. Only Faith had survived. And more than survived—she'd never need braces again.

Masking her somber mood with a smile, she flitted by the perfectly groomed three-decker homes that so typified the Southie neighborhood of Boston. She hurried beneath a canopy of trees where mothers chatted and toddlers played peekaboo around their petticoats. A tiny terrier yipped and danced in circles, coaxing a grin to her lips, while little girls played hopscotch on cobblestone streets dappled with sunlight.

In the tranquil scene, Faith saw no hint of impending

troubles, no telltale evidence of "the Great War" raging in a far-off land across the sea. But the qualms of concern were there all the same. Insidious, filtering into their lives like a patchy gloom descending at will—in hushed conversations over back fences or in distracted stares and wrinkled brows. The question was always the same: would America go to war? One by one, the neutrality of European countries toppled like dominoes. Romania, who had entered the war with the Allies, was quickly overrun by German forces. Now, within mere days, Italy had declared war on Germany as well, sucked into the vortex of hate known as World War I. Would America be next? Faith shivered at the thought and then gasped when she nearly collided with a freckled boy darting out of Hammond's confectionary.

"Sorry, miss," he muttered as he clutched a box of Cracker Jack against plaid knickers.

"No, it's my fault." She rumpled his hair. He smiled shyly, breaking through her somber mood. Flashing a gap-toothed grin, he flew off to join his friends. Faith laughed and rounded the corner, then sprinted into O'Reilly Park. She breathed in the clean, crisp air thick with the scent of honeysuckle, then exhaled and felt the tension drift from her body.

Oh, how she loved this neighborhood! This was home, her haven, her own little place of belonging. She loved everything about it, from the dirty-faced urchins lost in their games of stickball, to the revelry of neighborhood pubs whose music floated on the night breeze into the wee hours of the morning. This was the soul of Irish Boston, this south end of the city, a glorious piece of St. Patrick's Isle in the very heart of America. And to Faith, not unlike a large Irish family—brash, bustling, and brimming with life.

Out of breath, she choked to a stop at a wall of over-grown forsythia bushes that sheltered her from view. Emptying her arms, she snapped the blanket in the air and positioned it perfectly, then smoothed the wrinkles before tossing her journal and prayer book to the edge. She kicked off her shoes and flopped belly down, popping a pencil between her teeth. Thoughts of Collin McGuire suddenly blinked in her brain like a dozen fireflies on a summer night. Her teeth sank into the soft wood of the pencil. She tasted lead and spit.

No! I don't want to think of him. Not anymore. And especially not with her. Out of the corner of her eye, she glimpsed the fluttering pages of her prayer book, conspicuous as it lay open at the edge of the blanket. Her chest heaved a sigh. *I've gone and done it again, haven't I?* She glanced up, her lips quirking into a shaky smile. *People always seem so taken with my green eyes, but I don't suppose "green with envy" is too appealing, is it? I'll get this right, I promise. In the meantime, please forgive me?* She breathed in deeply, taking air like a parched person gulping cool water. Her final prayer drifted out on a quiet sigh. *And yes, Lord, please bless my sister.*

She reached for her journal and flipped it open, staring hard at a page she'd penned months ago. Her vision suddenly blurred, and she blinked, a tear plunking on the paper. *Collin.* She traced his name with her finger. It swam before her in a pool of ink.

Dreams. Silly, adolescent dreams, that's all they were. She had no patience for dreamers. Not anymore. After years of pining over something she could never have, she would choose to embrace the cold comfort of reality instead. No more daydreams of his smile, no more journal entries with his name, no more prayers for the impossible. She would not allow it.

She flipped the page over and closed her eyes, but it only produced a flood of memories. Memories of a gangly high school freshman, notebook in hand and heat in her cheeks, trembling on the threshold of the St. Mary's *Gazette*. She could still see him looking up from the table, a pencil in hand and another wedged behind his ear. He had stared, assessing her over a stack of books.

"Uh . . . Mrs. Mallory said . . . well, I . . . I mean she said that I was to be on the paper, so I—"

Recognition dawned. His eyes softened and crinkled at the corners just a smidge before that slow smile eased across his lips. "Little Bit! So, you're the young Emily Dickinson Mrs. Mallory's been going on about. Well, I am impressed—we've never had a freshman on the staff before. Mrs. Mallory told me to take you under my wing." He pushed pencil and paper across the table and grinned. "Better take notes."

And, oh . . . she had! In the year they'd been friends, she'd taken note of that perilous smile whenever he was teasing or the fire in his eyes when somebody missed a deadline. She adored that obstinate strand of dark hair that tumbled over his forehead when he argued a point. And she loved the way his voice turned thick at the mere mention of his father. His love for his father had been fierce. He'd often spoken of the day they would finally work side by side in his father's tiny printing business. McGuire & Son—just the sound of the words had caused his eyes to moisten.

The death of his father a week before graduation had been a shock. Collin never showed up to claim his diploma. Someone said he'd found a job at the steel mill on the east side of town. Occasionally rumors would surface. About how much he'd changed. How wild he'd become. The endless string of hearts he always managed to break. Almost as if his passion and kindness had calcified, hard and cold, like the steel he forged by day.

Faith laid her head on the blanket and squeezed her eyes shut. Despite the warmth of the sun, her day was completely and utterly overcast. How dare her sister be so familiar with the likes of Collin McGuire? How dare he be so forward with her, in broad daylight, and right under their mother's nose? Faith was disgusted, angry, and embarrassed all at the same time. And never more jealous in all of her life.

With coat slung over his shoulder, Collin whistled his way to the corner of Baker and Brae. Slowing, he turned onto his street, keenly aware his whistling had faded as he neared the ramshackle flat he shared with his mother. At the base of the steps, he glanced up, his stomach muscles tensing as they usually did when he came home.

Home. The very word was an obscenity. This house hadn't been a home since his father's last breath over three years ago. She'd made certain of that. Collin sighed and mounted the steep, cracked steps littered with flowering weeds. His eyes flitted to his mother's window as he sidestepped scattered pieces from a child's erector set. The crooked, yellowed shade was still down. Good. Maybe he could slip in and out.

He turned the knob quietly and eased himself into the front room, holding his breath as he closed the door. The click of the lock reverberated in his ears.

"It's a real shame you don't bother to dress that nicely for the good Lord."

Collin spun around, his heart pounding. He forced a smile to his lips. "Mother! I thought you might be in bed with one of your headaches. I didn't want to wake you."

"I'm sure you didn't." Katherine McGuire stood in the doorway of her bedroom with arms folded across her chest, a faded blue dressing gown wrapped tightly around her regal frame. Her lips pressed into a thin line, as if a smile would violate the cool anger emanating from her steel-gray eyes.

When his mother did smile at him, an uncommon thing in itself, one could see why his father had fallen hopelessly in love with her. At forty-one, she was still a striking woman. Rich, dark hair with a hint of gray only served to heighten the impact of the penetrating eyes now focused on him. Before she had married his father, she had been a belle of society. The air of refinement bred in her was evident as she stood straight and tall. She lifted her chin to assess him through disapproving eyes.

"She's too good for the likes of you, you know."

He stared back at her, a tic jerking in his cheek. He clamped his jaw to bite back the bitter retort that weighted his tongue. No, he would not allow her to win. Ever. He tossed his coat on the hook by the door and turned, a stiff smile on his face. "She doesn't care, Mother. She's in love."

"Her father will. It's not likely he'll want a pauper courting his daughter."

Collin shook his head and laughed, but the sound was hollow to his ears. He avoided her eyes and headed to his room at the back of the flat. "I won't be a pauper forever," he called over his shoulder. "I've got plans."

"So did your father. And you saw where they took him."

Collin stopped, his back rigid and his eyes stinging with pent-up fury. He clenched and unclenched his fists. *How had a man as good and kind as my father allowed her to control him?* His mouth hardened. It didn't matter. She would never control him. Not in his emotions, nor in his life. He exhaled slowly, continuing down the shadowy hall. "Have a good day, Mother," he said. And closing his bedroom door behind him, he shut her out with a quiet click of the lock.

"But, Mother, it's not fair! Why can't Faith do it?" Charity demanded, wielding a stalk of celery in one hand and a paring knife in the other.

Marcy O'Connor didn't have to look up from the cake she was frosting to know she had a fight on her hands. Usually she enjoyed this time of day, when the coolness of evening settled in and her children huddled in the warmth of the kitchen near the wood-burning stove. Tonight, five-year-old Katie sat Indian-style, force-feeding her bear from an imaginary teacup while her brother, Steven, a mature eight years old, practiced writing vocabulary words on a slate. On the rug in front of the fire sprawled eleven-year-old Elizabeth, a faraway look in her eyes as she lost herself in a favorite book. Marcy sighed. Soon, her husband and oldest son, Sean, would be home from work, and her family would be complete. She set the finished cake aside and reached for the warm milk and yeast, then poured it into a bowl of flour and began rolling up the sleeves of her blouse.

"I don't understand why Faith can't do it. She doesn't have anything else to do." Charity turned back to the sink to assault the celery with the knife.

"But, Mother," Faith said, "you know I'm reading to Mrs. Gerson this evening or I'd be happy to stay with the children." Her tone sounded cautious as she appeared to devote full attention to chopping carrots for the stew. In unison, both girls looked up at their mother.

Marcy couldn't remember when she had felt so tired. Her eyes burned with fatigue as she kneaded the dough for the bread she was preparing. With the back of her hand, she pushed at a stray wisp of hair from the chignon twisted at the nape of her neck, feeling every bit of her thirty-eight years. She eyed her daughters with a tenuous smile, her mind flitting to a time when she'd been as young. A girl with golden hair and summer-blue eyes who'd won the heart of Patrick Brendan O'Connor and become his "Irish rose." Marcy sighed. Well, tonight the "rose" was pale, wilted, and definitely not up to a thorny confrontation between her two daughters.

She paused, her hands crusted with dough. "Tell me, Charity, why is it so important you're free on this Saturday night, in particular?" Marcy didn't miss the slight blush that crept into Charity's cheeks, nor the look on Faith's face as she stopped to watch her sister's response, cutlery poised midair.

"Well, there's a dance social at St. Agatha's. I was hoping to go, that's all."

Marcy resumed kneading the dough with considerably more vigor than before. "And with whom will you be going, may I ask?"

"Well . . . there's a group of us, you see . . ."

"Mmm. And would a certain Collin McGuire be among them?" Marcy's fingers were flying.

Charity's blush was full hue, blotching her face with a lovely shade of rose. "Well, yes . . . I think so . . ."

A thin cloud of flour escaped into the air as Marcy slapped the dough from her hands. "Charity, we've been over this before. Neither your father nor I are comfortable with you seeing that McGuire boy. He's too old."

"But he's only three years older than Faith," Charity pleaded.

"Yes, and that's too old for you. And too old for your sister when it comes to the likes of him. Absolutely not. Your father will never allow it."

"But why, Mother? Mrs. McGuire is a good woman—"

"Yes, she's a good woman, who, I'm afraid, has let her son get the best of her. Ever since his father died, that boy has been nothing but trouble. He's fast, Charity, out for himself and willing to hurt anyone in the bargain. You can't possibly see or understand that now because you're only sixteen. But mark my words, your father and I are saving you a lot of heartbreak."

Marcy dabbed her forehead with the side of her sleeve while Faith scooped up carrots and plopped them into the boiling cauldron of stew. The kitchen was heating up, both from the fire of the stove and Charity's seething glare.

"It's because of Faith, isn't it?" Charity demanded, slamming her fist on the table.

Marcy whirled around. "Charity Katherine O'Connor!"

"It's true! You don't want me entertaining beaus because poor little Faith sits home like a bump on a log and couldn't get a suitor if she advertised in the *Boston Herald*!"

Faith's mouth gaped open. Her knuckles clenched white on a carrot, which she stabbed in the air. "I could have more beaus too, if I flirted like one of the cheap girls at Brannigan's!"

"Faith Mary O'Connor!" Marcy exclaimed, her fingers twitching in the dough. The kitchen was deathly quiet except for the rolling boil of the stew. Katie began to whine, and Elizabeth bundled her in her arms, calming her with a gentle shush.

Charity leaned forward. Her lips curled in contempt. "You couldn't get beaus if you lined 'em up and paid 'em!"

"At least I wouldn't pay them with favors on the side porch . . ."

Marcy flinched as if she'd been slapped. "What?" she breathed. She turned toward Faith, whose hand flew to her mouth in a gasp. Charity's face was as white as the flour on Marcy's hands. "With whom?" Marcy whispered.

"Collin McGuire," Faith said, her voice barely audible.

It may as well have been an explosion. Marcy gasped. "Is this true, Charity? Look at me! *Is this true?*"

Charity's watery gaze met her mother's, and she nodded, tears trickling her cheeks.

Marcy barely moved a muscle. "Faith, take the children upstairs."

Faith was silent as she picked Katie up to carry her from the room. Elizabeth followed with Steven behind. Charity was sobbing. Without a word, Marcy walked to the sink to wash the dough from her hands, then returned to her daughter's side, wrapping her arms around her. At her touch, Charity crumpled into her embrace like a wounded child. Marcy stroked her hair, waiting for the sobs to subside. When they did, she lifted Charity's quivering chin and looked in the eyes of the daughter-child who so wanted to be a woman.

"Charity, I love you. And that love charges me with responsibility for your well-being and happiness. I know you can't understand this now, nor do you want to, but you must trust us. Collin McGuire is not the boy for you. He's trouble, Charity. Behind that rakish smile and Irish charm is a young man whose only thought is for himself. I've seen you smile and flirt with a number of young lads, and I suppose with most young men, that's innocent enough. But not with him. It's stoking a fire that could burn you. Now tell me what happened on the porch."

Charity sniffed, wiped her nose with her sleeve, and straightened her shoulders. "He . . . he wants me to go to the social, and he . . . Mother, it was only a kiss!"

"Yes, and I'm only your mother. I love you very much, but you'll not be going to the social this Saturday nor anywhere else for the next month. You will come straight home after school each day and complete your studies. And you will have the chore of doing the supper dishes for four weeks." Marcy's tone softened. "But only because I love you."

Charity's eyes glinted as she spun on her heel and headed for the door. "I could certainly do with a little less love, Mother," she hissed.

Marcy couldn't help but smile to herself. She had been sixteen once.

The door flew open, and a blast of cool air surged in. Faith braced herself. Charity stood wild-eyed, hands fisted at her sides. "I hate you!" she screamed. She slammed the door hard and leaned against it, her chest heaving from the effort. "I will never forgive you for what you did. You are a wicked, evil person, and I hope you die an old maid!" She lunged and knocked Faith flat on the bed, yanking a fistful of hair.

"Ow!" Faith hollered. Pain unleashed her fury. She kneed Charity in the stomach and rolled her over, pinning her to the bed. "Stop it, Charity—I mean it! I never meant to tell Mother anything, and you know it. But you were so mean and hateful, it just popped out." Her breath came in ragged gasps. "Look, I don't want to fight with you."

Charity scowled. "Fine way to prove it. I still don't know if I'm going to forgive you. You've gone and ruined everything with Collin. It's going to be twice as difficult to see him now." She tugged her arms free and pushed Faith away.

In slow motion, Faith sat up on the bed, incredulous her sister would even entertain the thought of defying their mother. "But you're not supposed to. Not now, not ever—that's the whole point Mother's been making. Don't you understand that?"

"Yes, I understand that," Charity mimicked. "My head knows it, but I'm afraid my heart's having a bit of a problem." She stood up from the bed and smiled. "But then you wouldn't understand, would you, Faith? I love him. It's as simple as that. Mother may forbid me from seeing him, but she can't forbid me from loving him." Charity posed in the mirror, then hugged herself and whirled around, her golden hair spinning about her like a fallen halo.

"You can't love him! You don't even know him!"

"Oh yes I do," Charity breathed, "and he's wonderful!" She gave Faith a sly smile. "You know the studying I've been doing at the library? Well, I've been studying, all right—my favorite subject in the whole world."

Faith's facial muscles slacked into shock, prompting a peal of laughter from her sister. Charity plopped on the bed and grabbed her hand. "Oh, Faith, he's amazing! He's funny and bright, and all I know is I'm happier than I've ever been."

Faith snatched her hand away. "You didn't look so happy on the porch this afternoon."

A flicker of annoyance flashed on Charity's face and then disappeared into a sheepish grin. "Yes, I know, he can be maddening at times. It's part of his charm, I suppose. But I can handle him." Charity stood and reached for the hairbrush. She began stroking her hair in a trancelike motion.

"You didn't appear to be the one doing the handling . . ."

The brushing stopped. Charity turned around slowly, all smiles gone. "I know what I'm doing, and I'll thank you to stay out of it." She tossed the brush on the bed and turned to leave, but not before bestowing one final smile. "I trust you, Faith. We're sisters." One perfectly manicured brow jutted up slightly. "And sisters love each other, right?"

Faith gritted her teeth. The Bible she read to Mrs. Gerson every Saturday night claimed "love never fails." She certainly hoped not.

2

Patrick O'Connor knew he could count on two things when he arrived home from work each evening. Without exception, the warmth and hum of activity in the kitchen would escalate to a near-frenzy of children's greetings and giggles. This was accompanied by the excessive barking and tail wagging of the family's golden retriever, Blarney, who insisted on being the focal point of his master's attention. But before coat and hat were carelessly flung on the cast-iron rack and children petted and hugged, Patrick would seek out his own focal point—the soft and smiling face of his "Irish rose." To him, Marcy O'Connor was the woman who made life worthwhile, and whose startling blue eyes still had the power to make his heart race.

From the moment he first laid eyes on her, Patrick knew he'd never wanted anything more. But she hadn't come easily, not like the endless parade of females who had jockeyed for a position on the arm of the Southie's leading Lothario. No, it had been a fight, a struggle that forced him to woo and win her like he'd never done before. He'd been annoyed at first, confident that she, like all the others, would eventually fall under his spell. But it almost appeared as if she didn't notice him at all. And for Patrick Brendan O'Connor, the annoyance hardened into sheer determination to conquer this soft-spoken beauty who seemed to prefer an evening with a well-worn book to him.

She stared at him now from across the crowded kitchen. Exhaustion in her blue eyes belied the soft smile on her lips while Katie tugged insistently at his trousers. "Daddy, Daddy, happy birthday! I drew a picture for you."

Patrick hoisted his youngest daughter to his shoulders, his eyes never straying from Marcy's. "Is that so? Well, now, it better be good, missy!"

"Children, it's time to wash up for dinner." Marcy placed two freshly baked loaves of bread on the table. The heavenly smell rumbled his stomach.

"But, Mama, Daddy's giving me a piggyback ride," Katie insisted.

Patrick deposited her firmly on her feet and gave her a playful swat. "I suggest you mind your mother, young lady, if you know what's best."

Katie screeched and darted from the room, little-girl giggles ringing through the house.

"Marcy?" Within three great strides, he had her in his arms. A heavy sigh escaped her lips when she leaned her cheek against the nubby weave of his vest. His grip tightened protectively.

"It's not anything horrible, not really, I suppose," she was quick to reassure him. "It's just that Charity has been seeing that McGuire boy despite our warnings, and, well, apparently Faith saw them kissing on the porch—"

"They were what?" Patrick's hands fell from her shoulders. His jaw hardened, and he pulled back, staring at his wife in disbelief.

"Well, yes, Charity admitted they'd been kissing and—"

"Kissing! And what's next, I ask you, with the likes of him? That girl needs to suffer some severe repercussions!" He began to pace.

Marcy reached for his arm. "Patrick, my love, I think we have to remain calm in our dealings with Charity. After all, we are the adults, and she's just a child—"

"Saints almighty, Marcy, she's a child with the look of a woman, and I can tell you sure as I'm standing here what that young bloke sees in her." He swore out loud as he kneaded the back of his neck, then stopped when he saw the shock on her face.

The soft blue of Marcy's eyes turned flinty. "Patrick O'Connor, there is no call for profanity, and I am just as well aware of what that boy may be thinking as you. But severe discipline taken against a lovesick girl will accomplish nothing more than ushering her into harm's way. She's much too old for the strap, and this is far too delicate a matter."

He stormed to the cupboard and pulled out a glass, slamming the cabinet closed. After filling it with water, he drained it in one long gulp. He plunked the glass on the counter and turned to face her.

"Marcy, I just don't think that—" He stopped when he saw the firm lift of her chin, then released a heavy sigh and scrubbed the back of his neck. He took a deep breath and exhaled to force the frustration from his lungs. Walking to where she stood, he drew her close and cleared his throat. "You're right. We have to be calm but firm in our insistence that she stay away from him." He lifted her chin to gaze in her eyes. "I'll talk to her privately after dinner, when my belly is full and I'm not so prone to growl. You'll see, I'll handle it calmly and rationally." He cupped her face with his hand. An impish smile tugged at his lips. "And if that doesn't work, sure as St. Patrick is Irish, I'll just lock her in her room."

Marcy blinked, then smiled and shook her head. He folded her in his arms. Burrowing his face in her hair, he laughed—a rich, throaty sound that echoed through the still of the house.

Faith nipped at the nail on her pinky and paced the room. Why did it always have to be this way with her sister? Surely with her strong faith in God, she could overcome this urge to . . . what? Disengage a fistful of golden curls from her sister's head? Apply a bit of blackening around those luminous blue eyes?

She groaned and dropped on the bed. She supposed it wasn't Charity's fault she'd been born to turn heads at such an alarming rate. But this jealousy was not an easy thing to conquer. Even so, she believed she'd been making progress. Praying for God to bless Charity, just as Mrs. Gerson had taught her from Matthew 5:44. *Pray for those who persecute you.* And she'd done it—over and over again.

She vaulted from the bed to study herself in the glass that hung on the wardrobe. Resting her hands on her hips, she tilted her face as if she were one of the ravishing models peering from the pages of *Harper's Bazaar*. *I'm not completely unattractive*, she thought as she piled her auburn hair on top of her head. She struck a dramatic pose. True, some might call her pretty, one or two might consider her beautiful, but few would ever admit she was as striking as her sister.

She turned sideways to survey her slight figure. Even at almost nineteen, she was a mere shadow of a woman next to Charity. Her brow furrowed as she assessed her slight frame, a stark contrast to Charity's ample bosom and shapely hips. "I hope she gets fat!" She collapsed on her bed and closed her eyes to relish the thought.

Fury is cruel, and anger is outrageous; but who is able to stand before jealousy? Her eyes blinked open. A sick feeling crawled in her stomach. The words of her blind neighbor, Mrs. Gerson, came back to haunt her.

"My dear, anger is a natural human emotion we all experience," Mrs. Gerson had told her. *"The Bible says to be slow to anger and sin not, making it clear anger in itself is not a sin. It's what we do with it that's right or wrong. Do we become bitter or do we forgive? Ah, but jealousy, now that's a horse of quite a different color. Jealousy is a condition of the heart involving so many things that stem the flow of God's blessings—self-pity, an ungrateful heart, bitterness, and a lack of faith that God knows what's best for you. Understand me, Faith, few people can stand before jealousy."*

Puffing out a sigh, Faith reached for her pillow and jabbed it a few times. She curled into a ball. As usual, Mrs. Gerson was right. "Forgive me, Lord," she whispered. "Help me fight this jealousy, please. I have so much to be grateful for."

She sat up and stared wide-eyed at the girl in the mirror, suddenly feeling much lighter. She took a deep breath and released it again, a look of amazement on her face. How could it be that within several shallow breaths, her whole world could shift so dramatically? Only seconds ago, she was sick with self-pity and weighted with jealousy. Now, the girl in the mirror blinked back, peace flooding her soul. *His* peace.

She closed her eyes and lifted her chin to the ceiling. "Okay, God, it's me and you. We're going to slay this dragon of jealousy if it takes sewing my mouth shut to do it! I'm counting on you to keep me steady and strong no matter how long it takes." Her lips quirked into a crooked smile. "And Lord, don't fail me, please—we both know I can't sew to save my soul."

"Marcy, darlin', I've been dreaming of your Irish stew the whole day long. It's a birthday feast fit for a king, I can tell you that. So, how is my family today?" Patrick doled out stew and smiles around the festive table set with Marcy's china and Irish lace tablecloth reserved for special occasions. He surveyed his wife and children, and a profound sense of gratitude swelled in his chest. His gaze flitted to Faith and Charity. Both looked rather sullen. *And well they should.* His smile tightened on his lips.

"I learned to spell *cat* today, Daddy. Do you want to hear? Cat, c-a-t, cat. What do you think of that?" Katie was quite pleased with herself. Her blue eyes sparkled as she pursed her rosebud mouth into a satisfied smile.

"Well, I think you may be ready for school before too long. What a bright young thing you are, Katie girl! And how is your bear today?"

"He has a cold, and I'm afraid he's quite a bother when he's sick."

Patrick laughed as he chomped on a piece of bread. "Ah, but I'm quite sure he'll recover nicely with such a wonderful mama taking care of him." He took a gulp of his coffee before turning his attention to his youngest son. "And how are your vocabulary words coming along, Steven? Ready for that spelling bee next week?"

"That's all he does is write his words, Daddy. He won't even play with me." Katie's sigh was as long as her face as she poked at the food on her plate.

Patrick eyed his daughter with a degree of tolerance. "Now, Katie, Steven's a big boy who goes to school. He has to work hard if he wants to be the best he can be. Soon you'll be in school, and you'll have to work hard too."

"But I work hard now," she reasoned. "I take care of my bear all day long."

Patrick's brow arched slightly. "I suggest you work hard on that stew, young lady, while I have a conversation with your brother." He turned back to his son. "How have you been doing in the trial bees, Steven?"

Steven's blue eyes lit with excitement. He was slight for his eight years, with a generous spray of freckles that imparted an elfin quality to his delicate face. "I've won every one, Father, and Mrs. Broyles says I'm the best speller in three years! I do hope you'll be able to come to the spelling bee next Thursday after school."

"Steven, your father will be working," Marcy reminded him gently.

Patrick saw disappointment in his son's eyes.

"How about I come in Father's place?" Sean asked, eyeing his younger brother.

Patrick glanced at his eldest. At the age of twenty, Sean was a stabilizing force among the O'Connor siblings. Tall and lean of stature with a shock of blond hair neatly combed back, Sean possessed Marcy's blue eyes, infused with the playful twinkle of his own.

"Thanks, Sean, but I have every intention of being there." Patrick reached to tousle Steven's red hair until it stood up on his head.

Marcy started to object, but Patrick gave her a look of warning. "I'll simply tell Ben I have a personal matter of great importance to attend to—case closed." Patrick pushed his empty plate away and stretched comfortably back in the chair.

Marcy stood up from the table with a noticeable sigh and headed to the kitchen. "Charity, I need your help with dessert, please. Faith, your night to clear the table, I believe?"

Charity jumped up in a rush, bumping her elbow into her sister's arm as Faith guzzled the last of her milk. Faith groaned when a spray of milk sloshed up her nose.

"Oops, sorry," Charity muttered.

"Sorry, my eye, you did it on pur—" Faith stopped midsentence, her gaze meeting her father's. She clamped her lips shut while milk dribbled from her chin. She swiped it with the sleeve of her blouse and rose from the table. In stoic silence, she collected dirty dishes and piled them high until Patrick could no longer see the scowl on her face.

He shook his head and turned his attention to Elizabeth, his shy daughter with the violet eyes that often held a faraway look. An avid student of literature, Beth reminded him of how Marcy might have been as a child. For that reason, among others, he fostered a great affection for this soft-spoken daughter of his. Leaning across the table, he stroked her cheek with his hand and was rewarded with a gentle smile.

"And where have you been today, Beth, in your great world of literature?"

All shyness vanished as Beth shared the adventures of Miss Jane Eyre. Patrick listened attentively while Katie sat with hands folded on the table and eyes rolling upward.

"All she does is read, read, read!" Katie complained. "When I grow up, I won't just read about things, I'll do them!"

"Don't be precocious, Katie," Patrick reprimanded.

"I already am, Daddy, there's nothing I can do about it." Katie's tone was matter-of-fact.

Patrick bit back a smile before turning to his eldest son. "Tell me, Sean, how is business down at Kelley's?"

A conversation ensued about the nuts and bolts of the hardware store where Sean worked. Suddenly the lights dimmed, and Marcy reappeared carrying a cake aglow with candles. Faith and Charity followed, plates and utensils in hand.

"Happy birthday, Father!" the family chimed in unison as Patrick made great show of extinguishing the candles that lit up the room.

"Did you make a wish, Daddy?" Katie demanded. "'Cause you have to make a wish."

"Yes, Katie, I did indeed. But it's hard to believe any wish I could make would be better than this—breaking bread with the woman I love"—Patrick winked at Marcy—"surrounded by the children born of that love."

"Daddy," Katie said with no small exasperation, "it's cake, not bread, and why on earth would you want to break it? Mama and I worked very hard to make it."

Laughter filled the room, and Katie was clearly annoyed. "What? What'd I say?"

"Katie, love, it's from sheer delight of your adorable ways that we laugh, I can assure you. Now get over here, little girl, and give your daddy a birthday kiss." Patrick held out his arms. In a squeal, Katie was wrapped inside them, giggling and laughing with the others.

"Mother, you've outdone yourself—this cake's delicious!" Faith said after taking a bite. She licked icing from her finger. "If only I could bake like you."

"Goodness knows you'll need something to catch a husband," Charity muttered.

Patrick looked up from his dessert. The smile faded on his face.

"You're just jealous 'cause I can eat whatever I want," Faith whispered back.

"Eat as much as you like. Maybe it'll find its way into a figure—"

Patrick slapped his napkin on the table. "What the devil is going on over there? Faith, Charity, I'll have none of your squabbling on my birthday, do you understand?"

"Sorry, Father," Faith said.

"Sorry, Father," Charity echoed. "But she started it."

"I did not!"

"Enough! I'll see you both in the parlor after your chores. Go on now, get busy."

Charity rose and bolted for the kitchen while Faith began clearing the dessert plates from the table. She brushed past Patrick, gently touching his shoulder. "Sorry, Daddy," she mouthed, reverting to her childhood name for him.

Patrick grabbed her in a sideways hug. "I love my girl."

"I love you too, Daddy," she whispered back.

Patrick pushed his chair back from the table. "Katie Rose, where's that picture you promised me?" he bellowed.

His inquiry sent the five-year-old scurrying into the parlor in search of her present.

"Sean, are you up for a game of chess tonight? I'm feeling a bit like an old man. I sure could use a victory."

Sean rose to the bait with a lopsided grin. "I'll tell you what, I'll let you win as a birthday present. How's that?"

"I said old, my boy, not dead!" Patrick said. He laughed as he made his way to the parlor with the younger children close behind.

For the first time in her life, Charity took her time doing the dishes. There was no need to hurry through this, the most hated of household chores. She had no visits to the library planned, no clandestine meetings with a forbidden beau to rush off to. Not tonight. No, tonight—despite the fact it was her father's birthday and a most joyous occasion—would not be a good night for Charity Katherine O'Connor.

Charity had no doubt her mother had already shared with her father the news of the kiss. Everyone in the house had heard his shouted profanity, a completely infrequent occurrence, which only further underscored the true seriousness of his anger. Over a kiss!

Charity closed her eyes to recapture the sweetness of the memory. *Oh, but what a kiss!* The soft touch of Collin's lips caressing her neck had sent shivers down her back. Was there any man on the face of the earth so handsome and wonderful as Collin McGuire? Charity doubted it. She sighed and opened her eyes to a sink full of dirty dishes.

She washed and dried them slowly, wondering what she

could possibly say or do to convince her father that Collin McGuire wasn't the rogue they both knew he was.

If I were Faith, she thought to herself coldly, *I could get Father to do whatever I wanted.* Charity blew a strand of hair from her eyes and tackled the dirty stew pot. She scrubbed ferociously, wondering for the thousandth time why things had turned out as they had. Why had God allowed polio to take the life of her older sister, Hope—Faith's twin— and then cripple Faith too? Charity felt sorry for Faith, to be sure. Losing her best friend and twin at the age of nine was certainly awful, and then to be forced to live in a strange hospital for over a year. But it wasn't like Faith hadn't been loved through it all. Why, Father and Mother had traipsed to the hospital every chance they'd gotten, focusing only on her.

Charity pursed her lips into a tight line. And when Faith finally came home, Father had treated her like some price- less treasure, hovering over her, laughing with her, calling her "his girl" when he thought Charity couldn't hear. But she had.

Yes, if she were Faith, she could probably finagle her father into anything. But then again, if she were Faith, she would have never caught the eye of Collin McGuire. And that was a trade-off that carried too high a price. Charity tossed the dish towel over the chair and took a deep breath. "Into the lions' den," she muttered, completely certain it was well worth the fight.

The scene was too cozy to disrupt. Her mother rocked Katie by the fire while Elizabeth and Steven lay on the floor, tending to their studies. Faith huddled in a blanket on the love seat, engrossed in her writing while Patrick and Sean debated good-naturedly over chess. But disrupted it must be, Charity concluded when her father glanced up from his game. Despite the blazing fire, she felt a sudden chill in the room. Her mother rose with Katie asleep in her arms.

Sean jumped up and reached for his sister. "Mother, I'll carry her for you. She's getting way too big."

Marcy's smile was weary. "Thank you, Sean. She's already had her bath. Just put her in bed. Goodness, where did the evening go? Beth, Steven, it's time to head up. Faith, Charity, I'll kiss you good night upstairs." Marcy bent over her husband and kissed his cheek. "Good night, my love."

"I won't be long, my dear." Patrick reached for his pipe.

Charity could feel the uneasiness in the room as everyone cleared out. She sat ramrod straight in the chair, waiting for her father to begin.

Patrick stood, walked to the hearth, and leaned to light his pipe. The sweet smell of tobacco filled the room. Puffs of smoke swirled above his head. He turned to Faith.

"Faith, you're the oldest girl in this family, so you have to set an example. I'm asking you from my heart to work on your relationship with your sister. We are family, and a family loves each other. There will be no cutting words spoken here. You'll both get enough of that in the world. This is our home, our haven—treat it as such and treat each other as the precious gift you are. You're sisters. Few bonds are stronger than that. Do you understand?"

Faith nodded.

"Good, then come kiss your tired old father good night so I can have a word in private with Charity." Patrick embraced his eldest daughter and kissed her lightly on top of the head. "Good night, Faith," he whispered. "I love my girl."

"Good night, Daddy," she answered softly. "Sleep well." Faith glanced at Charity and gave her a nervous smile.

Charity nodded stiffly. She watched her father take a deep breath before he turned his full attention to her.

"Charity, your mother and I love you very much . . ."

Here it comes. She fixed her gaze on a spot in the carpet, the one where she'd spilled hot chocolate at the age of six.

"And it's because we love you that we are so strict regarding, well, certain things."

"You mean certain people, don't you, Father?" Charity never looked up, continuing to trace the chocolate stain in her mind.

She heard her father shuffle and glanced up to see him puffing on his pipe as if he wished he could lose himself in its smoke.

"Well, yes, as a matter of fact, I do. Look now, Charity, apparently your mother and I did not make ourselves clear when we tried to dissuade you from your interest in this McGuire boy. But, darlin', I want there to be no mistaking what I'm putting before you now. You're to have no association whatsoever with that boy. He's a wild one, Charity, the kind better suited to taking up with the women at Brannigan's Pub, not a sixteen-year-old girl from a family where morality and honesty are expected."

She stared straight ahead, her face serene like the stone bust that graced her mother's mantel. Cool and unaffected—except for a single tear trailing down her cheek.

Her father laid his pipe aside and moved to where she sat in the chair. He stooped to his knees, a pained expression on his face. He clutched her hand. "Charity, I love you more than I can say. I was Collin's age once. For pity's sake, I *was* Collin once. I know what goes through his head when he sees a pretty girl. I know how strong the desires can be for a boy like that, a boy who can turn the head of every lass in Boston Town. He's trouble, trust me on this. Promise you will heed my words and honor me. If you defy me, I'll be forced to take strong measures. I don't want to do that, darlin', but I've got to be sure you understand the severity of the situation."

His grip tightened on her hand. He seemed to search her face for any clue of consent. "Promise me, Charity. Give me your word you will stay away from Collin McGuire."

Charity lifted her chin to smile into his anxious eyes. "I promise, Father." Her voice sounded smooth to her own ears, as if she were discussing the weather.

Patrick scooped her up in his big arms and squeezed her tightly. "That's my girl! Everything's going to be fine, you'll see. There'll be another beau who will turn your head soon enough, I can promise you that."

Her face felt like a mask as she stared over her father's shoulder and fixated on the stain on the floor. He had called her "his girl," but that was a lie. She had never been his girl. His girl was Faith.

3

Faith couldn't remember when she'd been this excited. She studied herself in the mirror. What kind of impression would she make? With an approving eye, she surveyed her hair, which was neatly swept into the latest style—a twisted knot at the back of her head. Her starched, choker-necked blouse was crisp and clean and quite professional, especially with her mother's velvet ribbon around the fluted collar. The perfect look, she hoped, for the newest member of the *Boston Herald* typing pool.

Never was a first impression more critical. There would be veiled looks of jealousy to contend with, airs of skepticism to deflect, and respect to be earned. She was, after all, the daughter of Patrick O'Connor, assistant editor of the *Boston Herald*. If she were going to succeed, she'd have to demonstrate talent and ability far beyond bloodline advantage.

She lifted her hand to the porcelain brooch pinned to the ribbon. Her mother had insisted she wear it. It had been passed down by Faith's great-grandmother, Mima, years ago in Ireland when her own daughter—Faith's grandmother, Bridget—had chosen to flee a homeland ravaged by the potato famine. Even now, when Marcy told the story, tears would well and her voice would waver. The famine had killed Faith's great-grandfather, as well as one in nine of his countrymen, devastating Ireland's economy. Her grandmother experienced the heartbreak of leaving her mother and homeland behind when her husband insisted they seek a life in America. And so they'd left, along with a million of their countryfolk, taking their meager belongings and their young daughter, Marceline, to the Promised Land across the sea.

When Bridget had kissed Mima good-bye, Mima had pressed the brooch into her daughter's hand and begged her to return someday. Hand painted with a picture of their cottage home, the brooch had been one of Faith's grandmother's most precious keepsakes. Years later, following the death of her husband and with Marcy grown and married, Bridget returned to her beloved Ireland and to Mima. The day she left, she squeezed the brooch into Marcy's hand as they parted on the pier, their eyes as misty as the thick fog that rolled over the restless sea.

Nine years had come and gone, and now Marcy had pinned the same brooch on Faith. "This is a big day for you. School is behind, and a new life lies ahead. Be patient, work hard, and someday, after you've proven yourself, you'll get the opportunity to write—I can feel it." Her mother stroked her face with a tenderness that made Faith feel safe inside. "This brooch is not meant to be a good-luck charm, understand, but I do want it to remind you that you're not alone. You are greatly loved—by God and by us. You will remember that, won't you, Faith?"

Faith nodded, and Marcy gave her a peck on the cheek. "Good girl! Now hurry downstairs. You don't want to keep Father waiting." She disappeared, leaving Faith standing before the mirror. Gently she touched the brooch one last time—this rite of passage from mother to daughter—and felt at peace. This precious heirloom seemed an unspoken prayer, sending her into a new world with the knowledge that there was a place to return to, a haven of warmth and solace, if needed. Faith took a deep breath and one final glance. There was little doubt that she would.

Never had Faith seen anything throb with such restless energy as the newsroom of the *Boston Herald*. She stood on its threshold in awe, hand splayed on her chest and mouth gaping. The electricity of the room, with its sea of desks shrouded in a haze of smoke, sent waves of excitement coursing through her. Reporters and copywriters crowded the room, barking orders, screaming into telephones, and pounding typewriter keys with the same ferocity as they puffed on stubs of cigarettes and cigars. Amid the smoky maze, copyboys and typing-pool girls scurried, pencils behind ears and papers in hand, seeking to placate the edgy tempers of those provoked by the demons of deadline. To Faith, the very hum of the place was melodic: typewriter keys clicking and telephones ringing in exhilarating harmony with hushed tones and booming voices. Desk drawers slamming, doors flying open—it was a hive of people pulsating with life, and now she, too, was part of its wonderful frenzy.

Timid, she followed behind Patrick as he wove his way through the swarming throng, dispensing greetings as he went.

"So that's your eldest girl, is it now, Patrick? She's a pretty young thing." A tiny man with a voice too booming for his size grinned at Faith, causing those within hearing distance to turn and gawk. Patrick beamed.

"She is at that, Duffy, my man, but she's a hard worker too, the likes of which we could use around here."

Hand on her shoulder, Patrick steered Faith to the back of the room where a bubbled glass door sheltered the calm of the typing pool from the chaotic pace of the smoggy newsroom. Halting, he kissed her lightly on the forehead.

"Now you go on in and introduce yourself to Hattie. She runs the pool, and she'll get you started."

Faith chewed on her lip.

Patrick patted her arm. "You'll be fine, darlin'. Hattie is a kind woman. You'll like her. But I think it's best you go in alone, since you're my daughter. There's no need to rub that in anyone's face, now is there?" Patrick smiled, his eyes soft with understanding. "Go on, now, you'll be fine. Sure, you'll be running the place in no time."

Faith reached for the knob.

"Oh, and, darlin' . . ."

She turned and looked into her father's eyes.

"I love my girl," he whispered.

Faith lifted her chin and nodded, stepping through the doorway. On the other side she encountered a more peaceful existence, devoid of smoke as well as excitement, crammed wall to window with several rows of tiny typing tables. Each was occupied by a stone-faced girl with fingers flying over typewriter keys and attention focused on a steno pad before her. The white paint on the walls had long since yellowed to sallow. Veins of occasional cracks fanned between jaundiced editions of the *Boston Herald*, haphazardly hung. In contrast to the near-pandemonium of the newsroom, the drone of this room was deafening in its monotony. Nothing but the click-click-clicking of typewriters. And the silence of boredom. Faith swallowed her disappointment.

Miss Hattie Hayword, matriarch of the pool, sat at a decidedly more important desk at the front of the room. Her salt-and-pepper hair wound into a tight bun perched on the back of her head like an oversized donut. She was far too large for the delicate chair in which she sat, causing it to groan and squeak at her slightest movement. Absorbed in the galley sheets before her, she didn't notice that anyone had entered the room. Faith inched her way to Hattie's desk.

"Excuse me, Miss Hayword, I'm so sorry to interrupt . . ." Faith tried to calm her voice, hoping it sounded steadier than she felt. "I'm Faith O'Connor . . . and . . . I believe I'm scheduled to begin work in the typing pool today."

Hattie looked up, her broad face breaking into a warm smile. She extended a chubby arm, shaking Faith's hand with such enthusiasm that the heavy fold of her forearm swung back and forth. "Yes, you are, Miss O'Connor, and I'm quite pleased to have you. Your father is a fine man and a mainstay here at the *Herald*, I can tell you that. He tells me you like to write."

The knot in her stomach unraveled. "Yes, yes, I do, Miss Hayword. Someday . . . well, I hope to become a copywriter here at the *Herald*. But that's down the road, of course. For now, I'm committed to proving myself as a typist."

"And so you shall, young lady, so you shall." With considerable effort and strain on herself and the chair, Hattie rose and toddled around her desk. She grabbed Faith's arm to usher her to the front of the room. "Come now, we must introduce you."

Faith's chest tightened. "Uh, Miss Hayword . . . if you don't mind, I would prefer you didn't introduce me as Patrick O'Connor's daughter."

Hattie seemed puzzled. "But, my dear, all the girls will know eventually. You can't keep something like that quiet, you know."

"I know. I just don't want special attention because of it. I'd much rather, well, earn the respect on my own, if you understand my meaning."

"I do, and I applaud you for it, my dear. Come, I will introduce you to the girl who will assist in your training. She's one of our most experienced typists."

Hattie maneuvered Faith to the back of the room like a

tugboat pushing a barge, creating a ripple effect of curious eyes. She halted in front of a pleasant-looking girl with a persistent spray of freckles and a wild mane of tawny curls restrained by a black barrette. The girl smiled, and the freckles made way for dimples.

"Maisie, this is Faith O'Connor, our newest member of the typing pool. Faith, this is Maisie Tanner. She'll get you set up. These are Underwood machines. I understand you were trained on Royals in school, is that right, dear?"

"Yes, ma'am."

"Well, they're basically the same with a few minor differences, but Maisie can run you through all of that. This section of the pool is responsible for typing and proofing all copy from the obituaries to weather. The other section handles art through music—it's alphabetically divided, of course. A few copywriters prefer to type their own copy, but most will give you sheets and sheets of chicken scratch, which you will become quite adept at deciphering." Hattie's puffy hands fluttered in the air while her twinkling eyes rolled in Maisie's direction. "When you can't make heads or tails of it, you'll find Maisie's help invaluable. She's a wonder at reading their minds."

Maisie nodded and smiled, wisps of stray curls bobbing in agreement.

"You're assigned to the day shift, 9:00 a.m. to 5:00 p.m. Maisie will show you where to clock in. Lunch is at noon; you get thirty minutes. I have a few papers for you to sign before you leave today, but that about covers what you need to get started. I'll leave you with Maisie. Good luck, young lady." Hattie waddled to her desk, where the squeaking commenced once again.

Faith stooped to store her purse on the small ledge beneath her typing table, her stomach a jumble while Maisie rattled on. All at once, Maisie patted her arm. "First-day jitters—everybody gets 'em. You're gonna be fine."

Faith's smile was weak. "Do you really think so?" she asked, poising her fingers over the keys of her very own Underwood.

Maisie grinned. "Sure, once you get that shaking under control. Yeah, you're gonna be fine."

Faith sighed. Oh, how she had missed this—the heady warmth of the early autumn sun on her face, the crisp, earthy scent of fall in the air, the riotous blaze of color. It was hard to believe only two weeks had passed since she'd been here last, her favorite spot in O'Reilly Park. Only two weeks since she had begun her job at the *Herald*—two weeks that had changed her life so completely.

She lazed on the blanket like a contented cat, prayer book, journal, and pen by her side. Closing her eyes, she tilted her face toward the warmth of the sun. Oh, there were so few days like this left! The mournful echo of a loon filled the autumn air, its melancholy song bittersweet to her ears. It was a new season, and in some small way, she mourned the passing of the old—the summer, her school years, her adolescent daydreams.

But the new was certainly not without promise. Turning to lie on her back, she thought about her first weeks at the *Herald*. True, it had not been as exciting as she had hoped—passion was hard to come by when typing obituaries and weather eight hours a day. But it was, in a way, rewarding.

It was strange. Only two weeks had passed, and yet she felt so different, older, more alive. In a mere eight days—on September 30—she would be nineteen, but it was more than that. A feeling of importance, of contribution. She was, after all, part of the inner workings of one of the finest newspapers in the country. A minute role, to be sure, but a cog nonetheless in the wheel of a great machine. One that kept its fingers on the pulse of one of the grandest cities on the Eastern Seaboard.

Faith breathed in deeply, the expanse of air filling her chest with a sense of pride. Despite the monotony of her job, she rather enjoyed it. Well, perhaps not the job as much as riding the trolley to work with Father each morning. She loved listening to tales of his early days or colorful commentary on co-workers. She'd always been close to her father, but within the last two weeks, she sensed something new in their relationship. Over and above their love as father and daughter, they now had a common bond, a kinship that had nothing to do with blood. They were newspeople who loved the smell of ink and the demand of a deadline.

Then there was Maisie. Never had Faith met anyone who made her laugh more. Throughout high school, Faith had developed several friendships, but none even came close to what she and Maisie had shared in two short weeks. They had connected immediately, babbling on about the latest fashions, and Mary Pickford's hairstyles, and their dreams for the future. At the most inopportune times, Maisie's droll sense of humor would make Faith giggle out loud, catching the disapproving eye of Miss Hayword, who would tap a chubby finger against her lips in a scolding fashion.

Faith smiled. Everything was perfect. Or almost perfect. She rolled on her side and felt her smile stiffen.

Except for Briana. The image of the typing pool's resident bully invaded her thoughts. A hardened beauty from the wrong side of town, Briana reveled in picking on Faith. The moment she'd learned Faith was Patrick's daughter, she and her sidekicks had taken every opportunity to bombard her with insult and innuendo.

Faith sighed, remembering the knock-down fight that had finally resulted after a week on the job. The memory of Briana sprawled in a sea of trash flashed before her, and

Faith couldn't help the smile that twitched on her lips. For a solid week she had taken the bullying, biting her tongue so many times her teeth ached. She'd even managed to hog-tie Maisie when Briana's words had been particularly nasty. And then it happened—Briana breached the bounds of Faith's temper, striking at the soft underbelly of all that Faith held dear: *her father*.

With frightening speed, Faith had rammed the palm of her hand against Briana's chest, felling her like a tall, leggy oak. Briana toppled against a row of overflowing trash cans lining the dock wall, her face frozen in shock. She attempted to rise, smelling faintly of sardines.

Mortified, Faith reached to help her up.

"Don't you touch me! You better believe Miss Hayword is going to hear about this. Let's see what your precious daddy thinks of his little girl bullying her fellow workers."

Briana's cronies brushed bits of trash off her clothes as she stood to her feet. "Get out of my way," she rasped, pushing past Faith while her entourage trailed behind.

Faith had been aghast, but the moment she spied Maisie's red face, the two of them had howled until they cried. In the end, she had received a gentle reprimand from Miss Hayword, who never even mentioned it to her father. Apparently she didn't like Briana either.

Feeling a wee bit guilty, Faith squeezed her eyes shut. "Okay, okay, bless her, Lord," she muttered through clenched teeth. She shifted to lie flat on her back, then stretched lazily to soak in the surprising warmth of the late-September sun. With eyes closed, she kicked off her shoes and hiked her green muslin skirt above her knees. She shimmied out of her navy stockings to bare her legs. Thrusting her crisp, white shirtsleeves up, she clasped her hands over her head and breathed in deeply. Oh, how she cherished moments like this! To lie here in her own personal haven, hedged by massive forsythia bushes that spilled over a peaceful pond. It was the perfect place for reflection.

Through her eyelids, she could feel rather than see the flickering sun as it danced and shimmered between the fluttering leaves of the massive oak overhead. Intermittently its warmth was stolen for a moment, as it was now, by a stray cloud in an otherwise perfect sky. Somewhere high in the canopy of boughs, a mockingbird chattered, luring a smile to Faith's lips as she rested, content in her wait for the warmth to return.

"You know, there's a good chance you could burn those beautiful legs."

Heaven help her, she was paralyzed, unable to move anything but her eyelids. They flew open in utter horror, and she blinked, sunlight blinding her eyes to a shadowy figure standing over her.

Collin McGuire.

He assessed her bare legs with a grin, which promptly produced an onslaught of heat in her cheeks. "I'd be careful, you know. Looks like your face is pretty red too."

Faith yanked her skirt down and shielded her eyes from the sun as she looked up at him. *Please don't let him see me shaking.* With a sweaty palm, she clutched at her dress.

He sat down on the blanket beside her, his long legs stretched out next to her own. He leaned back, tugged at a piece of grass, and put the stem in his mouth. He chewed it slowly, deliberately.

Her breath hitched in her throat. "What are you doing?" she stuttered, inching to the far edge of the blanket.

Collin turned to face her, his gray eyes nonchalant. "Sittin'." He looked away and tilted his face to the sun as if being there were the most natural thing in the world.

Warmth washed over her. Her pulse raced chaotically. "I don't understand. Did you follow me?"

"Uh-huh."

"But why?"

He sat up straight and shifted to face her. The blade of grass continued to rotate in his lips. He plucked it from his mouth. "Honestly? I came here to vent. I was pretty mad that you made it difficult for me to see your sister. I'm quite fond of her, you know, and hope to see more of her. Why'd you tell your parents you saw us on the porch?"

Faith blinked and looked away. She felt as if he could read her mind, and it made her uneasy. She shivered. "I didn't mean to, honestly I didn't. It just . . . well, it just came out. We were fighting, and Charity said something hurtful. Then I did."

When he didn't answer, she straightened her shoulders and thrust her chin to stare at him boldly—then caught her breath. He was only inches away, and she'd forgotten the mesmerizing effect of those eyes, so serene and light. They were a striking shade of gray, not quite blue, and as clear and deep as the purest spring. Her mother often remarked how eyes were the windows to the soul. Faith stared into the depths of his now and felt as if she were staring into the inner sanctum of Collin McGuire. The blade of grass was back between his teeth. His gaze locked with hers, and a strange calm came over her. At the same time, her heart accelerated, a paradox that confused and frightened her.

His smile faded as he stared back, transfixed, almost as if he too felt the startling connection. Abruptly, she turned away, her fingers grasping at her hair to push it from her face. "I suppose it shocked me . . . seeing you with Charity like that. She's only sixteen. And you're twenty-one . . ."

He didn't respond, and she looked up. The deadly smile had reappeared. Another rush of warmth invaded her cheeks. "My parents aren't comfortable with that," she said.

Collin reached for an acorn and rolled its nubby hull between his forefinger and thumb. He certainly hadn't expected this, to find himself enjoying Charity's meddling sister. Suddenly he was following her every move. He tossed the nut in the air. "And what about you? How's your comfort level?"

It was like watching a scene in a play. He remembered her from high school, of course, and the memory broadened the smile on his lips. But he hadn't noticed then how pretty she was.

She'd grown up a lot since then. Gone were the steel braces that had shackled a little girl who'd looked as if the next breeze would wisp her away. As a freshman she'd been skinny and gangly with haunting green eyes. But now . . . He grinned, allowing his eyes to rove the length of her. He could tell by her blush that his gaze made her uncomfortable. He didn't care. It was too much fun studying her—the slightly upturned nose, the delicately sculpted face, the glint of sun in the red-gold hair. And the eyes—as green as a field of grass with tiny specks of gold scattered throughout.

Her head jerked up, and the green eyes glittered. "Me? I don't give a fig what you do or with whom you do it," she snapped. "Except for Charity. She's too young."

The eyes had him riveted. There was something about Faith O'Connor that stirred him, and he wasn't sure why. Charity's appeal far surpassed that of the pretty girl who sat beside him, and yet . . . there was something deeper he couldn't explain. Something he'd never experienced in the countless encounters he'd known. It thrilled him—and scared him—all at once.

He batted the acorn high in the sky and looked away, squinting at the sun. "Too young?" He spit out the chewed blade of grass to emphasize his point and felt his heart beating faster than usual. "Not from my vantage point."

With great difficulty, he kept his breathing steady and calm, his eyes indifferent. *Well, well, Collin McGuire, this is certainly uncharted territory for you*. And although he desperately wanted to explore it, something stopped him cold. Faith O'Connor seemed like the kind of girl who could put a stranglehold on his heart. And that was something he preferred to avoid. His smile eased into arrogance. "As a matter of fact, I'd say she's the perfect age."

She shot off the blanket and glared down at him, elbows flaring at her side. "You leave her alone! She's not one of your common girls at Brannigan's. She's a good girl. Too good for the likes of you."

"Too good for the likes of you . . ." The words of his mother assaulted his memory, flaming the fuse. Springing to his feet, he towered over her and gripped her shoulders, fingers digging in. For an instant, it appeared as if she didn't dare breathe.

"Don't ever say that again," he whispered. Fury pulsed in his temple. He tightened his grip. "Too good for the likes of me, is she now? Well, then, what about you, Faith O'Connor? Are you too good for the likes of me?"

She caught her breath just before his lips found hers, and he felt the fight within her as he locked her in his arms. The taste of her mouth was so heady to his senses that a soft moan escaped his lips at the shock of it. She shivered before she went weak in his arms, and instinctively, he softened his hold.

She lunged back and clipped the edge of his jaw with a tight-fisted punch, her breath coming in ragged gasps. "How dare you!" she sputtered, her green eyes full of heat.

He grinned and silenced her with his mouth. She made a weak attempt to push him away, but he only drew her back with a force that made her shudder. He felt her pulse racing as his lips wandered her throat. The scent of her drove him mad. He kissed her with renewed urgency, the taste of her making him dizzy. And then, before she could catch her breath, he shoved her away, his heart thundering and his mind paralyzed.

Faith reeled, nearly losing her balance. She swayed on her feet, breathless and weak, not trusting herself to speak. She had dreamed of his lips on hers, written pages of poetry about it. And now here it was, and she couldn't utter a syllable. Collin seemed bewildered, almost disoriented, rubbing his jaw with the side of his hand. His breathing was shallow and rapid, and she could tell he was trying to compose himself, to regain the casual confidence so much a part of who he was. His voice was gruff when he spoke.

"Look, I'm sorry . . . you made me angry." He glanced at her out of the corner of his eye. His mouth slanted into a wary smile. "Again." He took another deep breath, then exhaled. He appeared back in control. "But, you're right, you know. Your sister is too good for the likes of me. Unfortunately, that's not going to stop me. She's beautiful, smart, and most necessary of all, she loves me. And that, Faith O'Connor, is just too good to pass up."

He studied her as if he didn't know what to make of her. "You're a bit scary, you know that?" He leaned close, his voice low and husky in her ear. "Something tells me in my gut I'm way ahead sticking with the younger sister." He touched her cheek, his fingers lingering on her skin. And before she could open her mouth, he turned and was gone, leaving her as cold and still as the statues scattered throughout the park.

A chill swept her. Goose bumps prickled her arms. Shivering, she pulled her sleeves down and rubbed to bring back the warmth, then stopped. The thought of him produced another flash of heat, and instantly she felt lightheaded.

She was ruined. The stark realization filled her with dread in the pit of her stomach. For years he'd possessed her dreams, but she'd been the master of those dreams.

Now, he possessed her memory, and there was nothing she could do about it.

Faith stooped to pick up her pad and pencil, and in the next moment, she slumped to the ground, tears rimming her eyes. How was she to cope with this? Schoolgirl dreams were one thing—harmless reverie. But how was she to cope with the memory of his touch on her skin, his lips on hers, which even now produced a surge of warmth? If she never saw him again, perhaps the memory would fade. But then, he had no intention of going away. He wanted her sister. The only man who had ever turned her head, raced her heart—that man wanted her sister. The reality all but crushed her. It seemed to be the recurrent theme in the life and times of Faith O'Connor, and bitterness poured forth in the overflow of her tears.

As she lay there, the sky clouded over and the false warmth of Indian summer gave way to the chill of autumn. She rose to her feet and gathered her belongings, tilting her face to the sky. Frequent had been the times she had called on the faith her parents had instilled, and countless were the prayers she had cried to the God of that faith. But never had she needed him more.

Faith clutched her prayer book and journal to her chest and straightened her shoulders. It was really quite simple. She would do the only thing she knew to do. The only thing that would matter in the end. She would put herself and the situation in God's capable hands. At the thought, a holy peace flooded her soul, as familiar as the warmth of the sun. She knew then she could face whatever lay ahead, and she wouldn't do it alone. Faithfulness was a strong bent of this God of hers.

"We're a mite glum this evening, aren't we, Collin, me boy? So what's the matter—Charity's daddy won't let you see his little girl?"

Collin turned to give his best friend a withering look before draining the last of his beer. He reached into his pocket, threw some change on the counter, and grabbed his jacket. "Leave me alone, Jackson. I worked three double shifts this week. I'm tired."

"And lonely. Come on, there's plenty of ladies achin' to keep ya company."

Collin looked around. For once the allure of his favorite haunt failed him. The tiny bar was crowded with its usual patrons, rowdy and ravenous in their pursuit of pleasure. But tonight, the appeal of friendly banter and even friendlier women seemed diminished.

In his usual corner sat Tommy Thomkins, caressing the keys of a battered-looking piano as he crooned a stirring rendition of a favorite Irish ballad. Singing along were a number of ruddy-faced regulars, whiskey in one hand and a pretty woman in the other. A haze of smoke, sweetened by the stale scent of perfume and whiskey, hung in the air like a fog, creating the illusion that those in its midst were happy.

Collin turned his attention back to Jackson, who was watching him with more than a hint of curiosity. He grinned to deflect his friend's stare. "Don't think I'm up to it tonight, ol' buddy. But cheer up—that should give you a chance to make some headway with the ladies." Collin slapped him on the back and started for the door.

Jackson grabbed his sleeve. "Come on, Collin, it's too early to go home. I know you'd rather be with Charity, but don't underestimate the affections of a pretty young thing to get you through the night. You know for a fact Bree still has it bad for you. She never has gotten over it. Come on, now, she's just waiting for a chance."

Jackson cinched Collin's coat and bellowed across the room. "Hey, Bree, get yourself over here; somebody needs cheering up." Collin gave him a pained look, which apparently had no effect as Jackson pushed him back on the stool. "Come on, now, dance a little, laugh a little. You'll thank me for it in the morning."

Jackson patted the stool next to Collin's. A shapely blond sat down. "Well, hello there, Collin," she said, her voice husky, hopeful. "So you need cheering up, do you?"

"Bree, me girl," Jackson interrupted, "our friend Collin's having a bad time of it, I'm afraid. Seems he's been smitten by a lass whose father can't abide the sight of him. So ya see, he's sadly reduced to spending his nights heartbroken and lonely. And an unholy shame it is at that."

Collin rolled his eyes and shook his head. Jackson was an idiot, he thought, smiling despite himself.

And Bree was nothing if not a girl of opportunity. Fluttering her lashes in surprise, she scooted her stool close and leaned against him, her hand on his arm. "Heartbroken? Lonely? My, that's hard to believe. But I'm more than happy to do my part to help an old friend in need." She reached up and kissed Collin full on the lips.

He heard her soft moan as she pressed against him, and for the briefest moment, he froze. In his mind's eye, it wasn't Bree's lips he tasted but Faith O'Connor's. An unfamiliar ache stabbed within. *Where the blazes did that come from?* One brief encounter, and some woman had him thinking about her? Wanting her? Well, it wasn't going to happen. He would be the one who decided whom he wanted and whom he didn't. As long as he had a breath in his body, no woman would control his thoughts, and certainly no woman would possess him.

The ache was replaced by an icy anger that stoked a cold resolve within. He wanted to push Bree away, to tell her that her kiss produced nothing but contempt. That neither she nor any woman, least of all Faith O'Connor, would ever own him. But he didn't. Instead, he jerked her close, his lips returning her passion with a hard fervor. And in the heat of their embrace, in the smoky midst of Brannigan's Pub, he quickly seared the memory of Faith O'Connor from his thoughts.

"My beloved put in his hand by the hole of the door, and my heart was moved for him. I rose up to open to my beloved; and my hands droppeth with myrrh, and my fingers with liquid myrrh, upon the handles of the bolt. I opened to my beloved; but my beloved had withdrawn himself, and was gone."

Faith's voice faded to silence, leaving the words of Song of Solomon hanging in the air like a lament.

Mrs. Gerson leaned forward in the chair, her brow furrowed with worry. "Faith? Are you all right? You don't seem yourself tonight, dear. We can do this another evening, if you like."

Faith looked up, her breath catching in her throat. "No . . . no, I'm all right."

Mrs. Gerson clucked her tongue, shifting her vacant eyes in the direction of Faith's voice.

Faith sighed. Mrs. Gerson's physical sight might be minimal, reduced to the movement of shadows, but the vision of her soul was remarkable indeed. "I'm sorry, Mrs. Gerson. I shouldn't have brought my problems here tonight. I'm all right, really I am. I'll do better. I promise."

"If you're going to promise anything, my dear, promise to tell the truth—now *that* would be doing better." Mrs. Gerson, a devoted Protestant, settled back in her wing chair and rested her hands on one of the many Bibles she possessed. She often remarked how she enjoyed touching its smooth leather binding as Faith read its words. "Like I'm reading it myself," she would say with a chuckle. She waited calmly, her gnarled fingers clasped in expectation.

Faith closed the Bible in her lap, the rustle of its pages followed by a soft thud. Her weighty sigh darkened the mood of the room like a shadow.

"My dear, I've never known you to be like this before. Please tell me what's wrong."

"I'm embarrassed to talk about it, Mrs. Gerson."

"Why? Has someone hurt you?" The tiny woman leaned forward in her chair, a note of alarm in her voice.

"No . . . I mean yes . . . in a way. But mostly I've caused my own pain. I don't know, Mrs. Gerson, it seems so silly to put into words."

"Suppose you give me the gist of it."

The springs in the sofa squeaked as Faith fidgeted. Mrs. Gerson remained silent. A loud ping escaped into the air as Faith sank back in the sofa. She took in a deep breath, then exhaled. "When I returned to school after the polio, no one would even speak to me. I was an outcast, a cripple. One day, this older boy defended me from a bully." Faith looked up, grateful the old woman couldn't see the wetness in her eyes. "He was kind, and I was lonely. I missed my sister Hope so much I thought I would die." Faith swallowed hard. "That boy's one moment of kindness was balm to my soul."

The sofa rattled as Faith jumped up to roam the parlor. "In high school we became friends for a brief time. Suddenly, he was all I ever thought about, dreamed about, wrote poetry about . . ." Faith stopped to catch a breath, expelling it with a shudder. "Even prayed about. It sounds obsessive, I know, and I suppose it was. But I kept thinking I would get over it, honestly I did. Then his father died, and he changed, and I thought, this is it! Collin McGuire, the all-American boy with the winning smile, is gone. All that's left is this cocky rebel who runs with a rough crowd." Faith paused. "I thought that would do it. It should have done it."

"Done what, my dear?"

"Taken the feelings away! I'm not ten anymore, I'm almost nineteen. I'm tired of the feelings, and I'm tired of the jealousy."

"The jealousy?"

"He wants Charity, Mrs. Gerson. They all want Charity."

"I see." The old woman set her Bible on the table and folded her hands in her lap.

"Wait . . . I haven't told you everything." Faith's voice broke as she sat back down.

Mrs. Gerson rose and crossed the room to sit beside her. "My dear, nothing's so terrible that God can't deliver you." She pulled a lace handkerchief from her sleeve and handed it to her.

Faith sniffed and blew her nose. "I know, and I would be crazy with despair if I didn't realize that. But what do I do? When it was just girlhood dreams, it was safe. But now . . ."

"My dear Faith, what in the world happened?"

Faith sucked in a deep breath. "He followed me to the park . . . and he made advances. He kissed me, and God help me, I can't get it out of my mind. I'm so ashamed because there isn't a minute I can't feel his touch, and yet I'm sick inside because . . . Mrs. Gerson, I *want* his touch! Never has my heart soared so, and yet I know it's wrong." Her voice bubbled into a sob.

Mrs. Gerson gathered her into her arms. "There, there, my child, everything's going to be fine. The Lord sees your heart. He knows how you long to please him."

"But these feelings are wrong, aren't they? Even if the impossible were true and Collin wanted me instead of my sister, aren't these feelings wrong?"

"Faith, my dear, feelings in and of themselves aren't wrong; it's what we choose to do with them that makes them wrong or right. Obviously you've been greatly stirred by this young man. Right or wrong, he's now fixed in your heart. As you read Song of Solomon tonight, your heart was reminded of him. Tell me, my dear, do you have any idea why the Bible would speak of these things in such a bold manner?"

Faith said no and wiped her nose with the handkerchief.

"Because, my dear, God is love. Not just maternal or fraternal love but romantic love as well. Song of Solomon was written to show what the love between a husband and a wife should be, but it was also written to emulate the depth of feeling and love God has for each of us. As intense and wonderful as this young man's kiss made you feel, more so is the passion and love God has for you. No, your feelings aren't wrong, but perhaps the timing is."

Mrs. Gerson tilted Faith's face in her hands. "Dear Faith, those same wonderful feelings will knit you to your husband some day in a romantic bond that God intends. The feelings you experienced when this young man kissed you—the racing heart, the lightheadedness, the overpowering warmth and sense of the moment—these are all good things. Created by a God whose love for you, if you can imagine, far surpasses how Collin made you feel. God intended for these wonderful feelings to be experienced between a man and his wife. But we live in a fallen world, my dear. Many choose to pursue such feelings outside of God's intent."

Mrs. Gerson sat back and sighed. "True enough, the passion and excitement are often as potent whether one is in or out of God's will. But a word of warning, my dear. The true depth, fulfillment, and joy you're searching for, such as what your parents experience, can only be found when God is part of the equation. When we seek such feelings and relationships outside of his will, I'm afraid we leave ourselves open to mediocrity and, more often than not, heartbreak."

Faith sniffed. "I believe that. But what do I do with these feelings for now? I can't seem to fight them."

Mrs. Gerson chuckled. "Oh, you'll fight them, all right. In a manner that will infuriate the devil more than you can know. You will, my dear, pray for this young man. Each time the feelings come, chase them away by praying that God will bring this Collin McGuire to his knees before the throne of God. Oh, the devil will hate that! With each prayer spoken, you'll find the heartache slowly receding. Trust me on this, my dear; when you pray for those who hurt you, remarkable things happen."

"Mrs. Gerson?" Faith's tone was troubled. "I desperately want to have strength . . . should he ever confront me again."

"Not to worry," Mrs. Gerson said as she rose to her feet. She toddled toward the kitchen with a mischievous smile on her lips. "That prayer belongs to me, my dear. And we both know how much I enjoy giving the devil his due."

Collin might have heard the church bells pealing if his brain wasn't pounding in his head. As it was, the blinding glare of the sun peeking over the horizon was the only reminder he'd stayed too long at Brannigan's Pub. His hands were sluggish and clumsy as he fumbled with the key in the door, and he was making far too much noise for someone who hoped to maintain a degree of stealth.

Before he could turn the knob, the door swung open. In an instant, he knew his hopes for avoiding confrontation with his mother were not based in reality. He blinked and tried to smile despite the throbbing in his head, but she only stared at him coldly. Her eyes were puffy and ringed with dark shadows, suggesting a fitful night's sleep. Or none at all.

"Mother, you're up. I hope I didn't wake you."

"Of course I'm up. It's morning, Collin. You promised me you would be home early. You promised. But obviously you've the same talent for breaking promises as your father."

Her words were a punch to the gut. He bit hard on his tongue, fearful he would say something he would regret. She was his mother, after all. He owed her that. He pushed past her to his room.

She followed, jerking his arm to spin him around. "You're worthless, just like your father, you know that, Collin? I should have never married him. I could have avoided all of this. Instead, I'm living in a rundown flat in a wretched part of town." She flung his arm away and stepped back, the rage in her eyes tempered by a gloss of tears. She shivered. "With nothing to my name but the shame of a son with the morals of a cat."

He stared, his anger suddenly melting into empathy. She was alone. Her bitterness cut her off from anyone who might attempt to love her. His father had tried and failed. She had been the world to him, the love of his life. But it hadn't been enough. He'd given his love, and she took until she owned him. Collin reached for the door, his fingers taut on the knob to keep from slamming it closed.

"Good night, Mother. I'm sorry for disturbing you." With deadly calm, he quietly clicked the door in her face. He flipped the lock. She was all he had. And so when he rose from his much-needed sleep, he would make peace, exchanging civilities and common courtesies as most families did. Until the next time.

4

Faith couldn't resist a tiny smile. She watched Maisie harpoon the last piece of sponge cake on her plate. Finally, she'd been able to get her best friend over for dinner so her family could meet her—and love her—just like Faith did. Maisie seemed delighted to meet them as well. After chuckling at one of Sean's corny jokes, she ducked to whisper something in Katie's ear.

Faith fought the urge to emit a deep sigh. Her gaze flitted from face-to-face, each rosy and smiling in the glow of flickering candlelight. Family. Good-natured teasing, the synchronized voices of children and adults laughing and sharing. She knew Maisie had never experienced anything like it before. Unless you counted Thanksgiving at Aunt Edna's, which, according to Maisie, consisted of Maisie and her parents sitting around a sparsely set table with her poor, near-deaf aunt. The meal would usually progress in silence, occasionally punctuated by inane topics such as Aunt Edna's arthritis or the neighbor's fondness for gin. As an only child of immigrant parents, Maisie Tanner was obviously mesmerized by this nerve center of perpetual motion known as the O'Connor family.

Washing her dessert down with a gulp of milk, Faith turned to her mother. "I know it's my turn to clear the table, but Maisie needs to do some research at the library for a night class she's taking. Would you mind if I went with her? I've arranged to read to Mrs. Gerson tomorrow night instead."

Marcy smiled. "No, of course not, Faith. Beth can clear the table for you tonight, and you can take her turn next week. Is that all right with you, Beth?"

Elizabeth nodded, giggling at Steven as he sculpted un-eaten mashed potatoes on his plate.

"Mother . . ." Charity's voice sounded tentative. "I have a paper to write also. May I go?"

Faith felt her breath hitch in her lungs. Her gaze darted to her mother's face, then to her sister's. The hopeful look on Charity's face was more than convincing.

Her mother seemed hesitant, no doubt contemplating the month of confinement she'd given Charity three weeks earlier. "Well, I suppose it wouldn't hurt . . ." she began, glancing up at Patrick. The smile died on her lips.

A muscle jerked in her father's jaw. "I think it would, Marcy. The answer is no."

"But Patrick, it's just the library . . ."

Something cold slithered in Faith's stomach when his lips flattened into a tight line. Faith peeked at Maisie out of the corner of her eye, then shifted to stare at her plate, awaiting her father's reply. There was none.

An awkward laugh gurgled from her mother's throat. "Patrick, she's been cooped up for three weeks now and only has a few days left on her punishment. I know we haven't discussed it, but I'm sure it will be fine to let her go."

He remained silent. Faith sensed the drama in the room, keenly aware that Charity also observed the silent debate between her parents.

Like a spring-propelled toy, Charity shot from her seat. "Oh, Mother, thank you so much! I've been going stir-crazy, and I really need to get out. I love you!" Before her mother could speak, Charity hugged her, then smiled at her father. "Thank you, Father." She blew a kiss in his direction, causing his lips to compress even more. "Faith, can you wait until I finish the dishes?"

Faith's eyes widened. "No, that will take—"

"No need, Charity." Her mother's voice was strained. "I'll do your dishes this evening."

Charity appeared skittish with excitement. "Mother, you're wonderful! May I be excused?"

Marcy nodded, and Charity flew from the room.

Maisie cleared her throat. "Dinner was wonderful, Mrs. O'Connor. Thank you so much. I'll help clear the table." She rose, stacking Katie's plate on top of hers, followed by utensils.

"No, you two get going; you've got a lot of research ahead of you." Patrick avoided his wife's eyes. "We enjoyed having you for dinner, Maisie. Please come again." He pushed his chair from the table and stood, his smile cool. "Marcy, may I see you in the kitchen?"

The unease in the room was as thick as the mashed-potato sculpture on Steven's plate. Faith stood and clamped a hand on Maisie's arm, dragging her from the room while she waved her good-byes. In the hall, Maisie cocked a questioning brow, but Faith simply put a finger to her lips while she ushered her friend to the parlor to wait on Charity. Faith's stomach felt as jumpy as water drops on a heated cast-iron skillet. She released a quiet sigh. Turmoil or no, Charity or no, family was family. And she wouldn't trade hers for the world.

Her heart raced like a frightened bird's as she ran to the phone and cranked its handle. She gave the operator Mary Flannery's phone number and waited for her friend to answer.

"Hello?"

"Mary? It's me, Charity. I have another favor to ask.

Would you mind running next door and giving Collin a message for me?"

Mary giggled. "You know I never mind having an excuse to talk to that man, Charity."

"Great! Would you tell him the book he's requested is in?"

A sigh drifted over the line, edged with tease. "That man sure reads a lot of books."

It was Charity's turn to giggle. "Yes, he's very well-read. Thanks, Mary. I owe you."

Charity returned the receiver to its cradle and leaned against the wall, eyes closed and hands pressed to her chest. She could hardly believe in less than an hour she would be with him again. A shiver of delight tickled her spine. She reminisced about the day on the porch and the kiss that possessed her thoughts the last three weeks. Goose bumps popped at the memory.

Inhaling a deep breath, she composed herself and opened her eyes. *I must contain myself.* Collin was five years older than she was, not one of the simpering schoolboys always vying for her attention. He could have any woman he wanted— she had to make sure it was her. He must see her as mature and desirable. Taking another deep breath, Charity ducked out of the kitchen and vaulted up the stairs two at a time.

She knew she could do it; doubt never even entered her mind. It was time she was concerned about. She needed time with Collin. And her parents had seen to it she had precious little of that. But she did have tonight. That is, if Mary managed to get the message to him. After tonight, she would simply take it a day at a time.

Charity entered her room, grinning. She could do that. One day—or one kiss—at a time.

Marcy knew she was in trouble when Patrick dismissed the children and began to clear the table himself.

"Father, don't you want me to do that?" Beth asked, brows furrowed in confusion.

"No, Beth, you and Steven take Katie in the parlor and read to her. I want to talk to your mother."

Marcy's stomach knotted as she watched her husband silently carry dishes and utensils to the kitchen. Reluctantly she followed, feeling as if she were treading on uncertain ground. Patrick and she seldom argued, and their relationship knew little strain. This was all so new to her—he was not a man of silence. Marcy stood at the door, almost timidly, then entered the kitchen, allowing the door to swing closed behind her. Patrick turned, and her heart thumped. The tenderness that always accompanied his gaze was gone. In its place was a spark of angry fire, the only sign of energy in his weary-looking body.

"Marcy, am I or am I not the head of this household?" His voice was quiet—too quiet. She nodded.

"Well, then tell me," he continued in a monotone voice, "why did you break with Charity's punishment without consulting me?"

"Patrick, I'm sorry, I know we agreed—"

"Yes, we did. And now my daughter has had it reaffirmed to her once again that all she need do is smile a pretty smile and flutter those lashes, and she can get her way."

"Patrick, you're being ridiculous."

"Am I, Marcy? Charity's a very bright girl who knows how to use her wiles to manipulate a situation. She wants control, and we cannot afford to give it to her."

Marcy's jaw tightened. "Don't you think you're carrying it to the extreme? She's a child of sixteen, not a con artist trying to pull the wool over our eyes."

Patrick slowly loosened his tie and rubbed his neck, his eyes locked on hers. "We must present a united front, especially where Charity is concerned. We have never wavered from that in the discipline of the children, and we must not start now. We cannot, and will not, waver with Charity. I won't allow it."

She felt the blood rushing to her cheeks and found she had little control over the hurt and anger that spewed from her lips. "You won't allow it! I've been married to you for over twenty-one years, Patrick O'Connor—don't start dictating to me now how to raise my children." She shivered as she stood there, arms clenched at her waist.

In several abrupt steps forward, he loomed before her, his eyes intense. He didn't touch her but pressed uncomfortably close, hands fisted at his sides. "When it comes to the welfare of my children, Mrs. O'Connor, you will, in the future, consult me regarding your decisions. Am I making myself perfectly clear?"

For a moment her breath wedged in her throat before spilling forth in a rush of angry defiance. "And you, Mr. O'Connor, in the future, can find somewhere else to sleep! Am I making myself perfectly clear?" Her tone was shrill.

He flinched as if she'd just spat in his face. For a brief moment, hurt flecked in his eyes before giving way to the coldest of steel. She watched in disbelief as he reached for his coat and jerked the door open wide, the wind banging it against the wall.

"Patrick, wait . . ." she heard herself say, but the door ricocheted and slammed shut on her choked words. Marcy stood dazed, hot tears pooling in her eyes. *What just happened?* She ran and flung the door open, calling his name, but her words were only met by a bluster of wind. She shivered, the chill of the air as cold as the chill in her heart. Her hands trembled as she slowly closed the door. She moved like a sleepwalker toward the table and sat down. Her heart felt so empty—like her bed would be tonight, she thought. The realization hit her hard, causing a fresh wave of tears.

Her hands were like ice as she leaned on them to pray. "Forgive me, Lord, for losing my temper and hurting my Patrick. Please Lord, soften his heart and help him to forgive me." Wiping the wetness from her cheek, she blew her nose. *Dear me, what would I do without the Lord?* She blinked, and fresh tears glossed her eyes. *And dear Lord, what would I do without Patrick?*

Boston Library was one of Faith's favorite places. From its graceful, curved archways to its gleaming chandeliers and stately pillars, it was to Faith one of the most beautiful buildings in the world. A place where one could lose themselves in the great classics of literature and escape to a peaceful respite in an otherwise hectic day. And certainly, Faith decided, a place where one might happily wile away the hours of a Saturday evening.

The moment they entered the building, Charity was off "researching Latin" in the world language department, promising to meet in the entryway when the library closed. Maisie and Faith headed to the research department, opting for a table by the door.

"So . . . are you all right?" Maisie ventured, brows wrinkling as she eyed Faith. "I mean, you were awfully quiet on the way here. Is there something going on between you and your sister? I thought you were going to bite her head off over her remark about the library being the only place you spend a Saturday night."

Faith shrugged, trying to act nonchalant. "Just good old rivalry between sisters. Consider yourself lucky to be an only child." She took off her coat and threw it over the chair.

"Well, I don't—consider myself lucky, that is. Goodness, Faith, you've got everything I ever wanted in a family."

Faith sighed and rubbed her face. "I know. I'm sorry. I do have a wonderful family. But don't be fooled. Even wonderful families have their problems."

"What's yours with your sister?"

Faith frowned. "What, are you studying psychology now? My sister and I get along most of the time. We just don't see eye-to-eye on everything."

"Okay, okay . . ." Maisie shook her head, rifling through her bag for paper and a pencil. "I'll tell you what, she sure is beautiful."

"Yes . . . she *is*." Faith tried to keep the edge out of her voice but didn't succeed.

Maisie looked up, shocked. "You're jealous!"

"What are you talking about? Yes, she's pretty, I'll grant you. But there's more to happiness than catching the eye of every male in Boston."

"I'm sorry," Maisie said. "I didn't mean to upset you."

"I'm not upset."

"Yes, you are. Why don't you admit it?"

Faith glared. "You know, you're a really pushy friend."

"Emphasis on *friend*. Come on, out with it." Maisie steeple-folded her hands on the table and arched her eyebrows in expectation.

Faith leaned over the table and pursed her lips. "All right, okay, I'm jealous of Charity. Always have been, probably always will be. There! You happy?"

"Not particularly. So why are you jealous of Charity? I mean, she's pretty, but so are you. It's gotta be more than that."

"What is it with you tonight, Maisie? You're annoyingly analytical."

"I'm waiting . . ."

"For what? For me to say I'm jealous of my sister because she's beautiful and gets all the attention from men?

Or because I look sixteen and she looks nineteen, which is probably why . . ."

"Why what?" Maisie arched a brow. "Mmm . . . something tells me there's a man involved." She wrinkled her nose and leaned forward like a dog on the scent. "She's caught the eye of someone you like, hasn't she?"

Faith gaped. How did she do it? She hadn't breathed a word to Maisie about Collin—before or after the kiss. As far as Maisie knew, he didn't exist. And yet, here she was, her prying finger neatly on the pulse of Faith's beating heart. Faith closed her mouth.

"I'm right, aren't I? Oh, Faith, this is so exciting! Who is it, do tell!"

"I can't believe I opened my mouth."

"Oh, but you didn't have to. Do you think I didn't notice you sulking all the way to the library? I know we've only been friends for three weeks, but I feel like I've known you forever. You're the best friend I've ever had."

Faith forced a weak smile. How could she be angry with Maisie? She was the best friend she'd ever had too. Faith sunk into the chair and stared glumly ahead, hands limp on the table. She shot a furtive glance at the few other people in the room before fixing her gaze on Maisie. "I've never told this to another living soul, except my dear neighbor who is more like a grandmother to me."

Maisie nodded.

Faith took a deep breath and proceeded to unravel the whole sad tale—from the schoolgirl crush to the pivotal kiss in the park. Her friend sat wide-eyed as Faith spilled her heart. When finished, she felt lighter, as if sharing the burden made it more bearable.

Maisie shook her head in amazement. "And to think I thought you were this brainy bookworm with little or no experience with men."

"But I am, that's just it. At the end of this week, I'll be

nineteen, and that was my first kiss ever." Faith's shoulders sagged. "That is, if you don't count Peter McKenna in the third grade."

Maisie rolled her eyes. "Oh, but what a kiss! I'd pay a week's salary for a kiss like that."

Faith made a wry face. "Well, I wouldn't. It's my sister he wants."

"I wouldn't be so sure."

"Anyway," Faith said, quickly dismissing the notion, "one thing I am sure of is Collin McGuire is trouble for both me and my sister. My head—and my heart—tell me loud and clear to stay away from the likes of him."

Maisie suddenly jolted upright in the chair. In a scrunch of freckles, she peered at Faith. "Hey, Charity was awfully anxious to spend the evening in the library. You don't suppose . . ." She bounced up and started for the door.

"Suppose what? Wait! Where do you think you're going?"

Maisie wheeled around, grinning like a pixie. "I need a book from the language department."

"Oh no you don't!" Faith said as she ran after her.

"Oh yes I do. I need something on the language of *love*." She drawled out the word so ridiculously that Faith couldn't help a little giggle as she ran to keep up with her.

"Maisie, you're crazy!"

"Hush! The esteemed department of language lies just beyond those doors. Do you want to stay here while I explore?"

"No, I'll come. If he's here, I'd like to embarrass him— both of them." Somehow the thought of Collin and Charity together didn't have quite the sting to it with Maisie by her side. They tiptoed into the cavernous language department, which was dimly lit and mostly deserted this time of night. An elderly gentleman sat reading in a far corner while two students appeared to be studying—each other more than the books strewn on the table before them.

Maisie motioned her head toward the bookshelves in the loft area overhead. Faith nodded. The two crept up the staircase like burglars on the prowl. Faith shadowed her friend while she peeked around each and every bookcase. All at once, Maisie lunged back, colliding into her. With a look of smug victory, she put her finger to her lips and pointed. Faith took a deep breath. It jammed in her throat when Maisie yanked her into the aisle where Collin McGuire hovered over her sister. His hands were pressed against the wall on either side as if caging her in, but Charity seemed anything but trapped. She smiled up at him beneath thick lashes. Faith heard Collin laugh, and her body went cold as she shrank out of sight.

"Look, Faith, I found her!" Maisie announced, causing Charity to gasp and Collin to swear. He spun around.

"Mmm . . . nice research," Maisie said. She stretched her hand toward Collin, who stood speechless. "You must be Collin McGuire. I'm Maisie. It's nice to meet you," she said.

Maisie reached back and jerked Faith into open view. She wanted to die. There she stood, face-to-face with the man who had occupied most of her thoughts—and prayers—for the last seven days. Faith was as crimson as Charity, who stood in shock, her back hard against the wall.

Collin appeared immobilized for the briefest amount of time before he visibly relaxed. A shadow of a smile formed on his lips. "Hello, Little Bit," he said softly.

"You know my sister?" Charity asked, a slight razor edge to her voice.

Collin never took his eyes from Faith's. "We've met. Let's see, I believe it was in the—"

"High school," Faith interrupted. "It was in high school."

His smile flickered at the corners of his mouth.

He's enjoying this! Instinctively, her lips clamped tight. He laughed out loud. "And just what is so incredibly funny?" Faith demanded.

He laughed again. "You. You're the same funny little girl you were then."

Faith was appalled, Charity seemed relieved, and Maisie appeared to enjoy every mortifying moment. Collin turned back to Charity. "Enjoyed the book. Let me know when the next one comes in." He reached to pull her close and kissed her soundly.

Faith looked away with heat scorching her cheeks. Collin turned and edged by, resting a hand on her shoulder in a fraternal fashion. He leaned close to her ear. "What about you, Faith? Read any good books lately?"

He's a devil, she thought, her heart thundering in her chest.

With effortless charm, Collin turned to Maisie. He nodded his head toward her. "Nice to meet you too—Maisie, is it? Have a good evening, ladies."

And with that he was gone, leaving, as always, bewildered women in his wake.

5

Patrick tried to remember the last time he'd crossed the threshold of Brannigan's Pub—certainly not within the last twenty years. There'd been no need. From the moment he had laid eyes on Marcy, she had been all the intoxication he needed. But tonight . . . well, tonight he needed more, and with lips leveled in a hard line, he once again returned to the dark and smoky confines of the pub that had once been a second home. He looked around. Almost nothing had changed, except for the faces and style of clothing the patrons wore. They still crowded around the same rickety piano and leaned against the same endless cherrywood bar, which looked as if it were polished to a gleam twice a day. The smoky haze was the same, the smells were the same, and the lure and promise of trading in one's problems for a night of revelry was as strong as ever.

Patrick only recognized a few faces, such as Lucas Brannigan, the proud owner of this, the most successful pub in the Southie neighborhood. And, of course, there was Tommy Thomkins, minstrel to those who found themselves alone and miserable, catering to anyone who would drink up his melodies along with bottomless mugs of beer.

Patrick found a vacant barstool and wearily sat down, wedged between a bloke passed out on the bar and a young couple so entwined they only required a single stool. The sleeping man beside him was snoring loudly, cheek pressed hard on the cherrywood bar. Drool funneled from his mouth into a pool of saliva. Patrick forced himself to stare straight ahead at the endless rows of bottles overhead, each reflected in the smoky mirror behind, each a tonic of choice for various problems of the afflicted. The couple to his right disengaged momentarily to sate their thirst, and Patrick caught the nauseating scent of perfume mingled with sweat and stale beer. The whiff of it reminded him just how much Marcy had changed his life for the better.

The thought of her now brought a strange mix of sadness and longing, and more than a bit of anger. They'd had their arguments over the years, but she had never done this before, never questioned his authority or spoken to him with anything other than the utmost respect. And certainly, she had never turned him out of her bed before. Patrick nodded to the bartender who pushed a foaming mug toward him, the frothy rise of beer tumbling over the edge before slithering into a puddle on the bar.

He brought the mug to his lips, and the biting brew tasted strong and good going down. So much so, he was shocked when he emptied it. He would have only one more, he vowed to himself. This wasn't the end of his life, after all, only an argument, a minor interruption in a twenty-one-year love affair that was the impetus of everything good in his life. She would know by his absence just how much she had hurt him, and she would be sorry and ready to welcome him back. Patrick signaled for another, then sipped it slower this time as he mulled over his thoughts. He downed the dregs of the mug and blinked in surprise when the bartender magically produced another, its glorious overflow enticing him to succumb.

His sweaty palms hovered around the glass. He was wrestling with pushing it away when he felt the presence of someone standing close, lodged between the hopelessly entangled couple and himself. He blinked up at a pretty woman in her midthirties, and his fingers recoiled as if he'd touched a hot stove. Her dark hair billowed loosely about her shoulders while her green eyes assessed him with open curiosity.

She nodded at his beer. "Drink up—my treat. And tell me now, sweetness, where in the world have you been keeping yourself!" It was a statement of pleasant surprise rather than a question, and Patrick could do nothing but stare, completely caught off-guard by the woman before him. Her smile broke into a delighted grin at the effect she seemed to be having, and she sidled closer until barely inches away, her gaze level with his. "What, cat got your tongue? The name's Lucy, and it appears you could do with some company. We have a table over there—why don't you join us?"

She waited while he grappled with his response, then noticed the ring on his left hand. If she was disappointed, she never let it show as she rested her hand on top of his.

"Look, it's only a beer with some friends. We'll send you back to your darlin' wife with your virtue intact, if that's what's worrying you."

Patrick knew in his gut he should turn and go. Something within him desperately wanted to walk away and return home to Marcy, work things out and hold her in his arms once again. But as the beer took effect, the allure of home seemed impaired, temporarily overshadowed by the irrefutable charm of this place and the woman before him.

Lucy seemed to be holding her breath as she awaited his answer. When a smile pulled at his lips, she exhaled slowly, carefully. Her eyes were gleaming. "I hope that's a yes!"

"It is, at that. One beer with you and your friends. Then I'll be on my way."

It was only an innocent drink with friends, he reasoned, nothing more and nothing less. Within the hour, he would be back home with Marcy where he belonged, where he would be right now if she hadn't turned on him so. She had provoked him to this end, he decided, and she would soon realize just how much she'd hurt him.

"Everyone, this is—" Lucy turned to Patrick, an unabashed grin on her face. "Saints alive, I completely forgot to get your name."

"It's Patrick . . . Patrick O'Connor. It's a pleasure to meet you all."

"Oh no, Patrick, you have it all wrong. The pleasure is all Lucy's!"

The group broke into uproarious laughter as Lucy punched the arm of the sloshed man who'd spoken. Someone ordered a round of beer. They raised a toast to Patrick, and then one to Lucy, and then to no one in particular. Their laughter was contagious and their beer ever flowing, and before long, Patrick found himself wondering why he'd stopped coming here. Through the fog in his mind, he felt someone tugging his sleeve. He looked up and saw Lucy in a blur, smiling like a trio of angels.

"Let's dance," she said.

And so he did, unsteady on his feet as they slowly moved to the melancholy sound of Tommy Thomkin's soulful ballad. She burrowed in his arms, startling him when the scent of her perfume aroused his senses. She lifted her gaze to his mouth, her lips parted slightly. Closing her eyes, she waited for the kiss she seemed to expect. Painful seconds passed as a war waged within him, and Patrick could hear the blood rushing in his ears. Suddenly, his arms went slack at her waist. He faltered back.

Lucy opened her eyes to see his retreat, and before he

could turn her away, she kissed him. Abruptly, he shoved her away, a mixture of arousal and shame in his gut. He stood there, weaving, sweat trickling inside his collar.

Somewhere in the back of his mind, beneath the numbness the beer created and the passion Lucy ignited, an appalling guilt began to gnaw. He thought of Marcy, alone and asleep in his bed, their children slumbering in the rooms down the hall, and a sense of shame began to counter the intoxication of Lucy's seduction.

What had possessed him to do this? He hadn't touched another woman for over twenty-one years, hadn't sought it out or even wanted to. But tonight he'd fallen. The virtues he espoused to his own children now returned, a bitter derision of his own failure. *Dear God, forgive me, I've been a fool.* But, surely a fool who could put an end to his folly. Patrick stared at Lucy, his eyes too clouded to see her face. He hesitated before touching her arm. "Lucy, I'm sorry, but I should go. Lucy . . . I love my wife."

Lucy's lips quivered into a weak smile. She put her hands on Patrick's face. "That's as plain as the nose on your face, Patrick O'Connor." Stepping on tiptoe, she kissed him lightly on the cheek. "Go on with you, now."

Patrick nodded, lowering his gaze from her eyes. His body went to stone at the sound of a voice from behind.

"Well, good evening, Mr. O'Connor! Hello, Lucy."

Patrick's stomach rolled. Slowly he turned to look into the smiling face of Collin McGuire.

"You two make a lovely couple," Collin remarked.

A rush of hot blood flooded Patrick's face as he confronted the man who had been the source of so much grief. He wanted to slap the smirk off his face, to berate him for enticing his daughter and driving a wedge between them. He wanted to hurt him because he stood there judging him for this moment of failure, just as Patrick had always judged him. Patrick felt the sweat crawling down the back of his neck.

Collin offered a smug smile while Lucy blinked, totally bewildered. "Collin, do you know Patrick?"

"Lucy, do you know he's married?"

Patrick started to lunge, but Lucy held him back.

"Yes, I know he's married! You think I'm blind, do you?"

"This isn't as it appears . . ." Patrick's breathing was heavy, his face hot. He hated himself for being in a position where he felt the need to explain himself to this rabble. And he hated the superior look on the rabble's face even more.

"Is that so? Well, you know, that's often the case, isn't it, Mr. O'Connor? For instance, it certainly looks for all practical purposes as if you were—shall we say dancing?—with a woman who's not your wife."

Patrick winced as if Collin had struck him.

"But we both know despite how it looks to the naked eye"—Collin paused, his eyebrows arched in apparent assessment of the situation—"we can find not only a perfectly innocent explanation, but ourselves in grave danger of misjudgment, wouldn't you say?"

Patrick's humiliation was complete. Suddenly he felt very tired, very sober, and completely drained of all energy. Shame weighted him down like a ton of steel. Resigned, he turned to Lucy. "Lucy, I owe you an apology, I owe Collin an apology, and most of all, I owe my wife an apology. I should have never come here tonight. I love her, and I let momentary anger get in the way of that. I was wrong to succumb to your obvious charms. Please forgive me."

Lucy managed a sad smile. "Oh, go on with ya now, Patrick. It was me who came after you, now didn't I? I saw the ring on your finger, plain as day. I was just hopin' it didn't mean all that much, that's all. Go on, hurry home to that wife of yours. I swear by St. Patrick himself she's one of the luckiest women in all of Boston. And don't you know I'm giving her fair warning. If she ever treats you badly, I promise I won't be letting go quite so easy." Lucy grabbed Patrick's coat from the chair and threw it at him, a feeble attempt at a smile on her face. "Go on, get out of here!"

Patrick caught his coat and nodded before turning once again to Collin. "There's not much I can say, Collin. You're right. I have judged you—a most common error, I suspect, among fathers of the sixteen-year-old girls you've pursued. I apologize for that. And I apologize you had to see me make the biggest mistake of my life. But I don't apologize for being Charity's father. That in itself entitles me to decide whom my daughter may court and whom she may not."

Patrick put his coat on. "You know, Collin, I was a lot like you when I was your age; had quite a way with the ladies, if you will. I certainly broke more than my fair share of hearts, much as I suspect you do. As Charity's father, I prefer you break someone else's heart other than hers. For goodness sakes, she's sixteen and very vulnerable. I know she looks like a woman, but she's just a little girl—*my* little girl."

Some of the arrogance faded from Collin's face as he watched Patrick through wary eyes.

Patrick continued. "You're a man. You need to find the love of a good woman, not a young girl. I found the right woman, and it changed my life forever. Filled me with contentment and happiness I never dreamed possible."

"*Except* for tonight." Collin's voice was quiet.

Patrick's countenance fell. "Yes, except for tonight. Tonight something happened that hasn't happened in over twenty years of marriage. We fought bitterly. Tell me, Collin, do you know what we fought about? Would you like to know what shattered our evening and sent me bolting into the night? Well, I'll tell you. We fought over Charity. Over whether or not she should have the right to go out tonight. Could we trust her? Was the discipline of confining her to the house for three weeks enough to impact her? These are questions that race around in a parent's mind, sometimes creating an environment of volatility. And so we fought—over whether or not the punishment we gave for seeing you behind our backs was enough. Enough to let her know we loved her, and as her parents, knew what was best for her. Maybe you can tell me. Was it?"

Collin's eyes filled with surprise. "Why don't you ask your daughter?" he said, his tone belligerent. "She's your little girl, after all."

Patrick's anger surged with renewed fervor. "I'm giving you fair warning, McGuire. Stay away from my daughter."

"Or what? How can you stop me except by making it a little more difficult? I have a lot of feelings for your daughter, Mr. O'Connor. She's not just another conquest to me. Charity loves me, and that's pretty tempting for someone who's never had a lot of that in his life. I don't want to be at odds with you, truly I don't. But don't think you can cut me off from Charity's love."

"And what's more important? Charity? Or the fact that you think she loves you?"

The truth of his query seemed to catch Collin square in the gut. For a moment, his gray eyes widened, then clouded to charcoal as he brooded over Patrick's words. Collin cuffed the back of his neck and cursed under his breath. He peered at Patrick, a muscle twitching in his cheek. "It doesn't matter. Charity loves me. And nothing— not the fact I may or may not love her, nor the fact she's only sixteen, nor the dictates of her father—*nothing* will stop that girl of yours from seeking me out, nor me her.

It's a fact of life, Mr. O'Connor, and one I'm afraid you'll just have to get used to."

Patrick looked at the young man before him and tried very hard to dislike him. He was too good-looking for his own good, too confident and too cocky. But for all his air of superiority and all the problems he posed to Patrick's peace of mind, Collin was not unlike a similarly cocky Irishman of twenty years past. Before he found the love of a good woman and before he relented to the hand of God in his life. Patrick sighed and put his hand on Collin's shoulder. At his touch, Collin stiffened.

"Nothing?" Patrick's voice was strangely unaffected. "Well, make no mistake about it, Collin, I will fight you every step of the way on this. And I'm very sure you and Charity will do the same. However, my boy, I'm afraid you're forgetting one very important thing." Patrick slapped Collin on the shoulder, then buttoned his coat and headed toward the door.

Curiosity apparently got the best of Collin McGuire as he grabbed Patrick by the arm. "And what might that be, Mr. O'Connor?"

The faint smile on Patrick's lips felt almost peaceful. "Never—and I repeat, never—underestimate the power of a father on his knees." And with that he left, leaving Collin, despite the warmth of the pub, very much out in the cold.

Patrick entered the dark foyer and glanced at the clock on the parlor mantel. His heart sank—1:07 a.m. The reality of what had taken place tonight settled over him like a shroud, blacker than the gloom of his house as he slowly made his way up the steps. At the top of the stairs, Blarney met him, his tail wagging to let him know someone was glad he was home, even if Marcy wouldn't be. He scratched the dog under the neck for a moment, then glanced down the hall at the door of his room. Would Marcy be awake? He hoped not. He desperately needed some hours of sleep before facing her. But face her he would, come morning. The very thought caused his stomach, full of beer and bitter regret, to churn within. As if in a trance, he moved to the bathroom, where he quickly washed his face and brushed his teeth before continuing down the hall to their room.

Carefully, Patrick turned the doorknob to his bedroom and cautiously pushed the door ajar. He peered into the dark and strained his eyes until he saw her small form in the bed. She was buried beneath the mound of covers that always occupied her side. Patrick stopped and listened. The faint rhythm of her breathing could be heard, the mountain of covers slowly rising and falling in harmony with the sound. He removed his shoes and trousers and then his rumpled shirt and tie. He reached for his pajamas from the hook on the wardrobe and put them on. He walked to the nightstand and poured water from the pitcher into a glass, then added a small amount of Marcy's perfumed water. Swishing the concoction in his mouth, he glanced at the bed and swallowed hard. He prayed it would disguise the smell of beer on his breath. Silently, he crossed the room to his side of the bed, gently lifting the covers. Marcy never moved a muscle, except for the imperceptible motion of the covers as they rose and fell. Patrick eased his way into the bed, gradually stretching his legs to the bottom edge. With a silent sigh, he tentatively began to relax, the peace of sleep quickly pulling at the corners of his consciousness.

Somewhere in the dark recesses of his mind, he heard something move. And then, before the escape of sweet sleep could steal him away, she pounced. Her eyes blazed and her fingernails slashed like a cat stabbing its prey. Bolting up in bed, Patrick fended her off as her hands flailed in the dark and she spat whispered screams. He grabbed her wrists and shoved her back on the bed, holding her down.

"Marcy, listen to me, please . . ."

She sniffed in the air. "Sweet saints, Patrick, you've been drinking! You reek of smoke and . . . is that perfume?" He had never seen her eyes so wild. "Let me go, Patrick, let me go!"

Her voice was so shrill that Patrick glanced at the door in alarm. "Marcy, you'll wake the children. Can't we talk, please?"

Marcy squeezed her eyes shut, as if to make him disappear. "I don't care if I wake the children. Let them see what kind of father they have—a man who stays out all hours of the night doing the devil knows what! I can't even stand to look at you."

"Marcy, please . . . I'm so sorry. I was wrong, so wrong. Please forgive me. I love you." Patrick's words were coming in short raspy sounds, fraught with repentance.

Marcy's eyelids flew open. "You love me? You have the nerve to say you love me, and this is how you show it? You go and get drunk and let women fall all over you? You know, it's funny, Patrick, but that doesn't exactly say love to me."

"I'm not drunk. I've had a few beers, yes, but I did nothing wrong," Patrick lied, and Marcy seemed to sense it the instant the words were out of his mouth. All at once, as if the wind had been sucked from her, she went limp, a look of pain on her face as tears welled in her eyes.

"You're lying. You . . . did something tonight, didn't you?" Her voice was barely a whisper. She searched his face as if looking for something, anything to tell her it wasn't true. Patrick lowered his eyes. Marcy wrenched from his grasp and huddled to the other side of the bed. She jumped up, her hair tumbling about her nightgown like a banshee.

Patrick's heart felt like a boulder in his chest. He got up from the bed and walked toward her.

Marcy stepped back, her hand in front of her. "No! Don't touch me. I never dreamed you would do . . . anything . . ." She seemed at a loss for words.

He stood there, staring with sorrowful eyes. For a moment, she seemed to sway, appearing about to faint. In slow motion, she moved toward the bed and sat down, as if in a trance. Tears streamed freely down her face. Without uttering a word, Patrick quietly sat beside her, attempting to encircle her with his arms. At his touch, she began to pummel him with her fists, a broken wail heaving from her chest. All at once, she collapsed, and her sobs retched against him. Patrick held her tightly. The sweet scent of lilac soap filled his nostrils, causing his heart to ache for her. He longed to tell her she was everything to him, that no other woman could even come close. That he would be nothing without her by his side, loving him, supporting him. And, yes, despite his many frailties, helping him to be the man God intended him to be. But for the moment, in his abject failure, he remained silent, clutching her until the last whimper subsided.

When they did, he lifted her chin to stare into her swollen eyes. "Marcy, look at me, please. Nothing happened. Yes, it's true I had too much brew. And yes, I did dance with a woman." He swallowed hard. "But it meant nothing, Marcy. Nothing. I turned her away. But I was wrong to go there, wrong to leave you. So wrong. Please forgive me. I was angry. And then the drink, it . . . it took hold." He shivered involuntarily, clearing his throat in embarrassment. He grabbed her by the shoulders. "Marcy, you have to believe me. Now more than ever, I realize how much you mean to me. How much I need you." A lump formed in his throat, forcing his voice to crack.

She remained limp in his arms, and so he caressed her

face with his lips. He whispered his sorrow, telling her he loved her, cherished her, needed her. His lips brushed against hers, and he could feel the fire of his passion burn deep inside. With renewed fervor, he kissed her again. He felt her relent with a startling hunger of her own. Sweeping her up in his arms, he laid her gently on the bed, his lips never wavering from the sweetness of her mouth. In one beat of his heart, he was overcome with love for her. An intense rush of emotion flooded his soul for this woman who possessed his heart so completely. He stroked her face, her neck, her arms with such impassioned tenderness that a soft moan escaped her lips.

"Marcy, I love you," he said, his voice a hoarse whisper, "more than life itself."

She met his mouth violently with her own, and he knew in that one action, she forgave, allowing the intensity of their love to carry them away.

Marcy was tired but content as she moved about the kitchen preparing breakfast for her family. For a brief moment she paused and stood in the middle of the room with a stack of plates in her arms, thinking about what transpired just a short time ago. How could it be, she wondered, that only hours ago her heart had been so incredibly heavy, sick with pain, broken? And then, in a blink of an eye—or a kiss—suddenly the same heart felt so incredibly light, so free and so alive.

Marcy set the plates on the table and slowly distributed them, each to its proper place. She already knew the answer. She had done what she'd been taught to do. To do what was, after all the tears and heartbreak, the only thing she could do. She gave it to God—her anger, her hurt, her marriage. After hours of weeping, she had taken her heavy heart and placed it in the hands of her loving God, and finally she was able to drift off to sleep. And as the soft light of day had gently spilled into the room, her heart remained in his loving grasp, peaceful and whole as she'd lain in the arms of the man she loved.

The memory brought a rush of warmth to her heart and heat to her cheeks. Marcy closed her eyes. They had made love and then talked until the first glimmers of dawn crept across their sill, bathing the room with its pale light. It had been a time of healing . . . of rediscovery . . . of prayer. And when it was over, they made love again. To Marcy, it had been a completely cathartic experience, a sacred renewal of vows. She had not believed she could love Patrick O'Connor any more than she already did, but she had been wrong.

Theirs had always been a marriage of love and tender passion, but over the years, her true appreciation had diminished somewhat. She realized now she had taken it all for granted—taken him for granted. Her heart skipped a beat as she thought of him—his slow, easy smile and rugged good looks. And it stopped altogether at the idea of another woman holding him in her arms, kissing his lips. The very notion sent a jolt of fear and pain ricocheting through her. When had she lost sight of it all, even for a moment?

Lost in her reverie, Marcy failed to see Patrick enter the kitchen. She jumped as he embraced her from behind, wrapping his strong arms around her waist and burrowing his lips in her hair. She put a hand to her stomach, hoping to quell the hot flood of passion he stirred, while her cheeks reheated with embarrassment. *Saints alive, woman,* she thought to herself, *wasn't last night enough?* She took a deep breath. "Patrick! The children will walk in any moment."

Patrick's hands slowly brushed up the side of her waist, past her breasts, to her throat where his fingers began to trace, feathering her skin along the neckline of her blouse. "You weren't worried about the children last night . . ."

Marcy slipped from his grasp and turned to face him. Her heart melted at the smile on his lips and the sparkle in his eyes. She steadied herself. "Last night I was angry . . ."

Patrick's eyes never left hers as he took a step forward. "And now?"

Lord, the man is attractive! When did I lose sight of that? "Now, I'm so much in love with my husband I can't seem to get breakfast on the table."

In one quick reach, she was back in his arms, his lips on hers and the fervor of the night rekindled. Never had Marcy wanted to return to their bed more, to take their fill of love until they exhausted their passion. Oh, how she wanted to allow the children to fend for themselves! But she was a mother as well as a wife and needed to feed her children far more than her passion. Breathless, she pulled away.

"Good morning, Mother, Father. What a beautiful day! Did you sleep well?" Charity seemed oblivious to the blush Marcy felt on her face. Her daughter took her place at the table, humming softly under her breath.

The kitchen door was still swinging behind her as Patrick cleared his throat and sat down, a twinkle in his eye. "Good morning, Charity. Yes, we did sleep well, as a matter of fact. Best ever, wouldn't you say, Marcy?"

Marcy turned her back to retrieve the bacon and eggs keeping warm in the oven. "Yes, one of the best nights I've had in years." She smiled warmly at her daughter, careful to avoid Patrick's eyes lest they prompt another telltale blush. "You're certainly in a wonderful mood this morning," Marcy observed as she brought the utensils to the table.

Charity bounded up and took them from her. "Oh, I am! You can't imagine how caged I felt staying home for so long. I hate to say it, but I think the restraint did me good. I wanted out so badly, even the library was a thrill."

Marcy pushed the kitchen door ajar and called the others to breakfast. Within minutes, a stampede of hungry O'Connors descended on the kitchen while Marcy poured steaming cups of coffee for Patrick and herself.

"Mama, Faith won't let me wear my red dress to church this morning." Katie's mood was clearly not as jubilant as Charity's.

Marcy smiled patiently at her youngest daughter. "Katie, you wore the red dress last Sunday; your blue dress looks lovely, dear."

"But I like the red dress, and what's more, God likes it better too!" Katie was quite adamant, arms crossed and tone unyielding.

"Katie, stop complaining and sit down." Patrick's tone was as obstinate as Katie's. "Your mother's fixed a wonderful breakfast, and I'd just as soon avoid indigestion before tasting it."

"What's inde-jest-shun?" Katie wanted to know.

Patrick gave her the eye. "An upset stomach . . . not unlike," he continued, "an upset bottom after a spanking."

Katie got the gist and scrambled up into her chair, a truly angelic look on her face.

"Mama, I forgot to tell you Sister Cecilia says we need to bring money for the pagan babies," Steven said, grabbing his milk.

Marcy nodded as she spooned eggs on his plate. "Sean, will you be a dear and reach behind you for the toast? It's right on the counter. Does everyone have what they need? Are we ready to say grace?" Marcy sat down, took a deep breath, and smiled at Patrick.

He smiled back and bowed his head in prayer. "Lord, we thank you for this bountiful breakfast and for the beginning of another wonderful week in our lives. Our gratitude knows no bounds for the blessings"—Patrick glanced up at Marcy and grinned—"and the mercy you've so lavishly bestowed. Amen."

After the prayer, Patrick began loading his plate with bacon. "So, Faith . . . how was the library?"

Charity choked on a piece of toast, and Marcy patted her back while she coughed for several seconds. "Charity, are you all right?"

She nodded, her face flushed. "Yes, Mother, I'm fine. Just went down the wrong pipe."

Faith's eyes narrowed as she looked at her sister, but Charity avoided her gaze altogether. Patrick munched on his bacon, apparently still awaiting an answer. Faith sighed and frowned at her plate. "It was fine, I suppose. I mean, I love being with Maisie because she's so much fun, but I guess I just wasn't in the best of moods."

"You seemed fine when you left. What happened?" Patrick asked.

Charity chewed her bacon slowly.

"Oh, nothing, really. It's just Maisie and I spent so much time talking, I felt badly she didn't get much research in. Seemed like a wasted evening for her, that's all."

"Cultivating a friendship is never a wasted evening, darlin'," Patrick said, reaching for more toast. "Besides, young girls are entitled to a little fun on a Saturday night. How about you, Charity—did you get much research done?"

The tone of his voice caused Marcy to look up. He was studying Charity closely, as was Faith. Charity appeared cool and unruffled as she responded to her father, her smile stage-perfect.

"Yes, I did. I'm nearly done with my paper, as a matter of fact," she said. "Thank you for letting me go, Father. I feel worlds better today. Is anybody going to eat that last piece of toast?"

Marcy put a piece of bacon into her mouth and chewed,

looking across the table at her husband. A frown furrowed her brow as she detected a slight scowl on his lips. His pensive gaze flitted from Faith's deadpan expression to Charity's smiling face, then back once again. Marcy stopped chewing. Faith seemed fidgety, pushing at the untouched food on her plate, and her face was flushed. "Faith, are you feeling all right?" Marcy asked.

Faith dropped her fork on her plate with a clatter. Blushing, she suddenly shot up from the table and glanced at her father before attempting a feeble smile in Marcy's direction. "No . . . no, Mother, I'm not. May I be excused? I think I'll go and lie down before we leave for church, if you don't mind."

"Let me feel your head." Marcy put her palm on Faith's forehead for a moment, then gently stroked her daughter's cheek. "You feel okay, but you really do look flushed. Go and lie down, and I'll be up shortly. If you're not feeling better, I think you need to stay home."

Faith nodded and fled from the kitchen. Marcy looked up to see Patrick's gaze follow her out the door. His eyes seemed distant.

"Patrick, are *you* feeling all right?" There was the slightest hint of alarm in her voice.

Patrick looked up and smiled. "I'm fine, Marcy. How could I not be?"

The look of tenderness was back. Marcy returned his smile. Indeed, she thought to herself, how could either of them not be?

6

Her father was quieter than usual this morning. Faith stole a glimpse at him out of the corner of her eye. It was Monday, of course, she reasoned to herself, always a difficult day to get moving again. But still, he was definitely more pensive as he sat, arms folded, beside her on the trolley that bumped along Portland Street en route to the *Herald*.

"Father, are you all right?"

A shadow of a smile flickered on his lips as he glanced at her with a tender look. "Yes, darlin', I'm fine. Just a few things on my mind, that's all."

"Are you worried about the election . . . and the war in Europe?"

Patrick sighed and grabbed the pole when the streetcar lurched to a stop. His brow wrinkled slightly. "Yes, of course I am. I'm fairly confident President Wilson will win reelection, but I can't help but be concerned about our involvement overseas."

Faith's stomach tightened, both from the jostling of the trolley and her father's words. "You don't think we'll go to war, do you, Father?"

Patrick's look was sober. "I can't help but believe it's inevitable. I hoped it wouldn't be, but when the *Lusitania* was torpedoed by that German sub last year, well, I'm afraid my hopes sank along with it. I know the president has been trying to keep us out of the war, to maintain a position of neutrality, but I suspect it's only a matter of time. Of course, when the Germans sank the *Sussex* earlier this year, President Wilson did manage to get their pledge not to sink merchant vessels without warning, and certainly without saving the lives of those aboard. But, I'm afraid I hold out little hope of their compliance. We're hanging on to our neutrality by a thread. Wilson will probably be reelected because he kept us out of the war, but it's likely to be a hollow victory."

Faith stared out the window, the prospect of war whirling in her brain. "But haven't the Germans kept their pledge so far?" She turned to face him. "I mean, they have, haven't they?"

Patrick shifted closer to Faith to allow a heavyset man to pass as he made his way off the trolley. "Yes, they have, darlin'—so far. I just don't know how long we can trust them."

"If they do break the pledge, will we go to war with them?"

"More than likely."

"And will you have to go? And Sean?" She held her breath.

Patrick squeezed her hand. "There's always that possibility. But you listen to me. No matter what happens, we can get through anything, anything at all. We're a close-knit family with a very deep faith. If it happens—and I do mean *if*—then with God by our sides, we'll get through it, do you hear me?"

Faith nodded stiffly.

"That's my girl." He smiled and released her hand. "Now, before we get to our stop, there is something else on my mind."

The minute the words were out of his mouth, Faith suddenly became enamored by the passing scenery. "I hope it's nothing too serious after this last conversation," she teased, praying her father would think twice before broaching the subject of Collin McGuire.

He didn't return her smile as the car rumbled toward Herald Square. The pensiveness was back. "There is something else I'm concerned about. It's Charity. I can't seem to get through to her. She and I have never . . . well, I guess we've never had the closeness you and I share. I regret that, I really do, and no matter how hard I try, I can't seem to fix it." Her father rubbed his face with his hands, then leaned forward. "I've got to know. Is Charity still seeing Collin McGuire behind my back?"

A wave of warmth assailed Faith's cheeks. "I . . . I really can't say, Father." She looked at other passengers, at the back of the conductor's head, out the window—anywhere but at her father's face.

He sighed heavily. "You don't have to. I'm afraid it's written all over your face." He patted her hand. "You know, darlin', it's awfully good you're not prone to lying, because you really are terrible at it." The trolley jerked to a stop, and he stood and took her arm firmly in his. He guided her down the aisle with a gentle hand to her back and nodded at the driver before alighting from the car. "Let's go punch that clock before they dock our pay."

Faith cleared the last step, then turned to look at him. "But, Father, wait—what are you going to do?"

He latched on to her arm again and began walking quickly, dodging an elderly man toddling with a cane and a paperboy tugging a wagonload of newspapers. "Well, I suppose we'll need to restrict her a bit more, watch her like a hawk as much as we can, and then do the only thing that's really going to matter anyway." Patrick smiled at his daughter. "No question your mother will be lighting a lot more candles at church, and I'll be saying a few more prayers."

Faith blinked, holding on to her navy blue hemp-braided hat as her father tugged her along. "And me? What do you want me to do?"

He barely slowed as he smiled down at her. "You? Well, I'm counting on your prayers as well, darlin', along with something else."

She blinked up at him expectantly.

He pursed his lips together into what appeared to be a cross between a grimace and grin. "When it comes to Collin McGuire being alone with my daughter, you have my permission—indeed, my most sincere request—to become the biblical thorn in Charity's side." And tightening his grip on her arm, he wasted no time ushering her through the mahogany and plate-glass doors of the imposing six-story *Herald*.

"You're kidding!" Maisie gasped. She took a huge bite out of the apple she was eating, her eyes as big as the piece of fruit in her hand. "What did you say?"

"What could I say? Sorry, Father, if it's all the same to you, I'd rather not follow Charity around because, you see, I'm rather crazy about Collin McGuire myself." Faith blew at a stray hair and finished her banana. "What do you think I said? I said I would." She tossed the peel into the trash can by the loading dock and sighed. "I feel sick," she announced.

"Oh, Faith, I'm so sorry!" Maisie exclaimed, finishing her apple and flicking the core into the trash. "But you have to admit that this is exciting. I mean, talk about a love triangle! I'll tell you what, my life got a whole lot more interesting when you became my friend. So what are you going to do?"

Faith considered the question. "Well, I'll have to step up the prayers a notch, I suppose, and then . . . then, I will obey my father. And in doing so, take considerable satisfaction in becoming a bigger thorn in Collin McGuire's side than he is in mine."

"That's the spirit," Maisie said with a grin. Her expression turned serious. "Are you doing okay, you know, with your feelings for him?"

Faith ignored the twinge in her heart and forged a bright smile. "Better, I think. I've been doing what Mrs. Gerson told me to do, and I'll tell you what—that man's got some changes coming if my prayers have anything to say about it. But in the meanwhile, I intend to do everything in my power to keep him away from Charity."

"And from you?" Maisie's smile was wicked.

Faith scrunched her nose. "That's not even funny, Maisie," she muttered.

Maisie laughed and jumped from the loading dock to stand. "Hear ye, hear ye—let the record show that today, October 6, 1916, Collin McGuire will rue the day he fell in love with Faith O'Connor's sister!"

"It's your sister he's in love with?"

Faith and Maisie whirled around at the same time to stare in stunned silence at the girl behind them. The surprise on Briana Muldoon's face was at least equal to theirs.

"You know Collin McGuire?" Faith and Maisie asked in unison.

"Know him! I do a lot better than know him. I'm the girl who got the best of him, if you know what I mean. At least I did, until your sister came along."

"How . . . where?" Maisie managed to get a few words out. Faith was speechless.

The surprise on Briana's face twisted into a smirk. "Oh, Collin and I go way back. We met at Brannigan's, and I could see right away he was a bit of a scoundrel with the ladies, that's for sure." Her face softened. "But then we got together, and for a while, it was quite lovely."

It was the first time Faith had seen Briana devoid of her

usual hardness and sarcasm, and something tugged at her heart. Briana continued, her voice barely a whisper.

"I guess I still care for him because I can't seem to get over it, even though he's made it pretty clear how he feels about me." She looked at Faith with haunted eyes. "Do you have any idea what it's like to want somebody so much you ache all over? And know you'll never have him because he's in love with someone else?"

Faith glanced at Maisie, then swallowed a lump in her throat.

"And what do I do?" Briana continued, as if talking to herself. "I just keep going back, taking whatever he'll give and giving whatever he'll take."

A sharp pain sliced through Faith at the meaning of Briana's words. Her cheeks heated with embarrassment and anger at how casually Collin McGuire trampled women's feelings to satisfy his own. Her own hurt began to fester. She reached out and took Briana's hand. "Briana, I'm so sorry, really I am. He's not worth it; you deserve so much better."

Briana looked up with sadness in her eyes. "No, I don't." Her voice was weak, resigned.

Faith grabbed her by the shoulders. "Look at what he's done to you! The same thing he's trying to do to my sister. Only we aren't going to let him. And you aren't, either." Faith ignored Maisie's raised brows.

Briana shook her head. "No, you don't understand. I can't seem to stop myself. It's like he possesses me . . ."

"In a way he does, Briana, but only because of the liberties you've given him. You want to be loved, and there's nothing wrong with that. God made us that way. But you can't do it your way. It has to be within God's timing and will, or you'll reap the consequences. The Bible says to flee sexual sin. Do you know why? Because he made us, and he knows when a man and a woman enter that level of intimacy, the two become one. It's right there in the Bible, honestly. You're tied to Collin, Briana, because of the intimacy you've given him, and you won't be free from the pain—or find the type of love you really desire—until you do it God's way."

Briana stared, eyes wide and lips parted in amazement. Maisie appeared stricken dumb for once, her freckles dark against the pale shade of astonishment on her face. She probably couldn't believe Faith was preaching to the likes of Briana Muldoon. Well, Faith couldn't believe it either, but somehow the words had spilled out so freely. She knew she was right. Mrs. Gerson had been so good for her—teaching her, guiding her, leading her through God's Word. And now Briana needed God's direction for her life too. Desperately.

All at once Briana began to cry, and Faith put her arms around her, an unbelievable tenderness welling up inside.

"I want to do what's right, really I do. I'm just not sure I can." Briana's tears grew into sobs, and Faith held her tighter.

"Yes, you can, Briana, trust me. And I know just the person to show you how."

The shrill wailing of the whistle could be heard above the deafening drone of the boiler room, a welcome signal that it was the end of another long and productive workday at Southfield Steel. The second shift filed in, occasionally nodding to first-shift workers who lumbered out like zombies, exhausted and soaked with sweat.

Collin didn't mind the heat of the boiler room; in fact, he almost enjoyed it. Of course, Jackson thought he was out of his mind, but then Collin thought that about Jackson as well, so they pretty much called it even. Several times in the last three years at Southfield, Collin had been offered the opportunity to work in other parts of the mill, but he always refused. There was something about the heat that appealed to him, as if it purged him, his tight muscles layered with sweat while straining within its stifling inferno. He wasn't afraid of hard work and was often amazed how the suffocating heat seemed to feed his strength rather than sap it.

Collin headed for the door, where Jackson caught up with him. "Hey, buddy, are we on for tonight? I could do with a few tall ones."

Collin hesitated. It certainly wasn't unusual to spend three or four nights a week at Brannigan's. But lately, with such limited access to Charity, he found himself spending every free moment there, a development that was quickly taking its toll—on his sleep, his money, and his mother.

Collin paused, and Jackson's eyebrows raised in surprise. "And don't say you're thinking of staying home. I know Charity's out of the picture since her old man hates you."

Collin scorched Jackson with a glare. "You're really an idiot, you know that, Jackson?"

Jackson appeared hurt. "Come on, Collin, you know I don't mean anything by it. All I'm trying to do is get your mind off of her. I've never seen you like this before; it's not like you. What, you in love with this one or something? Is that it?"

Collin clinched Jackson's arm and slammed him hard against the wall. Jackson's mouth fell slack, his blue eyes widening in surprise. Strands of blond hair tumbled over his forehead.

"I'm not in love with anybody, ya got that?"

Jackson gulped. "Look, Collin, I didn't mean anything by it. I'm just worried about you."

Collin dropped his hold, suddenly very tired. He draped his arm around his friend. "I'm sorry. It's me who's the idiot, not you. And you're right—I have been acting differently. This whole thing with Charity has me kind of mixed up inside, you know? I mean, I want her . . . but then I don't want her." Collin sighed. "I don't know, I just feel less alone when I'm with her. If that's love, well, then I guess it is."

Jackson slapped Collin on the back, his eyes sympathetic. "Sounds to me like ya got it bad for her. It's a downright shame her old man is being such a hard nose."

Collin grabbed his time card and shoved it in the machine to punch out, then threw it in the bin. "Yeah, but for some reason, it's not Charity who has me so crazy."

Jackson punched his card and flipped it on top of Collin's. "What d'ya mean?"

Collin stopped and turned, his lips jabbed into a scowl. "It's the older sister—the one who got Charity in trouble over me."

"Hey, buddy, you got enough problems with the old man. Forget the sister."

"That's just it—I can't." Collin slung his jacket over his shoulder and kept walking.

Jackson grabbed him. "What's that supposed to mean?"

Collin peeled his friend's fingers from his arm and flicked them away. "It means she's driving me crazy. I keep thinking about her, and it's really starting to get on my nerves."

Jackson gaped, then started hooting and hollering as he slapped Collin on the back. "Now that's the Collin I know and love. So you're wantin' to double dip in the same family, are ya?"

Collin smiled patiently at the excitement on Jackson's face. "Okay, now the 'idiot' remark still stands. No, it's nothing like that. Believe me, when it comes to beauty, Charity has it all over her, but this one—something about her just raises my blood pressure, that's for sure. I mean, I wanna tell her off, and then in the next minute, I wanna grab her. I'm telling you, Jackson, this one's nothing but trouble."

"Hey, is she pretty? Maybe you can introduce me."

Collin laughed out loud. "Yeah, right. I'd say your chances are slim to nil. She's real different and too good for you." Collin felt a smile flicker on his lips. "But yeah, she's real pretty—not like Charity, of course, but the greenest eyes you've ever seen and a temper like a wet hen."

Jackson's eyes rounded. "Well, I'll be doggone! You got it bad for both of 'em."

"Aw, you're out of your mind, you clown. It's Charity I'm after. The other one's too scary for me. A girl like that . . . well, let's just say she's too prim and proper for me."

"But she's on your mind now, isn't she?"

Collin blistered Jackson with a look. "Not for long. Once I see more of Charity, the sister'll fade real fast, I'm sure."

"How sure?" Jackson was notorious for tweaking Collin when he was so serious, which of late, was probably more than Jackson liked.

"As sure as I am that I'll be at Brannigan's tonight, drinking you under the bar. Is that sure enough?"

"Exactly what I wanted to hear, as a matter of fact," Jackson said, tipping an imaginary hat as they headed out the door.

It was pure, breathless magic. Gliding on Katie's swings, Faith grinned at her sister Hope, the two sailing side by side into the heavens. They pumped in perfect harmony, breeze lashing their hair and toes poised and skimming the sky. Higher and higher they flew, their bodies taut with exhilaration. Their laughter floated on the wind as they thrust themselves into the blue, embracing the sun and the flood of its warmth. Faith's heart, like her body, was soaring with joy. Never had she felt so free, so peaceful . . .

"Higher, Hope! Higher!" Faith said, but her sister's swing slowed, breaking their bond and their rhythm. In a sweep of the sky, Hope's magical swing split wide, flinging her into the air. Terror seized Faith's throat. "No!" she cried. But her screams were only silent echoes while her sister plummeted in the dark . . .

Faith jolted up in her bed and clutched her nightgown, her heart thundering in her breast. Across the room Charity slept soundly, the rhythm of her breathing in stark contrast to the panic choking the air from Faith's lungs. Taking a deep breath, she looked at the window, an ideal canvas for the sliver of moon that hung in the sky. It had to be past 2:00 a.m., she thought with a shudder. Slowly she laid her cheek on the pillow, all sleep gone from her eyes.

All at once, she sat up again. What was that? She strained to listen. Was it raining? She glanced at the window and blinked at the soft shaft of moonlight streaming across her floor. And then she heard it again—the faint clink of something against glass. She hurried to the window and stood to the side, peeking out at the backyard.

Her mother's lovingly tended garden was bathed in moonlight. Katie's rickety wooden wagon stood beneath the rope swings that hung from the massive oak, the one her mother always begged her father to trim. "Patrick, my garden needs sunlight," she would argue, and Father would give her the stern eye, followed by a somewhat intense discussion, the closest thing to an argument Faith ever saw between them. But tonight, all seemed quite peaceful and still as her eyes searched in the dark for some sign of intrusion.

And then she saw him. Her heart clutched in its usual exasperating fashion. He was standing there, bold and motionless in his stance, coat slung over his shoulder and hip cocked. His handsome face was illuminated in the moonlight as he peered up at her window. Faith's eyes flitted to Charity's bed. The breath, thick in her throat, slowly released when her sister didn't stir. Shifting back to the window, she carefully raised the sash.

He lifted his hand to shield his eyes. "Charity, is that you? I need to see you." His voice sounded different, a slow drawl, almost slurred in speech.

Faith struggled to restrain her panic. "Collin, go home! You'll wake my father. I'm serious—please leave!"

She heard his familiar laugh, slightly muffled and completely indifferent to her plea. In brazen arrogance, he tossed his coat over a limb and leaned against the oak, legs casually crossed and arms folded. "Nope, not goin' anywhere, not 'til I can see you, touch you, feel your lips on mine . . ." His teasing tone increased in volume with each word spoken, causing a chill to ice her skin.

"All right, Collin, please hush! I'm coming!" She closed the window as quietly as possible and stole one more glance at Charity's bed. After reaching for her robe and slippers, she tiptoed toward the door. Except for the deafening pounding of her heart, all was quiet in the house as she made her way down the stairs to the kitchen. Blarney was close on her heels, tail wagging with curiosity.

"Stay, Blarney," she whispered as she silently opened the door to slip outside. The chill of the night air shivered through her, and she pulled her robe tighter about her, bracing herself for more than the cold. She stared out at the oak, and her heart skipped a beat when he wasn't there.

Stepping forward on the porch, she strained her eyes to catch sight of him. And then, like a thief in the night, he was behind her, his strong arms encircling her waist and his lips lost in her hair. He was kissing her, whispering things that caused her cheeks to flame in the glow of the moonlight. The heat of his touch felt like fire. *Oh, God, I need your help!*

And then, somewhere deep inside, beneath the passion he stirred, she could see things clearly once again. Yes, she wanted this—and she wanted it with him. But it had to be God's way, not hers and certainly not Collin's.

With a calm not experienced in his presence before, Faith pried his arms from her waist and slowly turned, hands propped on his chest to push him away. The startled look on his face almost made her smile as she stepped back.

"It's you!" he muttered, clearly taken by surprise, and she noticed his reflexes were a bit slower than usual. The easy smile was conspicuously absent, and he seemed shaken.

"Did you think I was going to send my sister down? Are you crazy . . . or just not very bright?" This was fun. It felt wonderful to get the best of Collin McGuire.

Collin blinked, and then instinct kicked in with the slow smile. His eyes traveled from her face, down her body, and back up again. Even in the moonlight, he could see her blush.

"No," he drawled, "I just thought you wanted me for yourself."

She caught her breath and jerked her robe around her shivering frame. "You are the most egotistical, low, selfish human being—"

"Well, you might have me on egotistical and low, but lady, on the selfish, I'm afraid you got it all over me."

He heard the soft catch of her breath as her lips parted. "Me? Over you? You must be drunk!"

Collin chuckled to himself and ambled over to the porch swing to sit with his long legs sprawled out before him. "Yeah, I've had a few, no question about that. But I'm not drunk—at least not too drunk to see things the way they are." He watched her from the shadows of the swing, taking in the way her hair glinted in the moonlight and spilled over her shoulders. Her slight form shivered in her thin robe, which she clutched tightly with pinched fingers.

"And what way are they, exactly?" Her tone was curt.

Collin took his time answering. Never had he derived so much pleasure from rattling a woman. She was this sweet, demure little thing whose temper could be tripped faster than flipping a switch. A pretty powder keg, to be sure, righteous and noble until you lit the spark that made her blow. And then the fun began. He cocked his head and looked up, his lips easing into a knowing smile.

"Well, I'm not the one who's keeping her sister from spending time with the man she loves." He paused for effect, then continued. "Nor am I the one telling Bree Muldoon she's on the path to hell if she, shall we say, spends time with me?" His smile flattened, replaced by intense scrutiny as his eyes pierced hers. "I'm not sure, but it looks to me like one of two things. You either are the most selfish thing around or . . ."

Her eyelids flickered and her mouth opened slightly, as if she couldn't breathe.

"You want me for yourself. So which is it? Tell me, Faith O'Connor, have I gotten to you?" It grated how his heart hammered in his chest whenever she was near, but he truly relished the effect he obviously had on her. He was glad he could get some of his own back. She had possessed his thoughts too much of late, and he wanted her to pay. She had no right to interfere in his relationship with Charity—or in his thoughts. He watched her now, a frail thing shuddering in the wind, all defenses stripped, and fought the urge to jump up and grab her in his arms. He swore softly under his breath. *Why does she make me feel this way?*

She looked sick standing there, the frigid wind whipping at her hair. Without a word, she moved to the door, then turned to confront him, her back stiff and her face set. "You know, Collin, I feel sorry for you. You think every woman will collapse under your spell. The charming Collin McGuire, so irresistible to women. Well, you're wrong. Not every woman chooses to do so, at least not this one. I'm looking for someone I can give my heart to and know it will be safe. Someone strong and good and moral. You—you're just bent on your own quest of misguided lust, and I doubt if you will ever be satisfied."

She turned the knob, and in a split second he was there, his face inches from her own. She turned away as if she could smell the liquor on his breath. "Pretty high and mighty, aren't we, Faith O'Connor? I think you're lying. I think I have gotten to you, only you don't want me to know it. Why don't we just see?"

He pressed her back against the door, his lips muffling her response. He kissed her long and hard until the fight faded away. Only then did his lips leave her mouth to stray along the curve of her chin and nip at her earlobe. She moaned, her passion igniting him like no other woman had ever done. He was breathing hard and fast as his lips smothered her neck, and the ecstasy of it all was so staggering, he thought he would lose his mind. *What am I doing?*

She seemed so weak in his arms but somehow managed to pull away, and when she spoke, her whisper was an urgent plea. "No! I don't want this—please, Collin, no!"

His eyes were on fire. "Yes, you do! I can feel it! You can't lie to me, Faith, I feel it!"

She opened her mouth to protest, but his lips silenced her, softening against her own. The sweetness of her kiss mingled with salty tears that glistened on her cheek. Stunned, Collin tilted her face in the moonlight.

"You're crying!" he uttered in surprise. Silently, and with more tenderness than he intended, he wiped her face with his fingers. "I'm sorry," he whispered gruffly, "I didn't mean to be rough, but you got under my skin." He cupped her chin firmly with his hand, gentling his tone. "I know you're feeling the same thing I am, Faith. Why are you fighting it?"

She sniffed and leaned against the door, wiping her nose with her sleeve. She looked like such a little girl standing there, and Collin knew he was treading on dangerous ground.

"Because I really don't want to do this. I . . . I do feel wonderful things when you kiss me, Collin, I won't lie to you. But it can't happen again. I don't want it to happen again, please."

He felt a sharp pain in his gut. What was she saying? There was something remarkable between them—they both felt it. Was she going to walk away from it? He shifted, keenly aware of her gaze. He fanned his fingers through his hair, then rubbed at his temple. "Because of Charity?" he asked, his eyes back on hers.

"No . . . I mean, yes, of course because of Charity. But not just because of her."

"What, then?" He stepped back, thrusting his hands in his pockets. He suddenly felt like such a little boy—so unlike himself—and horribly awkward as she stared up at him.

"Because of Charity, yes, and because of my father, but mostly because of the way you make me feel. I . . . can't afford to feel that way, Collin. The feelings—they scare me."

He grabbed her shoulders, relief flooding through him. "They scare me too, Faith, from that first moment in the park. I'm not sure what's going on, but there's something here, a pull between us. I felt it then when I looked in your eyes, and I know you felt it too. I don't know why or how, but it's there and it's real, and I can't fight it anymore. Any more than you can. Why do we even have to?"

She swallowed hard as she looked up at him. "Because these feelings—as wonderful as they are—they're not right. Not now, maybe not ever."

A muscle twitched in his jaw. He dropped his hands to

his sides, and she rubbed her arms where his warmth had been. "What are you talking about, Faith? You've got me out of my mind. Do you want me or not?"

She took a deep breath before answering. "No. Not this way."

The impact of her words was like a physical blow. He bent over slightly, all arrogance crashing to the ground. "Why?" His voice was a whisper.

She reached to gently touch his arm. "Because I want it to be right. That's more important to me than anything in the world. Yes, I feel the fire when you touch me, but I need more than that. I need more than the physical aspect, hard as that is to resist. As much as I . . . want you . . . I have to be sure it's also what God wants."

He couldn't have been more stunned if she had slapped him. "God? What the blazes does God have to do with it?"

Her green eyes bristled. "Everything. I don't want anything or anyone unless it's what God wants."

"And what does God want?" he asked, his tone mocking.

"He wants you, Collin. He wants you to pursue him instead of your lust."

He could feel his anger flare. Pressing toward her once again, he ran his hand up the side of her robe. He laughed when she caught her breath. "Oh, really? And this God of yours, is he going to keep you warm at night?"

She thrust his hand away. "You are something, Collin McGuire. All you think about, care about, is your desire for the moment. Well, I want more, much more. I'm looking for something you don't seem to know a lot about—genuine love, like the kind between my parents. And yes, Collin, the kind of love where God is at the center. That's the only thing I'm going to settle for, and I guarantee it'll have more passion than you'll know in a lifetime."

"I doubt that. And who's gonna give you this passionate love—God?"

"Someone will . . . someone who loves God as much as I do. I'm saving it for him, Collin. All the passion you provoke in me, it all belongs to him, wherever he is."

"You go right ahead, lady," he said, his eyes stinging with fury. "You save all that holy love of yours for God. But I'll lay good money on the table that says you're gonna end up a very bitter and a very lonely old maid."

Thrusting her chin, she stared boldly into his eyes, a faint smile on her lips. "No, I don't think so. I think you have the future all wrong. Someday, twenty years down the road, when you're still looking for love in the arms of any girl, you and I will probably meet again. And, I think you'll know me. I'll be the one with the smile on my face."

And before he could grab her once again, she turned and slipped inside, quickly locking the door behind her. Collin stared after her, open-mouthed and totally bewildered. Dramatic exits usually belonged to him. But for once, like it or not, he'd finally been upstaged.

7

Something was wrong. Charity wasn't herself. All she'd done all morning was mope around, never saying a peep, not even the usual gibes as Faith sprawled on her bed writing poetry. She seemed almost meek, so unlike Charity. She sat on her bed, staring blankly out the window.

Faith stopped writing. "Are you all right? I mean, you haven't said a word to anyone all morning. I thought you would be at the library today, or at least out with someone . . ."

Charity slumped against the headboard. "I'm just a little down today, I suppose."

Faith searched her sister's face. "What's wrong? Is it Collin?" she asked against her better judgment.

Several seconds passed before Charity nodded. Faith pushed her journal aside and rose, moving to sit next to her sister. "Did you have a fight?"

Charity shook her head and sniffled.

"Then what?"

Her sister swatted a tear from her cheek and slowly sat up on the bed. "I haven't seen him. Not once for over a month now. I've sent messages through Mary, but he never came. I don't know what's wrong. Oh, Faith, what if there's somebody else?"

Charity turned, her face stricken with fear, and Faith

put her arms around her. She closed her eyes. It had been exactly a month since her encounter with Collin on the back porch. Surely he wasn't avoiding Charity because of her? Faith opened her eyes again. Well, if he was, it was an answer to prayer. She felt sorry for Charity, but in her heart she was grateful. Collin McGuire wasn't good for her sister. And until God got ahold of him, if he ever did, Faith was afraid Collin McGuire wouldn't be good for anyone.

"Charity, I didn't want to tell you this before, but I think I need to now. Once I do, you'll understand why it's better you don't see him anymore."

Charity pulled away. "Tell me what?"

Faith went to her drawer, plucked out a handkerchief, and handed it to her sister. Charity took it and blew her nose, her eyes riveted to Faith's face.

"Charity . . . Collin sees . . . other women."

Charity's eyes went wide. "You're lying!"

Faith felt a blush rise in her cheeks as her sister stared at her in disbelief. "No, I'm not lying. I know for a fact he does. There's this girl at work—her name is Briana—and it seems she's in love with him too. Only . . ."

Charity stood up. "You're lying! Collin cares for me; he's told me so. And I know it in my heart. He couldn't be in love with anyone else."

"I didn't say he loved her, Charity." Faith hesitated as she searched for the right words. "I just know that . . . well, Briana told me that . . ."

"Told you what?" Charity looked as if she were going to shake her.

"Briana told me she and Collin, well, they're intimate. At least they were when we last spoke. Charity, listen to me. Collin *uses* Briana. Do you understand what I'm saying?"

Charity sank to the bed, her face turning a sickly pale.

"Charity, he's no good for you. Father's right—Collin's only out for Collin. He'll tell you he loves you, just like he used to tell Briana, but in the end, it's just to get what he wants."

Without saying a word, Charity rose. She squared her shoulders and lifted her head. "That may be true for your Briana, but it's not true for me. Collin does care for me; I know it. We've kissed, but he's never, ever crossed the line with me. I know in my heart he's not using me to get what he wants." Charity started for the door, then turned to give Faith an icy look. A lump shifted in Faith's throat as Charity's chin jutted in defiance. "But, if that's what it takes . . ." She turned to leave.

Faith couldn't believe her ears. She ran to grab her sister's arm and spun her around. "What are you saying? That you're going to try to win him like Briana did? Are you out of your mind? It didn't work for Briana. What makes you think it will work for you?"

"Why not? I love him." Charity's voice chilled the air.

"Because it's wrong! It's against everything we believe in, everything Mother and Father have taught us. It's against God, Charity. It's not what he wants for you, and you know it."

"So what? I know what I want for me, and that's all that matters. You and your oh-so-devout faith in God. Well, it hasn't done a whole lot for you when it comes to Collin McGuire, now has it, Faith?"

Faith went cold. "What are you talking about?" she whispered.

Charity's smile was mocking. "I'm talking about the undying love you've had for Collin for years now, only he doesn't even know you exist."

"You're out of your mind . . ."

"Am I? Like you're out of your mind with love when you write pages and pages of poetry about him?"

"You've . . . read my journal . . ." Faith's voice was barely audible as the realization sunk in. The blood rushed from her face.

"Of course I have, for years now. At first, I only read it because I was bored and thought it was funny. All you ever wrote about was Collin, Collin, Collin. Then I found out who Collin was, and suddenly, I didn't think you were so crazy anymore. So you see, big sister, I actually have you to thank for my unceasing devotion to the man I have every intention of marrying—one way or the other. And there's nothing you, Mother or Father, or God can do about it."

Charity opened the door. With a regal toss of her head, she glanced back, and for the briefest of moments, a glimmer of sympathy flickered on her beautiful face. But just as quickly as it had come, she seemed to dismiss it, leaving their room in considerably better spirits than when she had arrived.

Jackson was worried. Never in all the time he'd known Collin had he seen him like this. That covered a lot of territory—since the fourth grade at St. Stephen's when Collin had shoved Johnny McGee against the blackboard for giving Jackson a bloody nose. From that moment on, Jackson had sworn his allegiance to the tall kid who had a way with the nuns. It had been fun—a virtual whirlwind—riding on the coattails of this handsome charmer, along with the girls who always seemed to be hanging on too. Despite sporadic bouts of being overly serious about life and his occasional somber moods, Collin was to Jackson the best friend a man could raise a toast to and the brother he never had. He knew most everything about him—how he felt when his father died, what he thought of his mother, his favorite drink, his favorite women, and when he was or wasn't happy. And Jackson was worried. Collin wasn't happy.

Nobody noticed but Jackson. Everyone else just thought

he needed the money from the double shifts he constantly requested. Sixteen straight hours of sweat pouring off muscles so tired and sore, his body looked like a limp rag when he dragged it to the door to punch out. Eight o'clock in the morning to midnight spent hoisting containers of coal to feed a fire hot enough to melt steel—and maybe burn away some memories in the process.

It was a minute before midnight as Jackson waited outside the back entrance of Southfield Steel, shivering and rubbing his hands against the sleeves of his thin jacket. He leaned against the brick wall and tugged his coat tighter. The sound of a whistle pierced the night air. Within moments, men—or shells of men—trudged through the corridor toward the doors, dazed and lifeless, their energy spent in the bowels of Boston's most prolific steel mill. Jackson watched for Collin, his gaze darting from face to face.

He was the last to the door, whether too exhausted to hurry along with the others or because he had nowhere in particular to go, Jackson wasn't sure. All he knew was he had never seen his friend so listless, so removed from the Collin he loved. His eyes were tired, and the flesh on his face seemed to sag, aging him at least ten years. He didn't smile when he saw Jackson, only stared and nodded, as if Jackson were a mere acquaintance.

At that moment, Jackson would have given anything to get his hands on Charity's sister. She had done this to his best friend, he knew it, because ever since that night outside her house, Collin hadn't been the same. He had been a madman when he stormed into Brannigan's just before closing, ready to pick a fight and not a bit particular about with whom.

"If ever I wanted to put a woman in her place," he hissed, "it would be that one." He ordered a beer, then argued with Lucas Brannigan when he wouldn't serve it.

"It's late, Collin, go home; you've had enough," Lucas said.

Jackson had to hold Collin back from jumping the bar to take Lucas on.

"Collin, come on, buddy, let's get out of here. I'll take him home, Lucas."

Jackson pushed Collin toward the door, talking fast, desperate to calm him down. "Who, Charity? What did she do?" Jackson asked, running to keep up with Collin as he tore down the street.

"No, her holier-than-thou sister, that's who. I tell you, Jackson, I never wanted to put a fist through a wall so much in my entire life. She's a real loon. So help me, I gotta stay away from that family and anything even remotely related to that woman, including Charity. Or I swear, I won't be responsible for my actions."

"What did she do to you?" Jackson was dying to know what anyone could do to put Collin in such a state.

Collin stopped in the middle of the sidewalk and turned, his eyes blazing with anger. "She wants me to turn to God." He enunciated each word as if he couldn't quite believe any of them, his face as mocking as his tone as he raged on. "Can you believe that? She's a bloomin' fanatic, which is just another word for someone who tells you they're better than you are. I'm the unforgivable sinner, and she's the righteous Christian out to save me. Well, the only thing she can save is her breath because this guy is not gonna let any woman—or any god—push him around."

Jackson was dumbfounded. "She wants you to turn to . . . God?" It was more than he could handle. Poor Collin, out for a little fun and ending up at church! Jackson doubled over, his laughter echoing through the alleyway.

Collin stared, seeming annoyed, and then the whole thing apparently struck him funny as well. The two of them whooped so loud someone yelled out a window for them to shut up.

Since that night, four weeks had come and gone, and Jackson had seen precious little of his friend. Collin seldom met him at Brannigan's anymore. Most of his days and nights were spent working and sleeping, then working some more. Jackson couldn't take it. Something had to be done—Collin was way too close to the edge. He watched while Collin silently punched out, then Jackson swung his arm loosely around his friend's shoulder as he emerged through the door.

"Hey, buddy, I miss ya . . . and I miss the fun I don't have when you're not around. How about a late one?"

Collin was whipped. Without protest, he allowed Jackson to steer him along, almost as if he didn't have a mind of his own. Actually, he didn't. Not lately, anyway. His mind, his thoughts were all back there somewhere in a vat of liquid steel, and that suited him just fine. He didn't want to think, to allow his mind to follow its natural inclination of late, to think about her. He would do anything to drive her out of his mind—fill every moment with work until he was so exhausted he couldn't think of anything but sleep. And that was the irony of it all. Even when he slept, he couldn't escape her face, her words . . .

"He wants you, Collin. He wants you to pursue him instead of your lust."

Collin had never felt like this, and it scared him. *She* scared him, and he didn't want anything to do with her. From that moment in the park when he had kissed her, it was like he'd been possessed, cursed to dream of her, think of her, want her. He'd known women far more beautiful, far more accommodating, far more easy to control. But this! Two encounters and she'd traveled his system like poison, the very same poison that had killed his father.

It was moments like this he almost wished he believed in her God so he could pray to be rid of her. Yes, if truth be told, his soul craved to love a woman like that, to the depth of his being. But the risk was too high. That kind of all-consuming love could destroy him. *She* could destroy him. Better a love restrained, like his for Charity, than a love that controlled.

Collin exhaled deeply. He missed seeing Charity, but he needed time to sort things out, time to think about what to do, and time to break the spell her sister had cast.

"Collin? Did ya hear me? How about Brannigan's?" Jackson's voice broke through the stream of consciousness that had become a state of mind for Collin of late. Collin stared blankly.

"You know, Collin, you're really starting to scare me. You gotta snap out of it. No woman is worth this."

No woman is worth this. The impact of Jackson's words stung like a fist to his face. *No woman would ever possess him.* Thoughts of his mother and how she had destroyed his father came to him, and everything within told him he had to fight it, fight with every inch of his will. He would discipline his mind not to think of her. He would lose himself in Charity and insulate his heart with her love so completely that Faith O'Connor would never control him. Not in his thoughts—or in his heart—ever again. As if jolted out of a daze, Collin grabbed his friend at the waist and lifted him in a bear hug, taking Jackson by surprise.

"What the . . . Collin, are you crazy?"

Collin just laughed, the first deep-down belly laugh he had enjoyed in a very long time. "I love you, you know that, you big idiot!"

"You are crazy, I swear!" Jackson said, grinning. "A minute ago you looked like death; now you're lit up like a Christmas tree. Why the change of heart?"

Collin breathed in the cold night air, its briskness filling his lungs with energy. "Great choice of words, my friend. It is, indeed, a change of heart. And you're right once again, old buddy—no woman is worth this. I will have that drink with you, tired as I am. Let's celebrate!"

"I knew I could count on you. What are we celebrating? Your resurrection from the dead?"

Collin smacked Jackson on the back and swung his arm around his shoulder, grinning like the Collin of old. "Something like that. What d'ya say we drink a toast to marriage?"

"Marriage?"

"That's right, old buddy, marriage. I'm thinking of joining the club."

Faith never ceased to marvel at the warmth and intimacy of Mrs. Gerson's home, given the fact that Christa Gerson was nearly sightless. Softly hued walls were graced with pictures hung with near-perfect precision. Cozy furnishings, although dated, were tastefully arranged for both visual beauty and ease of movement throughout the parlor. The dining room table was covered with a hand-crocheted tablecloth and set with bone china and silver candlesticks in anticipation of a special dinner Mrs. Gerson insisted on preparing for Faith and her friends.

Faith watched her now as she bustled about the kitchen, a peaceful look in her vacant eyes, and once again marveled at the second thing that amazed her about this remarkable woman.

Despite the darkness she lived within, Mrs. Gerson always emanated a sense of peace. "My darkness is flooded with the light of Jesus," she would tell Faith, and Faith never saw evidence otherwise. Although a woman of considerable means and blessed with a number of good friends and neighbors to assist, Mrs. Gerson was quite alone in the world when it came to family. She had suffered more than her fair share of heartbreak. She had met and married her beloved Oscar at the tender age of sixteen back in the old country, and theirs had been a marriage made in heaven. They set out for a new life in America, Oscar hoping to capitalize on his skills as a master craftsman of fine clocks and watches. And so he had.

But despite their material success, both longed for a family. And finally, after fourteen years of marriage, Christa Gerson gave birth to their only child, Herbert Roland Gerson. Their lives were complete; no family was happier, until the day everything changed.

Sadness settled over Faith as she remembered the pain on Mrs. Gerson's face when she'd first spoken about it.

It had been a gloriously snow-laden winter, Mrs. Gerson told her, and Herbert had pleaded to go skating with friends at the lake.

"You may go, Herbert," she had lectured, "but stay to the sides of the lake; do not venture into the middle where the ice is thin. Is that clear?"

Herbert had nodded, throwing his arms around his mother with great passion. "I'll miss you, Mama," he said before dashing out the door. And then he was gone, both from the house and from her life—forever.

Never had she known such pain or darkness. But for all she felt, it had been Oscar who'd borne the brunt of the tragedy. He was never the same after Herbert's death, and although he was a relatively young man at forty-eight years of age, his health began to deteriorate, leaving Christa to bury her grief in the exhaustive care of her ailing husband.

When Oscar died several years later, Mrs. Gerson was bitter at life and especially at God. She closed herself off from the church she and Oscar had attended for so many years. But in her seclusion, she quickly found she had nowhere else to turn but to God. And then one day, she had reached for the Bible that lay on her mantel, sadly neglected beneath a layer of dust. The words she read were like a balm to her tortured soul, and she found she couldn't get enough of the tranquility they invoked in her heart.

Tears sprang to Faith's eyes as she now studied the woman who hummed about in her kitchen. That had been the true beginning of her life with God, she told Faith, the moment she dropped to her knees and recommitted her life to Christ. No longer could she live for Oscar and Herbert, so she would live for God. He became the only thing that sustained her, keeping her from the pain of the past and allowing her to remain, despite the onset of near blindness ten years later, in the glorious light of his unshakable love.

As Faith watched her now, she felt such an awe and respect for this woman whom Marcy had once coerced her to befriend. "But the Bible, Mother? She only wants me to read the Bible? Can't I take some of my favorite books to read to her?"

Faith recalled her mother gently cupping her chin. "She's asking for someone to read the Bible, Faith, nothing else."

"But, I'll go crazy, Mother! The Bible! It's so boring."

Her mother had smiled and gently pushed a strand of hair from Faith's face. "Not when reading it gives someone so much joy."

And so, with great reservation, Faith agreed to read to the blind woman weekly, thinking it would be good to give of her time to such a worthy cause. But as it always seemed to happen when God was involved, she ended up on the receiving end. This remarkable woman opened her young eyes to the depth and intensity of God's love for her. Throughout all the travail of adolescence and the insecurities Faith endured at the hand of her sister, the knowledge of God's personal love for her, Faith O'Connor, became an inner core of strength like nothing she'd ever experienced before. He was always with her, and the peace of his presence prompted her to commit her life to God, just as Mrs. Gerson had. It was a decision that never failed to bring her joy. It was Faith's hope that Mrs. Gerson could do the same for Briana.

Over the last month, Faith had gotten to know Briana better, only to discover that her involvement with Collin was the very least of her problems. When she was a girl, her alcoholic father had often come to her room at night, almost up until the day he died. Briana's mother had simply turned a blind eye to it all, and to Briana as well. Briana compensated with a hard veneer, which Faith managed to penetrate through prayer and persistence. It was slow, but they were becoming friends.

The dinner Mrs. Gerson prepared was magnificent, and Faith couldn't remember when she'd eaten so much. Apparently Briana and Maisie were feeling the same way. When the meal was over, all three moaned, pushing their chairs back from the table, stuffed but content.

Mrs. Gerson poured tea, obviously enjoying the role of hostess. Spooning a bit of sugar into her cup, she turned her full attention to Briana. "So, Briana, Faith tells me you are no longer seeing this Collin McGuire. That must be very difficult for you. I understand you care for him very much."

The relaxed smile on Briana's face faded as she shifted in the chair. "It is. But Faith has been praying for me, and I guess you have too, because somehow I've been able to do it. I haven't seen Collin since the last time I was at Brannigan's when I told him I couldn't . . ." Briana blushed slightly. "Well, you know . . . I told him no."

"And he hasn't bothered you since?"

Briana shook her head, a real sadness in her eyes. "No, he hasn't. Oh, he was angry with me at the time, almost like he actually cared, but he doesn't really. I think he was angry at Faith."

Faith stopped chewing, her jaw suddenly stiff and cheeks lumpy with one of Mrs. Gerson's sugar cookies.

"Angry with Faith?" Mrs. Gerson seemed confused.

"Yes, at least I think so. When he asked me why, I told him I had been talking to this girl at work and mentioned it was someone he knew. The minute I told him Faith's name, he went quite pale, and I don't think I've ever seen him so angry before. He slammed his beer on the bar, spilling it everywhere, all over me, all over him. I smelled like a brewery. He muttered something about . . ." Briana blushed, glancing at Faith. "Well, I can't exactly repeat the word he used, but something about 'that "blank" woman interfering in his life.' And then he left, just like that. That was awhile ago, of course. I haven't been to Brannigan's since."

Maisie and Faith exchanged looks.

"That's good, Briana," Mrs. Gerson said, pausing to reach for a cookie off the plate in the center of the table. "Briana, do you enjoy games?"

Briana blinked. "I suppose so, at least I did when I was young. Why do you ask?"

"Games are great fun, especially when you win. But, to win it takes great skill, and of course, you have to follow the rules." Mrs. Gerson munched thoughtfully, her tongue swiping a crumb from the corner of her mouth.

"Yes, of course . . ."

"You know, Briana, I think of life as very much like a game. The one who created it gave us the rules by which it is to be played, rules designed to help us win, rules to help us be happy. The problem is many times we choose to play by our own rules, and then we're at a loss to understand why we never win."

Mrs. Gerson leaned forward to stare straight at Briana

as if her vacant eyes could see her clearly. "God has a great deal of love for you, Briana. He made you, and he's given you his Word as the rule book for your life. He wants you to win, but to do so, you must follow his rules. Up to now, you haven't experienced a lot of genuine love in your life, but that's going to change. You've been looking for love in ways contrary to God's law. You thought you could find that love in an intimate relationship with Collin, but you found only heartache."

Mrs. Gerson paused to take a sip of her tea, then patted her mouth with a napkin. "The love you're seeking is available, Briana. In fact, it's exactly what God has in mind. It's right there in the rule book—the Bible. It says in Ephesians 5:22, 'Husbands, cherish your wives.' Tell me, Briana, do you know what cherish means?"

"To love and care for, I suppose." Briana's eyes were fixed on the old woman's face.

"Yes, my dear, and much more. It means to hold dear, to protect, to view as the most precious thing in your life. If it's in God's plan for you to marry, he wants it to be a man who will cherish you—love you to the depth of his soul, just like God does. But for that to happen, my dear, you must commit yourself to this God who loves you far more than any man ever could. And when you do and then follow his Word, it will lead you to the kind of love your heart longs for, not lustful love like you experienced with Collin. The Bible says the wages of sin is death. God's Word admonishes us to flee sexual sin. Why? Because he knows it's not only death to your soul, but death to the kind of love you're seeking. Death to the only kind of love that will ever make you happy. The choice is yours, Briana, but trust me, the strength to do it is all his."

Briana's eyes glistened with wetness as she stared at Mrs. Gerson. Her gaze flitted to Faith, then back to the old woman's face. Wiping her eyes with her hand, she sat up straight, pushing her chin out. "I want it, Mrs. Gerson. I want what you and Faith have. How do I get it?"

The old woman beamed and nodded her head. Faith stole a glimpse at Maisie, who was watching the entire scene with curiosity.

"It's simply a heart thing, Briana. All you have to do is acknowledge you're a sinner and that Jesus is your Savior. Then simply ask him to come into your heart and be Lord of your life. You'll never be alone again. I'll be delighted to lead you in prayer and then, if you like, you may keep one of my Bibles to see all he has in store for you. I can assure you, my dear, your life will never be the same." Mrs. Gerson took Briana's hands in hers. "Shall we?"

Briana nodded, her hands trembling. "Yes, please," she whispered.

With the softest of smiles gentling her lips, Mrs. Gerson nodded and led them in prayer, her voice strong and sure as they all bowed their heads.

8

Marcy was extremely worried about Charity. She'd never seen her daughter depressed for such a long period of time, and her concern was growing with each passing week. Patrick tried to comfort her, but Marcy knew he took a more practical view of his daughter's state of mind.

"She's a bit heartbroken over this McGuire boy, that's all, which is natural, I suppose, given the influence he's had over her. I'm just grateful it's over. She'll get past it soon enough."

His words did little to console Marcy as she lit the candles on Charity's birthday cake. "I hope you're right, Patrick. It just breaks my heart to see her like this, especially on her birthday. Seventeen! My goodness, where did the time go?"

"All to Charity, for sure, because it certainly hasn't touched you, my love." Patrick slipped his arms around Marcy's waist and buried his face in her hair.

Marcy gave him a wry smile. "Mmm, a case of being blinded by love, I think." She handed him a stack of plates to carry in.

Charity hardly seemed like a girl celebrating her birthday. She smiled as Marcy set the cake in front of her, but to Marcy, it was a hollow smile. She was thinner than she'd been, and more than Marcy liked. Most evenings Charity would sit quietly at the table and pick at her food, offering very little to the lively family conversations that always ensued in the O'Connor household. Even her complexion seemed to have lost some of its usual creamy glow.

"Don't forget to make a wish," Katie reminded before Charity blew out the candles. "You're gonna get your wish, you're gonna get your wish!" Katie was ecstatic as she bounced up and down on her chair.

Even Charity seemed brighter. "Oh, I hope so," she whispered, a bit of the glow creeping back into her cheeks. Marcy gave her a warm smile.

Everyone devoured the cake, including Charity. When plates were empty, Marcy jumped up from the table, eyes twinkling. "Ready for presents? Let's head into the parlor."

Charity positioned herself in the seat of honor—Marcy's rocking chair by the fire—while Marcy brought in an impressive stack of presents. With great fanfare, she placed them before the birthday girl, hugging her daughter tightly. "My little girl—a woman of seventeen!"

"Hey, I'm your little girl, Mama!" Katie's tone was indignant. Marcy scooped her up in her arms, tickling until Katie squealed with glee.

The family watched while Charity opened her presents one by one: a brooch from Sean, a poem from Beth, and a handmade clay dish from Steven—to put her hairpins in, he said.

Faith grinned when Charity opened her gift—a lovely red woolen scarf she had crocheted herself. "In place of the one you 'borrowed' from my drawer," she said with mock indignation.

A soft giggle escaped Charity's lips. She gave Faith an innocent smile. "Mmm . . . now I have two!"

"Open mine next!" Katie demanded, beaming with pride as Charity unwrapped her present—a picture of the birthday girl herself made out of navy beans glued to paper. Charity oohed and aahed with great relish, holding it up for everyone to see while Katie took a bow.

When Charity opened the last present, she seemed pleased with the new blouse and skirt Marcy had picked out for her. Nodding at her family, she smiled and thanked each of them again, appearing to be quite taken with their generosity.

"Well, that's it, I guess . . ." Charity said, stooping to retrieve bits of torn paper and bows.

Marcy grinned at Patrick, then rose from the chair. "Not quite." Pulling a tiny box from her pocket, she placed it in front of her daughter. "Happy birthday, darling," Marcy whispered. She stepped back to view the surprise on Charity's face.

Charity tore the paper off and lifted the lid, gasping when she saw its contents. In the box lay two delicate silver earrings. Slowly she lifted one to her ear, her face luminous. "Mother, they're beautiful . . . so beautiful!"

"They were your grandmother's. She gave them to me when I was your age. I've given her brooch to Faith and wanted you to have these. I hope you like them."

Charity bounced from the chair to fling herself into her mother's arms. "I love them, Mother, almost as much as I love you." Sniffing, she swabbed her face with her hands and approached Patrick. He seemed surprised as she hugged him at length. When she pulled away, his eyes were moist. "Thank you so much, Father. I love you too," she said in a husky voice.

Patrick squeezed her hand. "I love my girl," he whispered. Charity smiled at him shyly.

"Did you get your wish?" Katie asked.

"Not yet, but I have faith."

Patrick stood and stretched. "Okay, Katie, Steven, Beth—time for bed."

"I don't want to go to bed," Katie announced, clearly annoyed the festivities had come to an end. "I want to celebrate Charity's birthday some more."

Patrick heaved his youngest daughter to his shoulders. "You'll just have to celebrate in bed, young lady. Steven, don't forget your shoes."

"Up for a game of chess tonight, Father?" Sean asked.

Patrick hesitated for a moment, then shook his head. "No, better not, Sean. It was a tiring day at the paper. I think I'll call it a day. But maybe Faith will play."

Faith yawned. "Well, it's no fun beating him all the time, but I suppose I could give him a chance to redeem his pride."

Sean laughed and threw a pillow at her face. A knock sounded at the door. Charity looked up in surprise as Marcy hurried to answer it. Patrick stopped and turned on the steps while Katie dug her heels into his chest. "Giddyup, Daddy!"

"For mercy's sake, who do you suppose it could be at this late hour?" Marcy asked with a smile. She opened the door. Her fingers went cold on the knob, and a rush of air lodged in her throat. Collin McGuire stood on the stoop, polite expression in place and present in hand. Marcy's smile stiffened. Without a word, she turned to look up at her husband. Patrick slowly put Katie down on the steps, appearing oblivious that she squealed into the parlor once again. His eyes were flecked with granite as he stared, first at Collin, then at Charity to gauge her reaction.

Faith stood like stone, her face and fingers chilled. In her brain, the room stilled to a dreamlike state, words and movement coagulating into slow motion. She fixed her gaze on her sister, unable to shift it to where Collin stood at the door.

The look on Charity's face was truly a sight to behold.

The glow was back in full force, and her eyes were glittering like diamonds. Her beauty seemed intensified as she gazed at the man who held both of their hearts. Charity's lips quivered into a shy smile, and her fingers floated to the collar of her dress.

Clearing his throat, Collin addressed her father with a rare note of humility in his voice. "Mr. O'Connor, I apologize for barging in like this, I really do. But I couldn't let Charity's birthday pass without letting her know how much she means to me."

His words drew a gasp from Charity. Faith's gaze darted to her father, who appeared unflinching as his lips flattened in a hard line.

"Who is he, Mama?" Katie asked. Elizabeth watched the whole scenario with great fascination while Steven yawned. Faith forced herself to breathe.

"My name is Collin McGuire," he said to Katie, "and I'm in love with your sister."

Charity's fingers fluttered to her lips while the wind hitched in Faith's throat. She began to cough, her eyes watering as she glanced at Collin.

"Which one?" Katie wanted to know. A smile flickered on Collin's face.

"I thought I told you to leave my daughter alone," her father hissed. The gray of his eyes eclipsed to black. His mouth slashed into a scowl.

Collin turned to him without a trace of sarcasm. "Yes, sir, you did. And I've tried. I haven't seen Charity for close to two months now, and it's made me realize I don't want to go on without her. I know you don't like me, Mr. O'Connor, but I'm willing to do whatever it takes to win your respect."

"Whatever it takes?" Her father's tone was scathing.

"Yes, sir. I don't expect you to let me waltz right back into her life, but I do want you to know I've been working double shifts for a while now, and I'm saving real hard. I'm trying to be the kind of man you'd want for your daughter. I'll do whatever you want, Mr. O'Connor—follow any rules you set down—only please give me a chance. I love your daughter, sir."

Her mother stepped forward and gently touched her father's sleeve. "It is her birthday, Patrick," she said quietly. "At the very least, shouldn't we allow him to give her his present?"

Her father glared and waved him into the parlor, causing Charity to weep louder.

Collin grinned sheepishly. "Charity, don't cry, please. I'm not here to make you cry."

Charity laughed and pushed the tears across her face. Collin handed her a handkerchief. Like a little girl, Charity blew her nose loudly and laughed again, taking the gift from Collin's hand. Trembling, she opened the box and uttered a cry of delight as she held a beautiful mother-of-pearl comb to the light. The tears reappeared. This time, Collin grabbed the handkerchief and wiped the wetness from her cheeks. "It's not a lot, Charity, but someday I hope to give you much more."

Her father cleared his throat, and her mother shot him a pleading look. Faith, desperate to convey an air of calm, quietly moved to the love seat, where she sat ramrod straight, hands clasped tightly in her lap.

Charity looked radiant, clutching the comb to her chest. "I love it, Collin, more than anything in the world!"

Her father exhaled a hiss of air through clenched teeth.

"Mother, will you help me? I want Collin to see it in my hair. Please?" Charity turned to her father, her eyes entreating his permission. "Father, may I try it on . . . please?"

The breath stilled in Faith's throat. Her father finally nodded, causing Charity to squeal and snatch her mother's hand. The two skittered upstairs while her father sighed and picked Katie up in his arms.

Slowly, absently, Faith pressed a hand to her stomach to quell the nausea that was rising in her throat.

"Faith, would you be kind enough to get our guest a drink while I take Katie upstairs?" her father asked. "Beth, you too. Where's Steven?" His eyes scanned the room and spotted Steven asleep on the floor. "Sean, would you carry him up for me, please?" He turned to Collin. "You're welcome to take a seat. We'll talk after I put Katie to bed."

Collin nodded and perched on the arm of the sofa. Faith felt the heat of his stare as she rushed from the room. Inside the sanctuary of the kitchen, her mind hazed to a near stupor, her oxygen supply greatly impaired. How could this be happening? She leaned hard against the kitchen table, hands pressed white and knees teetering, then flinched when the kitchen door creaked open. She jerked and spun around too quickly. Her discomfort lured a smile to his lips.

"What do you think you're doing?" she asked, her breath thick in her throat.

Collin's eyes never left hers as he sauntered within inches of where she stood. "Getting a drink."

She stepped back and stumbled against a chair. He laughed.

"You're crazy!" she whispered.

He laughed again. Sliding a chair out, he sat and straddled it, arms relaxed as they hung loosely over the back. "You've called me that before, but now . . . well, now I think it's probably true." He cocked his head, his eyes dark pools of heat as he studied her. "I am crazy—about your sister. I'm going to marry her."

His statement found its mark, coldcocking her like an electric shock. She sank into the chair, her breath cleaving to her tongue. She licked the dryness from her lips and closed her eyes.

She heard him shift in the seat before he suddenly leaped to his feet. She opened her eyes to see him glaring at her, his eyes glinting like jagged quartz. He took a deep breath and bent over the chair, fingers bloodless as they gripped its back. "So help me, Faith, you provoke me—more than any woman I've ever met. I find myself wanting to hurt you, then end up getting hurt instead. Well, there's nothing you can do about Charity and me. She cares for me, just as I am. And I don't have to change one bit for her. That's more than I can say for you." He started for the door.

She looked up. Her voice was barely a whisper. "I've always cared for you—just as you are."

Collin stopped and turned, the color leeching from his face. "What? What did you say?"

It was an effort to stand, but she did, hand propped on the table for support. In hypnotic motion, her gaze lifted to his. "I said, I've always cared for you . . . since I was a little girl. You're everything I ever wanted, except . . ."

Collin looked as if she had spat in his face. His lips steeled into a slit. "Except I don't believe in your God," he hissed. The statement seemed to suck the air from the room. He took a deep breath and braced his hand against the door. "That doesn't matter to Charity."

"My father will never allow you to marry her, you know." Her tone was listless as she stared at the floor.

"Yes, he will. You underestimate the power of my charm. I'll become a changed man. You'll see, I'll win him over."

Faith looked at the man who owned her heart. A sad smile shadowed her lips. "You're willing to change. Just not for me."

The hard line of his chin angled as his gray eyes seared

hers. "I'll change on the outside to suit your father. I'd have to change my soul to suit you."

She nodded and stood. "It's going to be difficult, you know. I'll never get used to it."

His voice gentled. "You will, and so will I. I do care for your sister."

She tried to smile. "What do you want to drink?" she asked.

"What do you have?" he responded, and Faith walked to the icebox.

"Nothing strong enough to suit you." Her voice was flat, with just an edge.

Collin smiled. "That's okay. I'm thinking of giving it up."

Patrick watched from the bed while Marcy rigorously brushed her hair with the routine one hundred strokes, but it was one of the rare moments when his mind was not on his wife. It had been a very disturbing evening, to say the least. He cuffed his pillow then turned on his side to get comfortable, but it was useless. Sleep would not come easily tonight, not while he had the complexities of his daughter's love life weighing so heavily on his mind.

Marcy completed her regimen, turned out the light, and hurried to slip into the warmth of their bed. She leaned over to kiss him softly on the cheek. Instinctively, his arm reached to pull her to him, and she snuggled into the warmth of his embrace. "She looked happy, didn't she?" Marcy's tone sounded hopeful but cautious.

"Mmm," he responded, certain Charity's happiness over Collin was not a good thing.

"What are we going to do?"

"I don't know, darlin'."

"You know, Patrick, meeting him, talking with him, well, he really doesn't seem so bad."

"He's a man, Marcy. Charity's a child."

"She's seventeen, Patrick—she'll be graduating in May. We have to face the fact she's become a young woman." Marcy hesitated, obviously waiting for a response, but this time none came. She continued. "She loves him, Patrick, and he seems to care for her."

Patrick shifted away from his wife to punch at his pillow again. He turned to lie flat on his back. "She doesn't know the first thing about love, Marcy, and as far as Collin McGuire goes, it's not love on his mind."

Marcy sat up in the bed and reached for his hand. "Patrick, maybe if we took it really slow. You know, allowed him to come over to spend an evening with the entire family occasionally, maybe then we would get to know him, trust him . . ."

"There's no trusting a man like that."

Marcy lifted a hand to gently stroke his face. "You know, you were a man like that once, my love. Tonight when Collin walked through the door with steel in his eyes, he reminded me so much of you. My father didn't trust you either, if you recall. But you won him over—and me."

Patrick sighed and tugged her close. He buried his face in her hair, wondering for the thousandth time how he'd been so blessed to find her. Was it the same with Collin? Should he go against his better judgment and allow Collin to see his daughter? "I'm not comfortable with it, Marcy, not at all. But maybe you're right; perhaps we need to know him better. I promise I'll give it much thought."

"And prayer?"

He squeezed his wife. "That, my dear, goes without saying."

Charity was far too excited to sleep. And why should she when she could dream so happily wide awake? Her wish had come true—he loved her! She had seen it in his eyes, and he had professed it openly to her entire family. She heard Faith rustling in the bed across the room and knew her sister's reasons for not sleeping were far different than her own. The glow diminished slightly as she thought how Faith must be feeling tonight, knowing Collin would never belong to her. She would get over it quickly enough, Charity reasoned, and the glow returned once again. She would have to. Collin was going to be part of the family, and there was nothing Faith could do but accept it. Charity stretched beneath the cool sheets. Birthdays just didn't get any better than this. Unless, perhaps, you were celebrating them as Mrs. Collin McGuire! The mere thought silently took her away to sweet sleep with a smile on her lips.

Across the room, Faith lay quietly, listening to the even rhythm of Charity's breathing, which, at last, was regular and calm. She was dreaming, no doubt, about Collin. Faith blinked away the wetness forming in her eyes as she lay there, lifeless. Never had she felt so depressed. A shaft of moonlight split the room in two, flooding it with a soft glow, but to her it seemed darker than any abyss. How could it be all her dreams and hopes had come to this? She had tried to do the right thing, to seek God's way, but it had only inflicted the most excruciating heartbreak she had ever known. It wasn't supposed to be like this. She was supposed to have peace and joy—Mrs. Gerson had said so. But she didn't. All she had was despair, while her sister, once again, was blessed with the desire of her heart . . . and Faith's.

A surge of anger rose within. It could all be different, she thought. Collin could belong to her. The night on the porch, he'd implied that, hadn't he? They had both felt something, hadn't they? If she had relented to his kiss, things might be different tonight. He might belong to her and not Charity. But no, she had chosen to do what was right. But right for whom, she wanted to know. If this was God's best, as Mrs. Gerson was fond of saying, maybe she didn't want God's best!

Her mind began to race. Abruptly she sat up, pushing the hair from her face. She would tell him! She would let him know she wanted him, that it didn't matter if he believed in God or not. She would embrace his affections and allow the wonderful feelings to carry her away. Her heart rocketed at the mere thought of his arms around her, his hungry kisses . . .

And then all at once, beneath the warmth that thoughts of him always produced, a cold heaviness settled in. The hopelessness she'd felt only moments before now paled before the overpowering blackness that crept into her soul. It would never work. She would never be happy, and she knew it to the core of her being. She was trapped—cornered by a God who had taken her from the shadows into his glorious light. Yes, she had tasted the sweetness of Collin's kiss, but also the peace and joy of an intimate relationship with God, and it had ruined her for anything else. Faith sobbed into her pillow. She could never go back. Where was the free will in all this? *How can I choose to turn from you, God, when I know I will never be happy apart from you? Where is the choice?*

Faith wept until limp in her bed, and when her anger subsided, heartbreak returned with a vengeance. Never had she felt so incredibly lost.

The Lord is close to the brokenhearted . . .

Faith grasped her prayer book from the nightstand and frantically flipped its pages. Suddenly, she stopped and leaned forward to allow the moonlight to shine upon the passage from Psalm 34 that she had jotted down at Mrs. Gerson's.

The eyes of Jehovah are toward the righteous, And his ears are open unto their cry . . . The righteous cried, and Jehovah heard, and delivered them out of all their troubles. Jehovah is nigh unto them that are of a broken heart, and saveth such as are of a contrite spirit. Many are the afflictions of the righteous; but Jehovah delivereth him out of them all.

She fell upon the open pages with a broken sob. "Save me, oh Lord, for my spirit is crushed, and I am so broken-hearted." Faith's prayer poured from the depths of her soul, and the peace she'd become so dependent upon did not fail her. *He* would not fail her, she knew. Just as she knew in her heart she would let Collin go. She fell back on the bed, closing her eyes. With a purpose in her heart and a prayer on her lips, she finally drifted into a weary slumber.

9

It was Christmas Eve, and the O'Connor household was abuzz with holiday activity bordering on bedlam. In the kitchen, Marcy was dangerously close to the breaking point as she pulled another tray of cookies from the oven just as Katie knocked a bowl of icing onto the floor.

"Ooops!" Katie giggled as Blarney pounced on the gooey mess, tail wagging furiously at his good fortune. Marcy stood in the center of the kitchen, dumbfounded, a hot tray of cookies still in her hands. She cried out in pain as the heat penetrated the pot holders she held, and slammed the tray onto the counter. Tears stung her eyes when several cookies flipped in the air and crashed to the floor.

"Mama, are you okay? Did you burn yourself?" Katie's concern sounded genuine.

Marcy looked at her tiny daughter, who was covered from head to toe in flour and icing, then stared at her kitchen, which looked even worse, and wanted to cry. Christmas shouldn't be like this, she thought, nursing her burnt fingers.

In the next room, Faith grinned, watching her father point to a tree bough that needed decorating. The tree he'd cut down that morning from Holper's farm stood proud and tall in the far corner of the parlor while the rest of the family arrayed it with ornaments and cranberry garland. Pipe in hand, her father supervised from his favorite chair, and Faith shook her head and smiled, absently turning a page in the book on her lap.

Wonderful smells of Christmas filled the house, cookies and pine needles and orange-spice wassail. Everywhere you looked, homemade decorations hung, lending a festive air to rooms aglow with anticipation. Tonight, as O'Connor tradition would have it, they would concentrate on the birth of the Christ child, leaving the impending threat of war to another day.

"It's going to be another wonderful Christmas," her father announced as he bit into one of her mother's oatmeal cookies.

Faith wasn't so sure. She watched as Charity stood on tiptoe and giggled while reaching to hang a patchwork angel as high as she could. Behind her Collin hoisted Katie—now banished from the kitchen—well above Charity's shoulders to claim the honor of hanging the highest ornament. Elizabeth laughed as Sean offered a challenge, heaving Steven to his shoulders armed with a delicate glass dove, which Steven promptly placed on the highest bough. It was a joyful scene to all but Faith, who worked diligently at smiling along with the rest.

It had been over a month since Patrick had agreed to allow Collin to see Charity. The dictates had been strict— one visit a week, on Sundays, for lunch following church and staying through dinner. He was never to be alone with Charity, and under no circumstances could she go anywhere with him. And if either Collin or Charity broke any of the established rules, the relationship was over. Although her father had never suggested Collin join them at church each Sunday, he was always there nonetheless, standing in the back of the vestibule in his best suit, fresh-shaven and hair neatly combed. And so it went, Sunday after Sunday; Collin slowly became a part of their lives, a fact that suited almost everyone in the family.

Faith watched him out of the corner of her eye, pretending total absorption in her book. Collin had such a natural way with people when he put his mind to it, much like her father. He instinctively knew when to jump up and lend a hand to Marcy or tease Katie out of a near-tantrum. Sean seemed to enjoy his company, as Collin was always a ready and challenging partner at chess. He wrestled with Steven and talked poetry with Elizabeth, and yet somehow always managed to keep his eyes on Charity. Even her father had to admit that perhaps he'd been wrong about this man so intent on loving his daughter.

Through it all Faith remained in the background, never speaking to Collin, seldom looking his way, and more often than not, sitting up in her room or burying herself in a book. She noticed that he, too, seemed to avoid her, conveniently preoccupying himself with Katie, Steven, or the dog whenever she spoke. The first few weeks had been almost unbearable, but she found her faith seemed to grow to meet her need. Little by little, the dread that set in on Saturdays began to diminish, and steadily Faith could feel her enthusiasm for Sundays returning once again.

Collin was beginning to speak to her now, a word here, a question there, and she even found him watching her upon rare occasion. She could feel herself starting to relax when he was in the room, and it occurred to her that he had been right. She was getting used to it. And so was he, apparently. But there were times, she was reluctant to admit, when she would see him gaze into her sister's eyes and suspected it would be a long while before her feelings would wane. A very long while—and a lot of prayer—she realized as she got up to leave the room.

Her mother was finishing up the last of the dishes as Faith entered the kitchen. She seemed so tired. Faith walked up behind and put her arms around her shoulders. "Why didn't you say you needed help, Mother? I would have been in here in a heartbeat."

Marcy turned, her smile weary. "I know, Faith, but actually it was rather nice having a few moments alone. I don't know what's wrong lately. I seem to be much more impatient with Katie than I ever was with you and the others. It's just getting older, I suppose. I seem to wear out so easily these days."

Faith took her mother's arm and steered her into a chair. "Here, you sit down, and I'll finish up. Or better yet, why don't you go in and sit with the others?"

"Oh, that sounds so nice! I will, I think. Thank you, Faith. I love you."

Faith smiled over her shoulder. "I love you too, Mother. Now scoot. Go sit with that husband of yours."

"I'll be asleep within ten minutes, fifteen minutes at the most," she said, laughing as she headed through the door.

Faith shook her head and smiled as she reached for the mixing bowl. The kitchen door swung open again, and she lowered her voice to a threatening tone. "I'm warning you—don't make me carry you out of this kitchen . . ."

"I'd like to see you try," Collin said with that teasing tone of his. Faith's heart tumbled in her chest. She turned as Collin stood at the door, an empty glass in his hand, and a swell of the old familiar feelings tripped through her. *Why is this happening again? I've been fine for weeks, and now my stomach chooses* this *moment to do flip-flops?* She attempted a laugh, then turned to the sink, hoping he wouldn't notice that her hands were shaking.

"Oh, I thought you were Mother. You have to force that woman to take a break, you know." She put the shaking to good use by scrubbing a bowl with relentless determination.

She heard him walk to the icebox, open it, and pour himself a glass of something. Without a word, he leaned against the counter and sipped. She sensed his eyes and felt a blush warming her cheeks. *What in blazes does he think he's doing?* She attacked the next mixing bowl with even fiercer intensity, refusing to give him the satisfaction of her curiosity.

He drained the glass and ambled to the sink where he stood, glass in hand. Faith ignored him—and the flutters in her stomach—and reached for more soap. She put it in the water and swished with her fingers until bubbles puffed high.

"How are you at whist?" he asked.

"Excuse me?"

"Whist," he repeated. "Charity's convinced she can trounce me, and I need a partner." He handed her his dirty glass. "Wanna play?"

She snatched it from his hand and scrubbed as she had never scrubbed before.

"You may want to sterilize it," he said with a hint of a smile.

The heat in her face fanned to hot as she ceased her scouring. "I've got dishes to do."

"We'll wait," he said. "That is, if you're any good."

She turned to face him, eyebrow cocked. "Good? You want good? How do I know you can even keep up with me?"

He grinned. "My, we're a bit full of ourselves tonight, aren't we now?"

Her lips curved into a smile. "You should know." She dismissed him with a sweep of her hair and heard him laugh as her hands dove into the suds.

"I'll try not to disappoint you," he drawled.

The door creaked closed as he left, and she sagged against the sink, sucking in a breath. Her hands were shaking and her heart was pounding, but by gum she would teach him a thing or two about whist before she was through. And somehow, the thought cheered her.

It was a near-massacre. Collin worked hard to keep from breaking into an all-out grin. The look on Charity's face told him it would be unwise, so he jostled Katie on his knee instead. He wrapped his arms around the little girl as he positioned the cards in his hand. Glancing across the table at Faith, he fought the inclination to smile. She was a gritty-faced cardsharp, her green eyes focused as she surveyed her hand, picking up tricks as smoothly as a riverboat hustler on a peaceful river. She pursed her lips in satisfaction and carefully placed her trump card down.

Charity moaned as she pitched her remaining cards on the table and stood up. "Come on, Katie, I'll put you to bed."

Sean sighed and tossed his cards in as well. "I'm right behind you, Katie girl. I know when to call it a night."

"No! I don't wanna go to bed. I wanna watch some more."

"No, you're going to bed," Charity said, her tone as threatening as her mood. "Mother wanted you asleep a while ago."

Katie pasted herself around Collin's neck, a look of panic in her eyes. "No, Collin, don't let her take me, please!"

Collin flashed his little-boy grin. "Come on, Charity, it's Christmas Eve. Twenty more minutes won't matter."

Charity pushed her chair in abruptly. "That's what you said twenty minutes ago and then twenty minutes before that. No, Collin, don't try to get around me with that smile. She's going to bed." She reached to take hold of Katie, who clung to Collin like a newborn monkey.

Collin pried her arms from his neck and kissed her on the forehead. "Katie, you know what I forgot? Tomorrow's

Christmas, and if you don't go to bed, you might sleep through it."

Katie blinked. "I wouldn't do that," she whimpered.

"You might, if you don't get your sleep. I would hate for you to miss Christmas just because you're too tired to get up. Besides, you want to be a good girl for Santa, don't you?"

She nodded, and he gave her a squeeze. "That's a girl. Do I get a good-night kiss?"

Katie yawned before her little mouth puckered. She kissed him sweetly on the lips.

"What, no butterfly kiss?" he asked.

She giggled and pressed her cheek to his, fluttering her lashes against his face. A broad grin stretched across his lips. "Good night, Katie," he whispered, then handed her over to Charity, who groaned at the weight.

"Katie Rose, you're getting way too big for me to carry you."

Sean jumped up. "I'll take her up if you'll get her ready for bed. Good night, you two hustlers. I hope your conscience keeps you awake tonight."

"I'm sure you have plans to gloat while I put Katie to bed," Charity said with a smirk.

Collin laughed. "I promise, we'll get it all out of our systems before you get back."

She shot him a searing look before following Sean and Katie from the room.

Faith and Collin grinned at each other.

"We make a pretty good team," he said as he leaned back in the chair.

She smiled and nodded, appearing to avoid his eyes while she picked up the cards. "You kept up pretty well, I noticed."

"Where'd you learn to play like that?"

"School. You happen to be looking at the reigning champ of St. Mary's class of 1916."

"You don't show a lot of mercy for someone so devoted to God," he remarked dryly.

She was shuffling the cards with ease as her eyes suddenly locked on his. "Mercy's not exactly my strong suit," she said.

"What is?"

She grinned and cut the cards. "Well, I'm pretty good at self-control, and I suppose you could say I have perseverance. I've got a stubborn streak, so I guess it comes naturally. You wouldn't be interested in a quick game of rummy, would you?" Her green eyes issued a challenge.

He felt a smile slide across his lips. His pulse quickened as the color deepened on her cheeks. Her eyes quickly dropped to assess the cards in her hand, and all at once, he was as high-strung as a cat. He hated the way his blood was coursing through his veins without warning. Was he interested in a game of rummy? A swear word bubbled into his thoughts. No, he wasn't interested in rummy! And the cold realization did nothing to temper the heat he was feeling. After a month of devoting himself to Charity, a month of hoping these feelings for Faith were behind him, she still affected him more than any woman alive.

"Sure, why not?" He palmed the cards she dealt and breathed in deeply—quietly—as he arranged his hand. He willed himself to be calm and relaxed. Like her, he thought, stealing a glance. She was oblivious to the flood of feelings she'd just unleashed in him. Completely focused on the game, gauging her cards with a cool gaze, her face unreadable except for the slightest tilt of her lips. She picked up and discarded.

"Perseverance. Yeah, I'd say you have that in spades," he said, reaching for a card off the pile. "You were a plucky little thing, even with braces on your legs." He looked up, his eyes softening as they fixed on hers. "Charity told me about your sister. I'm sorry."

She nodded and took a deep breath, the bridge of her nose creasing while she scrutinized her cards. "Thank you."

"Do you miss her?"

She looked up. "Yes. Very much."

He stared back. There was heartbreak in those green eyes, but something else too. So much strength, so much inner peace . . . so much faith. He couldn't imagine two of her. He swallowed. "What was she like?"

A soft smile lighted on her lips. She gazed past him with a faraway look in her eyes. "What can I say? Hope was a part of me, my best friend, my 'other self.'" She smiled again, snapping out of her reverie. "Or, at least, that's what we used to call each other." She picked up a card.

He grinned. "Don't tell me—I'll bet you were the good twin."

She laughed. "You'd lose your money on that one, I'm afraid. No, I was the 'handful,' according to my father, the twin with the penchant for trouble." She glanced up, her eyes twinkling. "That wild temper, you know." Collin smiled, and she continued. "Hope was . . . well, she was one of the softest, kindest human beings I've ever known. Her voice, her manner, the way she walked, played . . . all spoke of a gentle heart."

Faith rested her hands on the table, cards braced low, almost facedown. The distant look was back in her eyes. "I remember playing dress-up with Mother's hand-me-downs. I'd parade around, stylish as you please, in the prettiest and fanciest clothes I could find, all heaped high with gobs of Mother's best jewelry. And Hope would take what was left, never complaining, never worrying about having the best. She always seemed the happiest when she could make me happy."

Faith took a deep breath, her gaze fading into a blank stare. "She was an angel from God. I loved her with all my heart . . ." Her voice trailed, and she suddenly blinked, moisture glazing her eyes. "Still do."

"So, what are some of your other strong suits?" he asked quickly, hoping to steer the subject away from the sadness he'd obviously inflicted.

"Well, I like to think I'm loyal, I have a deep faith in God, and I suppose I'm a good listener. Especially if you want to tell me what's in your hand."

He glanced up with a wry smile. "No, thanks. But I do seem to recall you made a pretty good sounding board when we were in school. Did I bore you to tears?"

"Of course not," she said with a laugh. "You were the exalted senior, and I was the lowly freshman. What else could I be but mesmerized?"

He picked up, frowned, then threw the card back down. "To tell you the truth, I don't even remember what I rambled on about."

She looked up, a slight blush stealing into her cheeks. "You don't remember? You had so many dreams, so many plans for your future. You had it all mapped out, as I recall. You wanted to work the printing business with your father. He was going to teach you, and you were going to grow it."

The muscles in his face tightened as he discarded. "Yeah, I remember now. What a pie-in-the-sky dreamer I was."

"No, you weren't! You wanted to make your father proud."

"Like I said—a dreamer." He snatched a card from the deck, then hurled it back.

"There's nothing wrong with dreams, Collin. You could still make him proud, you know."

He leveled his gaze on hers. "And how would I do that

now? He's gone, and everything is gone with him. The dream died when he did."

"I don't think so." She put her final card facedown on the pile. "The dream lives in you, not your father. Gin." She looked up with a touch of defiance in her eyes.

He tossed the cards on the table with a faint smile. "You haven't changed much since high school, you know that? I think you're a bigger dreamer than I was."

"Maybe. But I think you could have carried on with the business when he died. After all, you still had his shop, his equipment, and most of all, you had the fire inside to fuel it all. Honestly, Collin, if you could have seen the look on your face whenever you spoke about your future, you would have known you could make it a success."

He gripped the edge of the table and leaned forward, his eyes burning. "Do you think I didn't want to? You don't think I wasn't crushed? The person I loved more than anyone in this world died! And any chance I might have had got buried right along with him. Don't you understand? I didn't know enough about the business to turn on a machine, much less print anything."

Collin slumped back in the chair, his voice deadened. "He never wanted to burden me with working while I was in school. And summers . . . well, he said I should enjoy them, that there was plenty of time to learn the business once I graduated. Plenty of time, he said, to work the rest of my life." Collin looked up, his eyes stinging with anger and pain. "Only there wasn't. He left me alone, Faith, with no one to turn to."

She sat, her hands gently cupping the deck of cards as she watched him, her face full of emotion. "You weren't alone, Collin. God was with you every step of the way. He would have shown you what to do if you had asked. You could have learned the business from someone else, given yourself as an apprentice to someone who would run the shop, I don't know. All I do know is you have great potential, and if you would only turn back to the one who gave it to you, I know you could fulfill your father's dream . . . and yours."

Never did she radiate more beauty than when she spoke of her God, and never was his anger kindled more than when she did. It was the same seesaw effect she always had on him—a tug-of-war between wanting her and hating her. He stretched back in his chair and stared, his eyes angry slits as they took in the face aglow with hope and the eyes glimmering with promise. "And just exactly what would you know about *my* potential, Faith?"

She went red. "I just meant—"

"You meant well, I know, but keep in mind I'm not the only one running from potential."

Her cheeks flamed, and it gave him some small satisfaction to see her squirm.

His silence seemed to unnerve her further, and she suddenly stood, fumbling with the cards as she put them away. "Actually, Collin, I am pretty tired. I better head up."

"Why? My 'potential' too frightening a subject for you?"

Her green eyes narrowed. "No, I just don't know why you feel the need to ruin a perfectly good evening."

He let out a weary sigh and rubbed the back of his neck. "I'm sorry, Faith," he whispered. "You got a little too close to home, I guess. Sorry if I hurt you. Tonight . . . and in the past."

She averted her gaze while she brushed her hair from her face. "Don't be. Everything's fine, Collin. I'm getting over it, really I am."

"I hope so," he said without conviction.

She laughed, her voice shaky as she gathered empty glasses off the table. "Really, I'm fine. We had fun tonight, and that's good. It shows we can be around each other comfortably, without strain." She stared at the glasses in her hands, her voice fading low and soft. "You fit in well. The way you handle Katie, the way you tease and make us all laugh, it just feels right. I know you're going to make my sister very happy."

"Faith . . ."

She looked up into his eyes, and it was back, the memory of that day in the park flooding his senses with a strange connection as thick as the tension in the air. He could tell from her eyes she felt it too.

She straightened her shoulders and pressed her lips in a tight line. "Collin, I don't think it's a good idea for you and me to be alone like this. It's . . . well, it's very hard, and I think I do better when we avoid it."

He nodded without a word. So this was it, the self-control in action. The self-control that kept her at a safe distance, taught her to deny her feelings and then robbed him in the process. She turned and walked toward the kitchen. Collin jumped up. "Faith, wait—"

She stopped at the door, her back to him, when Charity's voice severed the air. "What's going on?"

Collin stiffened. "Just chatting with your sister."

Charity looked at him strangely, then glanced at Faith, who spun around, arms full of dirty glasses.

"I'll tell you what's going on. He's making me carry his dirty dishes without lifting a finger to help. It's best you know what a slave driver he is." Faith's tone was flip, and for that Collin was grateful.

Charity produced her most seductive smile. "Well, that's your problem, sis. You have to learn how to get a man to do for you." She raked her sister with a look of pity. "Maybe I'll give you lessons sometime."

Collin guessed it wasn't the first time Charity had humiliated her sister in front of people, but obviously it was one of the most painful. Faith's cheeks were crimson as she escaped from the room.

"Why do you do that to your sister?" For the first time since he'd known Charity, he was annoyed with her.

Charity blinked, her smile fading. "It's just a sister thing."

"It's not right."

She blushed. "Why do you care so much?"

"I don't."

"Really? It seems to me like you do."

Collin strode to where she stood and leaned a hand against the wall. He grabbed her chin with the other. "Charity, it's late and I'm tired. I don't give a whit what you say to your sister, as long as you say the right things to me. I need to be going. Walk me to the door?"

She followed him to the parlor while he said his goodbyes to Patrick, who was the only one still up. Patrick looked up from his newspaper. "Merry Christmas, Collin. See you tomorrow morning. Charity has something special under the tree for you, I think."

"I wouldn't miss it, Mr. O'Connor."

Faith slipped from the kitchen, leaned to kiss Patrick, then darted up the stairs.

Collin took a deep breath, grabbed his coat from the rack, and put it on. "Good night, Charity. Sleep well." He kissed her lightly on the forehead.

Her smile was tight as she opened the door. "I'll try to be nicer," she promised.

"Me too," he said, grazing her chin with his thumb. He descended the steps and heard the door click as he headed to the street. Pulling his coat tighter, he exhaled softly.

Another roadblock. Well, he'd just have to push it away, just like Faith did with the "potential" they held for each other. She wouldn't have him, but Charity would. The thought did little to ease the heaviness of his mood. He slammed his fists deep into his pockets and kicked an empty bottle lying in his path, hurtling it against a lamppost. It shattered to the ground.

When would he learn? He had watched his mother do this to his father—control him, destroy him—and he vowed it would never happen to him. But it was, and he had to do something to stop it. He forced himself to think about Charity, and a bit of calm came over him. She loved him, wanted him. He let his mind wander to thoughts of making love to her, and a smile creased his lips. Everything would be all right, he promised himself. Once they were married, his passion for Charity would consume him, save him. He inhaled deeply to fill his lungs with the sting of the frigid night air. And with a new confidence in his step, he headed for home.

"Mama, Daddy, wake up! He's come—Santa's come!" Katie's tone vibrated with excitement as she bounded into the room. "We have to get up! We have to have Christmas!"

Patrick's head was buried in his pillow, and Marcy never even stirred beneath the heap of blankets piled on her side of the bed. Obviously impatient with her parents, Katie leaned over her father's face, lifted his eyelid with her little finger, and stared into his bleary eyeball. "Daddy," she whispered loudly, "we have to get up—it's time!"

Never moving his head from the pillow, Patrick moaned, blindly reaching in the air until he found the alarm clock on his nightstand. He rubbed his eyes with his fist, squinted at the time, and moaned again. "Katie, it's only five o'clock in the morning—it's too early for Christmas. Go back to bed, little girl."

Katie remained undaunted. She tugged at his covers and managed to pull them back, leaving Patrick exposed to the chill in the room. She grabbed his hand in her two little fists and began to yank, eliciting more groans from her father. "Daddy, it's Christmas—Jesus's birthday! Don't you want to celebrate Jesus's birthday?" Her tone was accusing.

That did it. Somewhere deep within the mound of covers, Marcy's sleepy giggle erupted, and when Katie heard it, she vaulted on the bed with a squeal. Patrick felt Marcy's arms encircling as she cozied up behind him. Her soft lips brushed the back of his neck while Katie giggled and tunneled under the covers.

He sighed. Since Katie had been born, Christmas seemed to get earlier and earlier every year. He barely had the strength to get up, much less fight them both. "Katie Rose, it's an absolute wonder Santa brings you anything at all as demanding as you are, young lady."

"Well, he did! Lots and lots of presents. Just wait till you see. I'll wake the others. Hurry!" In the next breath she was gone, flying down the hall like a Christmas Paul Revere rousing the troops.

"Lord, please let me live long enough to see what becomes of that girl," Patrick muttered, "because I know it's got to be something truly amazing."

Marcy squeezed him tightly. "Merry Christmas, darling."

He rolled to face her, pulling her close. "They always are with you, Marcy," he whispered, her kiss warm on his lips.

For a moment they lingered, then Marcy shimmied free from her arsenal of blankets. "I suppose we better get downstairs. I don't know about you, but I don't want to incur the wrath of a strong-willed five-year-old, do you?"

Patrick laughed and swung his legs over the side of the bed, stretching his arms high in the air. "No, thanks, I've already had enough cold chills for one morning. What time is Faith supposed to collect Mrs. Gerson?"

Marcy pulled her hair into a chignon. "Christa said Faith

could come by anytime after six. What time did you tell Collin?"

"I told him we would begin Christmas around seven, breakfast closer to nine, then church at noon." Rising, Patrick walked to the closet to get ready, then returned to the bed to put on his shoes. In short order he stood up, completely dressed. He turned to his wife, hands on his hips. "So! What can I do to help you?"

Marcy smiled as she buttoned her blouse. "Well, you can light the fire in the parlor, of course, and then you can put all your energy into keeping Katie from tearing into presents. I've got the platter of cookies ready to go. All I have to do is put coffee on and start a few preparations for breakfast, but Faith and Charity can help me with that."

"Sure," Patrick teased, "give me the hard part!" With a wink, he adjusted his suit vest and turned on his heel, bracing himself for what surely would be the most daunting task of the day.

Collin was certain he had circles under his eyes—he hadn't slept a wink all night. It had been a very long time since he'd been this excited about Christmas. Surely further back to a time before his father died, and probably even longer than that to before he had first noticed the strain between his parents. He hadn't realized that a household could exist without tension until he met the O'Connors. The brief amount of time he'd spent with them had done more to restore his faith in marriage than anything he had ever seen.

He was enamored with the buzz and hum of this passionate family, often finding himself studying Marcy and Patrick's interactions with the interest of an avid student of psychology. Never had he seen such warmth and tenderness between two people married for such a long period of time, and it completely intrigued him. It seemed as if the entire family thrived in the glow that surrounded these two people, spilling over onto each as naturally as rain onto the earth. Collin had never experienced this before, and his hunger for it drew him like a moth to flame.

He grabbed his coat from the closet and headed for his mother's room. Pushing the door ajar, he tiptoed to her bed and leaned to see if she was awake.

"Are you leaving now?" The covers rustled slightly, and Katherine McGuire looked up, her eyes squinted with sleep.

Collin sat on the bed beside her and put his hand over hers. She looked so tired, like she used to when she waited up all hours of the night for him to come home. But it had been several months now since he had pulled a late-nighter at Brannigan's, which eased the strain with his mother considerably, and Collin wondered why she wasn't sleeping now.

"Yes, I am. Are you sure you don't want to come along? Mrs. O'Connor made a point of my asking you. I know they would love to see you."

Katherine McGuire shifted in the bed, attempting a faint smile. "No, you go alone. I'm not up to it today, Collin. I haven't been sleeping well. But you go and have fun. When will you be home?"

He kissed her on the cheek. "Should be back by early afternoon, plenty of time to help you get ready for our company tonight."

"Company . . ." she muttered. "I'd hardly call Uncle Sydney and Aunt Jane company, but I do appreciate your help. Will you be bringing Charity for dinner? I'm anxious to meet her."

Collin stood and pulled the covers over his mother's shoulders. "No, I don't think so, unless her father changes his mind. You get some rest, okay?"

His mother nodded and closed her eyes while Collin

shut the curtains. Silently, he left the room, sparing one last glance at his mother. How he wished she and his father could have known some of the joy he saw in the O'Connors. But, it wasn't to be, and for that, Collin felt a twinge of sadness, certainly not an uncommon emotion for him during the holidays.

He opened the hall closet door and lifted a paper bag filled with presents. There was a gift for each of them. They were practically family to him, after all. He wondered if they knew that, if they realized how starved he was for what they had to offer.

Faith's present caught his eye, and his mood ebbed. Would there ever come a time when the sight of her, the sound of her, would not affect him like this? He hoped to God there would. *God*—that was the root of the problem. If it wasn't for this God of hers, imaginary or real, he might be with her instead of Charity. But the thought of God angered him as much as Faith stirred him, and it would only be a matter of time before the relationship would feel the strain. Charity's belief in God seemed minimal, at most, and Collin was quite sure he mattered more to her than her surface devotion to a demanding deity. No, it was definitely for the best. It was much safer with Charity. He could be happy with her—in control with her—and that was certainly more than he ever believed he would achieve in the realm of love.

Collin thought about Charity, and a smile stretched across his face. She was beautiful. A bit of a brat, but truly beautiful, and he couldn't wait until he could really hold her in his arms again. But for now, pecks on the cheek would have to do. Nothing was going to jeopardize this relationship, he promised himself, and the thought infused him with the energy to control his passions—for the moment. At least, until the time was right. But the time would come, Collin felt quite sure, and he was counting on it heavily to douse any other flame that burned.

Faith was certain the parlor had never looked lovelier. She wished Mrs. Gerson could see it as she ushered her to a chair by the fire. Her mother had every oil lamp, candle, and light glowing, causing the tree to shimmer with a dazzling array of ornaments and candied fruit. The air drifted with the sweet scent of pine and cinnamon. Her father, chatting with Mrs. Gerson, stoked the fire while her mother divvied out mugs of steaming hot chocolate and coffee.

Under the tree, Katie was busy playing with the manger. She placed Mary and Joseph on their sides and covered them with her bear's blanket. Steven lay prostrate beside her, galloping the camel like a stallion. Katie snatched it away, a look of disapproval on her face. "Give me the horse. It's time for his nap," she said.

"It's a camel," Steven snapped, wrestling it from her hand. "Camels don't take naps."

"Mama, Steven took my horse!" Katie wailed.

Marcy knelt to pick her up. "It's okay, Katie. We're going to read about Baby Jesus now, so why don't you sit in my lap?" She carried Katie to the sofa and glanced back at Steven. "Steven, why don't you sit by me too?"

The doorbell rang as her father reached for the family Bible. Sean rose to answer it, and Charity jumped up at the same time. "I'll get it, Sean—it's Collin." She raced to the door and let him in, affording Faith a clear view of their warm embrace before they entered the parlor.

"Merry Christmas, everybody!" Collin shouted and was promptly greeted with matched enthusiasm. Charity tugged him to the love seat, while Faith ignored how closely they cuddled.

"Collin, I don't believe you've met our neighbor, Mrs.

Gerson," Patrick said. "Mrs. Gerson, this is Charity's beau, Collin McGuire."

Collin stood to his feet and smiled. "It's a pleasure to meet you, Mrs. Gerson."

"The pleasure is mine, young man." Her voice was cordial and warm, no hint at all that this was the man who'd caused Faith so much upset. "Aren't we the lucky ones, though, to be able to join this lovely family for the most blessed of holidays?"

"My thoughts exactly." He sat back down, and Charity leaned to whisper something in his ear.

Patrick opened the Bible to Luke 2, then looked up. "Collin, before we begin, can we get you a drink—coffee, tea, hot chocolate?"

Collin opted for coffee, and Charity fetched him a cup. He leaned back, his long legs extended as he sipped the steamy brew. Charity curled up on the love seat beside him while her father bowed his head in prayer.

"Heavenly Father, our joy knows no bounds on this blessed Christmas morn as we celebrate the precious birth of your Son amidst family and friends. We ask that you join us in our holy celebration, and we thank you for your incredible blessings. We love you and worship you. Amen."

A hush settled on the room as her father read the Christmas story. Collin closed his eyes to listen, his face calm. Faith found herself watching him, amazed at the way he seemed to fit in so easily. Her heart melted into an ache. All at once, his eyes opened and met hers. She dropped her gaze, heat fanning her cheeks. Out of the corner of her eye, she saw him draw Charity closer.

Following the Scripture reading, Sean was selected to play Santa, distributing presents, one by one, to each in the room.

"Mama, look at my pile—it's huge!" Katie said.

"Not as big as mine," Steven countered, stacking presents into a very shaky tower.

"Any idea what this might be, Beth?" Sean teased, holding a slim, rectangular present over her head. She snatched it from his hand with a giggle, then fingered it with care.

"Charity, one for you . . . and Faith . . . and Steven . . . nope, wait, this one's for me!"

Her parents looked on, sitting closely on the sofa, her father's arm snug around her mother's shoulders. Charity was busy poking fun at Collin because his pile was small while Sean tossed yet another box his way. When Sean had finished handing out presents, Mrs. Gerson was given the honor of opening hers first.

Her lips rounded in delight when she unwrapped Faith's present and the scent of potpourri escaped into the room. "Oh, Faith, how lovely!" She lifted the box to her nose. "It smells like oranges and cinnamon. I absolutely love it."

Around the room they went, each taking a turn opening one gift at a time to a resounding chorus of oohs and aahs.

"Oh, Mrs. Gerson, it's beautiful!" Faith said as she lifted a small silver cross and chain from the box Mrs. Gerson had given her.

"It was my mother's," she said with emotion. "It belongs to a daughter."

With misty eyes, Faith hugged her, telling her she would treasure it always.

A shriek of delight resounded when Katie tore open a beautiful Gibson-style doll with flowing blond hair. Elizabeth's usually shy smile almost gave way to a grin as she uncovered a book she'd been hoping for. And Sean seemed pleased with the new winter scarf he received, standing and posing with great drama.

The room was filled with paper and bows, laughter and love. Faith's mother and father exchanged a soft kiss before gazing about the room, a look of pure contentment on their faces. When Marcy's turn came, Patrick selected the present he wanted her to open first. She gave him a shy smile and took it from his hands. "What's this?" she asked, tugging paper off a small box.

"You'll find out soon enough," he said with a grin.

Her mother opened the box and gasped, almost dropping its contents. Her hand flew to her mouth in delight. With trembling fingers, she held up a hand-painted porcelain rose hung on a delicate silver chain. "Oh, Patrick, I love it!" Clutching it to her throat, she threw her free arm around his neck. "I've never seen anything lovelier!"

He laughed, seeming quite pleased with himself. "Well, I have, my love, and I'm afraid this rose pales in comparison." He kissed her full on the lips.

Katie groaned. "Mama, Daddy, stop it! There's no time for kissin' now. We've got presents to open!"

Everyone laughed, and the festivities continued: a new watch fob for Patrick, a tin of Marcy's special spritz cookies for Mrs. Gerson, and a chessboard for Collin—so he could practice at home, Sean said. And so it went until the piles of wrapped presents were replaced with piles of treasured gifts, each with special meaning for giver and recipient alike.

"Well, I suppose I should get breakfast on the table," her mother said, plucking torn paper from the floor.

Collin jumped up. "Not yet, Mrs. O'Connor, please." He slipped out the front door. A moment later he returned with a bag full of presents in his arms. "I wanted to surprise everyone. I hope you don't mind." His face glowed like a little boy's as he went about the room dispensing his gifts. "Mrs. Gerson, please forgive me. I didn't know you were coming, or I would have brought something for you too."

"Nonsense, young man. I think it's very thoughtful what you've done. I'm enjoying this."

"Collin, what's this?" Patrick said, a slight frown furrowing his brow. "You bought presents for each of us? You shouldn't be spending your money that way, son."

"No, Mr. O'Connor, I wanted to. You and your family have made me so welcome. I feel like I'm part of the family at times, and you can't possibly know how wonderful that's been. I wanted some way to say thank you."

One by one, the presents were unwrapped, each one significant to Collin and the O'Connor who opened it: a book on chess strategies for Sean—so *he* could practice, Collin said; a carved wooden tray for Marcy—for all those cookies she baked over the last few weeks; and a pen and pencil set for Patrick, because every assistant editor needed one.

Faith's turn came, and her stomach knotted as all eyes focused on her, particularly those of Collin McGuire. She kept her gaze low, attempting to steady her shaking hands while carefully removing the tissue wrapping. Pulling the paper aside, she held up a lovely, leather-bound journal and placed it on her lap. She looked up to see Collin watching her reaction. Slowly she opened its cover. *To Faith—a true woman of faith. Collin.*

"It's a journal, you know, for your poetry. Charity says you've written poetry for years."

There was no way to stop it. The tears were coming, and Faith could do nothing but let them fall. She was touched and embarrassed and heartbroken, all at once. He couldn't possibly know how a gift like this would affect her. Unless, perhaps, Charity had told him—told him he'd been the focal point of much of the poetry she had ever written.

Across the room, her parents watched with concern. "Faith, are you all right?" her mother asked.

She nodded and forced a smile.

"See, I told you she would love it," Charity said.

Faith wiped her face with her hand. "Yes . . . I love it. I need a new journal, Collin, truly I do. It's lovely. Thank you so much."

"You're welcome, Faith," he said quietly.

"Am I next?" Charity asked, eyes twinkling.

Collin reached into the bag, pulled out the last present, and handed it to her.

"It's so small. I like big presents myself," Katie announced.

"There's an old saying, Katie," Collin said with a smile. "Good things come in little packages. Look at you."

Katie giggled and squirmed into Marcy's lap. Collin turned his attention to Charity, grinning while she shredded the paper. With excitement in her eyes, she opened the tiny box and emitted a squeaky scream. Jumping up, she lifted a delicate diamond ring and screamed again.

Collin laughed and dropped to his knees, taking her hand in his. "Charity O'Connor, with your father's permission"—Collin glanced at Patrick, who nodded—"will you be my wife?"

Ring in hand, Charity bounded into Collin's arms, and the two toppled to the floor. Her father seemed amazed, her mother speechless, and the rest of the family jubilant.

All but one. Faith sat on the chair like a statue, her body cold and her eyes fixed in a stare. He had told her he would, but she had never really believed it. Somehow, she'd always hoped, sometime, some way, things might be different. But now, reality fisted her heart and nausea cramped in her stomach as the family gathered around Collin and Charity.

Faith rose like a sleepwalker, slowly moving toward the door.

Marcy was suddenly at her side. "Faith, what's wrong?"

she whispered, clutching her daughter's arm. "You look like death. Are you feeling all right?"

Marcy's voice was distant as Faith turned. She stared at her mother as if she were a stranger. Somewhere in the room, she sensed commotion and the faint sound of voices, farther and farther away until they disappeared altogether. And in a final swirl of darkness, with all energy depleted, she gave way to the spinning of the room, eyes flickering closed as she fell limp to the floor.

10

The room was so dark, and she was so tired, and something was terribly wrong. Faith strained to focus. The shadows of her bedroom came into view. Someone sat by her bed, hand on her arm, and she heard the imperceptible sound of lips moving. She tried to sit up. Fingers gently pushed her back. "Just rest, Faith. Your mother is preparing hot tea with honey, just as you like it."

The tension in her body melted at the soothing sound of Mrs. Gerson's voice, then seized in her chest as she jolted up in the bed. *Collin . . . Charity . . . married.* The thought of it was too much, and a choked sob wrenched from her lips.

Mrs. Gerson squeezed her hand. "There, there, my dear, God will see you through. 'Weeping may tarry for the night, but joy cometh in the morning.' This is the promise of the Lord. I know how difficult it may be to believe right now, that you could ever experience joy again in the midst of this hurt, but you will, my dear."

Her voice shook with pain. "No, I can't believe it. It hurts too much, Mrs. Gerson."

"I know, Faith, but you will get past it—you will."

"I've tried. And just when I thought I had, he speaks to me or looks at me, and I'm right back where I started. Even so, I believed I was getting better. And now this . . ."

Mrs. Gerson nudged a handkerchief toward Faith's clenched fist. Faith shuddered. "I . . . I was just deceiving myself. I thought if I did the right thing, God would let me have him, but he hasn't! Collin will belong to my family, Mrs. Gerson, but he will never, ever belong to me. How am I supposed to live with that?"

"Faith, I've told you many times, 'God causes all things to work together for good for those who love the Lord'—even pain. I believe in my heart he can use this painful moment as the very thing to liberate you from your struggle of the heart. Until now, you've held on to the hope Collin would come to God, and then perhaps . . . to you. And so, you never really let go. Now, you're forced to face the reality that someday soon, Collin will be Charity's husband, and you have no choice in the matter. I believe God will use the pain of it, the finality of this engagement, to help you let go."

A sigh quivered from Faith's lips as she dabbed her eyes with the handkerchief. "I know you're right." She lifted her chin, then sniffed. "I'm not happy about it, mind you, but I know you're right. I suppose I'm going to need your prayers now more than ever, Mrs. Gerson."

"Yes, mine, and those of your parents."

The breath stifled in Faith's throat. "No, I can't tell my parents."

"I'm afraid you have little choice. Collin will be a part of your family. You will need strength and support, both spiritually and emotionally. I think you must."

"But if they knew Collin made advances, and that I felt this way, it would only cause problems. They've just begun to trust him."

"Yes, and maybe they shouldn't, not quite yet. I don't think that young man even trusts himself, based on what you've told me. No, Faith, I think you need the deterrent of your parents' knowledge. And you certainly need their prayer cover. Promise me you'll tell them."

Faith cowered back. "Tell them what? I'm in love with the man of my dreams? Oh yes, there's just one problem— he's engaged to my sister!"

Marcy stood in the doorway, paralyzed, nearly dropping the mug of tea in her hands. *It can't be true!* But it was. She'd heard it with her own ears.

"Mother!" Faith's voice was breathless.

Mrs. Gerson pivoted toward the door, then rose. "Marcy, I'll leave you and Faith to talk. Would you be kind enough to call Sean to escort me downstairs?"

Marcy nodded dumbly, taking Mrs. Gerson's hand and ushering her to the landing. She summoned Sean before reentering the room. Silently she lowered herself to the bed.

Why hadn't she seen it? She'd noticed the stiffness between Faith and Collin as they spoke, when they spoke, but it never occurred to her why. She'd seen the sadness in Faith's eyes whenever he was around, but dismissed it as nothing more than Faith longing for a beau of her own. And the coldness between Charity and her sister, well, that had been going on for so long now, Marcy realized she had simply learned to accept it. Suddenly, it all came into focus, and the picture made Marcy ill. Without a word, she wrapped her arms around her daughter.

"I'm sorry, Mother. I wanted to tell you, but I knew how you and Father felt about him. It made you both so angry that Charity cared for him. How could I tell you I did too?"

"How long have you felt this way?" Marcy whispered.

"From the moment I first saw him, he's the only boy I've ever thought about, ever written about in my journal. We were friends, briefly, my freshman year. Oh, Mother, he was an amazing person before his father died. He was handsome and kind and gentle and good—everyone loved him. I couldn't help myself. I'd never met anyone like him before. He stole my heart before I even knew it. I hoped it was a schoolgirl crush that would pass. And it might have, if . . ."

Marcy sat up straight. "If what?"

Faith looked away.

"If what, Faith? You must tell me. Has something happened between you and Collin?"

Faith nodded, her gaze fixed on the handkerchief wadded in her hand. Her voice was barely a whisper. "He kissed me, Mother, more than once."

Marcy gasped. "When . . . where?"

"Once in the park. He followed me there, wanting to know why I had caused trouble between Charity and him. And then another time, late at night, on our back porch."

"What?"

"He threw a rock at the window. He wanted to see Charity, but she was asleep, and Father had asked for my help in keeping him away from her, so I went down instead."

Marcy stood, then began to pace. She wheeled to face her daughter, hands locked on her hips. "Faith, did you lead him on in any way?"

Faith's eyes widened. "No, Mother, I didn't, honestly. In the park, we got into an argument and then . . . well, it just sort of happened. I think he was as surprised as I was, really. And then . . . the night on the porch, it was late, and he'd been drinking. He came up behind me. He thought I was Charity."

"I knew from the beginning that boy was trouble," Marcy sputtered.

Faith reached for her mother's hand, pulling her to sit down. "Mother, please—inside Collin's a good man, I know it. I saw it, long before the pain of his father's death changed him. I couldn't have felt this way if he wasn't. Please don't tell Father; he would get so upset. I don't mean to cause trouble. I just want to get over it, but I don't know how. And now . . . well, now he's going to marry Charity, and he'll always be around." Her voice sank into a sob.

"Not necessarily," Marcy said, her tone dangerously quiet.

Faith's head jerked up. "No! I don't want to ruin what Charity has. Collin loves her. It's not his fault I have feelings for him."

Marcy's eyebrow slashed up. "Oh, really? And he had nothing to do with it, I suppose?"

Faith blushed. "Yes, he did, but he belongs to Charity now. He wants to marry her, and he should. She loves him. I don't want to cause any problem, Mother. I just want to be free from this. Will you help me? Please?"

For a moment, Marcy stewed, angry with Collin and heartbroken for her daughter. Then all at once, she folded Faith in her arms. "That young man is really something," she said, her tone as irritable as her frame of mind.

Faith leaned hard against her mother's chest. "He is at that," she said, gulping a shaky breath. "But for me, I pray he goes from something to nothing in record time."

Marcy tried to smile, but all she could think about was one thing: what in the world was she going to tell Patrick?

"How is she feeling?" Patrick inquired when Marcy reappeared. She noticed how quickly Collin glanced up from the chess game he was playing with Sean. Oh, how she wanted to shake him! He fit in so well, just like family, and now it hurt that she couldn't quite trust him.

She smiled weakly at her husband. "She's fine—just coming down with something, I think. I told her to sleep in through breakfast, and maybe even church." Marcy looked at the clock on the mantel. "Goodness, speaking of breakfast, I better start; you all must be starved. Charity, Elizabeth, I'll need your help."

"Mine too, Mama?" Katie was already up, bounding toward the kitchen when Marcy scooped her up and deposited her into Patrick's lap.

"No, darling, Daddy's wanting to read that new book to you. Will you let him?"

Katie giggled and burrowed into Patrick's lap as Marcy handed him the book. She kissed Katie on the head and Patrick on the cheek. He smiled.

The morning passed in a blur of activity. They enjoyed a leisurely breakfast, followed by more time in the parlor, talking, playing games, and admiring presents before Sean escorted Mrs. Gerson home and the family headed off to St. Stephen's.

The clock chimed 1:30 p.m. as they returned. Marcy checked on Faith, who had actually managed to doze. Although she seemed some better, Marcy was sure she was in no condition to face Collin quite so soon. She kissed her on the cheek and headed downstairs. On the landing, she spotted Collin and Charity standing in the foyer, putting their coats on while Patrick stood at the door.

"Where are you going?" she asked. Her high-pitched tone caused all three to turn in apparent surprise.

"Collin wants Charity to meet his mother," Patrick explained, his eyes puzzled.

"Oh! When will you be bringing her back, Collin?"

Collin appeared uncomfortable at Marcy's tense tone. He managed a nervous smile. "Mrs. O'Connor, I promise I'll have her home right after dinner, safe and sound."

"And what time will that be?"

He blinked, clearly taken aback.

Charity shot her mother a pleading look. "Mother, really!

We're engaged. Doesn't that change anything? Father, doesn't it?"

Confusion knitted Patrick's brow as he stared from Marcy's tense face to Charity's irked expression. Collin watched Marcy closely, not saying a word.

"Marcy, I told Collin since they're engaged, I would allow Charity to go out with him," Patrick said. "You don't have any objections, do you?"

Collin could feel his hands sweating. *Surely Faith hadn't said anything . . .*

"Marcy?"

She swallowed hard and shook her head. "No . . . I suppose not . . . as long as we take it very slow."

"Oh, Mother!" Charity groaned.

Collin gently touched her arm. "Charity, it's all right. You're lucky to have parents who care about you. And I'm lucky too, that they've been so gracious to me." He looked up at Marcy, his eyes intent. "But, it's their trust I want more than anything. If your mother's not comfortable . . ."

Their eyes locked, and Collin knew. Knew that Marcy was fully aware he was the reason for Faith's fainting spell. His heart constricted.

"Not completely, but I do want to trust you, Collin. I've grown quite fond of you; we all have. I would like to believe nothing would jeopardize that."

She spoke of Faith, and they both knew it. Collin nodded slowly, his eyes fixed on hers. "I understand, Mrs. O'Connor. Please believe me—I would never hurt your daughter."

"Mother, please!" Charity was on the verge of tears. Patrick stood holding the door, the bridge of his nose creased in unspoken question.

"I believe you, Collin. We'll see you after supper, then."

Collin took a deep breath and nodded. Turning, he shook hands with Patrick and quickly steered Charity through the door. Patrick closed it behind them and leaned back, his hand dangling over the knob as his brow quirked high. "And now, would you mind telling me, darlin', what was *that* all about?"

Marcy descended the steps to stand in front of Patrick. "Oh, I'll tell you, my love, but I'm not too sure you'll want to hear it." Taking his hand in hers, she led him upstairs to their room and shut the door behind.

Barely beyond the front yard, Charity grabbed Collin's arm and dragged him toward Mrs. Ellis's overgrown holly bush. In the process, he almost tripped, and Charity's giggle was pure mischief.

"What are you doing?" he asked, laughing.

She pulled him close, throwing her arms around his neck. "Kiss me, Collin. It's all I've been thinking about!"

For a split second, the breath stilled on his lips, and then slowly he brushed her mouth with his own. Thrusting herself against him, she returned his kiss with passion long overdue, and Collin's stomach rolled as he lunged away. "Charity, I made a promise to your parents. I need to win their trust . . ."

She tossed her hair over her shoulder with the degree of defiance he'd always found so attractive. The look in her eyes was hard to miss. "What about my trust, Collin? Win mine!"

He hesitated and then slowly wrapped his arms around her waist. Her lips were warm and moist as he caressed them with his own, and their soft touch should have ignited a fire in him. Instead, a cold wave of fear crawled in his belly as he found himself aching for her sister. He could hear Charity's breathing, rapid and intense, the way his should have been, and the fear exploded into anger. No! This was not happening! She was not going to do this to him. He was in control of his destiny. He would choose whom he'd love, not some make-believe god, and certainly not the woman who blindly gave her soul to him. Roughly he drew Charity in, kissing her with enough force to take her breath away. He felt a fire stir deep inside, and he kissed her again, pressing her close until his thoughts were consumed only with her.

Breathless, she leaned against his chest and gazed up. "I love you, Collin," she said, her eyes aglow with passion.

"I love you too, Charity," he lied and kissed her again, putting to rest for the moment any doubts she might have had.

The level of control Patrick maintained following a bout of rage never ceased to amaze his wife. She sat on the edge of their bed, hands folded quietly in her lap, watching as he calmly paced the floor. With his shoulders slightly hunched and his brow crimped, he seemed older than his thirty-nine years. Marcy sighed and patted the bed beside her. "Patrick, you've been pacing for twenty minutes now. Come, sit down."

Nodding, he settled beside her, and the two of them stared straight ahead into nothing. "How could this have happened, Marcy?" he whispered. "Our Faith—Collin hardly seemed like the type of man she'd be interested in."

"I don't know, my love. I think Faith has always seen in Collin what we've just begun to see. He's an incredible young man with great potential, just one who happened to get off track. He'll make a fine husband for Charity, I think. But I am very worried about Faith where he's concerned." Marcy idly rubbed her husband's hand. "Not just her feelings for him, understand, but perhaps that Collin may have feelings for her as well."

The folds on Patrick's brow deepened as he dropped back on the bed and stared at the ceiling as if it held the answers they so desperately needed. "It's a mystery, for sure. He's been after Charity so long, it seems certain she's the one he wants. If I didn't like that boy so much, I'd throttle him for toying with Faith's affections as he has. But it's been his nature up to now, I'm afraid, and I suspect that's exactly what he was doing—toying with her. I've got to believe it was before he made his commitment to Charity, before he asked her to be his wife. Surely that states his intentions clearly enough."

Patrick sat up. "Well, I will speak to him nonetheless, privately, of course. I will make certain he understands he's to stay as far away from Faith as possible. Not so much as an uttered word or casual glance, nothing that will make it any more difficult for her to get over her feelings for him. And she will—we'll see to that."

"How?"

Patrick's sigh was heavy. "I've been wanting to break Faith into copywriting at the *Herald*, but I must admit, I hadn't planned on doing it quite this soon. But now, I think I need to. It's important she occupies her mind with other things, and she's always loved writing. I'll talk to Ben about giving her some harmless stories to get her started."

"What about here at home, when Collin's over? He'll be around more than ever."

"We'll just have to limit him to Saturday evenings and Sundays. I don't think our trust factor should allow any more time with Charity than that. And as much as possible, for the time being, we'll make sure Faith has other places to be. Perhaps she can spend a few Saturday nights at Maisie's, and then switch her Bible-reading sessions with Mrs. Gerson to Sunday afternoons. We'll manage somehow."

"Patrick, do you think we need to talk to Maisie?"

Patrick's eyebrows arched in surprise. "Whatever for?"

"Oh, something Maisie mentioned awhile back about a young man at the *Herald* interested in Faith. Perhaps . . . well, perhaps she needs a little push in that direction. It certainly couldn't hurt, could it? She is nineteen, after all."

Patrick blinked, his stare going blank at the mention of Faith growing up, growing away. With Charity, he'd always expected it. But with Faith, well, she'd always been his little girl. Any thought to the contrary never even crossed his mind. Patrick shook himself out of his reverie and patted Marcy's hand.

"You're right, darlin'. I'll talk to Maisie as well. We'll get through this, I promise. And we'll get Faith through it too." He sighed again. "Now, dear Lord above, if you would be kind enough—please show us how."

11

For Faith, New Year's Eve came and went with minimal fanfare; she spent the evening with Maisie and her parents and Aunt Edna, sipping cider and playing pinochle until the stroke of midnight sent them to their beds.

Faith missed being with her family. In addition to a feast of wonderful dishes Mother always prepared, there would be traditional servings of red cabbage for good luck, pickled herring, and ham, of course, because her mother always said "the pig roots out the money." They would have greeted the New Year with a toast of hot cocoa for the children and spiced cider for her parents. It would have been an evening filled with games and music and memories of New Years past, and Faith ached at the thought of it. But her father had been right. She needed time to heal. Time away from Collin and Charity.

It had only been a week since she'd seen him on bended knee, offering her sister the life she had always dreamed of for herself. Now she berated herself for the child she'd been, wasting years on dreams devoid of anything but delusion. She vowed to put her schoolgirl fantasy behind and start anew. True, she couldn't avoid Collin forever. Within the year he would be married to her sister. But she could avoid him until then. Her faith was strong. She hoped that with the help of God and family, his hold over her would eventually be broken.

The days of January flew swiftly. More than ever, Faith struggled to immerse herself in her work at the *Herald*. The day the editor called her to his office had been a turning point. "Your father tells me you love to write," he began in a gruff tone. "Says you did quite a bit for the St. Mary's *Gazette*. Is it true you were editor your senior year?"

"Yes, sir," she whispered, her stomach aflutter.

"Well, then, I'd like to see what you can do in the way of feature writing, young lady." He tossed her a piece of paper. "Here's the name and address of a church parishioner experiencing miraculous luck at the weekly bingo meetings. Let's see how you handle this as a special-interest story. On your own time, of course."

Her hand had shaken as she'd taken the piece of paper. Her very own story! She could hardly believe it. Few women penetrated the ranks of copywriter at the *Herald*. She would, of course, he had emphasized, remain in the typing pool for the foreseeable future. And he could make no guarantees her story would even be published. But Faith had been elated, nonetheless. True, it was no more than a filler piece, an innocuous little story that would be lost, no doubt, somewhere between the store ads and the obituaries. But it was hers—all hers—and the realization certainly helped to put a new spring in her step.

Maisie had been elated. "I knew it wouldn't take long!" she said, beaming. "It's perfect timing. What better way to . . ." She hesitated as Faith threatened her with a look. "Get over things," she finished sweetly. "Of course, there are other ways."

Faith shot a look more menacing than the last. "Don't start with me, Maisie. Men don't hold any appeal for me right now."

"Only because you won't let them. I'll bet Danny O'Leary

has asked me at least three times if I thought you would allow him to call on you. He's a great catch. Why don't you give him a chance?"

"If he's such a great catch, why don't you go out with him?"

"Believe me, I would if I could, but he doesn't want to go out with me. He wants to go out with you! He's from a very devout family—your parents would love him. Come on, he's lots of fun."

"And how would you know that?"

Maisie's eyes twinkled. "I've tangled with him once or twice, and trust me, if I had a choice, I wouldn't be setting him up with you. But alas, he wants a good Catholic girl, not a Protestant, and let me tell you, I considered converting!"

Faith had to laugh. Maisie had a way of disarming her from the foulest mood and the most determined intentions. "Okay, you win. I'll go out with Danny O'Leary. Are you happy?"

Maisie frowned. "Not particularly. I really want him for myself."

"You are so crazy. So what are you going to tell him?"

"That you've been dying for him to ask—"

"I'll wring your neck if you do."

"Don't get your knickers in a knot. I'll tell him the truth. You're trying to get over someone, so you're not really interested in anything serious, but doing a few things together might be fun. How's that?"

"As good as it gets, I guess. Hey, Maisie, you'll come along, won't you? I mean, we'll do things in a group, won't we? I . . . I really don't want to be alone with him."

"You are such a chicken. You have to grow up sometime, Faith, and I'm afraid men are part of that process. I suspect they've always been interested in you, but you've had your nose buried so deep in a book or your journal, you haven't noticed."

The strain on Faith's face caused Maisie to roll her eyes. "Yes, Faith, I will tell him only group outings, all right?"

Faith nodded, her face relaxing into relief.

"When?" Maisie demanded.

Faith chewed her lip. "Give me a little time, will you?"

Maisie cocked a brow. "He won't wait a year, you know."

Faith gave her a playful swat and made a beeline for the door, hoping to buy time. It didn't work. Within the week, Maisie had arranged an outing.

Amazingly enough, Danny O'Leary turned out to be much better than Faith believed he would be. She had noticed his stares from time to time when she walked through the newsroom, but thought little of it. She wasn't used to the attention of men, and it hadn't occurred to her he might be interested.

Their first group activity had been skating in the park in late January. Faith was surprised at how much she enjoyed it. Danny wasted no time whisking her onto the pond, hand firmly in hers, his easy chatter dispelling any shyness she felt. Maisie was right—Danny was fun to be with, and it felt good reveling in the attention he lavished on her.

At twenty-three, he was the youngest copywriter at the *Herald*, a fact he mentioned no less than three times as they spun on the ice. He was tall and thin in a somewhat bookish way, with a shock of brown hair that fell across his forehead in disarray. He could have easily been mistaken for a poet or an intellectual, so studious was his manner—until he smiled. Never had Faith seen a smile transform anyone quite so much. It was a bit of a crooked grin that lit his face with a mischievous light, like a little boy about to misbehave. It was his smile Faith loved best, and it was his smile that eventually charmed her into seeing him again.

Each time they'd meet, they'd lose themselves in lengthy conversations about everything from Keats and Milton to what the Germans would do next. Before long, Faith found herself completely at ease in his presence. They laughed a lot, often at Maisie's antics or the droll looks she'd give them. In a matter of weeks, Danny had become as much a part of Faith's life as Maisie and Briana, and the four often ate lunch together and chatted away like lifelong friends. Friends who would prove to be a godsend, she prayed. And friends who would usher her into a new season of her life, hopefully keeping her mind from straying too far in the direction of her heart . . .

January gave way to February, and Patrick could tell Faith was happier. Her first piece on the bingo-playing parishioner had been well received by the editor, who was slowly assigning her additional filler pieces here and there. Her color was better; she had more of the usual glow back in her cheeks of late, and for that, Patrick was grateful to Maisie and Danny O'Leary. He liked this young man who suddenly hovered over his daughter at every turn. He had a lot on the ball, Patrick thought, and most importantly, he made his daughter laugh again.

Their plan had worked. Faith seldom saw Collin anymore, except on Sunday mornings at mass when Patrick and Marcy took great pains to position her as far from him as they could. Collin and Charity seemed to be growing closer all the time, exchanging knowing looks and holding hands. Patrick was grateful Faith was spared the closeness that was developing between the two. There would be time enough to face it down the road, when she was better able to do so.

Patrick sighed. He was certainly relieved things were

working well for his daughters; he only wished he could say the same for the state of affairs in the world. He didn't discuss much with Marcy as he didn't wish to alarm her, but he had an uneasy feeling about President Wilson's commitment to stay out of the war. At the beginning of February, Germany had declared submarine warfare against all shipping to and from Great Britain, a policy that quickly altered Wilson's pacifist point of view. Wilson broke diplomatic relations with Germany, and Patrick feared it did not bode well for U.S. peacemaking efforts. He was convinced they were straddled on a time bomb, one whose ticking had become dangerously difficult to ignore.

What would happen if the U.S. entered the war? The army was minimal at best, its population no larger than it had been in the year 1800. Without question, they would need an influx of men willing to fight. The mere thought caused his blood to run cold. No, he would not talk of his fears to Marcy, not yet. The time was all too quickly coming when she would learn of them soon enough.

"I don't know why I let you talk me into this." Faith was tense as she studied herself in the mirror. "We're just friends. We have no business going out alone together on Valentine's Day." She spun around to face Maisie, who sat cross-legged on her bed. "Hey, why don't you come along? Please, Maisie, it'll be fun!"

Maisie doled out one of her infamous looks of sarcasm. "By whose definition? Fun for you, maybe. Fun for Danny and me? Nope, don't think so. Come on, Faith, he's crazy about you. You do like him, don't you?"

Faith turned back to the mirror, fussing with her hair. "Of course I like him—as a friend. He's funny, charming—"

"Handsome."

"Mmm, that too. I'm just not sure . . ."

"Not sure? What's there to be sure about? You go out,

eat some dinner, laugh a little, and come home. Why is this so hard for you?"

"What if he kisses me?"

Maisie's jaw gaped. "So what! Enjoy it. Besides, you may find you like it. Won't know till you try. Faith O'Connor, you are such a chicken."

Faith took a deep breath and flopped on the bed. "Okay, okay." Suddenly, her eyes lit up. "Hey, wait a minute. Why don't I see what Sean is doing, and the two of you can—"

"Oh no, you don't!"

"Now who's chicken? Come on, I know you like him. And he thinks you're pretty cute."

"He does? Mmm, well, I guess I won't argue if you start inviting me for dinner on a more regular basis. That seems to be the only time that brother of yours is home."

"Oh, you've noticed?"

"Maybe."

Faith laughed. "Okay, he's home on Tuesdays, Thursdays, and Fridays—take your pick."

"How 'bout all three? He's real cute, you know."

"Yes, you're right. You'll need all three," Faith teased.

Maisie lunged at her just as Charity wandered into the room. "Honestly, whenever you two get together, you act like overgrown puppies," she muttered, interrupting their horseplay with a look of disdain. Her eyes suddenly narrowed. "What are you all dressed up for? You don't actually have a date, do you?"

Maisie settled back on Faith's bed, her jaw clamping tight.

Faith stood to smooth her dress. "As a matter of fact, I do."

"Well, fancy that—big sister is finally dating. I thought it was another 'group event.' Wonders never cease. Who is it, the copywriter?"

"If you ever paid attention to anything I said at dinner, you'd know his name is Danny O'Leary."

"Mmm, very nice." Charity's tone was borderline civil. "So, is this your 'official' first date, not in a group?"

"Yes, our first time out . . . alone."

Charity honed in on the tremor in Faith's voice. "Worried?"

"No, why should I be?"

"No reason. It's just I know you're very anxious to please God, so if he tries to kiss you, you'll want to make sure it's on the forehead like a good girl."

Faith took a step forward, her fingers curled in a fist. "Why do you do this? Why do you pick at me like you do? You have everything you want. Why attack me?"

Charity smiled easily as she selected her clothes for her date with Collin.

"I don't know, for sport, maybe? You're just so easy to pick on, I guess."

"Can't you be happy for me, just once? I'm happy for you."

Charity pivoted slowly, ice crystals in her eyes. "Are you, Faith? Are you happy I'm marrying Collin? Truly?"

"I am . . . for you." Faith swallowed hard.

"And for you?"

"Leave her alone, Charity. Danny O'Leary's done wonders to get Faith's mind off of Collin. He's crazy about her, and she's crazy about him."

Charity turned to Faith with grudging admiration in her eyes. "Well, big sister, I have to hand it to you—you certainly work fast. I'm anxious to meet him. Maybe we can double sometime." She grabbed her robe and sauntered to the bathroom while Faith glowered at Maisie.

"Crazy about him?"

Maisie giggled and stretched out on the bed. "Trust me, you will be. Once he kisses you!"

It was one of the best dates she'd ever had. Of course,

it was the only date she'd ever had, but that didn't matter—it was the best. Danny arrived promptly at 7:00 p.m., quite handsome in a charcoal-gray suit. He shook hands with Patrick, charmed Marcy with his boyish smile, then led Faith out the door to his father's automobile, on loan for the night. The Italian restaurant he'd chosen was enchanting, like him, and Faith listened with delight to his endless repertoire of stories, laughing until her sides ached.

In the car, he suddenly became very quiet, and Faith smiled shyly. "Not all out of stories, I hope?"

He flashed her a grin, but his tone was serious. "No, I just think it's time I do some listening. Tell me about you."

"Well, you've already heard all about my family, and you know my father . . ."

"No, I mean tell me about *you*, you and this guy you're trying so hard to forget."

Her stomach tightened. She had the sudden urge to throttle Maisie. "So, she told you."

"Afraid so. Said you were head over heels, but it didn't work out. Is that true?"

Faith shifted in the seat. "Something like that."

"Do you still care for him?" Danny's voice was quiet.

"I don't know. I'm desperately trying not to, but I honestly don't know. I don't allow myself to think about it. There are times when I think I'm over it, and then something happens and, well, then I'm not so sure."

Danny parked in front of the house, switched off the ignition, and turned to study her. "You still see him?"

She nodded.

"Why don't you just tell him to get out of your life? Why even let him come around?"

Even in the dark, she could see the pucker of his brow. Faith held her breath and then exhaled slowly. "Because he's engaged to my sister."

"What?"

Faith bit her lower lip and turned to face him. "He's engaged to my sister. Like it or not, he's going to be around for a long time."

The look on Danny's face was priceless. "Tell me you're joking."

"I wish I were, but I'm not. I had a crush on him long before he began seeing my sister, and when he did, my feelings started to grow. They escalated, I'm afraid, when he . . . well, we had several encounters when he . . ."

"He made a pass at you while he was seeing your sister?"

Faith nodded. Danny rubbed his chin with his hand and shook his head. "What a snake! What a two-timing, double-crossing snake. Do your parents know what he is?"

She nodded again. "It proves they were right to forbid my sister from seeing him, initially. But then things changed. He changed. He knew he had to if Father was going to allow him to come around. He's stopped drinking, as far as we can tell, and goes to church with our family every Sunday. He's a charmer, and he's won everyone over. Now we all love him." Her tone was edged with sarcasm.

Danny looped his arm over her shoulder. "Faith, I'm so sorry."

"That's okay. You've helped a lot, really. You've been such a good friend, and we've had so much fun together."

Danny inched closer, and Faith's heart stopped for a split second. "I hope we've been more than friends," he whispered. He kissed her softly on the lips.

"I . . . I don't know, Danny. Friends are good . . ." she sputtered.

"Yes . . . friends are good," he whispered, "but this is better." Gently he kissed her again, arms huddled around her.

All warmth evaporated into a cold chill at the sound of

Charity's voice. "So, this must be Danny O'Leary . . . at least, I hope you're Danny O'Leary."

Faith was certain she levitated several feet in the air as she whirled in the car, cheeks surging with heat. Charity exhibited one of her most becoming smiles while a stone-faced Collin looked on.

"Charity, you scared me! Why on earth did you sneak up like that?" Faith rasped. With shaky fingers, she swept away strands of hair from her face. She swallowed a lump and pressed toward the door. Undeterred, Danny scooted closer, hand possessive on her shoulder.

"Don't blame us," Charity said. "All we were doing was walking down the street. Hello, Danny, I'm Faith's sister, Charity. And this is my fiancé, Collin McGuire."

"Pleasure to meet you," Danny said. He smiled at Charity and gave Collin a curt nod.

Collin scowled. "It's better we startle you than your parents, wouldn't you say, Faith?" His eyes narrowed. "Besides, I thought this sort of thing was against your beliefs."

"We weren't doing anything . . ." Faith stammered.

"Excuse me, but we were," Danny said. A gasp escaped from Faith's lips as he reeled her into his arms, "We were doing *this*." Before she could object, he kissed her again as Charity and Collin looked on. When he let her go, Faith fell against the seat with a soft thud, breathless. Danny smiled at Collin. "Any objections?"

Collin grunted and jerked toward the car.

Charity gripped his arm. "Collin, no! It's not worth it." She looked at Faith, her eyes glazed with frost. "I don't have any, Danny, but I'm sure Mother and Father will. Let's go inside, Collin. It's rather chilly out here." She tugged him toward the house while he glowered at Danny. The door slammed behind them, and Faith finally exhaled.

She turned to Danny with fire in her eyes. "What in the name of sweet saints did you think you were doing?"

Danny grinned. "Putting those two in their place, I hope. Enjoyed it too."

Faith shoved at the door to get out, and Danny grabbed her arm. "Faith, I'm sorry. Please forgive me. It's just I would jump at any excuse to kiss you. I really care about you."

She swerved to face him. "Danny, I like you too, but this is going much too fast for me."

"Okay, Faith, we'll take it slow, I promise. Say you'll spend time with me again. I give you my word—nothing but pecks on the cheek, if that's what it takes."

She let him wait before she answered. "All right, Danny, but I want to be friends first. There's plenty of time for the other. Promise me."

"Okay, I'll promise, but I'm not sure I can keep it—"

"Promise me, Danny. I want it ironclad."

Danny sighed and dropped back in the seat. "Okay, Faith, I promise. Friends it is."

She smiled. "Then I will see you again, as friends. I had a lovely time, honestly I did. Thank you for everything."

Danny got out of the car and escorted Faith to the house. At the door, Faith looked up at him. "Would you like to come in for a while? You're welcome to."

"No, I don't think I'm up to facing those two again, but thanks. See you tomorrow?"

She nodded. Danny leaned to kiss her cheek. "Good night, friend." He turned and whistled all the way to his car.

Smiling, Faith entered the foyer. The sound of laughter was spilling from the parlor. She glanced at the clock—10:30 p.m. on a school night, and everyone was still up? Peeking in the parlor, she saw Sean and Father embroiled in a game of chess while Collin hand-wrestled on the floor with Steven. Mother was reading a book to Katie, who was half asleep in her arms, and Charity was braiding Elizabeth's hair.

Her mother looked up, a bright smile on her face. "Faith! How was your evening? I want to hear all about it. Danny seems like such a nice young man."

Faith smiled, careful to avoid Collin's probing stare.

Her father glanced up from his game. "I like that boy, Faith. He's a hard worker. I have a hunch he'll go far at the *Herald*. Did you enjoy your evening?"

"I did—very much. Danny's a perfect gentleman." She regretted the words the minute they were out of her mouth. Charity's smirk was positively annoying, and Collin's look was penetrating. Faith leaned to kiss her father good night.

"I'm very tired, so I think I'll head up. Mother, will you come talk to me after you've put Katie to bed?"

"I wouldn't miss it. I want all the delicious details," her mother said.

Faith felt a hot blush stain her cheeks when Collin chuckled. She shot him a scathing look. "Good night, everyone," she called, hurrying to the staircase. "Sweet dreams."

"Don't count on it, sis," Charity teased. "Tonight, they all belong to you."

Anxious for escape, Faith tore up the stairs two at a time, the sound of her family's laughter ringing in her ears.

"So tell me, how was it? Wonderful?" Maisie's eyes were glowing with curiosity.

"It was nice."

"Nice? It was nice? No, lunch with Mrs. Gerson is 'nice.' Dinner with Danny should be beyond nice."

"It was beyond nice, if you must know. I really like him. As a friend."

Maisie plopped back in her chair. "Then he didn't kiss you?"

"Oh, he kissed me, all right. Several times."

"And you still think of him as a friend? Impossible—that man is an amazing kisser!"

Faith smiled patiently. "He kisses nice, I suppose."

"That word again, *nice*! I know, I know—nice, but no bells, right?"

"No, not yet, anyway. But I really do like him. He's safe, I think."

Maisie laughed out loud. "Boy, oh boy, would Danny O'Leary really hate being referred to as 'safe.' There are girls at this paper who would kill to go out with him, and I'm at the top of the list. Trust me. One thing Danny O'Leary definitely is not, is 'safe.' He'll get under your skin, I can promise you that. You'll fall for him. All of us eventually do."

"I just like being friends with him. He calms me."

"So you're going to see him again?"

"Of course I am, as friends. It's the deal we struck."

"And he agreed to it?" Maisie's brows lifted.

"He promised—nothing more than a peck on the cheek."

"All I can say is he must be out of his mind with love. I can't believe he promised that. It'll be interesting to see if he sticks to it."

"Wouldn't tell you if he didn't."

"Oh, you'll tell me, all right. You tell me everything—such as there is to tell."

12

The crowd at Brannigan's Pub was in rare form tonight, and Collin was certainly up for it. There was no better place to celebrate St. Patrick's Day than here, with Jackson, and he wouldn't have missed it for the world. Charity pouted considerably, of course, but Collin was adept at handling her. Before long she was, once again, smiling and cooing, anxious to please.

Few things swelled his chest with pride more than being Irish. He loved everything about it—the people, the music, the dancing, the pubs. He'd forgotten how much he enjoyed sharing a cold beer with Jackson, flirting with a pretty girl, or playing a game of poker with old friends. It had been months since he'd been here, five to be exact, a fact that did not exactly endear the O'Connor family to his best friend.

Jackson had saved him a seat at the bar, one of the few left in the room. The tiny pub was packed bar-to-wall with apple-cheeked old women, pretty young things, and all ages of proud Irishmen raising toasts to their heritage. Collin jostled his way through the sea of green, occasionally greeting an old friend or enjoying a kiss from a lass in his path. He gave Jackson a bear hug and sat down beside him, then signaled Lucas for a beer.

"So, Collin, I thought you fell off the face of the earth."

Lucas shoved a foaming mug his way. "I swear my profits have dropped in half. Where you keeping yourself these days?"

Collin downed half the mug before wiping his mouth and answering. "Don't expect me to boost your profits any, Lucas. Haven't you heard? I'm going to be a married man."

"Jackson spread a nasty rumor to that effect, but none of us wanted to believe him. Especially the ladies. So, when's the big day?"

Collin chugged his beer, then pushed the empty glass toward Lucas. "Middle of September, if we don't go to war first."

Jackson punched Collin on the arm. "Come on, Collin, I don't want to be talking war. It's Saint Patty's Day, and I aim to enjoy it. Besides, that woman of yours doesn't let you out all that often. Let's make the most of tonight."

"Got you on a short leash, does she now?" Lucas grinned ear-to-ear, obviously tickled Collin McGuire would allow a woman to hog-tie him. He placed another glass with foam spilling down its side in front of Collin.

Collin shot Lucas a look that tempered his grin, then quickly drained half the mug. "Nobody's got me on a leash, Lucas. I've just got better things to do with my time than hang out with this riffraff." He flicked Jackson's head.

"Don't be a stranger, Collin. A wife needs to know a man's got someplace to go if she gives him any grief." Lucas grinned and worked his way down the bar.

Jackson watched Collin finish his second beer in record time. "Hey, buddy, take it easy. I know it's been awhile, but we have all night. I sure don't wanna carry you home. So, how's 'almost-married life' treating ya?"

Collin swiveled on the stool to scope out the scenery. "It's okay. You know what, Jackson? None of these girls can hold a candle to Charity. She's one beautiful woman. I'm a lucky man."

Jackson grinned and gulped his brew. "Now, why am I having trouble believing that?"

Collin glanced at him sideways. "What's that supposed to mean?"

Jackson almost choked on his beer. He wiped his mouth with his sleeve, then turned to look Collin straight in the eye. "Look, Collin, this is me, Jackson. I've known you since we were kids. You can't pull one over on me—you're miserable! What are you doing this for?"

Collin signaled Lucas for another beer. "Drop it, Jackson. You're just mad 'cause you lost a drinking buddy."

"Maybe." Jackson leaned against the bar, head cocked as he studied his friend. "I just hope you're not making the biggest mistake of your life. I've seen you happier."

"And drunker. But not for long."

"So, you know what you're doing, do you?"

Lucas pushed another brew his way, and Collin flicked the sweat from the side of his mug. He took a deep breath, then exhaled slowly. "Yeah, Jackson, I do. Charity's a great girl, and she's got the most incredible family. Bottom line? I'm happy when I'm there."

Jackson took another drink. "And the sister?"

Collin lowered his head, then looked up through hooded eyes. "She's an inconvenience, I won't lie to you. But that'll go away when Charity and I are married, if you know what I mean."

"The old man keeps pretty close tabs on Charity, does he?" Jackson eyed him closely.

Collin grinned. "Afraid so. She's off-limits until the gold band's in place."

Jackson chuckled. "Well, how do you like that? For the first time in his life, Collin McGuire's in the same predicament as me—love starved! Who said life wasn't fair?"

Collin laughed. "Yeah, but mine's by choice." His smile turned wicked as he took a sip of beer.

Jackson leaned close, a devilish gleam in his eye. "So whaddya say we do something about it? I hear Saint Patty's Day does strange things to the ladies."

Collin's eyes were slits as he studied his friend. The beer was beginning to take effect. He didn't answer right away. When he did, a mischievous grin spread across his lips like a little boy with one toe over the line. He turned to assess the selection of eligible females in the room.

"There's no ring on my finger yet, now is there?" Lifting his glass in the air, he made a toast. "To Saint Patrick of Ireland."

"To bachelorhood," Jackson replied.

Collin grinned, focusing on two pretty girls across the room. "To the best night of our lives," he muttered. They both downed their mugs and signaled Lucas for another.

"It's late, Danny; I better go in." Faith rose from the porch swing and smiled. "St. Pat's with your family was a lot of fun."

He reached for her hand. "Not yet, Faith, please? Look at that moon—it's amazing! When was the last time you saw weather like this in March? It must be sixty degrees. And tomorrow's Sunday—you can sleep in."

Danny's tone was earnest, and Faith could do nothing but relent. Shaking her head, she sat down again. He drew her close. "It is an amazing moon," she said as she rested her head on his shoulder. "Sent by St. Patrick himself, no doubt."

"Faith?"

"Yes?"

He stared at the moon, his throat bobbing before he spoke. "I know we're friends, but I swear, I've never wanted to kiss a friend so badly in my life."

She looked away. Over a month had passed since that night in the car. There hadn't been more than a peck on the cheek between them. "Danny, I . . ." She stopped and turned to face him. "I'd like that."

His arms tightened. "Oh, Faith, I'm crazy about you. Have been from the start." He leaned to kiss her, tenderly at first, then more passionately.

"Danny . . ." she whispered, pulling away. His arm tugged her back. Her palms flattened against his chest in protest. "Danny, please! This is exactly why I want to take it slow." She looked up at him. "I care about you, I do. More than as a friend. And I like kissing you. But all of this leads to feelings, to things we aren't ready for yet. Things I'm not ready for . . . at least for a while."

He stood and pulled her in his arms, his tall frame towering. "Faith, I know what your beliefs are. I know how important God is in your life. He's important to me too. I just didn't know how much until you came along. I'm not sorry I kissed you. Like I said, I'm crazy about you. But I can't just be friends—not any longer." He paused. "So what do we do now?"

Faith drew a deep breath. "Well, I guess it's too late for friends, anyway. I'm afraid Maisie was right. Your kisses are . . . very nice. But we have to take it slow."

"So . . . the kiss won you over, did it?" He reached to pull her close. She dodged him.

"Yes, and the kiss can push me away just the same. I think we better call it a night," she said softly. "And it's been quite a night, I think."

He smiled. "Good night, Faith." He gently grazed her lips with his. "Happy Saint Pat's."

"Oh, it is."

Danny's smile broke into a grin as he opened the door for her. She closed it again, took off her wrap, and glanced at the clock in the hall—almost midnight. She yawned.

Blarney ambled down the stairs to greet her, tail wagging and eyes begging for attention. Faith leaned to pet him, then jumped at a faint knock at the door. She opened it.

Danny stood there grinning like a fool. "Look, you're not going to change your mind, are you? I mean, we're more than friends, right?" He looked a tad like Blarney with his wide eyes and hopeful look.

She laughed and leaned against the door, nodding.

"Good!" He took a deep breath and kissed her again, allowing his lips to linger.

She fought a smile and tried to look stern. "Go home, Danny. It's late. Or it may change to friends before you reach your car."

He saluted. "Yes, ma'am! Sleep well. I know I will."

She closed the door again, suddenly drained. She was halfway up the stairs when she heard another quiet knock. She sighed and shook her head as she descended the steps. *Is he trying to make up for all the lost kisses in one evening?* She opened the door a crack. "Okay, what did you forget this time—"

"I thought he would never leave," Collin said. "Been hiding in those blasted bushes forever."

Even in the dark, she could tell he'd been drinking. A lot, from the looks of it. His speech was slurred, his eyes glassy, and his hair tumbled over his eyes like he'd just rolled out of bed. He swayed ever so slightly, despite one arm balanced against the door. "So, did you have a good time with Danny Boy?"

"Collin, you're drunk! Do you realize what will happen if Father sees you like this?"

He drooped against the door frame, head bobbing in slow motion. "Yessss . . . I do. But I have to see Charity. Right now."

Faith glanced upstairs, her heart jumping hurdles at the

prospect of her parents finding Collin like this. "Why? Is something wrong?" Her tone was urgent.

"Need to talk—hafta tell her somethin'." He was tilting more noticeably now, and Faith was terrified he would keel over. She shot a frantic peek up the stairs, then lassoed his waist with her arms. With a grunt, she shifted him from the door onto her small frame, then stumbled under his weight. Managing to steady herself, she weaved their way to the porch swing. The smell of beer and smoke assailed her as she unloaded him in the swing.

"A devil of a time t' come on t' me, Faith," he slurred. "You should be ashamed—I'm almos' a married man."

"Oh hush, Collin. You're drunk, and if my father sees you like this, there won't be any wedding."

"Aw, don' be mad. I guess maybe I had a little too much t' drink, but it's . . ." He blinked at his watch. "Or was . . . Saint Patty's Day." He propped his head back against the swing and sighed. "Guess I can't hold my beer like I used to."

"Well, you won't be holding Charity like you used to either, if you get caught. You need coffee. Promise you'll stay right here while I go brew some."

He nodded and closed his eyes. Faith watched him for a moment, her heart aching in her chest, then slipped back inside to get the coffee.

He was asleep when she returned, so she sat on the swing for a moment, the cup steaming in her hand. He looked like such a little boy, so innocent in sleep, his eyes fringed with the longest lashes she had ever seen. Her heart skipped a beat as she stared at him, and her breath accelerated as it always did when he was near. Never had she seen a more handsome man than Collin McGuire. He was well-suited for her sister.

Slowly, Faith stood and shook his arm. He mumbled

something indistinguishable and opened his eyes to stare blankly at her.

She held out the coffee. "Collin, take the coffee and drink it, please."

He stirred, recognition dawning on his face. He gave her a drowsy smile. "Faith . . ." His eyes widened as his memory kicked in. "Uh-oh. I didn't wake anybody, did I?" He tried to sit up, then slumped back in the swing, his hand flying to his head. "Sweet blazes, my head hurts!" He peered up from under those sweeping lashes. "Did ya say something 'bout coffee?"

She handed it to him, and he took it, his hands shaking as he bent to drink it. When he drained the cup, he handed it back to her. "Thanks. Got any more? I think I could use it."

She nodded and started for the door, turning as he reached out to touch her arm. "Faith . . . will ya stay up and talk with me a while? I really need to talk."

She looked at his handsome face in the moonlight and could think of nothing she'd rather do. He saw her nod, then dropped his grasp on her arm. Reclining once again, he closed his eyes.

She woke him again when she returned with the second cup. He took the coffee and drank it, slower this time, eyes staring ahead into the moonlit yard. She settled beside him, content, waiting for him to speak.

"So you and Danny—more than friends now?" He took another sip, his gaze shifting from the yard to the sky studded with stars.

"Just exactly how much did you hear?" she wanted to know, her voice chafing.

Collin turned and attempted a grin, then was caught off guard at just how pretty she looked with the glow of moonlight in her face. He averted his gaze, gulping his coffee instead of sipping. "Don't be mad—I didn't mean to spy. I thought for sure your good night would be brief." He glanced at her again. "I know how committed you are to . . . keeping it brief."

Even in the moonlight, he could see her blush, and his heart began to race. "Do you love him?" His question was barely audible.

She thought about it awhile before answering. "No, I don't think so, at least not yet. I mean, I really care about him. He's a very good friend who is suddenly becoming, well, more than a friend." She wrinkled her nose and smiled. "I suppose time will tell. So, Collin, what's bothering you enough to risk my father throwing you out on your ear?"

He took a deep breath and set the empty cup down on the porch. He pressed forward with his elbows on his knees, clasping his hands together to rest his chin. His eyes stared straight ahead and his voice was quiet. "I don't know if I'm doing the right thing."

"What are you talking about?"

"Marrying Charity—I'm just not sure."

Her lips parted, and he heard the soft intake of air in her throat.

"She deserves better, Faith," he continued. He buried his face in his hands.

Silence hung in the air. He heard her breathe in deeply several times. The gentle touch of her hand on his shoulder startled him. "What makes you say that, Collin? Charity loves you more than anything in the world. As far as she's concerned, there is no 'better' than you."

He exhaled slowly and leaned back in the swing, rubbing his eye with his thumb. "I cheated on her tonight, Faith."

He risked a glance at her and winced as she shrank back with her hand to her mouth. She sat there as if unable to move or speak. He continued on. "I never meant to, but I was drinking. And the pub was filled with pretty women who were drinking. One thing led to another . . ." His voice trailed off as he massaged his eyes with his hands. "Faith, I've done this so many times before, but I've never felt like this—sick inside, ashamed. Something's different. Suddenly I got a conscience, and I don't know what to do with it. Even though I've been committed to Charity for over six months now, and others before her, I've always had trouble saying no to a pretty face."

The shock in her face jarred him. He looked away. "I'm not proud of it, Faith, but it's part of who I am. Call it my own sordid quest for love, if you want. Whatever the motivation, it's never bothered me before. And then your family takes me in, I get engaged to your sister, and everything's different. For one moment, I step back into the old life of Collin McGuire, and suddenly I feel like a stranger."

He turned to her. "Faith, I don't know what's happening, but I don't ever want to do it again, so help me God . . ." He stopped when her eyes widened at his choice of words. He gave her a wary look. "Oh no. You're not going to tell me you've been praying for me, are you?"

She nodded.

He dropped against the swing and chuckled quietly. "Well, I'll be." He rubbed his jaw with the side of his hand. Leaning forward, he buried his face in his hands again. "While you're praying, Faith, pray I'll be a good husband to her, will you? Your family is the best thing that has ever happened to me. I'd hate to be a disappointment."

"I will, Collin. But you know, you can pray to him yourself. He would like that."

He glanced at her sideways. "You would too, wouldn't you?"

"It would thrill me to no end."

He smiled and lifted his hand to stroke her cheek. She

shivered. "You cold?" He raised his arm to extend it around her shoulders.

She shook her head, moving away. "What are you planning to do about Charity? Are you going to tell her?"

He sank back, exhaling slowly. "I'm not sure. It's so strange. All of a sudden, I have this horrible urge to be honest." He glanced at her. "Why, what do you think I should do?"

"Well, normally I'm a great advocate of honesty, but I think maybe in this case, saying nothing would be best. Did you mean it when you said you never wanted to, you know . . ."

"Cheat on her?" He finished her sentence, and she nodded. He smiled. "Yeah, I did. I think I found out tonight that when you're committed to someone, cheating on them is a lot like getting drunk—it's easy to do but hurts like the devil in the morning."

"Then, if you really mean that, let it go. It would only crush her needlessly. And not confessing means there's only one whose forgiveness you need. Why make it two?"

"Two? Who else?"

It was Faith's turn to look confused. "Why, God's, of course! Don't you go to confession?"

Collin laughed out loud. "What, you think because I was raised Catholic and go to mass with your family every week, it's a given I go to confession? What makes you think I even need to go? I don't feel I've done anything wrong."

"Oh, and you're proud of what you did tonight, I suppose?"

"No, I'm not particularly proud of what I did tonight, but I'm not ashamed of being a man, either. I have needs, and I know how to satisfy them. It's as simple as that. As far as I'm concerned, I'm doing what comes naturally, and I don't see anything wrong in that. At least, I didn't until tonight."

"Then doesn't that convince you it's wrong? Don't you understand that's why you have the sick feeling, the regret?"

"Maybe . . . but I'd rather not think about it in terms of hellfire and damnation like you do." His tone was nonchalant, which caused her to bristle. "That's the biggest problem between you and me, Faith. You see what I did tonight as sin, and you want me to grovel before God to obtain his forgiveness. I see it as simply living my life on my own terms, then wiping the slate clean when I've made a mistake."

"You mean sinned!" Her eyes blazed, but he only shook his head and laughed. "Don't you see, Collin, you're not wiping anything clean. Your 'slate,' as you call it, is black with 'mistakes'—closing your eyes to them doesn't make them go away. How can you ever know how to do the right thing in life if you can't even acknowledge the wrong? You want me to pray you'll be a good husband to my sister. Well, which good husband do you want me to pray for— the one according to Collin McGuire, or the one according to God? You can't have both."

Her words pricked him, and he stiffened.

"You want to be a good man, Collin, I can feel it. But the thing you don't realize is you can't be good without God. We're all sinners; the Bible says so. And I know firsthand that I am. You may want to be a good husband to my sister, and you may qualify that as one who doesn't cheat on her. But you're a human being, Collin, a sinner like the rest of us. One day, you may again do what comes 'naturally.' And when you do, your hopes for being a good husband will be dashed—along with your marriage."

Faith felt the charge of adrenaline flooding her veins as he glared, but she probed the depths of his gray eyes and knew he was finally hearing her words. Her heart felt light, full of hope, and she prayed God would pierce his with the truth. His gaze shifted away as he appeared to wrestle with the words she'd spoken. After a while, he nodded and hunched forward on the swing, head hanging as he stared at the floor.

"So, what do I do?" he asked gruffly.

She turned and grabbed his hands, almost breathless with joy. "Oh, Collin, I can pray with you! For God to come into your heart, into your life. To make you the man he wants you to be and the husband you want to be for Charity."

He studied her, not saying a word, and she could tell he was struggling inside. Silently, she prayed God would help him to make the right choice. He looked away again, pulling his hands out of hers. Moments passed before he answered. When he did, his voice was sober and low. "Do it," he said, so quietly she was afraid she hadn't heard right.

"You'll let me pray with you?"

"Yeah." He put his hands back into hers.

She was shaking. "Oh, Lord, thank you so much for this man before me. I know you love him. You've always loved him. He hasn't acknowledged you, Lord, because he's been hurt. But he wants the happiness you have for him, and I think he knows now you're the only way to get it. Help him, Lord. Help him to turn his life over to you, to be the man you want him to be and the husband Charity needs. In Jesus's name. Amen."

She opened her eyes. He was staring at her with a strange look and a faint smile. He squeezed her hand. "Thanks, Faith. As much as I hate to admit it, I actually feel better. I guess we'll see how much this God of yours listens to your prayers." The smile faded. His eyes became serious. "And, Faith, thanks for staying up . . . for being here." He bent to kiss her cheek.

The moment his lips touched her skin, a tingle of heat shot through her, causing her to gasp.

He stiffened at the sound and searched her face in the moonlight. "Faith?"

She dropped her gaze and backed away, her pulse sky-rocketing. *Why is this happening again?* She was over him, wasn't she? He wasn't supposed to be able to make her heart race like this. *Dear God, please—tell me I'm over him!* He lifted her chin with his finger, then his lips parted in surprise as if he could read her thoughts. She saw the look in his eyes and tried to escape. "Collin, no . . ."

He heard her words, she was certain, but they didn't seem to register as his lips tasted hers. A shock wave of heat rippled through her. All restraint apparently gone, he pulled her to him, his touch gentle and urgent at the same time. She melted into his embrace as if she belonged there, her lips responding with a hunger that jarred her.

"Oh, Faith, I love you. I can't help it, I do." His words tumbled out in a rush of husky rasps, between hungry kisses roaming the softness of her neck and her face. His hands pressed hard against her back, drawing her to him.

She wrenched herself from his grasp and stumbled from the swing, limbs quivering as she stood. "Collin, we can't!" she gasped, but the intensity in his face told her he wasn't listening. He rose and caressed her shoulders with his hands, eyes burning into hers until she thought she would faint. He bent to kiss her again. A riptide of heat swelled, causing her to moan as he pulled her back to the swing.

The Lord knoweth how to deliver the godly out of tempta-tion.

Lord, deliver me!

He seemed crazed with desire, breathing words of love in her ear as he kissed her. Neither heard the sound of the door as it quietly opened. But both heard a muffled scream.

As if in shock, Charity stood before them, barefoot and shivering, watching the man she loved . . . loving her sister.

Collin jumped to his feet, his face ashen. "Charity, no!" he moaned, standing there helpless.

Charity looked at Collin, tears coursing her face in the moonlight. "How could you, Collin? My own sister! How could you do that to me?" She sobbed, and he grabbed her and tried to restrain her as she struggled against him.

Faith felt dizzy as she stood. When she spoke, her voice was a lifeless whisper. "Charity, it was a mistake, a horrible mistake. Collin came looking for you . . . he wanted you. But he was drunk, and I was afraid Father would find him. So I gave him coffee and I . . . I stayed. I shouldn't have, but I did. We were just talking and . . . I'm so sorry. Please forgive me."

Her sister was weeping so loudly, Faith wasn't sure she had even heard her. Collin clutched Charity tightly and pressed his face against her hair, pleading his repentance. As he spoke, his eyes met Faith's, and pain splintered through her.

Nausea lodged in her throat, closing off her air. Turning away, she quietly slipped inside, leaving the only man she ever wanted where she knew he belonged—in the arms of her sister.

Collin wondered what time it was, but he dared not risk a glance at his watch. Charity was finally calmer now; the tears had subsided for a while, even though she hadn't spoken a word since she'd found him with Faith.

Faith. The mere thought of her brought a rush of sadness and pain unlike any he'd ever felt before. He had told her he loved her. Was it true? Or had it only been the heat of passion? Collin thought about this woman who was as passionate with him as she was fierce in her devotion to her God, and he suspected in his heart it was probably true. She stirred his mind, his body, and now his soul more than any woman ever had, and there was no turning back, no fighting it any longer. *God, what am I going to do?* The irony of his invoking God's name suddenly hit him square in the chest. All the times he had carelessly uttered it had been more as an epithet of profanity than a prayer. Now he was faced with one of the most difficult situations of his life, and he wondered if it hadn't been more of a cry for help through years of loneliness.

He thought about Faith praying for him. She didn't fight fair, that woman. He had wanted no part of her God or the control she exercised over his heart. He tried to fight her, but armed with her faith and her prayer, she managed to win anyway, getting him to invoke the very God who kept them apart. He wondered if the prayer she had spoken on his behalf would truly have any effect. He had felt peace at the time, but now he wasn't so sure. Pretty words, but could they change his heart? Apparently not, judging from the pain he'd caused—both to the woman in his arms now and the one who'd been there not long before.

Charity began to stir, and Collin gently lifted her face to his. He felt a stab in his chest as he looked at her tearstained cheeks and haunted eyes. "Charity, I don't know if you'll ever be able to forgive me. I've betrayed your trust, and to me, that's unforgivable. I don't know how it all happened, but one thing I do know is that I never meant to hurt you. I hope you believe that."

Charity nodded, her head languishing against his chest. He could feel her shivering, so he tugged her close.

"Charity, I swear—I came here tonight only to see you. But I was drunk and Faith just got home, so she tried to sober me up. You have to believe me—I had no intention of it ending up the way it did." He dragged a hand through his hair, his words coming out too fast. "I mean, you know Faith . . . what a fanatic she can be. One minute she's telling me about God and praying for me, and the next . . ."

"Collin? Do you . . . do you have feelings for Faith?" She sounded scared.

Collin was tempted to lie. He swallowed hard. "Yes . . . I do." He could feel her stiffen in his arms before she cringed back, eyes stunned and angry.

"How? When?"

Even in the moonlight he could see how white she was. He shook his head, not knowing how to explain it to himself, much less to her.

"Was it her? I know she's always been crazy for you. Did she provoke it?" There was a glimmer of hope in her eyes.

"No, Charity, she didn't—ever. It was me."

He could see the tears welling, and he hated himself for the pain he caused.

"Why?" she whispered.

He took a deep breath and exhaled slowly. "I don't know, Charity, I really don't. It just happened. I've been fighting the feelings for months now, but apparently to no avail."

She slumped back against the swing at the sound of his words. She closed her eyes tightly as if to block it all out. When she spoke, her voice was almost calm. "Do you love her?"

"I don't know."

"Do you love me?"

Her eyes were still closed, and he looked at her, thinking for the thousandth time she was one of the most beautiful women he had ever seen. Did he love her? "I don't know," he whispered, and he thought he saw her wince.

"What are you going to do?" she continued.

"I don't know."

Her eyelids flew open, and she leaned forward, eyes flashing. "Well, then, what the devil do you know, Collin?"

He blinked. The old Collin had always loved the wild streak in Charity—was that Collin still around or had Faith changed him forever? "I know you're beautiful, more beautiful than any woman I know."

"Is that enough?"

"I don't think so." His voice was quiet.

Never missing a beat, she laid her hand on his thigh. "Is this?"

Heat shot through him at her touch, and he caught his breath. "Charity, I need time. I'm confused. This will only make things worse."

Her finger slowly circled on his leg. "Worse for Faith . . . or worse for me?"

He grabbed her hand and held it behind her as he leaned over her, danger in his tone. "I don't take to teasing well."

"I'm not teasing," she said, peering from under heavy lashes. Slowly she lay back on the swing, her eyes fluttering closed. He saw the invitation on her face, and a fire raged as he wrestled with his conscience. The blue eyes opened, and she extended her hand. And the look she gave said it was only a matter of time.

13

She suspected sleep would punish her by its absence. From the moment she collapsed in the gloom of their room, both tears and prayers had been flowing. And although her exhaustion was complete, her heart was far too heavy to be stolen away by the peacefulness of slumber. It had been hours since she'd left them. She no longer spent what energy she had worrying her parents might find them. It didn't matter. How could it possibly be any worse than it was now?

She rolled on her back to stare blankly at the ceiling. He loved her. He said so himself, but for Faith, there was little joy in the declaration. There was such a strong physical attraction between them, she was certain it clouded his thinking, as it had hers. How much clearer could it be that God's Word was truth when it spoke of "fleeing sexual sin"? For the first time, she could easily see how it could make you say and do things you would later regret. No doubt Collin would regret the words he had spoken to her. If not tonight, certainly tomorrow.

Faith forced her eyes closed, desperate to shut it all out, but all she could see was Collin's head bent in prayer. For the moment, it had brought her such joy, and him such peace. Then it had been stolen away, rendered insignificant in what should have been one of the most important nights of his life. No doubt he thought her to be a complete fraud, espousing God and the avoidance of sin when she so readily fell into his arms, returning his passion with her own. The thought of it made her nauseous, a fine complement to the guilt and shame over what she had done to her sister.

The door creaked open. She froze as Charity crossed the room to her bed. Faith lay completely still as her sister disrobed and hoped Charity would think she was asleep. But her sister knew her all too well, apparently. Tossing her robe on the chair, Charity moved to the side of Faith's bed, sending a prickle of fear down Faith's spine. Her eyelids flickered open to see Charity standing over her, eyes candescent with cold rage.

"What a little hypocrite you are. To think all this time I actually believed you were this pure little Christian, so in love with God, so bent on doing the right thing." Her tone burned like acid. "But Collin told me how you've been chasing after him, teasing him, begging for his attention."

Faith jolted up in the dark, her fear fusing to anger. "You're lying! He never said that."

Charity's lips twisted into a savage smile. "Oh, but he did. He said he's tried to put you off, but you wouldn't leave him alone."

Faith's throat constricted, trapping her breath. Fear feathered her skin like spiders.

Charity laughed. "You can't accept the fact he loves me, can you, Faith? That it's me he's marrying, not you. Tell me, does it eat at you so badly you're reduced to making pathetic attempts to break us up? Because that's all it is. Don't you get it? Collin doesn't love you. He said he used you, just like he's used so many girls at Brannigan's Pub. Just like you said he would use me. Only, he's not using me, Faith—he wants me for his wife."

"No! He . . . would never say that . . ."

"Oh, but he did. I'd let you ask him yourself, only you caused us both so much embarrassment, he feels it's best if he stays away for a while. We'll tell Father and Mother we needed time apart, but we'll still see each other. So you see, your plan didn't work."

Faith shivered at the loathing in her sister's eyes. "Charity, what did I ever do to make you hate me so much?"

"Why don't you ask Father? He might have an idea." Turning on her heel, Charity walked across the room and slipped into bed, leaving the darkness of their room to settle like a shroud.

"What do you mean Collin won't be coming over for a while?" Patrick said, glancing up from his newspaper with a frown on his face.

Marcy halted in the middle of a stitch to stare at Charity, who clutched against the parlor door for support. She immediately put her sewing aside to go to her.

Charity teared up, then quickly straightened and blinked the wetness away. "Mother, I'm fine, really. Collin and I just decided to take some time apart, that's all."

Patrick leaned forward, the newspaper rustling to his lap. "What's going on, Charity? Two people in love just don't decide to take time apart. Did you have a fight?"

She nodded, and Marcy touched her arm.

"About what?" Patrick demanded.

Charity's eyes were blue ice. "I believe that's between Collin and me, Father."

"Not if it affects the whole household, it isn't. That boy is as much a part of this family as he is your fiancé. We all have a right to know what's going on."

"Why don't you ask 'your girl'?"

Patrick stood. The color in his face paled.

Marcy shot him a pleading look and pulled Charity closer. "Patrick, she's just upset. We all need to remain calm."

"You're both my girls," he hissed, stomping to the foyer, "although you both don't act like it." He bellowed at the bottom of the staircase. "Faith? Come down here—now!"

Faith appeared on the landing, her shadowed eyes a telling contrast to the pallor of her skin.

"I need to speak to you, please, in the parlor." Patrick marched back in, leaving Faith to follow. Her eyes remained downcast as she took a seat across the room. Marcy moved to the sofa while Charity remained at the door.

"It's been a week now that you two have been walking around here like death, and I want to know why. First, Collin is sick last Sunday and can't come over. Now Charity tells me they've decided to take some time apart. What's going on, Faith?"

She didn't answer.

"Faith? I want an answer—now!"

"Why ask me, Father? This is between Charity and Collin."

Patrick swore under his breath. "Answer me! Do you know what's going on?"

Marcy shook her head. "Patrick, there's no call for profanity—"

"Do you?"

Faith's gaze met his. "Yes."

"Are you going to tell me?"

"No."

Her jaw was set—just like his—and Marcy could see the danger in her husband's face. She jumped up. "Patrick, we're all upset. Please, can't we take some time to cool off?"

He stormed across the room to grab Charity's arm. "So help me, Charity, one of you will tell me what's going on."

"That would be 'your girl,' Father. Why don't you use your influence with her?"

The sound of his slap echoed like a clap of thunder.

"Patrick!" Marcy flew across the room.

Charity's hand trembled to her cheek.

"Charity, I . . . I'm sorry, darlin', I lost my temper . . ." He touched her arm and went white when she flinched. He faltered back. "Charity, I . . ."

"May I leave now, Father?" She shivered like a willow in the wind.

He nodded, and Marcy hovered as she led her from the room.

Patrick's shoulders sagged. He staggered to his chair, depleted of energy. He sat on the edge of the seat and buried his face in his hands.

He felt a hand on his shoulder. "Father, I'm so sorry," Faith whispered.

Patrick reached to cup her hand and held it against his shoulder.

"Me, too, darlin'—sorry two people I love are hurting so much. Sorry I've made it worse."

"Father, it's too painful to talk about right now. But we will, I promise. When we're ready. Until then, will you pray for us, please? All of us?"

Patrick stood and gripped her in his arms. "Dear God above, I never stop, darlin'," he whispered. *And dear God above . . . forgive me.*

For Marcy, the blackest day of the year was always Good Friday. More often than not, the weather was foul or overcast, and from childhood, she'd always felt a sense of foreboding on that day in particular. She'd never forgotten the mournful look on her mother's face when she said Jesus had hung on the cross from noon until three.

From that moment on, rain or shine, there were no more insidious hours in the year. She never understood until she was older just why it was called "Good Friday," for the mood of the day was anything but good.

Today was no exception, Marcy thought as she prepared breakfast. Except, perhaps, it could be called the second blackest Good Friday of them all. April 6, 1917—the day the United States of America would declare war on Germany. Only three days earlier, President Wilson issued a Declaration of War before the U.S. Congress, calling for a stronger navy and an army of five hundred thousand men. Today, before the whole world, it would be official—America was entering "the Great War." Marcy shuddered to think what such a turn of events might bring.

She reached for an egg, separated the yolk from the whites, and thought about Collin and Charity. Whatever the rift, it was enough to keep Collin away, and Charity and Faith in a state of chronic dejection.

"How long?" Marcy would ask, and Charity would attempt a smile that did nothing to cloak the sadness in her eyes.

"I don't know, Mother. All I know is he said he would call when he's ready, and he will. We just have to be patient." She would say nothing more.

Between the heaviness of impending war and the absence of someone they hoped would be one of their own, Marcy felt sure the season of Lent had never extracted such sacrifice.

Patrick's mood was equally somber as he entered the kitchen, the usual smile missing from his face. He kissed Marcy on the cheek, draped his suit coat over the chair, and sat down. Fatigue glazed his eyes, the result of too many sleepless nights of late. He worried incessantly how the war might affect Sean and Collin and knew that Marcy, in turn, worried about him.

"I really wish you weren't going in today, Patrick. You're so very tired, and I would feel much better if you stayed home."

He looked up from his breakfast. "Marcy, there's no place I'd rather be than by your side, today of all days. But I can't, darlin'. It'll be a busy day at the *Herald*, and I must be there. That's why I'm going in so early, darlin', instead of my usual time with Faith."

She nodded and turned away. His heart ached as he watched her while she worked at the sink. He knew she was crying. There had been more of that in their house over the last three weeks than he cared to admit. Patrick wondered when their lives would return to the joy and peace they'd once taken for granted.

He rose from his chair and crossed the room to where she stood and circled his arms around her waist. He buried his lips in the curve of her neck. At his touch, she sobbed openly and turned, clinging while her body quivered with weeping. Patrick stroked her hair and held her close. His heart felt as if it were being squeezed in a vise. What could he say that would stem the tide of her tears? How could he reassure her when he himself was so unsure as to what the future held for them all?

God is our refuge and strength, a very present help in trouble.

The first line of Psalm 46 from his morning devotional came to him in a rush, bringing with it a wave of calm. He tightened his hold on his wife and took a deep breath. "Marcy, everything will be all right. We have the Lord. He promises to be our refuge and our strength. We must put our trust in him—not what's going on in the world." He felt her nod against his chest as she gripped him. He led her to the nearest chair, then held her on his lap like a little girl, her head on his shoulder. "Let's not cry about it, shall we, Marcy? Let's pray about it instead."

A shaky sigh quivered from her lips, and she nodded again. Resting his head on hers, he closed his eyes and prayed. Prayed that God would give them peace in the midst of this storm, protect them, and keep them safe. He prayed for Collin and Charity and Faith, that God would give peace in a situation that had clearly shattered their joy. He prayed for God to give wisdom to President Wilson and his advisors, for victory to be swift and sure. When he finished, Marcy sniffed and wiped her eyes with her sleeve. Patrick smiled, a rush of love welling his heart. "Marcy, what if I took an extended lunch hour today? You know, between noon and three?"

She lunged, almost tipping the chair with her embrace, and kissed him with such passion that a soft moan escaped his lips. "Mmm . . . maybe I won't go in at all!" he teased, returning her kiss with equal passion. He paused and drew back, a brow shifting high. "You do realize, of course, I'll have to work a bit later tonight, don't you?"

She nodded and kissed him again, and he chuckled at her enthusiasm. Patting her on the leg, he resumed an air of responsibility. "I'd best be going, then; I'll need every minute I have at work."

Instead of getting up, Marcy pressed closer, her lips swaying against his.

Patrick groaned and nudged her away. "Marcy, you're a wicked woman," he said with a tight grin. "Darlin', there's no time—" He stopped, his heart flinching at the desperation on her face as her eyes pooled with dread.

"Patrick," she pleaded, "please . . . the world's being torn apart at the seams. I *need* to be close to you . . . to hold you. God help us, we're at war! And we don't know what tomorrow might bring . . ."

The reality of her words stung, and he felt his perspective

shift. He picked her up in his arms and kissed her again before letting her go. Pulling his suit coat off the back of the chair, he slung it over his shoulder and took her hand in his, quietly leading the way to their room.

The last three weeks had been the worst of Collin's life, except for those when he and his mother had buried his father. He was in a fog of confusion, deep in thought and yet thinking nothing at all. It was like one, long drunk he couldn't shake—a sick feeling in his gut and a dull ache in his head. Only this one hung over his heart and stubbornly refused to succumb to any remedy he might try.

He hadn't seen any of the O'Connors since that awful night, and today, with the solemnity of Good Friday and the gloom of war, it seemed an appropriate time to return to settle his business. He had done more than his fair share of drinking over the last three weeks, and even ventured a few prayers in the process. But in the end, he received more solace from the pub than the prayer, because at least the pub helped to dull the pain that was so much a part of him these days.

Collin kept his eyes down as he walked toward their house, his hands shoved deep in his pockets as he went over in his mind the words he wanted to say. They would be surprised to see him, he knew, for they would hardly expect him during the day when he was supposed to be at work. They would all be home, he hoped, except for Patrick and Faith and possibly Sean, and that suited him just fine. He could talk so easily to Marcy; it was much like talking to Faith, she was so caring and honest. But it would be hard to say good-bye to Sean, and especially difficult to face Patrick. Collin dreaded the look on Patrick's face when he told him. Patrick had become the father he'd lost, and he cared too deeply what he thought. It would crush Collin to see the pain in his eyes, just as he knew it would crush him to see Faith again. No, it was better this way, he thought—quickly, quietly, while all the world's eyes were focused on the reality of war.

Turning onto their street, Collin took a deep breath and braced himself to confront Charity again. His thoughts traveled to the night she offered herself to him. She had never done anything like that before. But she knew his weakness and felt no compunction in exploiting it. He had admired that once. She was more than well aware of the attraction she held for him. Like a skilled gambler in a game where the stakes were all or nothing, she played it for all it was worth. He couldn't seem to resist her, and Collin wondered if Faith had been right. Perhaps he was a sinner. But then surely a sinner who could never change. He recalled how, at the last moment, he finally denied her, a first in his young life. A faint smile flickered on his lips. Maybe he was changing after all. Certainly the old Collin McGuire would have never said no to a woman who was his for the taking.

Collin stood at the base of their front steps, wondering how Charity would handle it. The thought of her brought a sad smile to his lips. He did care for her. And the attraction was certainly there. But when he was with Faith, his attraction to Charity paled in comparison, and he knew it would be an emotional triangle Charity could never tolerate. She wanted to get married right away, but he'd told her he needed time to think. And so they agreed to separate for a time. The weeks had convinced him that, in the end, time would be his best friend, and he was quite sure he'd need a great deal more of it.

He ascended the steps with trepidation, as if scaling an impossible summit. He knocked on the door and waited, queasiness in the pit of his stomach. Somewhere within he heard Katie shriek. The door swung wide, and Collin froze.

Patrick greeted him, grinning ear-to-ear. "Collin! What a sight for sore eyes you are. We've missed you, my boy. Please, come in."

Patrick gave him a bear hug, and Collin tried to smile but was embarrassed at the wetness springing to his eyes. He returned the hug, clutching Patrick tightly, hoping the awkwardness he felt wasn't obvious. Turning toward the kitchen, Patrick called for Charity. The kitchen door flew open, making way for a parade of O'Connors bounding toward him. Marcy's eyes were sparkling as she pulled Katie off his leg, and Patrick demanded to know if his absence meant he was scared to lose at chess.

Collin smiled for the first time in weeks. "I think it's more of a case of my extending mercy to Sean, Mr. O'Connor."

Patrick laughed and slapped him on the back.

"It's good to see you, Collin," Charity whispered. He turned to look at her. She was a bit thinner, but it was nice, he decided. Her pale gold hair seemed even longer as it fell in loose curls over her shoulders and arms. He smiled, and her face glowed.

"It's good to see you too, Charity. I've missed you." He'd had no intention of saying that, but the words parted from his lips so easily. "I've missed you all."

"So, Collin, can you stay for lunch? Sean and Faith are at work, of course, but the rest of us are about to sit down for a light meal. It's not much, since we're fasting our full meal until this evening, but you're welcome to join us." Patrick looked tired, but his eyes were eager.

"I'd love to, Mr. O'Connor."

Nothing was said of anything that might have transpired three weeks earlier. The conversation was simply the usual banter he had grown to love in his brief time with this family. Patrick seemed careful to avoid talk of war while Katie babbled on about Easter and the candy she hoped to receive. Charity never took her eyes from his face while Marcy finished up the preparations for lunch. When it was ready, they all sat in the warmth of the kitchen to pray and eat, and in the midst of their warmth and love, Collin felt revived from weeks of death.

He had come here to end it, to say good-bye to the only real family he had ever known. Endless hours of whiskey and wondering convinced him there was no other way. How could he marry one sister when he was in love with the other? And how could he love the other at the expense of the betrothed, especially when he had no certainty the other would even have him? It was all too complicated, too painful to ponder, and it would be best, he decided, to simply do away with it all. But as he sat basking in the glow of this family he loved, he found he was reluctant to let them go. It suddenly occurred to him that, perhaps, time should make the decision for him, and Collin found his heart much lighter at the thought.

When the meal was finished, Marcy offered stout cups of coffee. Collin gratefully accepted, and he sipped it as they chatted on about Easter, school, and work at the *Herald*.

Collin put his cup down and took a deep breath. He pushed his chair back to give himself room to breathe. "Speaking of the *Herald*, Mr. O'Connor, I suppose it's abuzz these days with talk of the war?"

Patrick nodded. A slight pall seemed to settle on the room.

Collin pressed on with his point. "I wanted to come here today to tell Charity something . . ." He looked around the table. "To tell you all something. I've decided to enlist."

Collin felt as if he had just released the first of the wartime bombs that would shatter their lives. The deathly quiet of the room clotted the air in his throat.

"Collin . . . what are you saying?" Charity's color blanched to chalk.

Collin looked at her, his eyes tender as he put his hand over hers. "Charity, I've decided to join the AEF."

"What's the AEF?" Elizabeth wanted to know.

"It stands for American Expeditionary Force. It's our military force that will be fighting overseas."

"You're going to war?" Steven asked, his freckled face bunched in a frown.

Collin nodded, and Charity let out a faint cry.

"Collin, why enlist now, why not wait until you're called?" Marcy's voice wavered.

Patrick gave her a strong look. "Marcy, Collin has to do what he thinks is best. How we feel cannot factor in."

Collin glanced up at Patrick, his eyes stinging. "Oh, but it does, Mr. O'Connor. How your family feels affects me a great deal. I wouldn't be here today if it didn't. You're the family I never had . . ." He fought a tremor in his voice.

"Then why?" Charity cried.

"Because my country needs me, and because you and I need time to sort a few things out. My duty overseas will give us that time. And when it's over, God willing . . . I'll return, and we can see where things stand."

"Are you going to marry my sister?" Katie asked.

"I don't know, Katie," he whispered.

Charity began to cry.

"Collin, the problem between you and Charity—is there anything we can do . . ." Patrick seemed at a loss for words.

Collin shook his head. "No, sir. I just think it needs the test of time to make sure it's what we both want to do."

Collin turned to Charity. "Let's wait until after the war and see how we both feel." He stroked her wet cheek with his fingers. "If you don't want to wait, Charity, I'll understand."

She swiped tears from her eyes. "I'll wait, Collin," she whispered, "as long as it takes."

He wound his arms around her, cheek pressed hard against her hair, and all at once he felt as if a great burden had lifted.

"When do you think you'll leave?" Patrick's tone was sober.

Collin looked up. "The first troops will be in France by June for training. I hope to be among them, but I'll know for sure today or tomorrow as to exactly when."

"June! Will we see you until then?" Charity asked.

"Try and stop me," he whispered. She laid her head on his shoulder. Sitting there, holding her in his arms, Collin felt strangely at peace. He had come to end his relationship with this woman. How could it be that it felt so natural to be holding her again? He stroked her hair as she leaned against him.

His mind suddenly wandered to thoughts of Faith. Some of the peaceful feeling faded as he remembered that it always felt more natural with Charity when Faith was out of sight. Would there ever come a time when he'd be free enough to marry Charity? A part of him hoped so. But then, it was at war with a part of him that didn't.

"Collin, will you be joining us for Easter?"

The sound of Marcy's voice lulled him back to the present. He smiled. "I would like that, Mrs. O'Connor."

"Do you think your mother would be up to coming? We'll be going to mass at noon, then dinner is at four."

"She hasn't been feeling well, but I'll certainly extend the invitation."

"Good. I met her years ago, but it would be lovely to see her again. We'll have a full house, I can tell you that. Mrs. Gerson will be here, of course, and Faith has invited Danny and Maisie and . . . Briana, I think it is, to join us. Have you met any of them, Collin?"

He stiffened at the mention of Danny and Briana, as did Charity. "Yes, ma'am, all three."

"Good. It'll be fun, I think. And I suppose we could do with more of that lately."

"Yes, Lord, and amen to that, eh, Collin?" Patrick laughed, pushing his plate away.

"Yes, sir," Collin agreed, not sure how much "fun" would be derived from an encounter with either Danny or Briana again. But he smiled, nonetheless, at Patrick's words. In all his years he'd never seen such a family as this, and he doubted he ever would again. Where all things—whether run-of-the-mill conversations or matters of great import— were laid at the foot of the Almighty.

Faith opened her eyes to a room where the last remnants of moonlight were fading into the dusky light of dawn. Rising early on Easter had become a habit, she supposed, from years of sneaking out of bed at the first crack of light to see what the Easter Bunny had brought. A habit that lingered on, she found, long after the magic of the Easter Bunny faded.

The rhythm of Charity's shallow breathing harmonized with the soft ticking of the clock as she slept in her bed across the room. Charity had taken the news of Collin's enlistment hard, as they all had at the thought of someone they loved in harm's way. But for the moment, he was back. And the effect of that short reprieve could be seen in the soundness of her sleep.

Faith pulled the covers more tightly about her, curling up in bed and allowing her thoughts to drift. The timing for Easter couldn't be better, she decided with a bit of melancholy. Over the last few years, Easter had become a time of rebirth for her, much like the beginning of her new relationship with God. Her parents had raised her to know God and know about him, but it had been such a long-distance thing, too far away for her to touch or feel. And then she met Mrs. Gerson, and her eyes suddenly opened to the depth of God's love for her, personally. Faith had always known about Jesus, but for the first time he became her best friend as well as her Savior. Suddenly she understood his words to Nicodemus: "Except one be born anew, he cannot see the kingdom of God." For Faith, the change had been earth-shattering, taking her from the shallowness of the world to the depth of the spirit. She would never be the same again.

Though they never spoke in terms of a spiritual rebirth, Faith knew her parents embraced the same life-changing faith as she. It was evident in the strength of their marriage and the joy in their hearts, even in the midst of trials. Faith lay there in the early morning shadows, her eyes becoming misty just thinking about them. A swell of gratitude filled her soul. No one had to tell her how blessed she was to be a part of this family. She felt it to the core of her being. It was God's greatest gift, aside from his Son, to be surrounded and nurtured by the amazing love of these two remarkable people.

It was during moments like this that Faith had great difficulty understanding her sister. They were only a little over two years apart, born and raised in the same family, with the same loving parents and values, yet Charity was more of a stranger than a sister. A cold chill in an otherwise warm and wonderful existence. *A thorn in the flesh*, Faith thought as she remembered Mrs. Gerson's comments about St. Paul. Charity was definitely that. But no more, Faith supposed, than she was to her, especially where Collin was concerned.

Faith rolled on her back and shivered, sadness suddenly cloaking her like the weight of her blankets. A dull ache throbbed in her heart, and she wondered when she would ever be free from it, free from *him*. There was no question about it—it was the perfect time for Easter and the rebirth she hoped it would bring. Collin was leaving.

And although the thought produced a sick feeling in her stomach, Faith had no doubt at all it was exactly what she needed. Collin would leave, Charity would pine, and Faith would move on.

She thought of Danny, and a smile pulled at her lips. Who knows, perhaps he would be the one who would deliver her. She hoped so. From the start, Danny had such a soothing effect on her. True, he didn't elicit the passion of her star-crossed encounters with Collin, but with time and prayer, she believed she could love him. Perhaps then she would, as one of her favorite verses from Psalm 144 declared, "sing a new song." One whose melody would be as sweet as that of her parents'.

A squeal floated up from downstairs, and Faith knew slumber was short-lived now that Katie was up. Thrusting her covers aside, she sat up and glanced across the room.

"Charity, are you awake?" No answer. As quietly as she could, Faith dressed and headed for the door; she turned to look at her sister one last time before leaving their room. Charity's covers were still, with only the gentle movement of her breathing. "Happy Easter, Charity," Faith whispered, more to herself than to her sister. "I hope it's a new beginning for Collin and you." She closed the door behind her and sighed. *A new beginning for us all.*

Marcy had outdone herself. The dining room was aglow with the light of her prized candlesticks, and the lace-covered table was laden with the bounty of her kitchen. Her china sparkled in the candlelight, and the silverware was polished to a gleam, cushioned by delicate folds of lace-trimmed napkins. A profusion of Easter lilies graced the center of the table, their heady fragrance drifting in the air. Marcy herself was breathless and glowing. She hurried back and forth from the kitchen to deliver steaming platters of ham and turkey while Faith and Charity fetched bowls heaped high with vegetables.

A knock sounded at the door, and Sean jumped to answer it.

"That must be Danny with Maisie and Briana," Faith said, setting a basket of rolls on the table. "Right on time!"

Sean ushered them into the dining room, and Faith reached for Danny's hand. "Thanks so much for bringing Maisie and Briana. I really appreciate it."

Danny grinned. "I'd bring the pope if it meant I'd spend Easter with you," he quipped.

"Name-dropper," Collin muttered to Sean. Sean laughed.

Faith raised her voice over the commotion as she linked arms with Briana. "Everybody, this is Briana, a good friend of mine from work."

Briana smiled when introduced to each of Faith's family members, then blushed just a hint of rose when she came to Collin.

"And, of course, Briana, you know Collin."

Briana smiled shyly. "Of course I do. Hello, how have you been?"

Faith couldn't resist a peek at Collin. It was one of the few awkward smiles she'd ever seen on his face. She detected a sudden rash creeping up his neck. "Fine, Briana, and you?" He folded his arms, as if at a loss as to what to do with his hands.

"Never better," she said with a smile.

He nodded, his discomfort growing more obvious with each passing second. Charity stepped up and grabbed his arm, flashing a superior smile. "I've heard so much about you, Briana. It's good to finally meet you." There was the slightest note of disdain in her voice.

"And I, you," Briana responded in kind, causing Charity's smile to waver just a bit.

Briana leaned to hug Mrs. Gerson, who was already seated at the table, while Patrick ushered everyone in. Katie insisted on sitting by Maisie while Sean quickly claimed the other seat beside her and pulled out the chair for her to sit down. Danny did the same for Faith. He whispered in her ear, and she laughed, whispering back. Looking up, she saw Collin's lips tighten into a flat line as he seated Charity.

The meal began, as always, with a prayer from Patrick. "Lord, in the midst of a difficult time, we come together to rejoice in the resurrection of your Son. Thank you for sending him to die for us and then to rise again, offering each of us the joy of new birth, new beginnings. Help us to live for you, oh Lord, and guide us through the months ahead with your steady and loving hand. Amen."

Everyone consumed until full, both of the food and the intoxicating warmth pervading the room. They laughed as Patrick told stories of Easters past—of the time Faith and Hope had hidden chocolate behind the wood-burning stove to keep it from Sean, which resulted in a sticky mess for Marcy and a stomachache for Blarney. Or the morning Sean and Faith awakened to baskets filled with nothing but grass while Charity's fairly toppled with candy.

"So, that's why I wake up so early on Easter!" Faith exclaimed.

Everyone laughed, even Charity.

When the meal was done, Marcy rose and looked around the table. "So . . . who wants coffee? I also have tea, if anyone would like it."

"And hot chocolate?" Katie asked, her tone bordering on alarm.

"Yes, even hot chocolate, although my maternal instincts warn that a certain little girl may have already had more than her fair share."

"Who?" Katie asked. Marcy shot her a cynical look.

Mrs. Gerson rose from the table. "Marcy, would you mind terribly if I took my tea in the parlor by the fire? I'm afraid my rheumatism is not cooperating, and I think I would be more comfortable there."

"Of course, Christa," Marcy responded. "Maisie, Briana, would you mind escorting Mrs. Gerson to the parlor? I can bring your tea in there, as well, and you three can visit while Faith, Charity, and I do the dishes."

Maisie chuckled. "Oh, please, Mrs. O'Connor, don't deny me the dishes!" She rolled her eyes at Briana.

"You're just jealous 'cause I get to pick at the leftovers," Faith said with a smirk.

"Just one of many reasons, I'm sure," Maisie returned, winking at Danny.

The women left the room, and Patrick broached the subject weighing on his mind. "So, Collin, have they given you an exact date when you'll be leaving?"

Collin folded his arms and leaned back in his chair, a sober look on his face. "June 15."

Patrick nodded. "At least you'll be here for Charity's graduation. I'm glad."

Danny bent forward, one arm resting on the table. He looked at Collin in frank surprise. "Don't tell me you're going overseas to fight?"

Collin glanced at him, an amused look on his face. "As a matter of fact, I am. Why does that seem strange? Haven't you heard there's a war on?"

Danny shook his head. "It just doesn't make a whole lot of sense, that's all. You're engaged to a beautiful woman. Why risk getting shot when you don't have to?"

Collin's eyes narrowed as he gave Danny a cool look. "Because more than likely, we'll all be going sooner or later."

Marcy reentered the room with a tray of steaming coffee

cups, and Collin's smile was stiff. He thanked her and took a sip. Patrick nodded when she left, then stared blankly at his coffee, stirring in the cream. Sean stretched back in his chair and began idly tracing his finger on his mother's lace tablecloth.

Collin exhaled. "As you know, there's talk in Congress about something they're calling the Selective Service Act, which would mandate conscription—drafting men into the army. Right now, they're talking about registering men between the ages of twenty-one and thirty. If your lucky number is called, congratulations—you're a doughboy. Figured I'd get my bid in early."

"I'm willing to go, even if they don't call me." Sean took a gulp of coffee, then another. "Somebody's got to stop Germany from riding roughshod over the rest of the world."

Patrick glimpsed up with knitted brows. "You're right, Sean. Much as I hate to admit it, I don't think we can sit back on this one. I'll be going if called."

Danny's mood sobered as he stared at the untouched coffee before him. He looked up at Patrick. "I thought the draft was for the ages of twenty-one through thirty, Mr. O'Connor? Why would you be called?"

Patrick slumped in his chair and rubbed the back of his neck. "True enough, Danny. Right now they're going for the youngsters such as yourself, but I've heard rumors of extending the registration to all men between eighteen and forty-five. If that happens—which I suspect it might later this summer—well, then, I'm right there with you boys."

Sean turned to his father, his forehead creased with worry. "Father, if that happens, what would Mother do without your income?"

Patrick sighed and sipped his coffee. "I don't know, Sean. I've been pondering the possibilities since last year. With

Marcy's grandmother ailing, I'd originally thought perhaps Marcy and the rest of the family might go to Ireland to help her out. I thought we could put our house up for rent while they're gone. I even have an old friend who is the editor of the *Irish Times* in Dublin. I know I could get Faith on at the paper there, and Charity might get a job in a shop somewhere, I don't know. But now, with ship travel so dangerous, I'm not sure what I would do. It's something I haven't really figured out yet."

"Maybe your number won't come up." Danny sounded hopeful.

Patrick finished his coffee and rose. He pushed his chair in. "You know, Danny, I have a funny feeling it will. And if it doesn't, well, I might just go anyway. Sean's right. Somebody's got to do something. And I think the fight for freedom is a fight I'd rather not sit out." He smiled. "Anybody up for a game of chess? Suddenly I feel like kicking somebody's back end."

Collin laughed and stood. "Get in line, Mr. O'Connor; I've been feeling that way for over three weeks. But don't worry; I'll take your age into consideration."

"Fine. And I'll consider your inexperience. You'll need some excuse, I suppose, when you lose." Grinning, the two headed for the parlor, Patrick's arm draped loosely around Collin's shoulder.

"Mama, I don't feel so good." Katie groaned and slouched in the chair, her legs dangling as she hugged her stomach. Marcy turned from the sink to assess her youngest daughter, who sported telltale smudges of chocolate on her face.

Marcy sighed. "Katie Rose, have you been in the candy again?"

"No, Mama, just a little, bitty bite, not much at all. Ooooohhhh, but my tummy hurts . . ."

Marcy handed the wet dishrag to Faith, an apology on her face. "Faith, I'm sorry, would you mind taking over while I tend to Katie?"

"That's fine, Mother; we're almost done, anyway."

Marcy smiled and kissed her on the cheek, then turned and squeezed Charity's shoulder. "I love my girls so much," she said, scooping Katie up off the chair. "Come on, little chicken. Let's see if we can get your tummy feeling better." Marcy hurried out with Katie in her arms, leaving Faith to wash while Charity dried. Silence ensued.

Faith chewed on her lip, then ventured a peek at Charity out of the corner of her eye. She cleared her throat. "I'm glad Collin came today, Charity, for your sake."

Charity shot her a sideways glance. "I'll bet. We'd still be engaged if not for you."

Faith's stomach twisted. She scrubbed the turkey pan harder. "I know. I'm really sorry. There are no words to say how much." She rinsed the pan and handed it to her sister. "Will you forgive me?"

Charity didn't answer as she dried it and put it away. When finished, she turned, her eyes as hard as amethyst. "I don't think so."

Faith stopped washing, her brows knitted in hurt surprise. "Why?"

"Because you ruined my life. You've always ruined my life—first with Father, now with Collin. I don't think you deserve to be forgiven. I'd rather see your righteous little conscience drown in a sea of guilt over what you've done."

Faith's lips parted in momentary shock, then clamped shut. She hurled the wet dishrag into the dirty water. "Ruined your life with Father? And how have I done that? You're the one who defies him at every turn! And as far as Collin goes, I haven't done anything, at least nothing that deserves how you've treated me the last few weeks.

Collin kissed *me*! I tried to stop him, and he wouldn't. Do you really think I would try to steal my sister's fiancé?"

Charity crossed her arms and rolled back on her heels, studying her sister through slitted eyes. "You bet I do. You've been lovesick for Collin McGuire as long as I can remember. It just eats you alive he belongs to me."

"Well, he's all yours—take him! I'll be glad when he's gone so I can be rid of him." Faith trembled as heat stung her cheeks.

Charity grinned. "Good—I will!" She cocked her head, her brows slanted in contempt. "Tell me, Faith, you think you can manage to keep your hands off him while he's still here?"

Faith took a step forward. Her hands balled into fists. "How many times do I have to tell you? He . . . kissed . . . me!"

Charity's lip curled in scorn. "He's a man, Faith. You haven't had a whole lot of experience, I know, but I have. Let me tell you something I've learned—it's the woman who controls what goes on. You could have gotten up and walked away anytime, but you didn't. A while back, you told me about Collin and your friend Briana. You said Collin used her to get what he wanted. You were right. That's what men do when they don't care about a woman—they use them. Just like Collin used you that night. It was dark, he was drunk, and you, big sister, were nothing more than a convenient means of satisfying a need . . ."

Faith's face chilled as the blood leeched out. She lunged, her fingers aimed at the smirk on Charity's face. A creak sounded at the door. They both reeled to see Collin inside the room, his eyes burning in a face that was deadly calm. Charity caught her breath while Faith stood paralyzed.

"Charity—apologize to your sister." His tone was dangerously quiet. His eyes locked on Charity with an intensity that made her blush.

Faith stared him down, her hands on her hips. "Stay out of this, Collin."

His face was a mask as he stared back. "I'm just trying to defend you—"

"I don't need you to defend me!" she raged, fists clenched at her side. "And tell me, Collin, who's going to defend me from you?"

He blinked and went pale.

"Do me a favor. Don't come to me next time you need to 'satisfy your needs' or feel the need to 'do what comes naturally.'"

Collin looked as if she'd slapped him. He swallowed hard.

"Just stay away from me!" she hissed.

"Faith, it wasn't like that. It was a mistake—"

"Just like the mistake I made thinking God could ever mean anything to the likes of you. You were probably laughing inside the whole time you . . ." She hesitated for just a moment as a chill shivered through her, then continued on, her voice a hoarse whisper. "Poor, deluded Faith. I'll go along just to soften things up. I'll just do what comes naturally—"

"No! It wasn't like that. I was listening to you. What you said, it meant something to me." He took a step forward, and Charity moved between them, her eyes filled with steely fire.

"No, it didn't, Collin. You as much as said so when you called her a fanatic. You told me you only stayed because you were drunk, that all she did was talk about God. You said, 'You know what a fanatic Faith can be.'"

Faith's lungs closed in, trapping all air. Wet pain stung her eyes as she stared in shock. Collin's stricken face confirmed Charity's words. Faith's vision blurred as she stabbed a finger in warning. "Stay away from me, Collin. I mean it. Leave . . . me . . . alone!"

Charity spun, eyes flashing as she grabbed Collin's arm. "You leave him alone! He doesn't want you; he wants me."

Collin seemed bolted to the floor. A dangerous shade of red mottled his cheeks, and a muscle jerked in his jaw. He flung Charity's hand from his arm. When he spoke, his words were filled with venom, spewed forth in a deadly whisper. "To the devil with you both," he sneered. He bludgeoned his way through the door, leaving them singed by the heat of his anger.

14

It had to be a record. Charity had been crying for almost a week now, and Faith bordered on a depression ranging between listless and catatonic. Patrick was teetering on the brink of his sanity, and he and Marcy were at their wits' end. Both agreed—something had to be done.

It was anybody's guess what could have happened. One minute Collin was laughing and moving his pawn across the chessboard, the next minute he was charging through the parlor like a raging bull.

"Where are you going? It's your move," Patrick had said, amazed at the speed at which Collin thundered to the door.

Collin grabbed his coat and fisted it in the air. "I'm sorry, Mr. O'Connor, but I need to go home before I do something I regret."

That's all he had said, nothing more, before storming out the door faster than Patrick could say "checkmate."

Of course, Patrick had sprung from his chair into the kitchen only to find Charity sobbing uncontrollably at the table while Faith stood in a trance, face swollen with tears. Patrick had never seen anything like it—it was a vicious nightmare, and one they had yet to awaken from. There was no question about it. Something had to be done.

An uneasy feeling rolled over him as he opened the

door of Brannigan's Pub and his eyes scanned the room filled with people and smoke. Patrick could honestly say he didn't want to be here. But he was a man on a mission—the well-being of his daughters, not to mention himself—and nothing was going to deter him.

It didn't take long to spot him. He sat hunched at the bar, a near-empty drink in his hand, laughing with some sidekick friend while the bartender poured him another. Patrick took a deep breath and braced himself for an awkward encounter. He eased himself onto a stool. "So, Collin, my daughter's driving you to drink now, is she?"

Collin glanced sideways, then blinked. "Mr. O'Connor! What are you doing here?" he asked, his face stone sober, even if he wasn't.

Patrick turned and smiled. "Since you've made yourself rather scarce lately, I came looking for you. Your mother said you've been spending a lot of time here this week."

Patrick nodded to the scruffy-looking friend on the stool next to Collin. The friend wagged his head in return, then slapped Collin on the back and retreated to the other end of the bar. Patrick ordered a ginger ale and rested his hands at the base of the glass. Collin chugged his whiskey and pushed the empty tumbler toward Lucas. He stared at the cherrywood bar as if in a stupor, and Patrick wasn't all that sure he wasn't.

He laid his hand on his arm. "Collin, you're like a son to me. What happens between you and Charity happens to all of us. We all hurt inside. What's going on?"

Collin took a deep breath, then exhaled slowly, his eyes never wavering from the same sticky spot on the cherrywood bar. "I'm fed up, Mr. O'Connor."

Patrick took a sip of his ginger ale and sighed. "That makes two of us, then."

Collin swiveled to look at him, his eyes earnest. "Mr. O'Connor, your family means everything to me. More than anything in the world, I want to go on being a part of it." He turned away and grabbed his drink. "I just don't think it's going to work."

"What are you saying?"

"I mean, they're driving me crazy."

"*They're* driving you crazy?"

Collin glanced at Patrick as if trying to decide how much he should say. He hunched against the bar and laughed a hollow laugh. "Yeah . . . they're driving me crazy. They hate each other, and I'm the reason."

"I know Faith had feelings for you in the past, but I think that's over. She and Danny—"

Collin twisted on the stool. The look on his face squelched Patrick mid-sentence. "No, Mr. O'Connor, you don't understand. It's not that Faith has feelings for me. It's . . . well, it's like this. I desperately want to marry your daughter. I just don't know which one."

Patrick sagged against the bar. "How could something like this happen? What on God's green earth were you thinking, man?"

"I was thinking I wanted to marry Charity. But something happened . . ."

"Like you making advances toward Faith?" Patrick singed Collin with his glare.

Collin swallowed hard and took another drink. "I was pretty sure she'd tell you about that. It's true, of course, and I take full responsibility for it. I was wrong. It's just that . . ." Collin looked up, his eyes confused and almost pleading. "Sweet saints above, she drives me crazy! I mean, with Charity, I feel safe and warm and loved. But then Faith comes around, and I don't know what it is. She's got this exasperating way of stirring my blood along with my temper, and I don't know why." Collin slumped and swore under his breath. His gaze traveled to Patrick's face.

"Sorry 'bout that, Mr. O'Connor, but I can't help the way I feel. Believe me, I've tried."

Patrick leaned forward. "Are you telling me you're in love with Faith and not Charity?"

Collin was the picture of confusion, slouching at the bar, hands clutching his drink as if he were holding on for strength. "I don't know. I think so, but I'm not sure. You know, I've had a lot of experience with women, Mr. O'Connor, and when it comes to making love . . ." He hesitated, eyes flitting to Patrick's face.

The father in Patrick flinched.

"Well, let's just say, I know my way around. But when it comes to the real thing—I mean really *loving* someone— honestly, I'm just plain stupid. Do I want to marry Charity? I thought so. Do I love Faith?" Collin stared aimlessly at his drink. Seconds passed before he continued. "Heaven help me, I hope not."

Patrick sighed and swung his arm around Collin's shoulder. "I hope not too, for Charity's sake. No wonder you're going crazy. Makes me crazy just listening to you. Marcy and I knew how Faith felt about you but thought it was pretty one-sided. We were sure if we could just keep her from you for a time, she'd get past it. And she's done well, I think, especially with Danny in the picture." Patrick noticed the scowl on Collin's face. "Out of curiosity, Collin—how did Charity discover you had feelings for Faith?"

Collin shifted on the stool, averting his gaze.

Patrick waited, but Collin wasn't in a hurry to answer. "Collin?"

He exhaled slowly and rubbed his forehead with his hands, then dropped them, palms down on the bar. "I'm afraid she caught us," he whispered.

Patrick leaned close. "What?"

Collin turned and looked him in the eye. "Charity

caught us—together. You might say we were otherwise engaged."

Patrick sprang from the stool, his heart thundering in his chest. "So help me, Collin, if you took advantage of her . . ."

Collin's hand shot up to ward Patrick off. "So help me, I never took advantage of her. Please believe me! We just kissed—pretty intensely, I'll grant you—but nothing else happened. You have my word on that."

"I suspect with a ring on her finger, Charity thought she had your word too." Patrick couldn't help the sarcasm. The fact that Collin flinched satisfied him. "So, Charity found you like that? When? Where?"

"It happened Saint Patrick's night on your front porch. It had been so long since I'd been at Brannigan's, I guess it got the better of me. I came knocking on your door just as Faith got home. She could tell I'd been drinking and was afraid you'd see me." Collin's look was sheepish. "The truth is I was pretty far gone. She made me sit on the swing while she brewed coffee. I was upset about something and asked if she would stay and talk."

Collin stopped to gulp his whiskey. "She read me the riot act, I'm afraid, telling me I needed to turn my life over to God if I wanted to be a good husband to Charity. I have to say, she was wonderful. She actually got me to pray with her, if you can believe that. That's when it finally hit me what an incredible woman she is, Mr. O'Connor. And the next thing I knew, I was kissing her . . . and Charity saw it all."

Collin shoved the empty glass away, propped his elbows on the bar, and put his head in his hands. He moaned softly. "I am such a heel—the king of all heels! It's not bad enough I have to hurt one of your daughters; I have to hurt two!"

"That certainly explains the subzero temperatures around

the house lately. Well, son, I'm afraid you've got a decision to make, and you better do it fast. Faith or Charity—pick one and let the other one go. And trust me, Collin, the answer's not at the bottom of a bottle."

Collin nodded absentmindedly. "I know. But the decision isn't between Faith and Charity. Even if I did choose Faith, she still wouldn't have me."

Patrick squinted, bunching his brows. "Why not? Because of Charity?"

Collin shook his head. "No . . . well, yes, that's part of it, I suppose, but not all."

"Then what?"

"This is probably going to shock you, Mr. O'Connor, but I'm not real big on God."

Patrick looked at Collin and blinked. "I know you're no choir boy, Collin, but you go to church with us every week and pray at our table. I'm afraid I don't know what you mean when you say you're not big on God."

"I mean I don't have much use for him, at least not until I've been coming around your family, and even then it's been primarily pretense on my part. I don't even know if I really believe in him. You see, I would have done anything to get you to let me see Charity, and I did. I pretended to be a good Catholic boy so I could marry your daughter."

Patrick's smile faded. "I see. And Charity knows this?"

Collin nodded. "It doesn't matter to her."

"But it matters to Faith." Patrick's tone was matter-of-fact.

Collin stared straight ahead and nodded.

"Mmm . . . yes, I guess it would," Patrick said softly. "My Faith has a deep devotion to God. She reads the Bible to Mrs. Gerson every week and takes Scripture very seriously. Unfortunately for you, I believe it tells her to avoid being 'unequally yoked.' I'm afraid the man who wins her heart is going to have to go through God first to do it."

Collin wilted on the stool. "That's pretty much what she said, more or less. So you see, the decision isn't between Faith and Charity. It's between marrying Charity while being in love with Faith, or going away altogether." Collin sighed. "Not much of a choice."

"Which is why you enlisted?"

Collin's smile was weak. "Nobody would believe it was the coward's way out, would they? I thought it would buy me time to sort things out."

"There is a third choice, you know."

Collin almost managed a grin. "I refuse to enter the seminary, Mr. O'Connor."

Patrick grinned back and patted his shoulder. "Close. You could actually turn to God. Stranger things have happened. Look at me. I once felt a lot like you. Then I met Marcy, and the world changed. She made me want to be a better man. That's what the right woman does for you. Marcy's faith ignited mine, and it's been a flame that's burned brightly ever since."

"I don't know. It's so hard to believe. I'd like to, honestly I would, but I just don't. How am I supposed to change that?"

Patrick stood and reached for his coat. "I don't think you'll have to—he will. You see, Collin, war has a way of illuminating the face of God. But until then, life is short, so don't be a stranger. I want to see you at our house tomorrow for lunch after mass, no excuses. You will be civil to my daughters, and you will make it perfectly clear to both Charity and Faith regarding your true feelings. And you will apologize to both for the emotional turmoil you've subjected them to. Am I making myself clear?"

Collin nodded. He looked drained.

"And, Collin . . ."

He lifted his gaze, eyes sunken into ashen cheeks.

"The truth is, I've grown quite fond of you. Quite frankly,

you're a son to me, and I'm confident God will steer you right, if you let him. Rest assured, I plan to pray about it for you. But, bottom line?" Patrick tossed the payment for his tab onto the bar and buttoned his coat, giving Collin a thin smile. "See to it you marry one of my daughters."

Collin was there at mass the next morning, waiting in the vestibule as usual, and wearing his best suit. Despite a late night at Brannigan's, he seemed none the worse for the wear, except for the bloodshot eyes and somber mood—signs of his bout with the bottle that could easily be taken as the result of sleepless nights. *Good*, Patrick thought, pleased to see Collin was feeling the full effects of his misguided actions. He fought a smile as he ushered his family into the church.

Collin nodded at Charity, whose eyes rounded with surprise. "Collin, you came! I didn't know if . . . I'm so glad." She seemed nervous as she smiled in her most alluring manner.

"I needed time to calm down, Charity, but we need to talk." His eyes flickered past her to Faith. "I need to talk to you both, I'm afraid."

The smile faded on Charity's lips as she glanced at her sister. She nodded quietly and walked in ahead, leaving him to follow into the pew. Faith lingered behind, allowing the rest of the family to enter before her. Patrick watched the scene with a dull ache. Why did his daughters' affairs of the heart have to be so blasted complicated? Kneeling, he made the sign of the cross and turned his attention to St. Stephen, beseeching him on behalf of his daughters' happiness, not to mention his own peace of mind.

For the first time in a long while, Collin felt uncomfortable kneeling beside the O'Connors in the sacred shadows of St. Stephen's Church. Over the last six months, he had almost enjoyed coming here. The calm and peace of this hallowed place had filled him with a serenity he had seldom known in years of obligatory mass and forced catechism. But for some reason this morning, the things he'd taken pleasure in before, such as the shafts of brilliantly colored light pouring through the stained-glass windows or the sweet scent of incense in the air, now only served to provoke a cynicism within. One, he suspected, that had been resident all along but for a time had been quelled by the tranquility of this holy place.

It certainly didn't help that this morning's homily was Psalm 37:4. He shifted in the pew at the sound of the words. "Delight thyself also in the Lord and he shall give thee the desires of thine heart." *No doubt one of Faith's top-ten verses,* he mused with a degree of bitterness. Well, maybe she believed it, and Patrick as well, but Collin suspected it was going to take more than blind faith to convince him that this Scripture—or any other—bore much merit at all.

He leaned back and stole a glimpse at Faith out of the corner of his eye, his face angled just enough to bring her into view. She seemed oblivious to anyone else, lost in her God, he supposed, as she prayed with eyes closed and face lifted. There was an intensity in her manner that was so much a part of who she was. His lips steeled and his bitterness flared. He swore silently. Yes, he wanted her, but he didn't want her God, and she'd made it abundantly clear it was a package deal. Oh, he was a "believer," all right. He believed that slighted deity was making him pay, a thought that only served to harden him more.

Following mass, he accompanied them home, where lunch was filled, as always, with the laughter and easy banter of a meal shared in the O'Connor household. And yet, Collin felt somewhat removed, as if preparing to leave this refuge provided in his otherwise lonely existence. He almost wished his day of departure was upon him, so awful was the feeling of dread at its coming.

Patrick cleared his throat and gave him a look. Collin took his cue and stood to his feet. "Mr. O'Connor, I'd like to speak with Charity, privately on the porch, if I may."

Patrick nodded and excused Charity from the dishes while Collin walked to the door and held it open. She stood, glancing from her father's somber face to Collin's before stepping into the parlor, through the hall, and out the front door. She lowered herself onto the swing. Collin bypassed it altogether to lean against the railing. His long legs stretched out and crossed at the ankles as he folded his arms across his chest.

"Charity," he began, his gaze glued to the floor, "I care about you a great deal—"

"I love you too, Collin."

He looked up at her. "I care about you, Charity, I do. But understand me—I'm not sure if I love you."

She blinked, and he saw the hurt on her face. He continued, his tone softer. "I'm not ruling out marriage. I just don't know how I feel—about you, about Faith. What I do know is I owe you an apology for things I've done, things I regret." He took a deep breath and looked away, knuckles straining as he gripped the banister. He lifted a hand to rub at a tic vibrating in his cheek. "Especially the hurt I've caused because of Faith, because of feelings I have for her . . ."

"You told me you didn't love her."

His head jerked up. "I told you I didn't know . . . any more than I know if I love you. All I do know is I want to be fair—to you, to Faith, and to myself."

"You don't love me, then."

"I care about you very much . . ."

"Enough to marry me, Collin?"

He studied her without speaking, then looked down. "I don't know, Charity."

"Enough to marry her?"

He could feel the heat creep up the back of his neck.

She slowly stood, a stricken look on her face. "I see. And does she know you love her?"

He jumped to his feet and spun around to clutch at the porch railing. "Blast it all, Charity, *I* don't know that I love her."

"But you think you do, don't you?"

He turned to stare at her.

"Don't you?"

He didn't answer, and she collapsed into the swing. He took a step forward, even though instinct told him to stop. But the sight of her tore at his gut. Against his better judgment, he sat and folded her in his arms.

"Charity, the last thing I wanted to do was hurt you." He kissed the top of her head, then softly twined his fingers at the back of her neck. "I don't know what's going to happen, how I'll feel when I return. I need to sort things out. Europe will give me the time to do that. I can't promise it'll turn out the way you want. What I can promise is I'll think long and hard about it—about us, about what's best for you and for me." A smile pulled at his lips. "In fact, I'm pretty sure when I'm stuck in some vile trench somewhere, I'll be thinking very long and very hard about you." He lifted her chin. "Especially how beautiful you are."

She looked up from under wet lashes, lips slightly parted, and Collin found himself fighting the urge to kiss her. He started to stand. She gripped his arm. "Collin, we're good together! Nobody will love you like I can."

He pushed her hand aside and stood, eyes burning from anger and desire. "So help me, you O'Connor women are really something. Neither of you fights fair. I have you driving me crazy like this, and the other one driving me crazy with God." He swore softly as his fingers kneaded the back of his neck. "Blast it all, I feel like I'm already behind enemy lines."

He stepped back, his breathing labored. A faint smile trembled on her lips. He aimed a finger at her while a spasm tickled his jaw. "Look, Charity, I told you once I don't take kindly to teasing. I'm not going to tell you again. You just won't see me."

Her smile broke into a grin. "You just can't handle it because you love me," she said, confidence resurging in her tone.

He stopped and assessed her through wary eyes. "No, I can't handle it because I'm attracted to you. There's a big difference."

"Well, that's good enough—for now."

He silently cursed the fact she had never looked more seductive, with her golden hair disheveled and blue eyes wide and wet. Her lips parted, full and pouty, as she observed him from the swing, while her hand toyed with the button at the high collar of her dress. He finally shook his head and laughed as he leaned against the railing, eyes focused on her fingers.

"All right, Collin, I understand. You need time to make up your mind, so the engagement is officially off—for now. Shall we seal it with a kiss?"

The blood coursed through his veins as he watched her, and he nodded, almost oblivious to her question. His gaze fixed on the button now unfastened against her throat. Slowly she stood and moved to his side. His heart was pounding, and she smiled as if she could hear it.

"Kiss me, Collin," she whispered. "It's only a kiss, after all, nothing more."

Her eyes seemed to hypnotize, and he let her wait while he struggled with what conscience he had. Before he knew what was happening, the slow smile moved across his lips as if it had a mind of its own. He grabbed her, his breath hot on her face as he spoke.

"That's right, Charity . . . only a kiss . . . nothing more." He kissed her mouth, long and hard, then allowed his lips to brush across her cheek, caressing the delicate fold of her ear. He heard her soft purr of contentment and then pulled away and studied her. Slowly, he traced his finger along the gentle curve of her chin, down to the open button at the hollow of her throat. She shivered at his touch and closed her eyes. He nudged her away. "You know, Charity, two can play this game, but only one can win." He stepped back and reached for the door. "Something to think about, isn't it?" He opened it and went inside, leaving her wiser, he hoped, and certainly warmer than before.

Patrick looked up as Collin entered the kitchen. He and Sean were drinking coffee while Marcy and Faith finished the dishes. "Everything okay?" he asked. "You seem flustered."

Heat prickled the back of Collin's neck. He smiled at Patrick. "Yes, sir, I'm fine, and so is Charity. I think we understand each other now."

Patrick seemed relieved. "Good. Would you like some coffee, Collin? Marcy's kept some warm for you."

Collin nodded and gratefully allowed Marcy to fill his cup. "Thank you, Mrs. O'Connor. I think I'm going to miss your meals and your coffee more than anything."

She gave him a faint smile, then glanced at Patrick, who rose from his chair. "Up for a game of chess, son?" he asked Sean, who nodded and followed his father to the parlor.

Marcy turned to Faith. "Do you mind finishing up? I need to check on Katie. She's supposed to be straightening her room, but goodness knows what I'll find up there."

Faith nodded, and Marcy left them in silence.

Collin slumped at the table, staring at the palm of his

hand as he absently rubbed it with his thumb. His stomach was in knots. A hundred thoughts circled in his brain of things he wanted to tell her, but as he sat there, heart racing and hands sweating, he had absolutely no idea what he would say.

She dried the last dish, put it away, and neatly folded the dish towel before turning around, her small frame propped against the counter as if for support. For the moment, those green eyes were calm, resigned, and almost cold. But not quite, he noticed, as she quickly averted her gaze to the floor.

"You can't hate me, you know—it's against your religion."

He was teasing, but she didn't seem to care. Her head snapped up, and her eyes singed him. His heart started pounding, and his slow smile reengaged. She was like a chameleon—calm and placid one minute, all fire and flash in the next, and it never failed to rouse him.

"Get it over with, Collin. Father said you wanted to speak with me, so do it."

She was clearly not happy with him, and somehow it turned his smile into a grin, which only managed to aggravate her further. He tried to temper it a bit, but it was so blasted hard with her looking like that. A little girl with pouting green eyes and wild auburn hair tumbling her shoulders. Holy saints above, she was beautiful! Why hadn't he realized before just how much? Before he had courted Charity and set things in motion that were now too difficult to change? Things could have been so different, he thought, then frowned. No, they would have never been different. Something much bigger than an engagement to Charity stood in the way.

"Will you sit down, please? It's difficult to have a conversation with someone who looks like they're ready to bolt from the room."

Her gaze focused past him as she slipped into the seat farthest away and folded her hands on the table before her.

Collin cleared his throat and shifted in his chair. "I owe you an apology, Faith, and more than one, I suppose. I never should have taken advantage of you like I did. I regret it, I really do. Not just because of what it's done to you, but what it's done to Charity . . ." He looked away. "And to me."

He closed his eyes, leaned back, and massaged his forehead with his fingers. "I saw myself with Charity, Faith, I really did. I thought we'd marry, have lots of kids, and grow old together. But that day in the park, something happened. I don't know, I felt something—something strong—and it scared me. I hated it because it made me feel vulnerable. I didn't like that. But I couldn't stop thinking about it, either—about you—and believe me, I tried. I was certain if I could see more of Charity, if I could fill my mind with her love, I'd be fine. Only it didn't work that way. Then I thought, well, once Charity and I are married, I'll get over it . . ."

She watched him now, her face softening with concern.

"I was pretty slow on the uptake, I guess. It wasn't until the night on the swing that I realized I was falling in love with you."

He heard her sharp intake of breath as her eyes began to well, and he reached across the table to take her hand in his. "I love you, Faith. Marry me."

She jerked her hand from his. "I can't marry you, Collin."

He leaned forward. "I know you love me. Can you deny it?"

She didn't speak, and he jumped up, rounded the table, and gripped her arms to lift her to her feet. When she wouldn't look at him, he grabbed her chin and forced her. "Look at me! Can you deny you love me?"

She stared at him through a mist of tears. "Let me go, you're hurting my arm."

"Tell me you don't love me."

"I don't love you."

"You're lying, Faith. I would have thought better of you than that."

"Well, don't!" she screamed. "I'm not better than that. You've said your apologies, Collin, now let me go."

She tried to turn away. He jerked her back. "I know you love me. Don't you think I can feel it every time I touch you?" He pulled her to him, and she cried out before his lips silenced her with a savage kiss. She struggled to pull free, but he only held her tighter. The blood pounded in his brain. His mouth was everywhere—her throat, her earlobes, her lips—and he could feel the heat coming in waves as she melted against him. She was quivering when he finally let her go.

"You love me, Faith," he said quietly. "You know that, and I know that. Your heart belongs to me, and nothing can ever change that fact—not Charity, not you, and not your God."

A sob escaped her lips, and she collapsed into the chair, all fight gone. "I know," she whispered, "I know. Oh, Collin, if only you could tell me what I need to hear."

He was tempted to lie, to tell her anything to keep her. He had done it once—managed to convince her family he was something he wasn't; he could do it again. But somehow he knew, no matter how convincing the lie, she would know. Somehow that God of hers would trip him up, and then he would lose her forever. It was only seconds before he answered, but it seemed a lifetime. "I can't now," he said, his mouth dry, "but I don't know it couldn't happen. Maybe you'll save my soul, who knows?"

His attempt to be light fell flat, and inwardly he cursed at how hollow it must have sounded.

"What does it matter anyway? I won't stand in your way if you want to believe in your God. Please, Faith, just say yes!"

He was speaking too fast, as if he were desperate. He was. The only woman he had ever really wanted would not have him, and it was about to crush him. Never in his life had he ever begged a woman for anything. A sick feeling suddenly cleaved to his throat.

She started to cry, and he knew before she spoke what her answer would be. His hands dropped to his sides. Slowly, he walked to the sink to pour himself a glass of water. He emptied it and set the glass on the counter before turning to face her. When he did, he felt a spasm quiver in his jaw. His eyes itched hot as they pierced through her. "That's it, then? God wins and I lose? Well, I'm glad we settled that. It's been eating at me for a long time."

"Collin, please . . ."

"Please what? Go away so you don't have to face the fact you're in love with me?" He moved to his chair and slammed it against the table.

"It wouldn't work. It has to be right—"

"No! I don't want to hear it! I'm sick to death of hearing it, and I don't have to listen. We're oil and water, Faith. I'm in the real world, and you're out there somewhere in a world I don't understand." For a split second he stared past her before his eyes shifted back, finally resigned. "It's good for me to go away. You don't have to worry anymore, Faith. I don't need a ton of bricks to fall on me to know it's time to move on."

He squeezed his eyes shut and rubbed the back of his neck. "I suppose marriage needs more than passion anyway, doesn't it? It helps if you're on the same wavelength, at least, like Charity and me. We seem to understand each other, and then there's passion too." His voice sounded so strange to his own ears, a low monotone, emotionless, almost stream of consciousness.

He heard her move toward him. "You know, Collin, someday we'll be friends—good friends."

His eyes flew open, and he didn't blink once. "I don't want to be your friend, Faith. I want to be your husband and your lover."

A dark blush invaded her cheeks. She lifted her chin. "I want that too, Collin, more than anything in the world."

He heaved the chair against the table again, and the sound was as explosive as the fire in his gut. "That's a lie! But, it doesn't matter now, because I finally get it. I don't understand it, mind you, but it's finally sinking into this thick head of mine that we don't belong together. Not that what we have between us isn't strong and real. No, this thing is so real it makes us crazy every time we're near each other. It's what most people dream about, and we have it! But you—you'd rather turn your back on something so real for something that's only real in your own mind."

"It's not just real in my mind. God is real, whether you believe it or not."

"Yeah? Well, you can't prove it by me."

"Collin, please . . . don't do this! You can't possibly know how sorry I am."

"Yes I can, Faith." He started to leave.

"Collin . . ."

He stopped, hand splayed against the door.

"I am sorry, so sorry. And for what it's worth, I'll never stop praying for you."

He turned, all anger siphoning out. "Yeah, you do that." He took a deep breath and forced a faint smile. "Well, then, I guess that's that. Chapter closed. Man goes to war, ex-fiancée waits for him, and sister moves on with her life. Here's to a happy ending."

Tears streaked her cheeks. "I hope so, Collin," she whispered. "I'm staking everything on it. Somewhere in Mrs. Gerson's Bible it says, 'All things work together for good to those who love God.' I'd like to think that's assurance of a happy ending."

As he stared at her now, he almost envied what she had. Almost. He hung his head, then glanced up, his lips curved in a tired smile. "Well, one thing's for sure—I'm glad I'm leaving on good terms. If I'm going to be target practice for some Germans, I'd much rather have you praying for me than against me."

"Count on it," she said, wiping the wetness from her face. "And, Collin, I wish the best for you. I really do."

He studied her, completely certain she meant it. "Thanks, Little Bit." Without another word, he turned and left, causing the door to creak to an eerie stillness.

15

For Marcy and everyone in the O'Connor household, June 15 was a day of mourning. Collin McGuire was shipping out, and with him went the hopes and prayers of the family who claimed him as their own. The last month had been difficult for everyone concerned. Like clockwork, Charity would lunge into a crying jag following each of Collin's visits while Marcy tried to comfort her until it passed. Faith, although not as depressed as prior to her talk with Collin, wandered about in a mild malaise, which wasn't suspect at all as it merely matched the mood of the rest of the family.

Marcy knew Patrick felt as if he were sending a son off to war. And, indeed, the fear remained that soon they might be doing that as well. Just twenty-four hours prior, President Wilson had declared in his Flag Day Address that the initial American Expeditionary Force, of which Collin was a part, would soon be followed by more soldiers as quickly as possible. Marcy was sick with worry about Collin and fraught with dread for her own son. Her only consolation at this difficult time was that at least her husband would be spared from the greedy arm of the Selective Service. Never had she appreciated Patrick passing the draft age of thirty more than she did now. An appreciation that, she soon discovered, was destined to be short-lived despite her prayers. Shortly after the first troops arrived in France on June 26, General Pershing called for a U.S. army of three million men. Marcy could see in her husband's face what he refused to mention. The night he finally uttered it followed on the heels of the worst day of her life.

Her grandmother was dying and Sean had been drafted. Marcy had never known such fear and pain. Although she had never been a woman who stormed and raged, that seemed to be changing as she progressed in years. Suddenly she felt no compunction whatsoever at giving full vent to her anger. She lay on their bed, indifferent to the shards of broken glass strewn across her bedroom floor from the hand mirror she hurled at the wall. Her mother's letter was soggy and smeared from Marcy's hours of weeping. Mima's heart had weakened, Bridget had written, after becoming severely taxed by a serious bout with the flu. The doctor suggested that funeral arrangements be made as quickly as possible. As if that dagger had not been enough to gouge a gaping wound, a draft notice for Sean had arrived the very same day, inflicting the final death blow to Marcy's sanity and peace. She shivered uncontrollably despite the summer day, her pillow cold and sodden with tears as she awaited the sound of her husband's footfall.

Sean had met him at the door, and without a word handed him the notice he received in the mail. It was the ashen look on his son's face and not the notice itself that alerted Patrick that their worst fears had come true. He crushed his son in his arms before Sean could see the tears in his own eyes. His voice was thick when he finally spoke. "When?" he asked.

"August," Sean replied.

"Does your mother know?" Patrick's eyes searched the house for his wife.

Sean nodded. "She's been upstairs all afternoon, crying

her eyes out. She was the one who opened it . . . right after she opened Grandmother's letter that Mima is dying."

Patrick's heart squeezed in pain for his wife. *Lord, help me to help her, please.*

And so he found her, lying prostrate on their bed, her form lifeless and still except for an occasional whimper, painful residue left from hours of weeping. The room seemed dark, even though the late-afternoon sun streamed in, and Patrick felt sick as he crossed the room to lie beside her. The minute he did, she clutched him tightly, her sobs beginning in force. He held her close, and her head quivered as he stroked her hair. He stared blankly at the ceiling.

"Why, Patrick? First Collin, now Mima and Sean . . . Why would God do this to us?" She could barely voice the words for the tears.

His own vision blurred with emotion. "I don't know, Marcy. All I know is we have to trust him. We have nothing else . . ." He held her tighter, his voice steeled with purpose. "We don't need anything else."

She didn't answer.

"He didn't promise we would be free from trial, Marcy. He told us we would have tribulation, but to be of good cheer for he has overcome it. We have tribulation, my love, but he will see us through. We must trust him."

His words seemed to calm her, and he felt her relax in his arms. Reaching up, she put her hands on either side of his face, her eyes red and swollen as she stared at him. "Patrick, I don't know what I would do without you. You're my strength."

He felt his jaw twitch. "No, Marcy, I'm not your strength—he is."

She shot up and clenched his arm. "No! You are—you know that! You're everything to me, Patrick. I would die without you . . ."

"No, you won't!" The look on her face chilled him. He hadn't meant to say it like that, to imply she would ever have to, but it had rolled off his tongue before he could stop it, and the damage was there on her face.

Her knuckles strained white as she grabbed his shirt. "What are you saying, Patrick? Tell me this sick feeling inside my stomach is wrong. Tell me I have nothing to worry about, that you'll be by my side every day of this despicable war. Tell me, Patrick!" Her voice reached a level of hysteria as she searched his eyes for assurance he couldn't give.

He pressed her to him, holding her so tightly she couldn't move. "I can't tell you that, Marcy. I wish I could, but I can't, darlin'. I didn't want to worry you. But Marcy, the chance remains I may have to go."

She jerked away, her eyes crazed. "No! You're too old! Tell me, Patrick, you're too old!"

"Marcy, they're desperate for soldiers, so desperate they've extended the draft to forty-five. Marcy, if they call me, I have to go."

She screamed as she lunged, her fists striking his chest with a fury he'd seldom seen in this woman he loved. He grabbed her hands and pinned her flat on the bed, his breathing labored from the effort. She was like a mad woman, thrashing beneath his grip, and he found himself crying out to God to impart peace to her soul. Seconds lapsed into minutes before stillness came. When it did, she was limp in his arms, emotionally ravaged by the fear that possessed her. She was spent, and so was he. All that was left was a numbness buzzing in his brain as they lay side by side in a room filled with darkness, despite the sunlight of a summer day. They lay like that for hours, it seemed, while Faith, Sean, and Charity tended to the others downstairs.

When Marcy finally spoke, her voice was more like the woman he knew, despite a nasal tone from hours of crying.

"Pray with me, Patrick. Pray I can do this. Pray God will heal Mima . . . and that he'll keep you safe, along with Collin and Sean."

And so he had, invoking the name of the God they served. His voice was calmer as he finished, and he pulled her close. "You can do this, Marcy. He's your strength, not me. He promised we could do all things through Christ who strengthens us, even this. If I go, and we still don't know if I'll be called, you won't be alone. He said he would never leave us nor forsake us. We've lived our whole lives believing that. Now we'll learn how very true it is."

He lifted his head from the pillow to peer into her face. "Are you hungry?"

She shook her head against his chest before looking up, a faint smile creasing her lips. "No, but I bet you are, aren't you?"

"Not that holding you in my arms isn't sustenance enough, mind you," he began, a note of levity in his tone, "but it would seem if you don't want to lose me, you'd feed me before I fade away into nothingness on this bed."

"Worried about your stomach at a time like this, are you?"

"Worried I'll not have the strength for you at a time like this, my love."

"I love you, Patrick," she whispered. She leaned to kiss him gently on the lips.

With an energy that belied the emptiness of his stomach, he pulled her to him, his lips pressed hard against hers with a passion that had little to do with desire. It had everything to do with his heartfelt gratitude for this woman who shared his life, and to the God who had led him to her. "Woman, I love you . . . to the depths of my soul, I do."

She laid her head on his chest, clinging as if it were the last time, while fresh tears spilled onto his shirt. It was a bittersweet moment and one neither wanted to lose. And so they lingered, content to lie a few moments more while the shadows of dusk slowly stole away the light of day.

"I can't believe you're leaving! I'm going to miss you so much," Maisie cried.

Crying was the last thing Faith wanted to do as they stood in the middle of the newsroom, wrapped in a tight hug. But there was little either could do as the tears streamed freely with no regard for their weak attempt at composure.

"I can't believe your father is letting you go. It's just plain crazy, Faith, to even attempt ship travel right now. What about the German U-boat warfare? Isn't he afraid?"

Faith pulled back and took a deep breath. "Yes, he's afraid, but he's more afraid that Mother will have a break-down while he's gone. With Mima near death and Father drafted, Mother begged to go to Ireland. She simply wouldn't relent, and I think she just wore Father down. He contacted his cousin, Thomas, who owns a freight-ing company. Although all passenger-ship travel has been suspended, apparently freight shipping is going strong, especially in convoys. Thomas convinced Father that losses for ships sailing in convoys have fallen dramatically." Faith sucked in another heavy breath and lifted her chin. "So he agreed to take us. With God watching over us, we'll be fine."

"But Ireland—it's so far! Why couldn't your grandmother live in Dubuque? At least then I could take a train."

Faith laughed as she pushed the tears from her eyes. "Dubuque! You'd wish me destined to be a farmer's wife? Working the fields from sunup to sundown? Some friend."

"Well, at least we'd still be friends . . ."

"Maisie, we'll always be friends. Distance is not going to change that. I'll write you every chance I get, I promise.

Who else can I brag to when I start my new job at the *Times*?"

"You realize, of course, you won't have me around when some little hussy gets her Irish up because your daddy got you the job?"

Faith gave her a smirk. "I can handle myself. You forget I've spent the last year learning from the best. Besides, it won't be forever. As soon as the war is over, we're coming back. Father finally agreed that it would do Mother a world of good to be back in Ireland while he's gone. My grandmother could really use my mother's help, especially now. Somehow, in my heart, I feel that it's the best thing for her. It'll do her good to get away from Boston where everything reminds her of Father."

"And you? I suppose getting away wouldn't hurt you either, would it?"

Faith looked up and didn't answer, but they both knew she was right. Maisie tried to lighten the conversation. "Well, I'm sure I don't have to tell you who it is going to hurt. Have you said your good-byes yet?"

Faith shook her head, suddenly very uneasy at the prospect of telling Danny good-bye. She had tried several times to end their relationship months prior, but he'd insisted on friendship, a friendship she feared still harbored deeper feelings on his part. "No, he didn't want to say good-bye at the paper. He's coming over this evening, although I have a lot of packing yet to do."

"Are you going to miss him?" Maisie asked.

Faith laughed. "Yes, of course I'll miss him. Not as much as I'll miss you, but close."

Maisie seemed uneasy. "No, I mean really miss him, you know, pining-away missing?"

Faith grinned, and Maisie's spray of freckles disappeared into a sea of pink. "You mean, do I love him, or are you asking if you can have him?"

Maisie went scarlet. Faith laughed out loud and hugged her again. "Oh, Maisie, I'm gonna miss you something fierce! Who's gonna make me laugh like you? No, I've told you before—I don't love Danny, hard as I've tried. I've told him over and over again, even though he doesn't seem to want to hear it. And believe me, I have. It's much closer to friendship than love. Blame it on Collin McGuire, I suppose. But either way, dear friend, he's all yours. I know you want him. And I have a feeling with me out of the way . . ."

"Stop it! You know he's crazy about you. He only sees me as a friend."

"A friend whose shoulder he's sure to cry on, right? All you have to do is convert! Believe me, Maisie, my money's on that shoulder of yours."

Maisie started to cry again. "I love you, you goose," she whispered, swiping at her eyes. She picked up her purse. "You better write, or so help me . . ."

"Oh, I'll write, you can count on that. Can't wait to tell you all about the tall, handsome stranger I meet in Dublin. And, I expect progress reports as well, young lady."

"Done!" Maisie said as she blew her a kiss. "Till the war's over," she cried, escaping out the door as Faith spied a fresh wave of tears. She returned to the typing pool to collect her things. "Till the war's over," she whispered. "And may it end before our lives change forever."

The summer had been little more than a blur, and now here they were on a freighter on the Atlantic Ocean, embarking on a new life in a distant land. It hardly seemed possible Sean had left in August with Patrick following in October, both stationed in remote places in the French countryside. Before his departure, Patrick handled the details, so reluctant was Marcy to even acknowledge his leaving. Now their home on Donovan Street was comfortably occupied by the new interim associate editor, who paid quite handsomely to rent a furnished house within the Southie neighborhood.

It had been difficult for Faith to say good-bye to Mrs. Gerson, but the old woman had insisted she would only be "a prayer away." "God has something special for you in Ireland, Faith. Just delight in him while you're there, and he'll give you the desires of your heart. I can't wait to see what he does in your life, my dear. You must promise to write."

And so she had, and to Danny as well, although she knew for his sake, her communications would be brief. He had taken the news of her departure hard. Faith was shocked at the degree of affection he had developed for her, even though they were just friends. She regretted now ever allowing him to kiss her in the beginning, for every kiss had apparently led him to believe she would eventually be his. It had certainly seemed, for a while at least, as if he would win her heart. But the futility of that became evident as the tension between Collin and her had escalated over the last few months. Soon, it became quite clear to Faith that her depth of feeling for Collin, no matter how unfortunate, only served to extinguish any romantic feeling she may have had for Danny. The reality all but crushed him at the time, but they had remained good friends. Faith was grateful Danny had also developed a close friendship with Maisie. He would need a good friend, and there was none better.

She leaned against the railing of the freighter, the wind whipping her hair as she stared into the endless sea separating her from the life she had once known. On the day they had sailed, her mother worked at hiding her true feelings. But as she had ushered what was left of her family onto the boat, Faith suspected that underneath the forced smile and excited tone was an apprehension she seldom saw in her mother. Yet Faith knew even if Marcy herself did not feel strong, her faith in God was, which brought some semblance of comfort throughout the long journey to Ireland.

The week aboard the freighter had been shrouded in dreariness, from the endless raging of the waves to the damp sea mist that hovered in the air like a harbinger of gloom—a gloom only deepened by an underlying dread. In addition to the very real threat of German U-boats, Faith couldn't help but think of the "unsinkable" luxury liner, *Titanic*, that had fatally plunged into these same icy depths five years earlier. The memory weighed heavily on Faith as the convoy of freighters plowed an endless surge of whitecaps. Over 1,500 lives were entombed in the same gray, bleak waters now battering the hull of the ship, and Faith couldn't shake the uneasiness that hung heavily in the pungent sea air.

The day they finally sighted Ireland, it was as if the gloom lifted, allowing shafts of sunlight to peek through like the fingers of God directing them home. Faith had never seen anything so beautiful as Ireland drenched in sunlight, a vibrant patchwork of blinding green hills and fields rolling across the landscape into the restless sea. In the midst of it all rose Dublin, a warm and welcoming port, which each of them hoped held the promise of better days.

For the first time since her father had left, her mother's eyes shone with excitement as she gazed across the water at her homeland. Even Charity seemed enthralled with Ireland's beauty as the family stood side by side on the deck to catch a glimpse of their new home.

"Mother, it's so beautiful, it almost doesn't seem real!" Charity exclaimed, her blue eyes wide as she clutched her mother's arm. Marcy smiled and took a deep breath, her hands positioned tightly on Katie's shoulders as the six-year-old attempted to better her view by hoisting up on the railing.

"I can't see . . . I can't see! Mama, lift me up!"

Marcy boosted Katie in her arms and pointed toward the southern outskirts of the city. "Your grandmother lives over there, in a little cottage on Ambrose Lane." She turned to look at Faith, her eyes as excited as Katie's at Christmas. "Faith, do you have the brooch with you?"

Faith nodded and reached into her purse to produce the treasured keepsake her mother had given her on the first day at the *Herald*. Marcy lifted it to show Katie. "Look, little chicken, this is our new home. This is where your grandmother lives and your great-grandmother. So, what do you think?"

Katie frowned as she fingered the brooch, then grinned. "It's awfully small, Mama . . . are you sure we'll all fit?"

Her mother laughed out loud, and hope surged in Faith at the glorious sound. It had been too long since she'd heard the ring of her mother's laughter. Ireland would be good for her, as she hoped it would be for them all.

"No, silly, this is just a tiny picture of what the house looks like. Actually, it's quite a good size, I believe. I think we'll be most comfortable there." She turned to Charity. "It's in walking distance of several charming shops, Charity, and Father thought you might enjoy working in one. You're so bright and lovely to look at, you'd be a natural, I think."

Charity smiled and nodded, fairly glowing with the praise of her mother.

"Beth and Steven, you'll be attending St. Patrick's School, also within walking distance. Your grandmother went there, and I would have too, had we stayed in Ireland."

"Where will I go to school, Mama?" Katie asked.

"Next year, little one. This year you'll stay home to help us care for Mima."

"Mother, do you have any idea where the *Irish Times* is located?" Faith squinted hard at the city skyline, her heart fluttering at the prospect of a new job in a strange city.

"I think your father told me it was on Lower Abbey Street, in the business district. It's not within walking distance, I know, but it shouldn't be too far. Even so, public transportation is available, I believe." She glanced quickly at her daughter. "Are you nervous?"

Faith shivered as she nodded, and her mother squeezed her arm. "There's nothing to worry about, Faith—God's in control. That's what I have to remind myself every day, and you do too. He'll be right there with you, every step of the way. Aren't we the lucky ones, though, to know him like we do?" Her eyes were suddenly misty.

"We are, Mother. How do people do it without him?" Faith whispered. Sadness settled in at the thought of Collin. Shaking the feeling off, she smiled into her mother's eyes. "We're going to be fine, you know."

Her mother brushed a stray tear aside and nodded. "I know," she whispered, turning to gaze at the city. "Fine enough, at least, until the war is over. And then, when I finally have my husband by my side, and my son and prospective son-in-law home safe and sound, well, now, that will certainly be the true definition of 'fine.'"

When the door swung open and she looked into the face of her mother for the first time in nine years, Marcy knew it would be a moment etched in her memory forever. A moment of destiny, she thought, as she ushered her family onto the street where she had lived as a little girl.

Ambrose Lane was as charming as it sounded—a quiet street shaded by massive oaks arched over a narrow lane of cottage homes, each more inviting than the next. There was a distinctive scent in the air, a heady fragrance that Marcy identified as viburnum. The sweet smell of it would, from that moment on, forever remind them of Ireland. They stood, the six of them, on a somewhat rickety porch. It was thick with coats of white paint long since given way to the peeling and cracking so inevitable on the Irish seaboard. The large wooden door had not fared much better, speckled as it was with bits of the original white peeking through the most recent coat of green, which looked anything but recent.

Marcy knocked on the door timidly, holding her breath until it opened. When it did, she exhaled with a faint cry of joy as she beheld the face of her mother.

Bridget Murphy was still a handsome woman, by anyone's definition. She was slight of stature and strong of character, like her daughter. She looked at them now through the same clear blue eyes that seemed youthful despite an abundance of delicate lines and creases. At first sight of her family, her hand flew to her mouth, and the blue eyes pooled with tears as she echoed the faint cry of her daughter.

Marcy dropped her bags at her side and flew into her mother's arms. The two cried and laughed at the same time while the rest of the O'Connors grinned and looked on.

"Oh, Mother, I've missed you so much! I can't believe we're together again at last. Let me look at you." Marcy stepped back, her hands still clutching her mother's arms. She laughed from the sheer joy of touching her again.

Bridget's trembling smile was wet with tears as she squeezed Marcy's hands. "Marcy, I'd forgotten how beautiful you are." Her smile faded into a look of concern. "Tell me, have you heard anything from Patrick or Sean?"

Marcy shook her head. "I don't expect to for a while. Patrick only left a little over three weeks ago, and I'm sure he would have waited to write me here. I heard from Sean not long after he arrived in France back in August, but nothing since."

Bridget hugged her daughter again. "Now, you have nothing to worry about, Marcy. Patrick and Sean will come home to you again, safe and none the worse for the wear, you'll see. God wouldn't dare allow otherwise with all the candles I've been lighting, now would he?"

Marcy smiled, and Bridget turned to greet her grandchildren with a twinkle in her eyes. "Sure, it's expected for these grandchildren of mine to be so handsome, what with the comeliness of both you and Patrick, now isn't it so? Saints alive, Faith, I'd recognize that auburn hair anywhere! You're all grown up and quite the beauty. Why, you were just a shy little girl not ten years old when I saw you last." Bridget reached to stroke Faith's cheek, her eyes sobering. "My goodness, you were such a strong little thing, as I recall. First, losing your sister, then losing the use of your legs . . . and never once did I hear you complain." Bridget sighed, shaking off her melancholy. "And look at you now! No braces in sight and as robust as you please. And, Marcy tells me you're to start a job at the *Times*?"

Faith laughed and hugged her grandmother. "Yes, next week, as a matter of fact. Father arranged it with an old friend of his. We knew we would need income, and I love journalism. I've done a bit of feature writing at the *Herald*, but I'm hoping to have the opportunity to do a lot more here in Ireland."

"A writer in the family! I'm so very proud of you, my dear."

"I'm a writer too! I can write my alphabet all by myself, Grandma." Katie couldn't wait to be noticed.

Marcy's mother bent to give her full attention. "Why, you must be Katie! Your mama has told me so much about you, and what a big girl you are. Do I get a hug, big girl?"

Katie giggled and shot into Bridget's arms, prompting another stream of tears to streak her grandmother's face.

"Grandma, don't cry! Aren't you glad we're here?"

Bridget smiled at Katie, then glanced at Marcy. "Yes, dear, of course. It's just that I've waited so very long to hug you." She picked Katie up in her arms and turned to Charity. "This is Charity? Goodness, Marcy, beauty runs deep in your family. I'm afraid the young men around here will be love struck in no time."

Charity grinned and hugged her grandmother. "Thank you, Grandmother. Actually, I'm almost engaged, but he's in France."

Bridget touched Charity's cheek. "Yes, Collin, I know. Your mother wrote me. But, 'almost engaged' is not engaged, my dear. I don't want you pining away under my roof. You're young, and I want to see you meet friends here and have fun. Collin will still be there when the war is over, my dear."

"Yes, ma'am," Charity said, hugging her grandmother once again.

"And this must be Elizabeth, Marcy's bookworm, right?"

A shy smile creased Beth's lips as she nodded.

"Well, now, you and I will just have to talk literature, young lady. I've got a whole bookshelf of my favorites just waiting inside, and I fully expect you to reciprocate in kind by sharing some of yours. Agreed?" Elizabeth actually laughed as Bridget kissed her on the cheek and gave her a gentle hug.

"And last, but most certainly not least, is the man of the house—Steven. Well, young man, have you been taking good care of your mother and sisters?"

Apparently delighted by the referral as "man of the house," Steven grinned and nodded enthusiastically. He stuck out his hand to shake hers. Bridget laughed and grabbed it, pulling him into a hug while she kissed the top of his head. "Nonsense, young man, we're family here.

There will be no handshakes, only lots of hugs and kisses. Understood?"

"Yes, ma'am," Steven said with a grin, then looked up earnestly. "Grandma? Right now, instead of hugs and kisses, do you think we could have something to eat?"

Bridget laughed and winked at Marcy. "Isn't that amazing, now? I just happen to have a kitchen full of good things to eat. Let's get you inside and settled in, then we'll have a bite. How would that be?"

"Great!" Katie shrieked, tearing past her grandmother into the house with Steven in hot pursuit. The older girls picked up their bags and followed them in.

"Faith, Charity, would you mind finding something for them to eat while I talk to your grandmother?" Marcy slipped her arm around her mother.

"How are you holding up, my dear?" Bridget asked, the smile on her lips in stark contrast to the deep concern in her eyes.

Marcy sighed, so very grateful to allow someone else to be the strong one for a change. "I have my moments, Mother, but God has seen me through, along with my children. I try not to think about it, about what could happen . . ." She stopped, tears welling against her will. "I hope and pray God keeps them safe. I . . . I don't know what I would do, Mother, if anything happened. Sean . . . Patrick . . . they're my life."

Bridget squeezed her hand. "I know, Marcy, I know. And God knows too—trust him."

"Patrick's words exactly. And I'm trying, Mother, really I am. But it should be easier, now. Now that I'm here with you. How's Mima?"

It appeared to be Bridget's turn to wrestle with her fears. "Not good, I'm afraid. The doctor says it's just a matter of time. Her heart . . . well, it's quite weak and . . ." Bridget's voice wavered slightly as she continued. "I'm just trying to keep her comfortable as long as possible."

Marcy put her hand on her mother's arm. "Oh, Mother, I had no idea her heart was that weak."

Bridget nodded. "I know, dear; I didn't want you to know. I suppose I kept hoping it wasn't true myself, but that bout of the flu changed everything." She smiled a sad smile. "Who would have thought a war could be convenient? It brought you to me when I needed you most."

Marcy hugged her mother. "And me to you."

Arm in arm, the two made their way to the back of the cottage to Mima's room, but Marcy wasn't prepared for the change in her grandmother as she entered. It was the sunniest room in the house, cheerful and bright with a peaceful view of her mother's prized garden, but it was filled with the feel of death. Mima, not yet eighty, looked to be at least a hundred as she lay in the bed, a frail shell of her former self, her sunken eyes closed. Marcy's hand flew to her mouth.

All at once, Mima's eyes opened, and a ghost of a smile flickered on her lips. "My Marceline . . ." she whispered. "I've missed you."

Marcy sat on the bed and stroked her grandmother's face with her fingers. "Oh, Mima, I've missed you too!" She laid her head on Mima's chest. "How are you?"

The old woman smiled, then coughed before answering. Her eyes shone with a hint of a sparkle, the only sign of life in her otherwise ravaged body. "Better, I think, now that you're here. Where are those children of yours? I want to meet them."

Marcy smiled and pushed tears off her cheeks. "Oh, you will, I assure you. They're in the kitchen getting a bite to eat, but you may ask Mother to ship us back once you meet them. My six-year-old, Katie, can be quite demanding, I'm afraid."

"No more than the Marceline I knew at her age," Mima answered, patting Marcy's hand. "Go, get settled and have a bite to eat. I'll rest now. I can meet them when I awaken."

Marcy leaned and kissed her on the cheek. Mima closed her eyes, and Marcy's heart ached as she sat and watched her for a moment. She stood and took a deep breath, glancing at Bridget, who stood at the door. "You know, Mother, today . . . right now . . . there's no place I'd rather be than here."

Bridget lifted her apron to wipe the tears from her eyes. "I know, dear. And God knows. And that's why you're here, isn't it? Now, how about that bite to eat?"

For Marcy, it was one of the most remarkable weeks of her life, and who would have believed it? Mima was dying, Patrick, Sean, and Collin were at war, yet here they were, encased in this cocoon of warmth and new discovery—the perfect antidote to the heaviness they'd been carrying all too long. It was like one endless celebration, a bit of revelry in an otherwise dreary reality, and there was no question in Marcy's mind she had made the right decision in badgering Patrick to send her here.

Mima had taken to the children instantly, and they to her. Especially Katie, who was mesmerized by this tiny woman who seemed more like an oversized doll than a great-grandmother. She would lie beside Mima for hours, brushing her hair or pretending to read a book, plying her with questions that never failed to make Mima smile. It almost seemed that the gloom of death so prevalent upon their arrival had somehow dissipated, replaced instead by the warm sound of laughter spilling into the room along with the sunshine. Could it be, Marcy wondered, that

Mima looked better? Her previously sallow complexion was now more aglow, her former listlessness now sparked with new energy.

The evenings were filled with the delights of Bridget's cooking and Mima's spellbinding stories and childhood games, which Marcy now passed on to her own children. Even Blarney, after confinement on the ship, seemed happy with his new lot in life as the shadow of Marcy's mother, who shamelessly plied him with bits of soda bread dredged in bacon drippings.

Of course, the highlight was a letter from Collin. After months of training on the front lines, he'd earned a short leave to one of the small towns in southern France, where he managed to run into Sean. Both were doing well, according to Collin, who carefully chose to avoid any specific talk of war. Instead, he rambled on about Sean or the beauty of the French countryside, teasing that apparently Sean was better at soldiering than at chess, for he seemed none the worse for the wear. He talked of friends he'd made, and one in particular, he wanted Faith to know, was a devout Christian who carried his Bible with him into the trenches. Collin liked manning his post with Brady, he said, because he was sure it gave him a bit of insurance.

His letter was addressed to them all, and after a few paragraphs of general conversation, he included separate sections devoted to each, ending with several pages for Charity. After reading most of the letter aloud to the family, Charity excused herself and hurried to her room, where she pored over her pages until she had them memorized.

Even though it was early November, Ireland's mild temperatures lured the children outdoors for games of Red Rover and Snatch the Bacon while Marcy worked and chatted with Bridget in the garden. Beth, who was working her way through her grandmother's book collection, was delighted to discover a bookworm named Patricia who lived several houses down. They would debate plots of their favorite novels for hours, either lazing under the massive oak in Bridget's front yard or gliding on rope swings down at Patricia's house.

Even Charity had ventured out to explore the shops Patrick had told her about. It was no surprise to any of them—least of all Bridget, who forged a particularly close bond with Charity in one short week—that she came bounding home with news of her employment. She was to begin work on Monday, the same day as Faith, at a darling boutique that would also allow discounted purchases for herself and her family. Marcy had never seen Charity so excited, except, of course, where Collin was concerned, and her heart was grateful that things seemed to be working out so well.

Thank you, Lord, for your hand in our lives, she thought, and wished Patrick could be here to see it. But God's hand was, she had no doubt, upon her husband's life as well, and she longed for the day they would finally share all the wonderful things God had done. But for now, there was certainly no question about it. For each of them, it had been a most remarkable week.

16

"Why do I have to take her? Why can't Brune?"

Michael Reardon had never seen Mitch Dennehy quite this agitated. He wondered if he was once again disengaging himself from some lovesick girl who actually believed she could encroach upon his bachelorhood. Michael stared at his best department editor and smiled patiently. "Come on, Mitch, simmer down. It's not a big deal. Just give her what nobody else wants to do, and you'll be thanking me in the morning."

Mitch leaned his hands on Michael's desk and glared at his editor through blue eyes that seemed a bit bloodshot—or maybe he was just seeing red—and Michael could tell he wasn't buying it.

"The devil I will! Let Brune thank you in the morning. I don't have time to break in some kid still wet behind the ears. How do you know she can even write?"

Michael breathed in deeply and then sighed, too tired to take anyone on this morning, much less incur the wrath of his most bullheaded employee. There was clearly nothing to do but pull rank. He stood up from his desk, which was piled high with stacks of press sheets, ringed coffee cups, and dirty ashtrays, and glared right back into the face of the *Time*'s second most stubborn journalist. "You don't have a choice, Mitch. She's yours, not Brune's, and I'll be dashed if I'm going to stand here and argue with you about it. I've read a few things she's written, and they're not bad—"

"Not bad? Well, now that's just great! A glowing endorsement if I ever heard one."

"She's got a strong feel for special interest, Mitch. That's your department, and I want you to use her—case closed." Michael sat down and shuffled through the papers on his desk, hoping it was a clear dismissal to the man who stood glowering before him. He didn't hold out much hope.

"Okay, Michael, you win. I'll take her, but I'll warn you right now I'm not about to pussyfoot around some little princess who thinks she can waltz into our newsroom just because she happens to be a daughter of a friend of yours. I'm gonna work her hard, so hard she'll be crying to her daddy about how awful it is. And you, my friend, won't be able to yank her by the hair fast enough to fling her in the direction of Brune, guaranteed!"

Michael waited until Mitch stormed away before opening his drawer to reach for the aspirin. It wasn't particularly unusual for Mitch to give him a headache, but this one had the feel of a real doozy. He was glad he had a weekend to recover before the real migraine hit on Monday. Michael grabbed a cup of cold coffee, slammed the aspirin in his mouth, and took a swig. He hoped Patrick O'Connor's daughter was one-tenth the journalist her father was, or he would have to buy stock in aspirin. As it was, with Mitch around, he bought 'em by the gross just to get through a day. *Maybe*, he thought, *the headache will be so bad I'll have to stay home.* He smiled. Mitch Dennehy was one lucky character. Because if he wasn't the best journalist on the *Times*, he would have been history—and Michael Reardon headache-free—a very long time ago.

It seemed such an awful contradiction to Patrick—the ethereal beauty of the French countryside defiled by miles of makeshift trenches that snaked along the Marne River, uprooting its simple splendor. And yet Patrick feared the day coming when the contradiction would be greater still. For the moment, the trenches were used to provide soldiers with rigorous training for trench warfare that was sure to come. But he knew the day loomed when the exercises would not simply be for training but for the liberation of Europe, and the bullets and blood spent would be more than real.

He was, of course, grateful the commander of the American Expeditionary Force, General "Black Jack" Pershing, seemed bent on maintaining the integrity of the AEF until he deemed the soldiers fit for combat. After four short weeks, Patrick was already in better shape than he'd been in his life, gladly welcoming all training and conditioning the army chose to expend prior to his marching into battle in the spring.

Patrick was anxious to write Marcy. There'd been precious little time to do so upon his arrival, and he wanted to take full advantage now that his commander had afforded them the opportunity of a twenty-four-hour leave. He was quick to head to the billet, the farmland buildings that housed the soldiers, eager to stretch out in his bunk, even if it was only hay, to compose the letter he knew she would be waiting for.

"Hey, O'Connor, a group of us are heading to the big city for some fun. Why don't you join us?" LaRue, one of his bunk mates, was in great spirits as he poked his head in the barracks.

Patrick grinned. "Not tonight, I'm afraid. I've got to write a long-overdue letter to the love of my life. I don't think she'd take too kindly to my seeing the sights of Paris, at least not the sights you plan on seeing."

LaRue laughed. "Neither would my missus, but she's

not around, now is she? Come on, Patrick, you can write that letter anytime."

Patrick hesitated, then thought better of it. He'd heard stories about Paris, and all he wanted right now were moments alone to dream of Marcy and tell her how much he missed her.

"Maybe another time, LaRue. Right now, I'm too lonely for my wife."

LaRue shook his head. "I guarantee you, Patrick, this would be the cure for that, but don't say I didn't tell ya."

Patrick waved him off and closed his eyes to think of Marcy, an aching loneliness suddenly overwhelming him. He thought about the last night they'd spent together, and he felt passion enflame as he lay in the dirty confines of the billet.

"Oh, God, please give me the strength I need for this place, and give Marcy the strength she needs too." He reached for pen and paper and settled in to write his family, assuring them the only malady befallen him was the excruciating pain he experienced at missing them all. And aside from that, all was well on the Marne.

It was certainly a comedy of errors—Charity and Faith scrambling to get ready while their mother looked on, beaming with excitement while she helped Beth and Steven prepare for their first day of school. Faith stood, her stomach rolling as she banged on the door of the water closet currently occupied by Charity. A sour taste rose in her throat. She snatched the towel slung over her shoulder and pressed it to her mouth. After a moment, her throat cleared, and she took a deep breath. "For pity's sake, Charity, I don't feel well, and I'm going to be late. Open the door!"

"It's my first day on the job, and I don't want to rush it." Charity's voice was curt.

Faith's "Irish" flared. "It's mine too, and if you don't hurry, I won't have a first day on the job. Mother!"

Marcy came bounding down the hall, a serene smile on her face. Patting Faith's arm, she tapped on the water-closet door, her knock considerably more gentle than her daughter's had been. With a pleasant voice, almost sing-song in tone, she addressed the daughter in possession of the bathroom. "Good morning, Charity, open the door, please. Faith needs to use the privy too. You'll just have to share the bath this morning and work out your morning routine later."

The door swung wide, and Charity stepped out with a smug smile on her face, looking perfectly wonderful. "I'm ready, Mother," she announced, giving Faith a pointed look.

"You look lovely, Charity. Faith, it's all yours," her mother said with a smile.

Faith desperately wished she had some of the calm her mother seemed to exude this morning. She could certainly do with a bit of it, she thought as she looked in the mirror, aghast at the dark circles beneath her eyes. Never—since her affliction with polio as a child—had she been so scared. Not even her first day at the *Herald* came close to producing the nausea and fear now churning in her stomach. Starting in the typing pool at the *Herald* with her father close by for moral support was one thing. Taking a position as a junior copywriter on a strange paper in a strange city was completely and totally unnerving. Faith hoped and prayed she could get through the day without throwing up.

The stress she was feeling must have been written on her face as she entered the kitchen, because her mother shushed Charity as she started to comment. Taking her arm, she ushered Faith to a chair. "Here, sit down and eat your breakfast. I'll get you some coffee."

Faith perched on the edge of the seat, face ashen despite a healthy application of rouge.

"A little scared, are you now?" Charity asked with a smile.

Her mother shot Charity a look of warning and set the cup of coffee before Faith. "The first day is always the hardest, but God will see you through. Trust me, you'll be fine. More than fine, you'll be wonderful."

Faith took a deep breath, easing some of the tightness she felt in her chest. She nodded. "I know, Mother. Will you pray for me, please?"

Marcy reached for both daughters' hands and closed her eyes. "Lord, be with my girls today as they begin their new jobs. Don't let them feel alone. Be with them and guide them and give them your favor. Amen." Marcy's eyes popped open, her smile positively radiant. "You have absolutely nothing to worry about. God is going to bless you both. I can feel it!"

Thirty minutes later, Faith would have given anything to "feel it" as she stood on Lower Abbey Street staring up at the *Irish Times*. Unfortunately, the only thing she could feel was pure indigestion. She swallowed hard and unbuttoned her pleated woolen coat to better adjust her new green hobble skirt. She tried to tug it down; she was self-conscious over the new stylish length that fell to midcalf, exposing flesh-tone silk stockings. Her fingers trembled as she tucked her starched V-necked blouse in a bit tighter before nervously patting her loose chignon. Taking a deep breath, she forged through the front doors, praying the awful taste in her throat was only heartburn and not an indication she was about to be sick.

Her smile at the receptionist was shaky, at best. "I'm here to see Mr. Michael Reardon, please," she managed with no more damage than a slight blush to her cheeks. The woman smiled coolly and pointed her to the newsroom through a set of double doors. Once inside, Faith felt somewhat better as she encountered the familiar buzz of a newsroom. It was certainly not as hectic as the *Herald*, to be sure, but bustling nonetheless, alive with the frenzy of publishing the most important paper in Ireland. Faith stood there, entranced by it all, her nervous fear giving way to an edgy excitement at the prospect of what this building might hold for her.

"Hello! You must be Patrick's girl. Welcome, young lady."

She turned to look into the kindly face of Michael Reardon. Any trepidation she may have felt was ousted by the welcoming smile spreading across his broad face. He was older than her father, she guessed, by as much as twenty years, but his eyes had a youthful sparkle when he smiled, which immediately put her at ease. He was heavyset but somewhat small of stature, and Faith had the distinct feeling he garnered as much respect from his colleagues as a man ten feet tall. She liked him immediately.

"Yes, hello, Mr. Reardon. Thank you so much for allowing me to work here. I promise I will do my best not to disappoint you."

"I have no doubt whatsoever, young lady, that you will prove your father proud. Shall we step into my office and chat?" He held the door as he beamed at her, his pin-striped vest straining at the buttons.

An odd mix of anticipation and affection bubbled in her chest. "I'd like that, sir," she breathed, and sank into a chair as he closed the door behind.

Michael Reardon lounged in the chair, idly tapping a pencil against his lips. He observed her striking auburn hair pulled back into a neat chignon and her glowing enthusiasm, and immediately a sense of dread invaded his soul. She seemed so young, so fresh, so innocent—inevitably the type Mitch found himself attracted to before discarding as easily as yesterday's news. Perhaps Mitch had been right. Perhaps she should have been assigned to Brune. Michael thought about Patrick and wondered what he would want him to do. He blinked, suddenly aware Faith had stopped speaking.

Her brows crimped in concern. "Are you all right, Mr. Reardon?"

"Oh, I'm sorry, Faith. I'm afraid I wandered off, thinking about your father. He was a great friend of mine at the *Herald*, you know, and I was quite distraught to learn he went to fight in this nasty war. Have you heard from him yet?"

"No, sir, not yet. It's only been a month since he left, so we didn't expect to for a while."

"Yes, of course. Now, dear, what were you saying?" Michael gave her his undivided attention for a brief moment before his mind strayed once again. His arm swung to scratch the back of his balding head with a pencil. Patrick had written that she had just turned twenty, but she had this air of wide-eyed innocence that made her appear more like sixteen. Michael could tell she was going to bring out the father in him, especially where Mitch was concerned. The thought produced an immediate pain in his head.

"I'm very excited to have the opportunity to work here, Mr. Reardon. I'll do anything, anything at all. No job is beneath me, sir. I'm just so grateful for the chance to write. I'll do my very best, I can promise you that."

Michael stood and smiled as he extended his hand to help her up. "I don't have any doubt, my dear. Come, follow me." He steered her toward a group of colleagues gathered at the back of the newsroom. "You're just in time for your department meeting. I'll introduce you to the people you'll be working with."

"Good morning, Michael. You running the meeting this morning?"

Michael cocked his brow as he eyed Jamie, the man who addressed him. "What do you mean? Where's Mitch?"

"You tell me, Boss," Jamie said, his gaze traveling past Michael to Faith. Michael snorted. He pushed past Jamie, who leaned against the door, observing through horn-rimmed glasses.

Heat crept up the back of Michael's neck as he peered into Mitch's empty office. He turned to the group with a low growl. "Okay, everybody—inside. Does anybody know where His Highness is this morning? Bridie? Jamie? Kathleen?"

Michael surveyed the group, all of whom shrugged their shoulders and averted their gaze on anything other than his face. Hands on his hips, Michael zeroed in on Kathleen, whose gaze was, for the moment, completely captivated by a crumpled piece of paper on the floor.

"Kathleen?"

Her eyes flicked up, as if startled, and a soft blush oozed up her cheeks that came close to matching the rose-colored blouse she wore. "Honestly, Michael, I don't know where he is. Haven't seen him," she uttered softly, her gaze returning to the fascinating trash on the floor.

"Not since last night, anyway," someone muttered.

Michael shot a searing glance at Bridie, whose remark sent another shot of color into Kathleen's cheeks.

Bridie's hazel eyes flashed before they congealed to ocher-green. She smoothed a trembling hand against silver hair haphazardly flung into a makeshift topknot. "What? It's true now, isn't it? Everyone knows she was with Mitch last night at Brody's. He's probably just hung over, that's all."

Fatigue seeped into Michael's bones as he stared, first at Bridie, then at Kathleen, who still avoided his gaze. He rubbed the bridge of his nose with the palm of his hand and sighed. He could feel a headache coming on. "Kathleen, darlin', can you at least tell me if he's planning on gracing us with his presence today?"

"I think so," she whispered.

Bridie rolled her eyes.

"Okay, then, let's get this meeting over with so we can all go back to work." Michael pushed his way into Mitch's office and plopped into his chair. A high-pitched squeal sounded as he sloped back and propped his short legs on Mitch's desk, ignoring the galley sheets strewn across it. The rest of the crew filed in and dispersed around the small office, the ladies occupying the few chairs in the room while the men lumbered to the perimeter.

"The first order of business this morning is to introduce our newest staff member, Faith O'Connor. Faith comes to us from the *Boston Herald*, where she was a copywriter, and a mighty good one," Michael said, stretching the truth a wee bit. He nodded at Faith, which prompted a blush to burnish her cheeks when all eyes focused on her.

"She and her family are staying in Dublin with her grandmother while her father and brother are fighting in France. I don't know how long Faith will be with us; that depends on the war, I suppose. But we can certainly use some stretching in the special-interest department, what with the gloom of war on everybody's mind. And that's where we intend to use her. Any questions?"

"Special interest—that's my territory, Michael. Just exactly what is she going to be writing?" Bridie bristled.

"Now, don't go getting uppity on me, Bridie. You're my feature writer, and nothing's going to change that. All I'm asking is you show Faith the ropes and give her anything you don't want to do. She's willing to start anywhere."

"Yeah, well the loo could certainly use a good scrubbing," Bridie mumbled. Several of the men snickered.

Faith's cheeks continued to flame as she stared at the floor.

Michael's demand for respect was about to be engaged as he swung his legs off the desk and leaned forward in the chair, eyes locked on Bridie's face with deadly precision. "You presently work on one of the finest newspapers in the world, Mrs. O'Halloran, and it would behoove you to act like it. You're not slumming at Brody's, and I'm not an editor who takes kindly to petty jealousies. Do I make myself clear?"

It was quite obvious to everyone in the room that he did. Bridie nodded.

"Good. Now, let's move on with the introductions. Faith, this is the motley crew you'll be forced to work with. They may seem rough around the edges, and trust me, they are, but I think you'll soon discover why we keep them around. In this room are some of the finest journalists in Ireland, and I have no doubt whatsoever that you'll learn from each and every one of them." Michael turned and pointed to an elderly man leaning against a cabinet. "That's Aiden McCrae, our hard news and financial genius. Keeps us on top as one of the finest financial papers in the world."

Aiden nodded, and Faith smiled. Michael continued the introductions, wagging his hand next at Jamie, who was in charge of editorials and book reviews and one of the few in the room whose face reflected a genuine welcome. Several of the men grunted as they were introduced. Faith nodded politely at each while Michael went down the line, pointing out the names, talents, and sometimes humorous flaws of the ten employees in the room.

Michael introduced her to Jack and felt a quickening in his gut when Faith nodded abruptly. He noted that she quickly dropped her gaze to the floor. The young pressman lounged against the door frame, lips curled as he assessed Faith through hooded eyes. Michael cleared his throat and waved his hand at the women who sat on either side of her. "Kathleen is the proofreader for Mitch's department, and then, of course, you already know Bridie, our 'senior' feature writer."

Kathleen managed a shy smile as she coiled a thick strand of chestnut hair around her finger. Bridie merely grunted in the grand fashion of most of the men in the room.

"And that's everybody, except, of course, the man they all answer to . . . that is, when he's here." Michael had a habit of rubbing his head every time he spoke of Mitch, as he did now. "Mitch Dennehy is department editor for news, editorials, and features, and regrettably, one of the best in the business, or I would have fired his sorry—" Michael blinked, a colorful word stuck in his throat. "Well, let's just say he wouldn't be punching a clock at the *Times*." He slanted back in the chair with a loud screech, hands behind his head, and surveyed the room. His feet were back on the desk. "So, Aiden, on the McGettigan scandal—any new leads?"

Aiden proceeded to update them on the financial woes of one of Ireland's most prolific companies when the door flew open, causing a breeze—and according to rumor, a dangerously attractive man—to blow into the office. Michael frowned as all conversation and action came to a halt, not an uncommon thing when Mitch Dennehy entered a room. Michael's eyes flitted toward Faith, then back to Mitch. He squinted, attempting to see what others saw when confronted with Mitch for the very first time. He was tall and muscular, an obvious fact despite the stylish single-breasted sack suit he wore over a starched white shirt. He appeared to border on burly, rather like an overgrown man in a child's playhouse, and his black necktie was loosened as if it were the end of a day rather than the beginning. He carried himself with such an air of authority that people were prone to step back and let him pass, like the parting of the Red Sea. Michael's nerves itched as he glanced at Faith. She, too, was staring along with the rest at this charismatic man whom Bridie had once proclaimed "far too masculine a creature to have eyes so amazingly blue."

"Sorry I'm late," he stated without the least bit of repentance, "but I had to work late last night and needed to sleep in."

Michael regarded Mitch through narrowed eyes, struggling to keep his lips from twitching into a smile. In some ways, Mitch was like a son to him. Unfortunately, in many others, he was the bane of his existence. Michael elevated his chin in an effort to ward off the inclination to shake his head. So pervasive was Mitch's influence over his subordinates that not one of them was willing to utter the clever comments that surely rested on the tips of their tongues. Instead, each simply nodded their acknowledgment of his presence.

Michael coughed. "Mmm . . . yes, well, you were late and I'm running this meeting now, so lean back and listen. Maybe you'll learn a little something about managerial style." His tone had an acidic edge that stopped Mitch in his tracks as he crossed the room. It did nothing, however, for the look on his face, which was clearly annoyed.

"Michael, I'm here now. I'll take over," Mitch insisted.

Michael leaned forward in the chair, his eyes pure granite. "I *said*, I'm running the meeting now. You abdicated that responsibility when you came through that door forty-five minutes late. Sit down!"

Nobody breathed as Mitch propped enormous hands on the desk, his blue eyes volatile as he loomed over Michael like a plague. Their gazes locked for several seconds while friction sizzled in the air. Neither man blinked. With a ragged breath, Mitch slowly rose, towering to his full height. A low growl rumbled in his throat as he stabbed through his short blond hair in frustration, causing the natural curl to look even more disheveled. He sulked all the way to the back of the room, and Michael savored the victory with a silent sigh. It was a standoff that could result in only one winner. And other than Faith, everyone in the room knew that when it came to confrontation with Mitch, Michael was one of the few men who could walk away with the title.

Michael calmly continued on, conducting the business of the meeting to its completion while Mitch scowled in the back of the room. At its conclusion, Michael looked up and nodded toward Faith. "Mitch, this is your new copywriter, Faith O'Connor. I want her to tag along with Bridie this first week or so, just to get her feet wet." He turned to Faith. "Faith, *this* . . ." Michael said with a touch of drama, "is your manager, Mitch Dennehy."

Faith turned in her seat to acknowledge Mitch, whose frosty gaze shifted from her face, down to her new leather shoes, and back up again. His blue eyes assessed her so completely that her cheeks bruised crimson as she stiffened in the chair, chin thrust high. "Hello, Mr. Dennehy," she said, her tone polite but cool.

Mitch didn't say a word, only eyed her with practiced superiority, and the blush on her cheeks spread like blight in the rainy season. Michael watched in fascination as a smile fluttered on his department editor's lips. Mitch's penetrating blue eyes drifted from the tiny hands pinched white in Faith's lap to the soft tendril of hair that curved the nape of her neck.

"Michael tells me you were a copywriter at the *Boston Herald*, is that right?"

Faith hesitated, then sucked in a shaky breath. "Yes. I mean, I did write some copy . . ."

Mitch nodded. His cocky smile worked its way into a grin. "Some copy? Have you done any feature writing before?" He was waiting. They were all waiting.

The hot stain on her cheeks was a permanent condition now. "No, I haven't done much feature writing, exactly . . ."

"Any reviews, editorials, hard news?"

She tensed as if straddling a mule about to buck. "No, I'm afraid I don't have much experience doing any of that . . ."

"Well, then, Miss O'Connor," he mused, his eyes laughing at her, "tell me. Is there anything you can do?"

The air stilled to a deathly hush. Slowly, she lifted her chin to stare at him with as much defiance as she could politely display. "Yes, sir," she said, producing a smile that was anything but. "I can be on time."

It was a bombshell poor Mitch never saw coming, and the impact blasted his face with a ruddy shade of unease. Bridie couldn't contain herself and laughed out loud, creating a ripple effect of laughter that tittered through the room. It rose to such a level of hilarity that even Michael had tears in his eyes.

Reaching for his handkerchief, Michael stood, still chortling as he wiped the wetness from his face. "Well, now, I can see you do know how to run a meeting, Mitch, so my usefulness here is over, I suspect. Faith, I know it's hard to believe right now, but you'll learn a lot from this pigheaded editor of yours. Just let me know if he gives you any trouble."

He laughed and winked at her as he headed for the door, a smile permanently on his face for the duration of the day, he was sure. It wasn't often he got to witness Mitch Dennehy being put in his place by a woman. He suspected the experience was supremely more effective than aspirin in curing any headaches inflicted by his temperamental department editor.

He entered his office and sat down at his desk, exhaling deeply, feeling almost relaxed. He had worried about Faith

O'Connor, that Mitch might chew her up and spit her out, but the fear no longer needled him. She may be slight of stature and "still wet behind the ears" as Mitch had said, but she seemed more than enough woman to deal with the likes of him, and Michael relished the thought of further such encounters.

"She's a pistol," Michael said to himself as he thought of Patrick. "You did good, my friend, and so, I'm quite sure, will she."

17

"Well? How was it?" Marcy hurried into the room after tending to Mima, bubbling with excitement over her two girls' first days at work. She set plates of steaming lamb stew before each daughter and stepped back to wait, hands clasped in anticipation.

Charity's excitement seemed nearly equal to her mother's. She quickly divulged the full extent of her day—from her brief training on the cash register to balancing the ledger at the end of business. The highlight had been, she announced with pink in her cheeks, discovering that one of her sales had been the biggest sale of the day. "Honestly, Mother, I never thought I would like working so much. Mrs. Shaw is wonderful, so kind and encouraging. And the customers, my goodness, they were so pleasant! And prosperous, judging from the amounts they spent."

"Did you meet any young men, my dear?" Bridget asked in an innocent tone.

Charity gave her a teasing smile. "A few, Grandmother, but I already told you, I'm taken. Or, at least, 'almost taken.' And, after reading Collin's last letter, I'd say it's more likely I'm completely unavailable."

"Mmm. We'll call you 'unavailable' when there's a ring on your finger, my dear," Bridget remarked dryly. "Till then, you're too pretty to waste on 'almost taken.'"

Charity laughed, seemingly unaffected by her grand-mother's remark. "As a matter of fact, I did see a few young men who turned my head, and I theirs. I have to admit, Grandmother, it did feel good to have young men notice me again."

"They never stopped noticing," Marcy said. "Once Collin came into the picture, it was you who stopped noticing them."

"I know," she whispered, her thoughts obviously on Collin. She swooped up her spoon and smiled brightly. "Well, I suppose a little competition might do him good. He is rather sure of himself, isn't he?"

"*Cocky* sounds like a better word to me," Bridget said.

Marcy eyed her mother, raising her brows in warning. "Mother, please! I know what I've told you in the past, but Collin's nearly a member of our family. We all love him a great deal." Marcy winced as she noticed a rush of rose in Faith's cheeks. She clamped her lips closed.

"Mmmm . . . sounds a bit too much of a rogue to suit me, if you know what I mean." Bridget pursed her lips.

"Mother!" Marcy's eyes widened in shock. "Really, you forget that the right woman can tame the rogue in any man. Look at Patrick; you swore he would break my heart, and he's the love of my life."

Bridget smiled. "Yes, he is. And there's no doubt in my mind I was completely wrong about him," she said with a twinkle in her eye. "Either that, or the boatload of prayers I said took full effect."

Marcy's mouth dropped open before she closed it with a smile. She shook her head and laughed, reaching for a piece of bread. She ignored Bridget and turned to Faith. "And you, Faith, how did your day go?"

"I think it went well, for the most part."

"What do you mean 'for the most part'? What part didn't go well?" Marcy asked, buttering her bread.

"Well, I love the main editor, Michael Reardon—he's Father's friend from the *Herald*, you know. He's very kind and protective, and I really like that. Most of the people seem nice enough, I suppose. Although I don't think this older woman liked me at first." Faith stopped talking to swallow a mouthful of stew. "But then she seemed to warm up after our morning meeting, and I think I'm really going to like her. She's the one training me this week."

"What's her name?" Marcy asked.

"Bridie . . . O'Halloran, I believe. She's a widow who went to work at the *Times* a number of years back, not long after her husband passed away. I think he worked there too, and that's how Michael knew her. She has several older children, at least in high school. She's such a character, Mother. She made me laugh the entire day."

"Any young men catch your eye?" Bridget ventured, relentless in her pursuit of romance for her granddaughters.

Faith laughed. "Well, maybe. There's a young man named Jamie who happens to be our department editor's right-hand man. He's in charge of editorials and book reviews. He's kind of cute in a bookish sort of way."

"Anybody else?" Apparently Bridget had no time for subtleties.

"Not really, although there is this kind of rough-looking man named Jack who stared a hole through me. I suppose you could say he was handsome in a dark sort of way. He gave me the chills the whole time he looked at me, though."

"Was that the part that didn't go well?" Marcy inquired.

Faith scrunched her nose. "No, that wasn't it. I hate to say this, but I think I got off on the wrong foot with my immediate supervisor."

Marcy felt her heart catch. "What do you mean?"

Faith sighed. "Well, he came in forty-five minutes late for a meeting he was supposed to be running, only Michael had to fill in because Mitch wasn't there."

"Mitch?"

"Mitch Dennehy, my supervisor. Then, after Michael introduced me, Mitch started picking at me, asking what I'd done before. Honestly, Mother, the man was downright rude."

Marcy's spoon drifted to her plate as her eyes went wide. "Oh no, Faith, tell me you didn't mouth off to him. Please tell me you were respectful."

Faith's chin lifted. "As respectful as he deserved, Mother. He's arrogant and a complete bully. Everyone in the department is afraid to even open their mouths. Well, I'm not. He's nothing but an egotistical womanizer who just happens to have the good fortune of being a great journalist."

"No, he just *happens* to be your manager, young lady, and I think you need to adjust your attitude accordingly."

"A womanizer? How do you know that? What does he look like?" Charity was suddenly breathless with curiosity.

Faith shot her a scathing look. "You would be interested, wouldn't you? Well, he thinks he's God's gift to the women of Ireland—and probably the world."

"Is he tall, dark, what? Come on, Faith, what does he look like? Is he good-looking?"

"Yes, he's good-looking, all right? Very good-looking, if you must know—very tall, very muscular, and very blue eyes. But I'm telling you, his obnoxious personality ruins any attraction. All I want to do is punch the clock, do my job, and stay out of his way."

"Promise you'll be a good girl, Faith, please?" Marcy began, her tone pleading. "Promise you'll be nice to him? I know your temper can get the best of you sometimes."

Faith sighed and squeezed her mother's hand. "I promise, Mother. I'll do my very best to be civil to him, honestly I will."

"Sounds like a pretty tall order to me," Charity said with a grin as she buttered a piece of bread. "So . . . any chance we'll get to meet this man of the world?"

"In your dreams," Faith mumbled.

Charity laughed out loud. "Or your nightmares," she countered, and promptly helped herself to another plate of stew.

"Come on, Brady, you could use a night off from that Bible of yours. Don't you ever get tired of reading that thing?"

Collin looked at Brady, who was stretched out on his bunk with the Bible in his lap, and decided he'd never met anyone so absorbed in God. Except for Faith, of course. He wondered if that was the reason Brady fascinated him so. He had the same intensity and passion in his eyes when he spoke about God—which he did a lot—as Collin had seen in Faith over the many months he'd battled with her. Normally Collin wouldn't have chosen someone like Brady as a friend. But they'd been assigned to the same billet and the same trench, and in no time at all, Collin found himself drawn to this man, despite his obvious obsession with morality. In fact, he was closer to Brady than to any of his drinking buddies; sometimes the two of them would talk for hours on end about anything at all.

Occasionally, Brady broached the subject of God, and Collin would feel his defenses going up, prompting a grin from Brady. "Can't run away from it forever, Collin. Eventually you'll have to make your peace with God. Sooner or later, everyone does. I just hope it's sooner. Later would be a real shame."

And then Collin would get mad and storm out, opting

for an evening spent at the nearest place he could buy the most drink for his money. There were times when Collin would return to their barracks so drunk that Brady would hoist him up on his bunk rather than let him pass out on the dirt floor. Collin supposed it was during one of those moments of drunken rambling when Brady found out about Faith. The first time Brady mentioned her name, a cold chill slid through Collin like a slow-motion avalanche. He wondered how the man could even know about Faith when he hadn't mentioned her to anyone.

"So, this girl named Faith—pretty devoted to God?" Brady casually asked during one of their many training exercises.

Collin positioned his weapon, pretending not to hear.

"Who is she?" Brady asked again, causing a twinge in Collin's gut.

"Nobody," Collin snapped, his jaw tight as he peered through the sight of his gun.

"Yeah, nobody you just happen to talk about till you pass out in one of your drunken stupors. Come on, Collin, who is she?" Brady adjusted his own weapon, then looked up, his face pinched with impatience.

Collin sighed. "I would have never let them put me in a trench with you had I known you'd be so nosy. She's nobody—just the sister of my fiancée, or my ex-fiancée, I guess."

"You're engaged?" Brady's jaw sagged in shock. "And you're out every chance you get, looking for women?"

Collin grinned. "Why not? I'm a red-blooded American male, and I already told you, I'm not engaged anymore. At least, not till after the war."

Brady slumped against the trench as if Collin had shoved him there. He shook his head. "So help me, McGuire, I had no idea you were so mixed up. I thought you were just strutting your stuff till you met the right woman and settled down. But you—you met the right woman, and you're still on the hunt? When are you going to grow up, anyway?"

Collin laughed and slapped him on the back. "Never, I hope. I'm having way too much fun. And you could too, if you just cut loose every once in a while."

Brady stooped to pick up his gear. He glanced up at Collin, his eyes dark. "Is that why Faith wouldn't have you? Because you cut loose every once in a while?"

The smile on Collin's face slashed into a scowl. His eyes itched with fury. "You're a moron, you know that, Brady? What do you know about anything? She's nothing but a fanatic, just like you. You people make me sick, shoving your religion down everyone's throat. Well, I've had enough. Stay away from me, you got that?"

Collin hadn't lost his temper like that in months, not since he'd lost it with her. *Figures*, he thought as he climbed from the trench. *What is it with these people anyway that make me lose control like this?* Whatever it was, he was fed up with it.

He ignored Brady after that, as best he could, at least until the next drunk, when Brady would take care of him once again. After that, they slowly eased back into the same close relationship, except this time, Brady seemed a bit more selective about his choice of subjects.

Collin blinked back to the present and stood in the doorway, eyeing his friend. A grin pulled at his lips as he strolled to where Brady sat reading on the bunk. Leaning against the wooden bed frame, Collin used the toe of his boot to flip the Bible closed in Brady's lap. "I'm not taking no for an answer. You need a night out. You haven't taken one of the leaves they've given us. Besides, you can help keep me honest for my ex-fiancée."

Brady cocked his head. "Okay, you're on. Where we going?"

Collin laughed. "To heaven, Brady, to heaven." He slapped his arm around Brady's shoulder before his friend could change his mind and almost dragged him to the door. "Hey, lookie here, boys—we got ourselves a guardian angel," he called to a group of soldiers waiting on him. They started whooping and yelling.

Brady smiled and shook his head as he climbed into the mule-drawn wagon next to Collin. "Something tells me you guys need more than a guardian angel."

Collin grinned. "You got that right. But don't worry, old buddy. Where we're going there'll be plenty of angels, I promise."

"That's what I'm afraid of," Brady replied wryly, appearing to settle back to enjoy the ride.

Mitch hadn't been late for almost two months now. He didn't dare. The last thing he wanted was to encounter a smug smile on that pretty face of hers. Not that she seemed prone to that. On the contrary, since her first day, she'd been the model employee—always smiling, always working hard, *always on time*. Oh, occasionally he took pleasure in picking at her in the Monday meetings, just to see the sparks fly, but for the most part, she'd managed to keep that temper under wraps. It was enough to make him crazy. She had the knack of being as polite and courteous as he was gruff, but deep in his gut, he sensed she didn't approve of him. And that was a reaction he didn't get from many people, and even fewer women.

He had never had a woman stand up to him before, unless you counted Bridie, which he didn't. Bridie and he went way back. Her husband had been his best friend, a fact that allowed Bridie to think she could take more liberties with him than others did. Sometimes he let her, sometimes he didn't, depending upon his mood. Either way, Bridie was not the threat that Faith O'Connor seemed to be.

She actually could write, he discovered, and it surprised him how quickly she adapted to the pace and deadlines of the *Times*. She did, indeed, appear to have ink in her veins, as Michael liked to say, obviously inherited from her editor-father who, according to Michael, was one of the best in the business.

Despite the rocky start, she fit in well with his group. A little too well with Jamie, to suit his tastes. The two of them were almost inseparable. And he noticed Jack seemed to spend less time with the presses and more time sitting on her desk these days. It was natural, he supposed, that a pretty face would do that to the men in his department, but it galled him nonetheless. She was here to work, not to provide them with a social life, and he'd be hung up to dry if she thought she was going to hook a husband on his time.

She got on well with both Bridie, who took on the unlikely role of Mother Hen, and Kathleen, who thoroughly enjoyed jabbering with her. Although Mitch didn't have the slightest idea how they could gab through an entire lunch hour and then some. Without question, she got along famously with everyone—everyone except him—and for some reason he couldn't explain, it was driving him up the wall.

"O'Connor," he yelled, "get in here!"

Faith's head jerked up. She stared at Bridie with saucer eyes that strained wide with apprehension. She swallowed a lump in her throat. "It's five o'clock," she whispered. "What could he possibly want?"

Bridie grinned and hunched her shoulders. "Who knows, maybe he's going to give you a raise. You've been doing great, you know." She grabbed her coat and headed for the door.

"Bridie, wait! Are you sure?" Faith put a hand to her stomach and breathed in slowly.

"O'Connor, are ya deaf? Get in here!"

Bridie blew her a kiss. "Yes, Faith, I'm sure. See ya Monday—I hope."

Faith managed a smirk and adjusted her starched white blouse and plaid woolen skirt before tentatively approaching his office door. The moment she stepped over the threshold, she could smell the musky scent of the soap he used, and her stomach fluttered. He leaned back in his chair facing the window, a newspaper in his hands. He was so absorbed in what he was reading, he didn't look up, which was fine with her. For once, she could watch him unaware, something she seldom did, and in fact, took great pains to avoid.

Charity had been right. Mitch Dennehy was, by any definition, a "man of the world," and Faith hated herself for being so intrigued. Of course, the fact he was considerably older than she, quite attractive, and very bright had something to do with it as well. Sometimes she found herself wishing she worked for someone more like Michael, someone fatherly and comfortable. Mitch Dennehy was thirty-four—only five years younger than her own father—but working for him was anything but comfortable. For pity's sake, he was her supervisor! She didn't like the feelings he provoked—flushes and palpitations every time he looked her way. It was maddening, and Faith made a mental note to subject these annoying feelings to some serious prayer.

"O'Connor! Where the—" he bellowed without even looking up, and she cleared her throat, catching those blue eyes by surprise as he spun around in the chair. His face broke into a grin, and her pulse took off. *Probably because he scares me half to death*, she reasoned before something clicked in her brain. The last time her heart had raced like this was with Collin. Faith swallowed a gulp, realizing what that meant.

"Don't just stand there, O'Connor, come in and sit down. You look like I'm gonna bite your head off."

He grinned again, and Faith sat down, her nerves prickling under her skin like a foot fallen asleep. She perched on the edge of the chair, suspended between an adrenaline high and a bout of nausea. Her eyes focused hard on the wood grain of his desk. Her brain was whirling. *Okay, just keep thinking: he's almost as old as my father . . . He's almost as old as my father . . .*

Mitch studied her blanched face and was tempted to rile her, just to rouse a little fire in those green eyes. How she could go from this nervous, scared little thing to a spitfire in record time was beyond him. All he knew was when she did, he was so bloomin' attracted to her he couldn't think straight. He should have known this would happen. She was just the type that always managed to trap him. Thank goodness it was never for long.

He rose and ambled to the door to shut it, and the click of the lock drained all color from her cheeks. He restrained a grin as he returned to his chair to settle in. "O'Connor, I have to give it to you—you surprised me. Your writing is fresh and honest, and I like how you've managed to fit in." He hesitated, squinting at her. "Jack's not giving you problems, is he?"

She was just a desk away, and he could tell she was jumpy as she picked at her nails and straddled the edge of her seat. She usually managed to avoid being anywhere near him, except during the Monday meetings, which didn't matter because the room was filled with people. But now, here she was, barely inches away and so close he could almost feel her breath on his face. He leaned forward, and she shivered. "Is he giving you problems, O'Connor, 'cause if he is . . ."

She glanced up with wide eyes. "No! I mean, of course not. Jack's fine. At first, yes, he did scare me a bit, but now that I've gotten to know him, well, I think he's just fine."

Mitch sank back in the chair. "You and Jamie seem pretty close," he said, eyeing her carefully.

A weak laugh tripped from her lips. "Yes, we are. Jamie's great."

His jaw stiffened, and he forced a smile. "Good, good."

She straightened in the chair, raising her chin. "Was . . . there anything else you wanted to talk about, sir?"

She always called him "sir," had from the first day he laid eyes on her, and it never bothered him before. Suddenly it made him feel old, and he didn't like that one bit. Blooming saints, he was only thirty-four. And younger women were his specialty, weren't they? His mood darkened as reality cast a shadow on his conscience. Yes, but not this young, he realized. She was only twenty—and two months, to be exact—yet somehow it hurt too much to do the math in his head. He took a deep breath and pushed his chair back from the desk.

"No, O'Connor," he said, his smile gone sour. "That's all. Just wanted you to know you're doing a great job. Keep it up." He shuffled papers on his desk, avoiding her eyes.

She rose. "Are you all right, Mr. Dennehy?" she asked, searching his face.

His jaw locked tight, and he heaved a fist on the desk. She jumped, as if the explosive sound had goosed her in the air. "No, I'm not all right, O'Connor, ya got that? 'Mr. Dennehy' sounds like I'm your father. I'm not, by a long shot. So to you and everyone who works for me, I'm Mitch, not Mr. Dennehy!"

Her eyes widened with shock as she stood inert for several

seconds. She blinked, and her body visibly relaxed as a faint smile squirmed at the edge of her lips. With a gleam in her eye, she slapped her palms on his desk and leaned in. "Understood, Mr. Dennehy. And to you and everyone who works with me, I'm Faith, not 'O'Connor.'"

His eyelids flickered in surprise. A little-boy grin tugged at his lips. He stood up. "You hungry?"

She tottered back, a pink haze on her cheeks. "Hungry?" she stammered. "For what?"

"For food. What did you think I meant?" His eyes locked on hers as he put on his jacket.

The haze whooshed to scarlet. He laughed out loud and rounded the desk to stand in front of her. She looked scared to death. It made him want to protect her and take advantage of her, all at the same time.

She stumbled against the chair. "I don't know . . . I really should be getting home . . . but I suppose I could . . . I mean, if you're hungry and all . . ."

The smile on his face creased into a grin. He took a step closer. "As a matter of fact, I'm ravenous." Before the shock could register on her face, he pulled her into his arms and kissed her, feeling a charge between them before she slammed her hand to his chest. She pressed one palm to her flushed cheek while holding him at bay with the other. "Mr. Dennehy . . . Mitch . . . what are you doing?"

"Whetting my appetite."

Her chest heaved as she jabbed him away with her fist. "Well, stop it, now!"

"Only if you'll have dinner with me."

"Yes . . . I'll have dinner with you," she sputtered, "but understand me, please—I am not on the menu!"

She backed away, arching over his desk to put as much distance between them as she possibly could. It took all the restraint he possessed not to bend right over and taste those lips once again. Her eyes widened with innocence, an unsettling reminder she was only twenty to his thirty-four. And although she was making him crazy, he knew enough to know she wasn't his usual bill of fare. She was right to fend him off. Something told him that this time, the physical attraction would just get in the way. For now, at least through dinner, a little restraint might do him good. He stepped back and offered his arm.

"Deal," he said with a grin. "Let's eat, then let's talk. We can always discuss dessert later." And with a wink, he ignored the strain on her face as he firmly tugged her to the door.

It was Saturday, the only day of the week she could sleep in. And here she was, completely awake at 6:00 a.m., her mind racing and her heart close behind. Faith stretched beneath the covers before she snuggled up again, reflecting on the events of the evening before.

Never had she imagined the two of them together. Oh, she knew he was everything most women longed for—she wasn't blind, after all—only naïve, she suspected, for she'd never even entertained the notion. He was her manager, a person she found attractive, certainly, but not a man she could date. She chewed on her lip. For pity's sake, it couldn't be wise to date your supervisor, could it? And he was closer to her father's age than to hers, she reminded herself, facts that remained the only clouds in an otherwise blindingly blue sky.

The moment he kissed her had sent shock waves jolting through her, something she hadn't felt since Collin. The thought provoked a disturbing mix of feelings. She was scared. Mitch ignited passion she'd hoped to escape, at least for a while. And she was glad. Maybe it meant she'd finally be free, free from Collin. Most disturbing of all was the sadness, the aching hesitancy to allow any man to remove Collin from her heart altogether. And yet, she knew this Mitch Dennehy could do just that, and the realization left her trembling.

She closed her eyes and smiled. He was . . . so amazing! He'd practically carried her through the newsroom, allowing a brief call to her mother before he whisked her to his favorite pub and ushered her into a cozy booth. He was in charge, just like at the paper, only now he was selecting wines and requesting special dishes as he chatted easily with the waiter. He was a man who knew what he wanted. And for the moment, at least, he wanted her, and the memory caused her pulse to race.

They had talked for hours—over poached chicken and her first sip of wine—and she had been spellbound, more by his charm than the effect of the alcohol. Gone was the gruff Mr. Dennehy who had a habit of barking orders and storming into Michael's office. In his place was this incredibly handsome man with a teasing smile and penetrating blue eyes. Eyes that looked at her as if she were the next course. Eyes that made her wish she could be.

They talked about everything, from Bridie to Michael to the McGettigan scandal, and then they talked some more. He told her about his dear maiden aunt, now deceased, who had been more of a mother than his own. He had been shocked when she'd left him her entire fortune, which he refused to touch except for various charitable donations and his one extravagant purchase—his beloved Model T. He had learned from an early age to work for his money, not subsist on someone else's fortune.

He asked her about her family, and she unleashed a wealth of memories that brought warm laughter to his eyes and sometimes tears to her own. She told him about Maisie and Mrs. Gerson and the faith that meant so much to her. She never dreamed she could talk so freely about God with a man who didn't seem so inclined, but he listened as if it were the most important thing he'd ever heard.

She all but glowed when he told her about his own faith, instilled by his dear Catholic aunt, and she laughed out loud when he grumbled about never missing mass, not because it was a sin, he said, but because his aunt would hunt him down.

Once during dessert, he'd taken her hand to softly kiss it. "That's just to let you know," he whispered, "that I find spending time with you far more delectable than any dessert on Duffy's menu." Heat surged, causing her to quickly slip her hand from his. She wondered if he knew the effect he had on her, and suspected he did from the dangerous look in his eyes.

"Mitch," she whispered, "there's something we need to discuss."

He spooned a bite of dessert, then laid his utensil down, taking her hands in his. "Yes?"

She'd found it difficult finding the right words, but he waited patiently, fully attentive as he absently stroked the inside of her palms. The heat of his touch alarmed her, and she jerked her hands free to bury them in her lap. "Mitch, I . . . I enjoy your company, I do. And I hope we can go on . . . enjoying each other's company. But I have, well, convictions." Her hand flitted to the side of her plate, where her finger slowly traced its edge. She dropped her gaze to her half-eaten pie. "I hope you understand what I'm saying," she continued, cheeks stinging. "I'd very much like to keep our relationship . . . well, you know . . . friendly."

"Friendly," he repeated. She nodded. He reached for her hand and stared with lidded eyes while he brushed her fingers with his lips. A hot blush broiled her cheeks. She snatched them away.

"Yes, friendly! Which means, Mr. Dennehy, I refuse to get into this . . ."

"Into what?" he asked calmly.

Her chin jerked up. "You know exactly what, Mitch Dennehy."

"No, I don't," he said. "By *this* do you mean a relationship with your supervisor, or dinner with a friend . . . or enjoying the favors of a man you're attracted to?"

The heat he ignited converged to her cheeks. "The last one," she snapped, "although the first is coming in a close second."

A brittle laugh escaped his lips as he hunkered back in the booth and folded his arms. "Okay, Faith, I do know what you're talking about. So, what are you telling me? We can see each other, but hands off? I can't touch you or kiss you? What?"

She hesitated before answering, his sudden mood giving her pause. "Mitch, please understand, my faith means the world to me. I have every intention of saving my . . . well, my affections . . . for the man I marry. I want to see you, I do. But I can't indulge in 'favors,' as you put it, because they're wrong. That means if you and I are going to have a relationship, I need you to know I mean what I say. We can occasionally kiss, Mitch, but when I say no, the kissing is over. And if it isn't, the relationship is."

He stared as if she had just flicked food in his face, and she could only imagine the thoughts whirling in his head. Here she was, barely a woman at twenty years of age, dictating what he could and could not do. Without a word, he pinched the bridge of his nose with one hand and poured another glass of wine with the other. He downed a third of it before answering. His lips hardened to rock.

"Pretty presumptuous, aren't ya, Faith? I mean, you're assuming I want a relationship with you." He let that sink in, seeming satisfied when she sucked in a breath. He continued, glass twirling in hand as he relaxed against the booth. "But I don't think it would be too long before you broke your own rules. It only took one kiss to see the attraction between us. You know what I think? I think you'd relent, not me."

She flinched at the sting of his words. "You couldn't be more wrong. The man I love made that mistake. Do you really think you could get away with it?"

His smile cracked. "The man . . . you love? You're in love with someone else?"

"Yes," she said, her voice a hiss as she seized her purse in her fist. "I don't even know why I'm discussing this with you. You obviously don't take me seriously. I want to go home." She started to rise, but he reached to pull her back down. His blue eyes congealed to gray.

"You're not leaving, Faith, we need to talk." He pinned her arm to the table and leaned forward. "Who the blazes are you in love with?" he demanded, suddenly in one of his stormy moods.

"It's none of your business," she whispered, her eyes flitting to the other patrons in the room. "The only reason I mentioned it at all is because I want you to know I mean what I say. The choice is yours, Mitch." A nerve twittered in her cheek as she elevated her chin in defiance. She was sick of this, first with Collin, now with him. Somewhere there had to be a man who cared enough to respect her wishes. If Mitch Dennehy wasn't it, then good riddance.

For several seconds, he remained silent, his face livid as he stared her down. Finally, he took a deep breath and looked away. His tone was sharp. "Okay, Faith, you win." He faced her, his lips pressed into a mulish bent. "I want to see you, it's as simple as that. But there's a part of me so mad I want to tell you to take a flying leap. And maybe I will after we see each other a while. But for now, I guess, it's on your terms."

On the drive home, he'd been considerably subdued, but Faith felt as if a great burden had been lifted. "Mitch," she whispered at the door, "it's been a wonderful evening.

Thank you so much." She turned the key in the lock and opened the door. "See you Monday, Mr. Dennehy."

He nodded, a half-smile shading his lips as she closed the door. She caught her breath as his hand wedged in to block it. "O'Connor, you owe me an explanation. Not tonight, but soon."

"About what?" she asked.

"This character you're in love with."

"I will, Mitch, soon."

"And one more thing. If we start seeing each other—it better be me."

18

Marcy sat in the kitchen with Patrick's letter spread on the table before her, reading it for the sixth time. It was too early to be up, what with it being Saturday, but she couldn't sleep, at least not well, a symptom that coincided with the arrival of his letter earlier that week.

He sounded good, even though she could read the loneliness between the lines, and she detected a note of pride in his comments at how the army had shaped him up. He was stronger and leaner than when they had met, he claimed. The thought brought a rush of warmth to her cheeks and a desperate longing to her soul.

His days consisted of nothing but training, a fact most comforting to her. He'd made a number of good friends with whom he spent what free time they were allowed. But he missed her terribly, he wrote, insisting he was only a shell of his former self, going through the motions until he could return to her once again.

Marcy sighed and looked out the window, barely seeing the beauty of Bridget's winter garden, now bathed in the first shimmer of dawn. She managed to maintain a degree of contentment here in Ireland, one that, at times, bordered on happiness as she grew close to both her mother and Mima, whose health actually seemed to be improving. Their Christmas, though hauntingly lonely without Patrick,

Sean, and Collin, was pleasant enough, she supposed. The children seemed to understand nothing was the same these days, not even Christmas, and she was grateful they took it all in stride. All but Katie, of course, whose appetite for Christmas was second to none. "Why aren't Daddy and Sean and Collin here, Mama?" she asked, quite put off that Santa had refused her primary request.

"They can't, chicken. They're far away and wouldn't have the time to get here. But, we'll have Christmas together next year, I hope." Marcy had been relieved when Katie suddenly turned her attention to annoying Steven instead.

But the arrival of Patrick's letter only served to unearth the true depth of sadness she felt at his absence, and the malaise it inflicted was heavy, indeed. Marcy wiped the wetness from her eyes as she rested her head on the pages he'd written. A new year had begun, and for the first time in over twenty-two years, it had begun without him. "Oh Lord, I can't bear to think how long it might be before I see him again. Patrick's only been gone not quite three months, and already I miss him so. Please strengthen me, Lord, and strengthen him."

Marcy was weeping quietly when Faith entered the room and knelt beside her to wrap her arms around her mother. At her touch, Marcy looked up, trying to smile as she wiped the tears from her face. "Oh, Faith! It's so early. What are you doing up?"

"I think a better question is why are you crying, Mother?" Faith glanced at the letter on the table, and for a moment, a look of panic flickered in her eyes. "Is something wrong with Father or Sean?"

Marcy laughed and wiped her face with her apron. "No, Faith, there's nothing wrong. This is just the letter your father sent a few days ago. I like reading it, that's all."

Faith lowered herself into the chair and gently touched her mother's arm. "You miss him terribly, don't you?"

Marcy nodded, and fresh tears sprang to her eyes.

"Me too, Mother. But the time is coming, I know it, when we'll all be together again."

Marcy patted her hand. "I know, dear. Just this morning I read in my missal that 'God keeps in perfect peace those whose mind are stayed on him, because they trust in him.'" Marcy sighed. "I do trust him, Faith, but sometimes I'm afraid the peace seems anything but perfect."

Faith's smile twisted. "I think the 'perfect' part belongs to him, Mother, not us."

"I suppose." Marcy's tone was reflective as she stared at Patrick's letter. Suddenly, she looked up and grabbed her daughter's hand. "My goodness, I never even asked how last night went! Tell me, did you have fun?"

Before Faith even uttered a word, Marcy saw the glow in her eyes. She laughed and squeezed Faith's hand. "I just knew it! You like him, don't you?"

"I'm afraid I do. I never expected this, honestly I didn't."

"Where did you go?"

"He took me to this wonderful little pub called Duffy's, just around the corner from the *Times*, and we ate and talked, about anything and everything. He's Catholic, of course, and would you believe he actually has a spiritual side? He's so smart and funny and—"

"Handsome?"

Faith rolled her eyes, and Marcy chuckled. "Oh, Mother, you can't believe how much. It's been absolute murder trying to concentrate at work with him around. But, of course, I never let on. And, apparently, he's been feeling pretty much the same way. So here we are."

"And, where is that, exactly?"

"Well, seeing each other, of course." A hint of a frown shadowed Faith's face.

Marcy's brow shot up. "What?"

"Well, the down side, I suppose, is the fact that Mitch is my supervisor and that could certainly be awkward at work. And then, of course, there's the age thing . . ."

It was Marcy's turn to frown. "The age thing? Exactly how much 'age thing' is there?"

Faith jumped up to pour herself a cup of coffee. "Would you like a refill?"

"No, thank you, dear. How old is he, Faith?"

Faith stood at the counter, her back to Marcy as she stirred the cream in her coffee. "Thirty-four," she whispered.

"Thirty-four?" Marcy stammered, struggling with this new information.

Faith rushed to the table and knelt beside her mother. "Mother, I know he's older than me—"

"Older? Saints alive, Faith, he's only five years younger than your own father!"

Faith sat down and reached for her mother's hand. "I know, don't you think I haven't thought about that? I never dreamed something like this might happen. But I care about him, I do. Being with him last night was the first time I could finally believe I would be free from Collin. Mitch touches a chord in me, Mother, a chord I thought only Collin could."

Marcy glanced up, uneasiness gnawing her stomach. "With an older man like that, it's not the 'chord' that worries me."

Faith blushed. "I already set the ground rules, Mother, trust me."

Marcy wasn't convinced. "I do, Faith. But a man with as much experience with women as I'm sure he has, it just concerns me, that's all."

"He seems different, Mother, older, wiser than most men I've met. Oh, he was pretty put off when I told him that any kind of . . . well, overt affection . . . was out of the question."

"You told him that?"

Faith seemed hurt. "Of course I did. You know how I feel about that. And he didn't like it one bit, I can tell you that. But he came around."

"You think he means it?"

Faith looked up, considering the question carefully before answering. "I do. Mrs. Gerson told me she had a feeling something good was going to happen for me in Ireland. I think this might be it."

Marcy hugged her, her eyes misting up once again. "Oh, Faith, wouldn't that be something now? So, when do we get to meet Mr. Wonderful?"

Faith laughed. "Soon enough. But first, I have to get used to it myself. This has taken me by surprise, you know."

"You! I just found out my daughter's interested in a man almost twice her age!"

Faith grinned. "Yes, almost twice as old, but who knows? Maybe he'll make me twice as happy."

"I just wish your father were here," Marcy lamented. "He'd have something to say about it, I'm sure." A shiver skipped down Marcy's spine at what Patrick might have to say about such a development. "Of course, I'm not all that certain you'd want to hear what your father would have to say. I think perhaps in this situation, God knew what he was doing."

Faith nodded, then smiled. "Yes, I think so. Just hope I do."

Marcy nodded. Her thoughts exactly.

"I can't believe we're finally going to meet this man of the world," Charity said. She folded the lace napkins exactly as Bridget had shown her, placing them next to each china plate. "Why isn't Faith helping to set the table, Mother? This is her dinner, after all."

Marcy's mind jumbled with thoughts as she glanced up at her daughter, crystal candlesticks in hand. "Faith has already prepared a large part of the meal, Charity. I told her she could go up and get ready. The poor thing, I've never seen her so nervous. And, it's not like this is their first date. Goodness, they've had lunch together every day this week, and she's been out with him after work a number of times. But I suppose she's concerned about us meeting him and vice versa."

"What do you know about this young man, Marcy?" Bridget asked.

Marcy dodged her mother's gaze as she placed the candlesticks dead center. "Well, he's her manager, of course, which is not the best scenario, I suppose, but then who's going to complain? Faith tells me he's quite bright, outgoing, and one of the best editors at the *Times*. Oh, and apparently he's a good Catholic boy, Mother."

"Mmm." Her mother mulled it over, the wheels obviously gyrating in her brain. "Can't be too young if he's an editor at the *Times*. How old did you say he was?"

Marcy could feel the heat of her mother's scrutiny. She gnawed at her lip, feigning deafness.

"Marcy?"

"Yes, Mother?"

"How old is the boy?"

Marcy gulped, feeling as if she just swallowed a foot in her throat. She was trapped and knew it. When it came to her family, her mother was notorious for relentless pursuit of the truth.

"Well, he's not a boy, exactly . . ."

"Twenty-six . . . twenty-eight? Out with it, Marcy!" Both

her mother and Charity paused, staring with unrestrained curiosity.

"Thirty-four." There. It was out. Marcy peeked at her mother out of the corner of her eye. She bit her lip again when Bridget's jaw dropped. A fork slipped from Charity's hand and clinked on a plate.

"And you're allowing her to keep company with him?"

Marcy steeled herself. "I'm not any happier about the age discrepancy than you are, but Faith cares about him a great deal, and, quite frankly, I welcome anything or anyone who can get her past the heartbreak of Collin." Marcy shot a quick look at Charity before continuing. "I trust Faith. It's as simple as that. I trust her judgment, and I trust the decision she's made to have a relationship with this man." Marcy's tone implied finality of the discussion.

Bridget's lips gummed into a hard line. "Well, if you don't care about your daughter's reputation . . ."

Marcy spun around, her eyes spitting fire. "Don't you dare, Mother! Faith is my daughter, and I don't give a fig what anybody thinks. I trust her."

"I'll bet Patrick would feel differently," Bridget said in a clipped tone.

The blood whooshed from Marcy's face. "Well, Patrick's not here, now is he?"

Bridget backed down, whirling to rearrange utensils on the table. "Fine. She's your daughter, not mine."

"That's right, Mother, she is." Marcy turned to Charity, who quickly dropped her gaze to fidget with a napkin. "Charity, please go upstairs and waken Katie from her nap. She'll be needing a bath. I need to tend to Mima."

Charity opened her mouth to protest. She shot her grandmother a pleading glance. Bridget nodded and Charity sighed. "All right, Mother," she said, giving Bridget a pained look.

Marcy started for the kitchen, then turned at the door, her face like stone. "You will manage to treat Mitch with the courtesy due him as a guest in your home, won't you, Mother? I'm not asking you to like him, just leave him alone. Understood?"

Bridget stiffened, her blue eyes cool as her lip jutted forth. "Tonight, consider me a deaf mute, my dear, instead of your mother."

Marcy fought a smile as she looked at the resolute face of her mother the martyr, as stubborn a mule in all of Ireland. With head held high and face as stoic as she could manage, Marcy forged her way to the kitchen. Once inside, she exhaled, collapsing against the door as a grin infected her lips. She didn't know who was more the mule, she or her mother. And frankly, she hoped to high heaven she wouldn't have to find out.

Brady wanted to kick himself. He let Collin railroad him again. He watched McGuire exercise his charms on a saucy little thing who either didn't care she was about to be taken advantage of or hoped to steal the heart of a handsome doughboy. He swore after the last time he wouldn't be party to another of Collin's you'll-have-a-great-time-trust-me ploys. And yet, here he was, dead tired in a bar at 2:00 a.m., while Collin pulled out the stops to get lucky with yet another pretty face. It made Brady sick, and he was through putting up with it. It was time to go.

Rising to his feet, Brady plucked his jacket off the chair. Collin ceased nuzzling the girl in his lap to look up, the slits of his eyes rounding in surprise. "Hey, ol' buddy, where ya going?"

Brady finished off the last of his ginger ale, set the glass on the table, and put on his coat. "I'm heading back."

Collin laughed and reached for the starter handle to the motor lorry he and four other soldiers had been lucky enough to finagle for the evening. He waved it in the air. "Aren't ya forgettin' somethin', ol' buddy?" Collin's grin was as muddled as his words, and Brady could see his friend was on his way to another monumental hangover.

"I'll walk," Brady said in disgust and turned away, only to reel around and press his palms flat on the table. He focused on Collin's bloodshot eyes. "Come on, Collin, let's call it a night. The rest of the guys'll come along if you do. What do you say?"

The smile dissolved on Collin's face. "Come on, Brady," he slurred under his breath. "I'm 'bout t' get lucky here. Why don' ya give it a try? She's got a friend who's been eyein' you all night." Collin winked, then buried his lips in the woman's neck.

Brady was tired and didn't care anymore. There was only one way to get to Collin, apparently. "I wonder what Faith would say if she could see you now, ol' buddy."

Collin's reaction was swift for someone so inebriated. He pulled away from the woman's mouth and spat a curse into Brady's face. Rage opened the slits of his eyes to reveal red-rimmed whites. "Get out of here, Brady, or so help me I'll rip you apart. I told ya once never to mention her name to me again. Go on, get out! You're no friend to me."

Brady reached in his pocket and hurled a few coins on the table, his eyes as black as Collin's. He slammed the chair in, sloshing the beer in Collin's glass. "I am, you idiot, you just don't know it. Just like you don't know what the devil you're doing now. You sit here and treat these women like their only purpose in life is to gratify you. You think you're in control, but I got news for you—they're controlling you."

Collin cursed again and staggered up, toppling the woman to the floor. He blinked as if in a stupor, then extended a limp hand to help her up. She slapped it away in a tirade of high-pitched French, then picked herself up and stormed to the other side of the bar.

Brady braced himself as Collin weaved to face him, his face flushed with fury and his mouth twisted in rage. A vein quivered in his temple as he clawed the side of the chair to steady himself. "Get this, Brady, and get it good. No woman will ever control me," he hissed, enunciating each word with slurred emphasis.

"No, instead you'll let yourself be controlled by something that will destroy you even more thoroughly. Everybody's controlled by something, Collin, don't kid yourself. It may be your base desires instead of a woman, but it will enslave you nonetheless. You know, I would have thought you were smarter than this. Your drive for love is so strong, it's just a real shame your own ignorance will stop you from finding it." Brady chafed the side of his face and sighed. He held his hand out. "Give me the crank, Collin."

Collin's stare glazed past him. "Everybody's controlled by something," he repeated dully. He closed his eyes and slumped in the chair. All at once, he laid his head on the table and began to sob.

With his heart thudding in his chest, Brady eased into a chair and rested his hand on Collin's shoulder. Something told him this was a graced moment, that God was giving him a window of opportunity to impact his friend with the truth. *Lord, help me to reach him*, Brady prayed. Taking a deep breath, he pressed on.

"Collin, it doesn't have to be like this. You don't have to let this control you anymore. This is not the way to get the love you want. Faith knew that, and you can too. Trust me, Collin. I wouldn't steer you wrong, and neither would she. Faith loves you, and the only thing standing in the way is this—your rebellion against God and everything he represents. He wants you, Collin. He wants you to pursue him instead of your lust."

Collin might have been asleep, for all Brady knew, now lifeless and still and his head buried in his arms. But as Brady finished speaking, Collin's body stiffened, and when his head lurched up, Brady barely recognized him. His face, blotched and swollen, was pinched in shock as his bloodshot eyes fixed on Brady's. "What did you say?" he whispered.

Brady blinked. "I said it doesn't have to be like this . . ."

"No, the last thing—what was the last thing you said?" Collin's eyes were crazed.

Brady thought about it. "I said he wants you, Collin. He wants you to pursue him instead of your lust."

Brady watched as this grown man trembled before him. He had never seen Collin like this. For that matter, he had never seen anyone like this before, and he sensed something spiritual was going on. Collin's fingers shook as he ripped them through his hair. He seemed almost fearful as his eyes locked on Brady's.

"That's just what she said, Brady, word for word, the first time she talked to me about God. How could you know that? How could you?"

Brady exhaled slowly, a shiver traveling his spine. He smiled. "I didn't, Collin, but God did. What I want to know is, what's it going to take to get your attention?"

Collin sat there in a daze and shook his head. "I don't know," he said in a hushed tone, "but this is a devil of a start." He picked up the crank and held it out to Brady. "Do me a favor? Round the boys up, will ya? I got a feeling this is one drunk I'm gonna have trouble sleepin' off."

Brady reached for the crank and nodded. He couldn't agree more.

Bridget entered the parlor, jarred at the sight of Charity stretched out on the couch. She put a shaky hand to her chest. "Goodness, Charity, you gave me a start. I thought you were going out with that McClanahan boy tonight." Bridget took a deep breath and stooped to collect her knitting off the seat of her rocker. She sat, only to bounce right back up. She rubbed her backside. "Ridiculous needle," she muttered. She snatched it up in her hand and sat back down.

Charity glanced up from the *Harper's Bazaar* she was leafing through and smiled. "Honestly, Grandmother, you're going to hurt yourself one of these days. Yes, I was supposed to go out tonight, but I decided to cancel."

The needles were suddenly flying as Bridget commenced with her knitting. She eyed Charity over the pink sweater she was making for Katie. "Why, dear? I thought you liked him."

In a lazy stretch, Charity extended her arms overhead, and Bridget was grateful her granddaughter was not enamored with any of the several beaus who sought her attention. It was just as well, she thought, studying Charity's sensuous pose. This granddaughter of hers was too much of what most men were looking for. It might prove to be her undoing if she actually cared for one of them. Bridget sighed. Perhaps it'd be best for Charity to end up with that Collin character. After all, both Patrick and Marcy seemed to approve of him. Looking at her beautiful granddaughter now, Bridget felt sure she would be much better off safely married, out of temptation's way.

"I did at first, but then he started to bore me, just like all the others. None of them can even come close to Collin." She looked up, her eyes dreamy. "He's all man."

A frown wrinkled Bridget's forehead. "And what, pray tell, does that mean, young lady?"

Charity laughed and rolled over, her eyes mischievous. "Oh, come on, Grandmother, you know what I mean. Collin's not like these little boys that keep flitting around.

He's incredible! First of all, he's more attractive than any man I've ever seen, and the fact he's five years older than me is really quite nice. It means I can't push him around, although I have to admit, I've certainly given it my best shot."

Bridget chuckled. "Wonderful. My granddaughter's a vixen. I'm so proud."

Charity grinned. "I know you know what I mean, Grandmother. Didn't Grandfather make you feel all weak in the knees and warm inside?"

The needles stopped as Bridget thought about it. A faint smile flickered on her lips. "Yes, I suppose he did at that. He was older too, as a matter of fact, although not as old as Mitch Dennehy, for mercy's sake."

Bridget's reference to Mitch seemed to dampen Charity's good humor. She flipped over on her back to stare at the ceiling, her face pinched in a frown. "He may be old, but I'd let him put his shoes under my bed anytime."

"Charity!" Bridget ceased her knitting, startled enough to knock the ball of yarn off her lap onto the floor where it unraveled halfway across the room.

Charity blushed and jumped up to retrieve it. With a chastened look, she dropped it back in Bridget's lap. "I'm sorry, Grandmother. It's just an expression I heard at work."

"Well, it's crude, young lady, and quite inappropriate for a well-bred young woman. Don't ever use it again, understood? Saint's alive, your mother would have a stroke."

"Yes, ma'am, I'm sorry. It's just that it's so unfair. Things always work out for Faith. It's like she's got this fairy godmother watching over her, making sure everything goes her way."

Bridget studied her granddaughter for a moment, then laid her knitting needles aside. "Nonsense, Charity, you're being ridiculous. Why, you're the one who's almost engaged to the man of your dreams, not Faith. You're just as blessed as she."

"Am I? Here she is, working as a copywriter at the most important paper in Ireland, and what happens within two short months? She catches the eye of her manager, who just happens to be one of the most incredible men I've ever seen."

"I thought Collin was incredible," Bridget said with a wry smile.

"He is, Grandmother, but that's just it. He's not here and Mitch is. It's just not fair."

Bridget shook her head. "Charity, my love, I don't know what to do with you. Jealousy will get you nowhere in life. It will only hold you back. Besides, a girl as beautiful as you has absolutely nothing to be jealous of. I suggest you pray about it."

"Pray about it?" Charity gaped as if Bridget had taken leave of her senses.

Bridget couldn't help but smile as she walked to the couch and sat beside her. "Obviously something you're not used to doing, I think. Yes, pray about it."

"You sound like Faith, Grandmother. That doesn't make too many points with me, you know." Charity's tone was terse.

Bridget grinned. "I know, my dear, but it's not points I'm concerned with, now is it? When it comes to the happiness and well-being of one of my favorite granddaughters, points can go to the devil. I want results. Shall we?" She took Charity's hands in hers, closed her eyes, and began to pray, leaving Charity little choice but to bow her head and join her.

19

He was in love and he knew it. Certainly he'd been in lust enough times to know the difference. She was truly remarkable—a woman who had all the passion of a bad girl and all the restraint of an angel. For him, it was a deadly combination, and one that convinced him his days of bachelorhood were numbered.

The night she had "set the boundaries" all but put him over the edge, and he had never wanted to walk out on a woman more in his life. To the devil with her rules, he thought; he would do as he pleased. Who did she think she was? She was just a little girl, barely out of her teens. Certainly not woman enough to capture the heart of a confirmed bachelor. A bachelor who had no inclination whatsoever to put a ring on his finger . . . or one in his nose.

Mitch couldn't believe how much his life had changed in four short months. Once he had been a man about town, enjoying the company, among other things, of a host of eligible women. Now here he was, enamored with only one, who certainly gave him the pleasure of her company but only that, and he'd never been happier. She had transformed him, it seemed—from a man with little use for God to one who now reveled in the sanctity of worship. Gone were Sunday mornings idled away in bed as a reprieve from the night before. Now they were spent in communion with God, in a dim church pew with her by his side.

To him it made little sense, but the more time they spent without physical involvement, the more comfortable and relaxed he felt with her. It was the oddest thing. She had single-handedly put his raging passions, and her own, out of reach for the moment, and the effect was totally astounding. Suddenly his base desires weren't running amuck over the relationship. In their absence, he found himself focusing on her, on who she was as a person, and she him. And although the growth of affection was far slower than the many tempestuous affairs he had known, it was certainly steady and strong. A flame, he was sure, that would burn longer and brighter than any heated affair.

Not that he didn't have his moments. Just the touch of her lips on his was enough to make a grown man cry, and Mitch would have never believed he had it in him to refrain. But he did. And each time, he fell a little more in love with her and found himself a little more willing to wait. She was worth it.

The night she had finally told him about Collin had been difficult. They had been having dinner at Duffy's, sitting in the same booth as the first night, the memory of it lingering in the air like a heady perfume. He knew by this time his feelings were too deep to ever turn back; he couldn't even entertain the thought of being without her. He wouldn't have believed, with his appetite for women, that he could have ever been faithful to just one, but she made a believer out of him. Never had he wanted to tell a woman he loved her more, but he worked hard at fighting the impulse. He was afraid, afraid she wouldn't say it back, and afraid she was still in love with someone else. As he sat across from her that night, he knew he couldn't wait any longer. One way or another, he had to know.

And so he ordered their meal, along with a bottle of

wine, more for himself than for her. A little wine would give him the courage he needed, he decided, and maybe steel his nerves to hear the wrong answer. She watched as he poured himself a glass, and shook her head when he offered one to her. "Not tonight, Mitch. I'm so tired, I'm afraid it will make me woozy."

"Woozy might be nice, you know." He reached to twine his fingers with hers, and his heart quickened when a soft blush seeped into her cheeks. His tone stilled to a hush. "Faith, there's something I need to know."

She leaned close and smiled. "What is it, Mitch?"

His eyes burned into hers, vulnerable and unblinking. "I have to know. Do you still have feelings for this other guy?" He uttered the words quickly, as if he couldn't wait to get them off his tongue. When the smile faded from her face, his heart went cold.

"I don't know, Mitch. I hope not."

Her answer stabbed him. He dropped her hand and grabbed the bottle of wine to refill his glass, then drank half before slamming it back down again. He swore under his breath. "You hope not! You hope not! Confound it, Faith, what kind of answer is that?"

She stared back, her eyes blinking in surprise before narrowing. "I don't like it when you talk like that, Mitch, and I won't sit here and listen to it."

"The devil you won't! I love you, and all you can say is you *hope* you're not in love with someone else?"

It was the first time he had ever told her he loved her. The impact of his words could be seen in the trembling of her lips as they rounded into a soft "oh."

"I'm sorry, Faith, but it's true. I love you, and it infuriates me to think you might be in love with someone else."

"I think I may love you too, Mitch," she whispered, tears spilling.

"You do?"

"I do."

"And what about him? Who the devil is he, anyway?" The look on her face made him wince, and he quickly grabbed his glass to drain it. He reached across the table to wipe the tears from her cheek. "Sorry," he muttered softly. "You know, Faith, I've been talking like this all my life. It's going to take some time to change."

She nodded. "I know. It's going to take some time for me too, I'm afraid. I'm getting over him, but it's slow."

"Who is it?" he whispered.

Her gaze shifted to the plate before her. "He was engaged to my sister before the war."

"Was? What happened?"

"He broke it off."

"Because of you?"

She looked up, brows puckered in anguish. "I think so. He said he loved me."

"And you loved him? I don't understand, then why didn't you—"

"Because my faith in God is everything to me, Mitch, you know that."

His lips curved into a faint smile. "Yes, ma'am, I do."

She continued to stare at the plate before her, but her thoughts seemed far away. "Collin didn't feel the same way. I don't think he even believes in God." She looked up, and Mitch saw the hurt in her eyes. "How can anyone not believe in God? He's everything to me."

The intensity in her voice made him feel guilty. "I know, Faith."

"He asked me to marry him, but I told him no. It would kill my sister if she knew; she's crazy about him. So he broke off their engagement and promised he would think about it while he was away, that maybe they could start fresh when he got back."

Mitch reached for the bottle of wine to pour himself

another drink. "I don't like the sound of that," he said, his voice harsh.

"Why? She loves him. And I think, in his own way, he loves her."

He stared as if she'd lost her mind. "Are you serious? A man you love, who loves you enough to cheat on his own fiancée *and* your sister—in the family for the rest of your life?"

Faith leaned forward, her eyes intense. "I would get over it, Mitch. And so would he."

"And how could I be sure?" he asked, taking her hand in his.

"Because, if you and I were to end up together . . ." She hesitated for just a moment, as if to let the words resonate. "I don't have any doubt the passion between us would leave little room for anyone else."

He lifted her hand to his mouth and kissed it, his chest expanding with a rush of love. "I would certainly spend the rest of my life making sure," he whispered, stroking her palm with his thumb.

Faith shivered and pulled her hand away. "Yes, I'm quite sure you would," she said.

"Did he make you feel like that?" he asked quietly. He hadn't wanted to utter the words, but he had to know. He found himself holding his breath as he awaited her answer.

Her face went pale, and his heart stopped. But then she leaned forward, those green eyes glistening with wetness. "Yes, he did. But I turned him away because he cared more for his own lust than for me, more for himself than my God. While you . . . you have proven you care more for me, Mitch . . . and for God." She swallowed, then attempted a smile. "That, I'm afraid, has sealed your fate."

Exhaling slowly, he squeezed her hands in his. "Don't be afraid, Faith. I'm not."

"Did I tell you I love you, Mr. Dennehy?" she whispered.

"Not near enough."

She grinned. "Thank goodness you can't dock my pay for that."

"Don't be too sure, O'Connor. I'm the boss. I can do anything I want." His mouth tilted into a cocky smile. "Almost."

When he took her home that night, he had given her his usual gentle kiss.

"I'll see you Monday," she whispered, pushing the door ajar.

Something inside had compelled him to pull her close. "No, you'll see me tonight, in your dreams, and that's an order. But just to make sure . . ."

Never would he forget the look—eyes blinking wide as he dragged her to him, her soft lips parting in surprise as his mouth took hers with a hunger long suppressed. His hands wandered her back, urging her close while his lips roamed the curve of her neck and then returned to reclaim her mouth with fervor. For one brief, glorious moment, the terms were his, and by thunder, she would feel the heat of his kiss in her bones.

In a raspy gulp of air, she lunged back. "I can't believe you did that!" she gasped.

"Believe it," he quipped, his tone nonchalant.

"But why? After what I told you tonight, why would you do that?"

"Why? Let's just call it a bit of insurance."

"What?"

"Insurance. If the woman I love is going to have memories of passion, it's going to be with me, not him."

"I don't entertain memories of passion." Her voice was edged with anger.

"You will tonight," he said. And turning on his heel, he

left her—hopefully with a warmth that defied the coolness of the night.

"So what time did you tell Mitch to come for dinner?" Charity's tone was casual as she peeled the carrots.

Faith looked up from the dough she was kneading to glance at the clock on the wall. "Saints alive, he's coming at 6:00, and it's almost 5:30 now! I have to get ready. Although, the man is notorious for being late," she said with a chuckle, washing the dough off her hands.

Charity eyed her with curiosity. "You two pretty serious?"

Faith smiled. "I think so. He told me he loves me."

"I wouldn't put too much stock in that." Charity tossed another carrot into the pot. "Men have a way of throwing that word around when they want something."

Faith peered at her sister, her eyebrows arched in irritation. "Not a man like Mitch."

Charity turned. "Especially a man like Mitch," she drawled, smiling at how easily she could provoke her sister.

"He's not Collin," Faith snapped.

Charity's smile faded as her eyes hardened. "Don't be too sure about that, big sister."

Faith headed to the door. "I'm going up to get ready. If Mitch gets here early, will you let him in?"

Charity flashed a pretty smile. "It'll be my pleasure."

Faith left the room, and Charity turned back to the sink, a smile still on her lips. Mitch may have told her sister he loved her, but Charity knew enough about men to understand the way they looked at her. Especially the way Mitch looked at her the first time he had walked into the parlor over four months ago. She had been shocked at how handsome he was but smooth enough not to show it. He hadn't been quite so lucky when he had rounded the corner and seen her. She was certain he caught his breath, although he recovered nicely with a warm smile, extending his hand to shake hers. He seemed ill at ease, which was unusual for a man of his obvious good looks, and Charity reveled in the look of approval in his eyes.

Dinner had been pleasant enough, although Grand-. mother's usually chatty self was conspicuously absent. Katie had seemed especially geared up with the presence of an older male in the house once again. And Mima, of course, always enjoyed taking her dinner with the family when she felt up to it. It was one of the few joys she was afforded, and no more so than in the company of Mitch. He was as charming and warm as her sister had said, and his easy banter and teasing eyes had focused on each person around the table, especially Faith.

The memory of that night stirred a familiar knot of jealousy in Charity's stomach. She exhaled a heavy sigh. When it came to her sister, it was certain to be a chronic condition, she decided, despite the persistent prayers of her grandmother.

She tossed the last of the carrots into the pot and turned her attention to the unfinished bread. Pushing the dough with the heel of her hand, she thought of Mitch. She whacked the bread with several hard punches. How had her sister ever managed to attract the attention of someone like him? Faith would have never stood a chance, Charity assured herself, if she'd seen him first.

He seemed to care about her sister, she noticed, although he kept his distance. He seldom held her hand and never touched her. Whether out of respect for her family or out of fear of her sister's moral mandate, Charity wasn't quite sure. But one thing Charity was sure of—Mitch Dennehy was no different than the scores of men who had been mesmerized by her beauty. A fact in which she took great pleasure, and one confirmed by the way he avoided her eyes.

Marcy and Bridget interrupted her thoughts as they returned from the backyard, winter vegetables in hand and chatting about the summer garden they hoped to put in.

Marcy looked up. "Where's Faith?"

Charity told her as Katie and Steven shot through the door, squabbling over some toy Steven insisted Katie had stolen.

"Katie, so help me, if you've been into Steven's things again, young lady, you'll have dinner in your room."

Katie stopped dead in her tracks. "Mama, no! Mitch is coming."

"Mother, she took my best marble. My aggie."

Her mother stared hard at Katie, who for once had no defense, seeing as the marble was clenched tightly in her little fist. "Katie Rose, I cannot believe you would defy me after I specifically warned you to stay away from your brother's things. That's it, young lady, upstairs."

The wailing started, but not before Katie screamed that she hated her brother and hurled the precious aggie across the room. It ricocheted, barely missing her grandmother. Her mother swung into action, sweeping Katie up in her arms with a resolute look.

"Mama, I'm sorry! Please, I'll be good . . ."

Marcy's eyes burned hot as she carried Katie from the room, quite horizontal and quite distressed. "Mother, would you mind checking on Mima to make sure this hasn't upset her? You know how she can't bear to hear Katie scream."

Bridget nodded and hurried to Mima while Steven crawled on the floor in search of his marble. He whooped when he found it and jumped up with a look of supreme satisfaction. "Good as new!" he breathed, polishing it on his knickers. "I hope Mama gives it to her good."

"I don't think you have to worry about that," Charity said. She grimaced at the sound of Katie's screams reverberating through the house.

The doorbell interrupted and Charity glanced at the clock, butterflies flitting in her stomach—six o'clock! Right on time. She frowned, irritated that someone so habitually late could be on time to see her sister. She hurried into the foyer and glimpsed into the hall mirror, quite satisfied with the breathless girl who stared back. The gold in her hair glinted as it cascaded over her shoulders in soft, loose curls, and her eyes were truly a striking blue, even more remarkable than Mitch's own. Charity pinched the creamy skin above her cheekbones to enhance the already soft blush that was there, then pursed her full lips together in a skillful smile. She opened the door and draped against it, hands behind her resting on the knob. She savored the way his smile faded as his eyes raked her. "You're not supposed to be punctual," she said.

"Says who?"

"My sister."

"Do you believe everything your sister says?" he asked, striding into the hall.

"Of course not." She closed the door and turned to see him studying her. His eyes shifted away. She smiled.

"Will you tell Faith I'm here?"

She nodded and strolled toward the staircase, careful to brush his arm as she passed. She looked up the stairs and yelled for her sister.

Mitch laughed. "I could have done that."

Charity turned to face him. "I don't doubt you can do a good many things," she whispered. She knew she'd caught him off guard when he flushed. He stared at her, his eyes narrowing as if he didn't know what to make of her.

"I can at that. What, no date tonight?" His gaze locked

on hers as he slowly took off his coat and held it out for her.

She shook her head, fully aware her pale gold curls shimmered with the motion. She took his coat and idly fingered the soft material. "Not tonight. Too tired."

"From fending them off?" he asked, a dangerous smile on his lips.

She laughed. "Maybe. Or maybe I just wanted to see you—"

"Mitch!"

They both turned. Faith stood on the landing, beaming like the sun. "I can't believe you're on time! You've got my internal clock all thrown off." She scampered down the steps. "Hungry?"

He grinned, seemingly oblivious that Charity was still in the room. "That depends on what you're serving," he teased. Faith blushed and led him into the parlor.

Charity could hear them laughing as she entered the kitchen, and the sound of it blackened her mood. Maybe she would eat in her room along with Katie. Watching him with her sister was too unsettling, she thought, then changed her mind midstream. No, she was close; she could feel it. He was attracted to her, she knew it deep down inside. It was just a matter of time before she could return the favor her sister had paid her. Charity reached into the pot on the stove and popped a carrot in her mouth. Who said revenge wasn't sweet? The thought brought a smile to her lips that carried her through the evening.

Mitch wasn't exactly sure what to do. He was elated, of course—it was summer, and they were finally engaged. Everything was almost perfect. But it was the "almost" that bothered him, a condition that had nothing to do with Faith and everything to do with her sister.

From the moment he had laid eyes on Charity O'Connor,

he knew he had never seen a more beautiful woman, and something in that assessment produced a guilt that annoyed him greatly. He had done nothing wrong, he told himself, except admire the beauty of his fiancée's sister. And yet, inside, Mitch felt uneasy.

As much as he would have liked to, he knew he couldn't discuss it with Faith. Over the months he had known her, he quickly learned of the intense rivalry between the two, a rivalry that had already inflicted too much pain on the woman he loved. No, he would never even mention it to her. He wouldn't if he could. He didn't doubt he could explain the concern he felt that her sister might be flirting with him. But how could he ever let on about the desire she provoked in him every time she did?

Mitch dragged his fingers through his hair. Blast it all, it was one thing to stop seeing other women now that he had Faith, but it was something else altogether when the temptation was right under your nose, so close—and so willing—you could almost touch it.

Mitch sighed. There had been a time when he might have welcomed this—the rival affections of two pretty sisters, but the notion did little to thrill him now. He loved Faith, he knew it. He didn't relish the thought of anything interfering with a long engagement that would keep him at bay longer than he could handle. For pity's sake, it was almost July. They'd been seeing each other for six months now, and only God knew when the war would end and they could be married. He worried celibacy would take its toll, and that her sister was more than well aware of it. Something told him these sisters didn't share the same beliefs, a suspicion that made him skittish as a cat whenever Charity was around.

He glanced quickly at the clock and sighed. Well, there was little time to dwell on it now. He was to pick Faith up in an hour and didn't want to be late. He couldn't worry about it; he would simply have to take it one day at a time. After all, each day had enough trouble of its own. He smiled at the Scripture that came to mind. It didn't surprise him; Faith filled his ears with Scriptures a lot lately, all lovingly extracted from the now dog-eared Bible Mrs. Gerson had compelled her to take when she'd left Boston. Although he'd always believed, he'd never felt close to God until he saw him through Faith's eyes. There were times now that he even found himself occasionally reading the Bible she had given him, and with little or no prompting from her. He closed his eyes. What was the rest of that verse?

Be not therefore anxious for the morrow: for the morrow will be anxious for itself. Sufficient unto the day is the evil thereof. Mitch opened his eyes and smiled. That Bible said a mouthful.

20

Collin was shell-shocked. Not so much from the war, which had been raging around him for months now, but more from the letter he held in his hands while lying on his bunk in the dark. He heard Brady's quiet snoring beneath him as he stared into the rafters of the billet they shared, and knew sleep would not come easily tonight.

Charity's letter had been light and breezy, as always, filled with the adventures she enjoyed in her job or Katie's antics. She was always good about passing on news of Patrick and Sean, whenever their letters were received. He could tell she worked hard at sounding cheerful, something he needed after days buried in a trench reeking of urine and sweat and fear.

But he hadn't expected this, and he laid there, a numbness settling in his brain as he realized what it meant. Faith was engaged, Charity had written in a brief paragraph tagged on at the end of the letter, almost as an afterthought. His name was Mitch, and they planned to marry as soon as the war was over because Faith wanted her family together. The words had stunned, and he found himself reading them again and again, as if he couldn't comprehend their meaning. He closed his eyes, and her face swam before him, along with the memory of her words.

"You are something, Collin McGuire. All you think about,

care about is your desire for the moment. Well, I want more, much more. I'm looking for something you don't seem to know a lot about—genuine love, like the kind between my parents. And yes, Collin, the kind of love where God is at the center. That's the only thing I'm going to settle for, and I guarantee it'll have more passion than you'll know in a lifetime."

"I doubt that," he had sneered. "And who's gonna give you this passionate love—God?"

"Someone will . . . someone who loves God as much as I do. I'm saving it for him, Collin. All the passion you provoke in me, it all belongs to him, wherever he is."

Her words circled in his brain like a drunken dizzy spell, making him sick. The passion that belonged to him had finally slipped through his fingers. The same passion that had gotten him through the last month since Brady convinced him he could have her. Now, someone else would have it. The realization was like a knife in his chest. He would have given anything at the moment for one of those mind-numbing drunks he had so readily given up. And for what? So another man could have the only woman he had ever loved. The old anger at God flared as he stared up, his eyes burning with fury. "What good have you done me?" he whispered bitterly. "I give you my life, and you take away the only thing worth living for. What am I supposed to do?"

Delight thyself also in the Lord: and he shall give thee the desires of thine heart.

"She is the desire of my heart!" he hissed. He heard Brady rustle in the bunk below. Collin squeezed his eyes shut and tried to remember exactly what Brady had said. Something about delighting yourself in God and seeking him first. That when you did, your desires became one with his, and he gladly gave them to you. Unfortunately, Collin had learned that too late. He had spent his whole adult life seeking his own desires—in alcohol and women—and in the end, it had been nothing more than a chasing after the wind.

Collin vaulted off his bunk and bent in to where Brady slept, reaching for the Bible he always kept by his side. He clutched it to his chest and hurried outside the billet, the moonlight cutting shadows around him like the noon of day. His fingers fumbled the pages in a rush, seeking the Scripture he had read before his last shift in the trenches. His hand stilled as he found it, and for the first time, he understood its meaning with frightening clarity.

"For he giveth to a man that is good in his sight wisdom, and knowledge, and joy; but to the sinner he giveth travail to gather and to heap up, that he may give to him that is good in God's sight. This also is vanity and pursuit of the wind."

The verse pierced his heart. Overwhelming grief brought him to his knees in the dirt. He didn't care who might see or who might hear. He had spent his whole life chasing after the wind, and it had never yielded anything more than emptiness that blustered cold in his heart. *No more*, he thought. It was over. The life he led was over, and with God's help, a new one would begin. He had allowed the prayers of Faith and Brady to go forth on his behalf but had never uttered them himself. And looking up into the heavens, he cried out to their God, and in the instant it took for him to speak, that God became his. Like the shaft of moonlight washing over him, a holy peace flooded his soul. For the first time, he understood the fervor he'd seen in Faith, the peace he saw in Brady, and he was filled with awe. Every conversation he'd ever had with Brady convinced him he would never be happy until the desire of his heart was one with God's, just like Faith had said. Only, his heart had heard it too late to have her.

Slowly Collin rose from the dirt, astounded at the serenity he felt. He breathed in deeply to fill his lungs with the cool night air. He couldn't have her, but she would always be a part of him. He knew to the depth of his soul that it had been her prayers that had saved him. It was a debt for which he would always be grateful. He wished her well. No, he thought, there was no wishing to it. He would pray that God would bless her with the marriage she deserved. He owed her that. Quietly, he entered the billet and returned the Bible to Brady's side. He crawled into his own bunk, closed his eyes, and slept, finally, the slumber of a man with peace in his heart.

Faith stared at her friend's letter, absently toying with the ring on her finger as she thought about what Maisie had written. Maisie was, of course, overjoyed that Faith was engaged. Had they set a date yet, she wanted to know, and suggested, in not so subtle a manner, that the friendship would be dissolved if the wedding took place anywhere but Boston. Faith smiled, reminded of just how much she missed her friend.

Did Collin know? Maisie had inquired. The smile wilted on Faith's lips. She stared out the window into her grandmother's garden, which had burst from the soft colors of spring into the full-blown vibrancy of summer. She wondered how the news would affect Collin. She had purposely chosen not to let him know, specifically asking Mother and Charity to refrain from telling him in the newsy letters they both frequently wrote. She had been afraid. He was embroiled in the devastation of war; she didn't want to inflict further desolation, if he cared at all. If he didn't, well, he would find out soon enough anyway, and he and Charity could get on with their lives.

Faith gently touched the diamond shimmering on her finger and reflected on Collin fighting a war somewhere in the south of France. In a sense, she fought a war as well, and her heart ached for an armistice of her own. She believed she loved Mitch, more than she dreamed possible with Collin still in her heart. And yet, she knew he was, even now. Daily she wrestled with her own personal war within, wanting him gone but afraid to let him go. And she worried that somehow, some way, Mitch would sense it.

The thought of Mitch coaxed a smile to her lips. He was . . . wonderful. Sometimes cantankerous, frequently impossible, but incredibly warm and caring, and Faith was grateful for him in her life. She thought of the kiss he'd given her the night he asked about Collin. In the months they'd been courting, he had never once crossed the line and been so passionate with her. Although she had been angry at the time, she was, in fact, almost grateful he had done so. It convinced her that once they were married, after they explored the depth of each other's love without restriction, it would, once and for all, extinguish any fire that still burned for Collin.

Faith picked up the pages of Maisie's letter and reread her question. Did Collin know? No, he did not. And she prayed that by the time he found out, she would be irreversibly in love with the man with whom she would spend the rest of her life.

She was, simply, the most beautiful woman he had ever seen. It was, in fact, his depth of gratitude for her love that had brought him so completely to his knees before God. Patrick watched from afar as Marcy glided around the dance floor in his arms. He never felt it strange at all that she could dance in his arms as he observed the scene distantly at the same time, as if in a dream. Her flaxen hair fell about her shoulders like shimmering gold glinting in the moonlight as he spun her around. His heart ached to hold her, even as he whirled her through the mist, his sturdy arms grasping her tightly.

All at once the music stopped, and against his will, his strong arms dropped limp at his sides. In the catch of his breath, a stranger stood beside her, taking her hand in his as the silence gave way to an eerie melody. He could see them dance in the moonlight, and the anguish was so brutal that the breath left his lungs . . .

Patrick jolted up in his bed in a pool of sweat, his heart racing with fear greater than that extracted by the pain of war. God help him, he missed her to the point of excruciation, and it took all the strength of his soul to renounce the despair that washed over him. He couldn't lose her! No—never! She was his joy, his strength . . .

He dropped back on his bunk and closed his eyes. No, she was not his strength. He had said that once to her. Now the very words mocked him as he himself lay in a bed of hopelessness, not far from men who were dying, in a country ravaged by war. She was . . . the love of his life, but she was not his strength. Not since she introduced him so completely to her God, who now claimed him for his own. He would not fear, he told himself. "God has not given me the spirit of fear," he quoted, sweat dripping down his neck into the infested bed of hay beneath him, "but he has given me a spirit of power, love, and a sound mind."

Patrick opened his eyes once again and breathed deeply. He could feel God's presence around him as he stared at the rotting roof of the billet that provided respite from days of hell spent in trenches. Even in the trenches, in the midst of men's screams and decaying bodies, Patrick felt God's peace, as in the midst of a storm, or a war, or an unspeakable hell.

Whether from the fear of returning to the trenches in the morning, or from the coolness of the night air against his sweat-soaked skin, Patrick shivered. He thought of Marcy, and the aching returned, greater than the fear that barraged his soul. When would it be over? When would he see her again, hold her, love her . . .

"Oh, God," he whispered, "help me . . . it's been so long. When will it end?" Despair welled within him. How could he go on in the face of such terrifying loneliness and desolation?

"I will never leave thee, nor forsake thee."

Patrick closed his eyes, and as before, weariness filled his soul until he drifted off, once again to dance in the night.

Mitch felt his fingers twitching as he ran up the steps to Bridget's front porch.

The message had been specific—Faith needed to see him as soon as possible. "Who left it? Faith?" Mitch had asked, but Bridie had just shaken her head. "I didn't take it, Kathleen did, and she didn't say. Do you think something's wrong? Is she sick?"

He grabbed his coat and glanced at his watch. "No, she's not sick. She took a day of vacation to attend a summer festival at her brother and sister's school. But I don't understand why she would want me to come over there, unless something was wrong." He looked back at Bridie as he headed for the door. "Tell Michael I took a late lunch, will ya?"

"Don't forget you've got a meeting with the board at two," Bridie reminded. "What'll I tell him if you're late?"

Mitch flashed her one of his famous smiles. "Tell him Faith called about something important. He'll understand. He's crazy about her too."

Now, as he stood before her door, his fist banged with a heavy thud that matched the pounding of his heart. Seconds passed, but it seemed like hours before the door finally swung open. Mitch stood there, face-to-face with Charity.

"Where's Faith? Is she all right?" he asked, his voice edged with concern. All at once, Charity came into focus, and he could see she'd been crying. He stepped inside the door. "Charity, are *you* all right? Has something happened?" He glanced into the parlor, his eyes searching for Faith or Marcy or Bridget, anyone but his fiancée's beautiful sister.

Charity shook her head and put her hand to her mouth, rivulets of tears streaming her cheeks. Mitch felt his heart twist. He put his hands on her shoulders and looked into her eyes. "Charity, please tell me what's wrong. Is everyone okay?"

She pulled away and stepped back, wiping the tears from her face. She attempted a smile and failed miserably. "Yes, Mitch, everyone's okay. Nothing's wrong, at least not with Faith or Mother or anyone else. They're running late. Steven and Beth had a festival at their school today."

Mitch nodded. "I know. Why aren't you there?" He pulled a clean handkerchief from his pocket and handed it to her.

Charity took it, sniffed, and blew her nose, her tear-streaked face more like a little girl's than the sensuous beauty she always appeared to be. Mitch's heart softened.

"Someone had to stay with Mima . . ." she began, then blew her nose again, causing a smile to pull at his lips.

"Are you going to tell me what's breaking your heart like this, young lady, or will I have to coax it out of you?"

Charity looked up, her eyes wide and wet. She sniffed, then sighed, causing him to grin.

"That's an awfully big sigh for such a little girl," he teased, detecting a glimmer of a smile. "Aha! So it's not complete heartbreak. I do believe I see a semblance of a smile. What do you say you and I head into the parlor to tell old Mitch exactly what's bothering you?"

He put his arm around her shoulders and steered her to one end of the couch. She faced him and hovered on the edge of the seat. He sat on the other side and rested an arm on the back of the sofa. "So, come on, Charity, spill it. What's bad enough to ruin that pretty face of yours with a nasty bout of tears?"

She rubbed her face with her hands, then leaned back and closed her eyes. "I'm sorry, Mitch. I didn't mean to interrupt your work."

He bent forward. "*You* called?"

She looked at him with little-girl eyes and bit her lip. "You're not angry, are you, Mitch? I didn't mean to cause a problem at work."

He slumped back on the sofa, then looked up, a spasm working in his cheek. "Okay, Charity, what is so all-fired important that you call my office and pull me away from work?"

"Please don't be mad, Mitch," she pleaded. "I desperately needed to talk to someone."

His lips pressed to stone, like his jaw. "And you call me? Why? You can't talk to your mother . . . or your sister? For pity's sake, Charity, I'm your sister's fiancé, not your confidant."

"I know," she whispered. Her tears welled up, ripping his heart open. "Mitch?"

"What." His voice was terse, causing her to shiver slightly.

"I needed to talk to a man."

He glared out of the corner of his eye. "Why not call someone from your crowd of admirers?"

She faced him, and he perceived a spark of anger in those remarkable blue eyes. "I said a man, Mitch." She sank into the sofa once again and stared up at the ceiling.

He dropped back against the cushion and observed her. She was a study in sensuality—from the wet, doleful eyes to the sad, pouty lips—and he knew in his gut he shouldn't be here. It was playing with fire, being next to her like this, her hair untamed as it fanned over the back of the sofa and spilled down her shoulders. She had the body of a woman men dreamed about, and she used it to her advantage whenever possible. And never more so than now. She refixed her gaze straight ahead, as if in a daze.

When she finally spoke, her voice wavered, as if on the threshold of another onslaught of tears. "I was engaged . . ." she began.

"I know, Collin. Faith told me. I'm sorry."

She sighed, then dabbed at her eyes with the handkerchief. "So was I. But at least he agreed to think about us while he was away. He said maybe we could try again after the war."

Mitch nodded, never taking his eyes from her profile.

"He wrote me a letter." She looked at him then, her blue eyes tortured. "He's in love with someone else."

Mitch felt his heart constrict.

"He met her in Paris, and he's in love with her, not me."

The tightness in his chest relaxed, and a surge of relief flooded his brain. Suddenly, the relief turned to empathy as he realized how crushing this must be for her. Faith had said Charity was crazy about Collin. For a brief moment, he hesitated, then moved closer. His hand settled on her shoulder in an awkward attempt to comfort her.

"I'm so sorry, Charity," he whispered.

"What's wrong with me, Mitch? Why doesn't he love me?"

Sobs racked her body, and he was at a loss for words of comfort. "He's a fool, Charity, that's the only answer. He's gotta be."

She lunged away, her eyes wild. "No, Mitch, it's me! Why can't Collin love me? What's wrong with me?"

He couldn't stand what this was doing to her. He already hated Collin McGuire, but now the hate took on a dimension of rage at the toll taken on the girl before him. Mitch leaned close, taking Charity's tearstained face in his hands.

His eyes locked on hers. "Listen to me. There is nothing wrong with you. Collin is a fool. It's his loss."

She was trembling in his hands. He wanted to hold her but didn't dare. She sniffed and pushed the wetness from her eyes. He handed her his handkerchief once again, then bent down to examine her face. "Are you okay?"

She nodded.

"Is there anything I can do?" he asked, feeling helpless to soothe her pain.

She looked at him from under a sweep of heavy lashes. "Will you hold me?"

His heart stopped before it started pounding again. He took a deep breath and nodded, slowly wrapping his arms around her. She inched closer until her head rested on his chest, and he knew she could hear the chaotic beating of his heart. The delicious scent of her hair assailed him as he rested his face against it. A sensation of warmth flooded as she pressed in close, hands wound around his back as if she were afraid he would let go.

Alarm curled in his stomach, and he tried to pull away. She raised her head to look up, and he read the desire in her eyes. She wanted him to kiss her.

Faith had been a master at boundaries—it had been all too long since he'd been this close to a woman. The touch of her, the smell of her suddenly overpowered his senses. No, he wasn't going to do this, he told himself. He was in love with Faith. This was wrong, and it wasn't going to happen. But it was as if she willed it, so strong was the pull. The fire inside him was slowly raging out of control. *Push her away!* his mind screamed, but his body refused to listen. It wanted to taste those lips just once, please God, just once . . .

He jerked away and lunged to his feet, his jaw compressed in anger. "I have to get back to work. Cry on somebody else's shoulder." He turned to go, but she jumped up to stop him, her fingers clenching his shirt and her face contorted in pain.

"Please, Mitch, don't turn on me like Collin. Please . . ."

His eyes burned as he stared at her.

She blinked, sending a tear shimmering down her cheek. "Just hold me," she whispered. Her voice was a broken rasp. "Please, Mitch, I just need someone to hold me . . ."

He exhaled his anger and removed her hands from his shirt, every nerve in his body on edge. Against his better judgment, he slowly twined his arms around her, his mind reeling at the prospect of what he was doing. She moved in close, like putty in his hands, melting into him with a familiarity that shocked him. He squeezed his eyes shut. Lust warred within, its warmth colliding with the cold grip of guilt. *She just needs comfort*, he argued in his mind, *nothing more*.

He felt her move as she tilted her chin up, and he opened his eyes, regretting it the moment he did. Heat singed him as she moistened her lips before releasing a shuddering sigh.

"I don't think anyone will ever truly fall in love with me. My greatest fear is I will always be alone . . ." Her voice broke. "Even my own father has never really cared for me." She convulsed in his arms as rivulets of tears streamed her pale face. He stared at the fullness of her lips, wet and quivering as she wept, and his heart twisted.

"Stop it, Charity, don't talk like that." He couldn't seem to stop himself as he bent to kiss her wet cheek. When he did, she turned her face ever so slightly, her soft lips barely touching his. Heat engulfed him. "God help me," he whispered, and his mouth sought hers. He pulled her to him, burying himself in her hair and her neck, his breathing out of control. He was desperate to put words—anything— between them. He stroked her hair as he held her close.

"Not fall in love with you? Impossible. You're the most beautiful woman I've ever seen . . ."

Neither had seen her enter until they heard her cry, a pitiful gasp paralyzing him as he embraced her sister. A sharp pain jolted through him as he looked up. Faith's face was stricken with a look of horror he would never forget. *Please, no!*

Charity reeled and collapsed onto the sofa when he pushed her away.

"Faith!" he cried, his body cold as slate. He started toward her, and she stumbled back, her face crumpling into revulsion.

"No!" she screamed. "Don't you touch me! Not now, not ever! You just destroyed everything we had, everything we could have had . . ."

Mitch froze as the blood siphoned from his face. "You don't mean that. You can't mean that. You've got to let me explain. You can't just walk away." His voice came in hoarse rasps.

"I can and I will. We're through! I could never trust you again, never look at you without remembering . . . *this*. It's over, Mitch."

"Faith!" he shouted, but she fled the room. He panicked as he heard her race up the stairs and slam the door. He stood there, his heart sick in his chest, feeling as if he were going to vomit. She couldn't mean what she said. She was upset. He would give her time, and then he would reason with her. He put his face in his hands, a cold shiver traveling his spine. Slowly, he looked up to see Charity watching him, and the reality of what he had done began to sink in.

Charity forced herself to stand, her body pure lead. "Mitch, I'm so sorry." Strangely enough, she meant it. She was sorry—sorry she caused him pain. She never meant to do that to him. She hadn't thought it through, hadn't realized she would also inflict some pain of her own. She looked at him now, and something inside told her the plan had backfired. Oh, she accomplished what she had set out to do. But in the process, she set an emotional trap that managed to snare her as well. She had used him to hurt her sister. She hadn't counted on wanting him for herself.

He nodded as if in a trance and slowly made his way to the door. His eyes were lifeless when he turned to face her. "Tell her I'll call, will you? Tell her I love her," he said, his voice cracking. He left, and Charity put her face in her hands.

What had she done? What possessed her to crush her sister like this? Her grandmother had said jealousy would get her nowhere. She was wrong—it had gotten her the ultimate revenge against Faith. What her grandmother hadn't told her, however, was that revenge always partnered with heartbreak. Now that was a lesson she could have used.

21

Mitch was in a foul mood when he arrived to the meeting almost thirty minutes late. Michael had never seen him quite this bad. His face had a green tinge, and his eyes were sinking into their sockets as if he hadn't slept for days on end. His brain wasn't tracking, and he seemed distracted to the point of lapsing into moments of dazed staring. Several times Michael asked if he felt all right. Mitch would nod and put at least some effort into composing himself before wandering off again, clearly somewhere else. When the meeting ended, the men shook hands and departed. Michael tracked Mitch to his office.

"Michael, telephone," someone called. Michael scowled. "Take a message," he yelled as he tried to catch up with Mitch.

"It's Faith. She says it's important."

Michael paused, and Mitch spun around, his face completely devoid of color. "I need to talk to her," he rasped, racing to Michael's phone. Michael snatched it first, pushing him back.

"She asked to talk to me," he said, his hand over the mouthpiece. Bile rose in his throat, and a sick feeling burned in his chest. "What's going on, Mitch? You're not dumping her, are you? Because if you are, so help me God . . ."

Mitch kneaded his forehead with his palm. "No . . . no, I'm not dumping her. It's more the other way around."

Michael didn't believe him. They were made for each other—a sweet kid with a will of iron and the roving ladies' man who got his wings clipped. Michael had never seen Mitch happier. Since Mitch had been seeing Faith, Michael had reduced his aspirin intake at least in half. He glared and put the phone to his ear. "Yeah, Michael here."

"Michael? It's Faith." Her voice sounded nothing like her, far more nasal and completely void of its usual lilt.

"Faith, what's wrong?" Michael felt the heat of Mitch's glare and turned to stare out the window, his lips pinched tight.

"I . . . can't . . . come . . . back, *ever*. I'm giving you my resignation—now."

"What? No! You and I need to talk about this—"

"My mind's made up, sir, I'm sorry. But I will never forget your kindness to me . . ."

Mitch paced, ready to rip the phone from his ear. "I have to talk to her!"

Michael waved him off. "Faith, why are you doing this?"

"Personal reasons, sir, too painful to go into. I have to go now . . ."

"Faith, listen to me, please—"

"No, Michael, I'm sorry. Good-bye."

Michael stared in shock, the line buzzing in his ear. He carefully replaced the receiver.

"What? What did she say? Blast it all, Michael, don't just stand there like an idiot. What the devil did she say?"

He squinted up at Mitch, his fingers frozen on the phone. "She quit. Personal reasons." Michael scowled at Mitch, his temper kicking in. He could feel a headache coming on. "For the love of heaven, Mitch, what in the devil did you do to her?"

Mitch's face bleached white. "This can't be happening . . . one mistake, one lousy mistake!" He stared through Michael like a zombie, his voice barely audible. "I . . . I did something stupid—really, really stupid. I've got to fix it, Michael. I've got to see her." He bolted to his office to get his jacket, then bellowed something to Bridie before tearing out the door.

Michael watched the whole scene with nausea in his stomach. He hoped Mitch could remedy whatever was wrong. Speaking for himself, he would miss Faith terribly. She had been a breath of fresh air in an otherwise stale newsroom, and the thought of her gone did not sit well. And obviously, Mitch would be crushed. He'd never seen him fall quite this hard before, and the thought of the happy, easy Mitch being replaced by the old, cranky one was enough to push the nagging headache in his brain to the status of migraine.

Marcy was beside herself. She hadn't felt such a heaviness since the day Patrick had left, and other than pray, she was at a loss as to what to do. When she and Bridget had arrived home with the others, they discovered Faith locked in her room. Charity was sobbing in the parlor, unable to stop long enough to tell them what was wrong. Marcy sped up the stairs, demanding Faith open the door while Bridget checked with Mima to see if she could shed any light on what had happened in their absence.

Mima told them she'd been awakened by screams—it sounded like Faith, she said. She heard Mitch, but wasn't sure what happened until a door slammed. She suspected they had fought. When she finally managed to drag herself out of bed to see what was wrong, Charity was crying, and she refused to respond to Mima's queries.

Upstairs, Marcy pleaded for Faith to let her in, but was met only by the sound of her daughter's weeping.

Downstairs, she heard someone knocking at the door and hurried to the landing. Mitch entered, looking like an apparition with his bloodless face and sunken stare.

"I've got to talk to Faith," he stammered, starting up the stairs. Marcy blocked his path, her eyes like flint.

"No, Mitch! Not a step farther until you tell me what's going on."

He staggered back, a low groan issuing forth. "Faith and I . . . we fought . . . she doesn't want to see me anymore."

Icy cold needles flicked under Marcy's skin. "What are you saying? Why?"

He rubbed his eyes hard. "She walked in on us, Charity and me . . ."

"What? Are you saying that you and Charity . . ."

His gaze slowly lifted to hers, a mix of shame and grief on his face.

Marcy grasped the railing, dizziness swelling in her brain. "How? Why?"

He exhaled slowly. "I received a message Faith needed to see me. I came and found Charity crying. She was distraught. Collin wrote her that he was in love with someone else."

Marcy gasped.

"I swear, Mrs. O'Connor, all I was trying to do was comfort her. I don't even know how it happened, but it did . . . and that's how Faith found us."

Marcy doubled over, clutching her stomach as her fist tightened on the railing.

"Mrs. O'Connor, I love Faith more than anything. It was a stupid mistake. Please, I've got to talk to her."

Marcy shook her head. "No, Mitch. She won't talk to you. She won't talk to me. I think it's best you go now. We'll call you."

"No, I'm sorry, but I've got to talk to her. Now!"

He pushed past her and stood in front of Faith's door,

battering it with a ferocious pounding that echoed through the house. Somewhere downstairs, Katie began to cry. He screamed for Faith to open the door, but the futility of his demand became evident by her silence, which seemed to enrage him even more.

Marcy's eyes flashed. "Mitch, stop it! Please go—now!"

But he only ignored her, bludgeoning the door like a madman, his words full of pain and fury. "Faith, you can't do this. You can't run away. I love you! Please talk to me, hit me, anything, only don't shut me out."

He raged on for what seemed like eons, periodically sagging against the door, head hanging and arms limp at his sides. Finally, her silence appeared too much for him to take, and he relented, rushing past Marcy as he flew down the steps and out the door.

Marcy leaned against the railing, her body weak from the emotional trauma. She desperately wished Patrick were here, now more than ever. But he wasn't, and the burden fell to her to bind the wounds of a family badly bruised. Silently, Marcy said a prayer and straightened her shoulders. She would deal with it one daughter at a time, she decided. With a deep breath, she descended the stairs.

Her mind was numb. Never had she felt so totally depleted of energy and hope, and certainly tears. It was all gone, leaving her little more than a shell lying on a bed, staring at a ceiling she wasn't seeing, through bloodshot eyes that saw nothing but despair.

The picture played in her mind for surely the hundredth time, no longer accompanied by the sickening wave of nausea and tears long since spent. She saw him, the man with whom she hoped to spend the rest of her life, holding her sister, clenching her with an unspeakable passion that should have belonged only to her. His hands . . . touching, grasping, taking something that did not belong to him, and in the process, destroying something that did. Words spoken—which never should have been uttered, or whispered, or even formed in his mind—now circled in her brain like an endless dirge.

"... *the most beautiful woman I've ever seen* ..."

The ultimate betrayal, filling her with the ultimate desolation. She meant what she had said. She cared about Mitch, but the trust he inspired was now shattered, splintered like their relationship into a million irretrievable pieces. She thought of those easy good looks, those laughing blue eyes and the Irish gruffness so much a part of who he was, and a horrendous pain seared through her. Yes, she cared for him, and she had believed in him, defended him. Charity had said men knew what to say and do to get what they wanted, especially a man like Mitch. But she hadn't believed it. "He's not Collin," she had said. But he was—just like Collin—putting his own lust before her and before God.

The room was filled with the shadows of dusk when she finally rose from the bed, and the house was deathly still, free at last from the onslaught of both her mother and Mitch railing at her door. She had lain there for over five hours, leaving the sanctuary of her room only briefly after Mitch left, and only then to call Michael first, and then the shipyard to inquire about any passage she could get. She sobbed through the entire exchange with Michael, quite certain he must be thinking she'd come unhinged. She didn't care. She couldn't go back, ever, not as long as *he* was there. But she did want Michael to know how grateful she was, and that she was sorry, so very sorry.

Faith stood to her feet, her head aching horribly as she bent to light the lamp. Slowly, she made her way to the closet and caught a glimpse of her reflection in the mirror. The girl who stared back was ravaged but not defeated;

broken but not destroyed. No one could do that to her—ever. Not as long as she had a breath in her body. She reached into the closet and stood on tiptoe to pull her valise from the shelf, causing it to clatter to the floor. She picked it up and laid it on the bed.

There was no way she could stay. How could she live in a city where she would see him again? Live in a house where she was faced with the hate of her sister, a hate that had stabbed through her heart? She couldn't, and she wouldn't.

The silence was broken by a quiet knock on the door. "Faith, please . . . may I come in?" Her mother's tone was pleading.

Suddenly Faith was overwhelmed with the desire to have her mother hold her in her arms. She ran to the door and flung it open.

Her mother grasped her tightly. She closed the door and led Faith to the bed, where she clung with a ferocity that allowed Faith to go limp in her arms. She stroked her daughter's hair, whispering that she loved her, hurt for her. She knew, she said. Both Mitch and Charity had told her, and they were devastated, both of them.

"Faith," her mother whispered, "Mitch has been calling all day. I've never seen a man so broken. You have to talk to him."

Faith shook her head and lurched away, her eyes stinging with fury. "No, I won't talk to him! I can't. What he did . . . he might as well have put a knife in me. He knew, Mother. He knew all about the hurt Charity's caused me over the years."

"Faith, that's not true. She's your sister. Conflict is natural—"

Rage coiled like a serpent in Faith's stomach, ready to strike. "No, Mother! You've conveniently closed your eyes to it all these years. It's not natural. Charity hates me; she's always hated me. Mitch knew that, and he knew how I felt about morality. He's betrayed me on both counts. I will never trust him, nor will I ever give him the opportunity to hurt me again."

Faith rose, and her mother's eyes widened at the suitcase on the bed. She sprang up and grabbed her daughter's arm. "What do you think you're doing?"

Faith stared with deadly calm. "I can't stay. I need time away. Time to heal. I'm going home." The color drained from her mother's face as Faith continued. "Please don't fight me on this, Mother. I can't stay here, not now. I want to go back to Boston."

"You're just angry. You can't mean that. That would be wrong to do to Mitch, wrong to do to all of us. You can't run. You have to face it and deal with it, openly and honestly. No, I won't let you do this. You must face Mitch; you owe him that."

Faith flinched. An eerie vehemence settled on her soul like an icy mist. She saw her mother shiver. "I owe him nothing but perhaps a little of his own back. I want him to hurt. I want to tear his heart out like he did mine. I can't wait to leave! I hope and pray it crushes him like he's crushed me."

Marcy grasped her arm. "Faith! How dare you 'pray' that! Your anger at Mitch may convince you that you owe him nothing, but you owe God your obedience. You know better than anyone that the bitterness in your heart is sin, and you must deal with it."

"I don't owe God anything. Not anymore. As far as I'm concerned, when Mitch betrayed me, God did too. I'm through—through with faith in people and faith in God. From now on, I will live my own life, and I will live it in Boston."

Faith strode toward the dresser, jerked a drawer open,

and seized its contents in her arms. She flung the clothing into the valise.

Her mother appeared paralyzed, staring at the stranger before her. "I won't let you go," she whispered.

"You can't stop me," Faith said. A surge of power shot through her. It was hard and cruel and hurtful. And it felt good.

Her mother shrank back. "Where will you stay?" she asked, her voice barely a whisper.

"With Mrs. Gerson, if I can. If not her, then Maisie. I don't really know. But when the war ends, I'll see to it the renters are gone and the house is ready."

"When will you leave?"

Faith's eyes flitted to her mother's tired form bent over the bed. She felt a sudden prick of tears in her eyes. Her lips pressed tight. She could not allow her love for her mother to deter her from her rage. She must guard it at all costs—it made her strong. It ensured she would go. "This weekend," she lied.

Her mother nodded, slowly rising to her feet. "What will I tell Mitch?" she whispered.

Faith eyed her mother with cool indifference. "Tell him to go to the devil," she said, and meant it. And the look on her mother's face was worth the price.

Marcy considered bolting her in her room, but that wasn't the answer. Neither was talking right now. Hurt and bitterness had closed Faith's ears and heart to anything she or Mitch might say. There was nothing to do but pray her daughter would return to her senses.

Marcy entered the kitchen, where Bridget was preparing dinner. She would let Faith sleep on her anger, she decided. This was Tuesday. She had till the weekend to think of something—anything—to change her daughter's mind.

Totally drained, Marcy slumped at the table. Bridget

turned at the sink, her face etched with concern. "How is she?" she asked.

Marcy shook her head. "I don't know what to do, Mother. I've never seen her like this before, so full of fury, so cold. She's a stranger—angry with Mitch and Charity, angry with me, and especially God. It scares me. God has always been the most important thing to Faith. Now she's even turned on him." Marcy hesitated. "She's going back to Boston."

Bridget set a half-peeled potato down and wiped her hands on her apron, then moved to sit by Marcy's side. "Marcy, Faith has been wounded deeply. Of course she's angry with God. What human being wouldn't be? But she knows his goodness too, and in the end, it will woo her back. We have no choice but to trust him. She's his child too."

Marcy nodded, and Bridget reached for her hand, her eyes full of hope. "She will come through this, Marcy; I know she will. And do you know how I know?"

Marcy shook her head.

"Because God is faithful," Bridget said, as if stating a fact no one could possibly dispute. "Faith has served him with her whole heart, and he will not let her go. But I'm afraid you must. Let her go, Marcy, and trust him to keep her."

Marcy's head jerked up. "Mother, I can't!"

"Yes, you can. He won't fail you, and he won't fail her."

Marcy shivered, then finally nodded. "Mitch has a right to know, Mother. For all his stupidity and failing . . . he has a right to see her before she goes."

Bridget sighed. "Perhaps not. What he did . . . well, I'm not sure I would forgive him myself, nor ever trust him."

Marcy's eyes strained with fatigue as she looked up. "He deserves to be heard. I'll call in the morning. Perhaps . . .

perhaps even yet, he can change her mind." Marcy extended her hand. "Mother, can we pray together, please?"

Bridget smiled and placed her hands in her daughter's. "It's the only thing we can do, Marcy," she whispered. "But, it's more than enough."

It was still dark when Faith rose to carry her suitcase downstairs and hide it in the bushes of the neighbor's front yard. When she returned to the darkness of her room, she closed the door and lit the lamp, grateful Charity had found somewhere else to sleep. Apparently she couldn't stomach the sight of Faith anymore than she could her. Faith hoped guilt was eating at her, but she doubted it. Guilt was a tool Charity used to inflict on others, not something that would ever invade her own conscience, if she had one.

Faith walked to her bed and sat down with pen and paper to write her letters. First to her mother, then to the others, explaining why she needed to do this. A thought came to ask them to pray for her, but she dismissed it with a surge of anger. She had spent enough time and energy on the emptiness of prayers. She had neither time nor inclination for that now.

Putting the letters aside, she began to write a separate one to Charity. The venom flowed easily as she penned her hostility to this sister who had destroyed her life so completely. She would retaliate, she promised. She would write Collin about all Charity had done—how she had vowed to wait for him, then spent time with an endless parade of men, culminating in the very seduction of Faith's own fiancé. "And one more thing," Faith wrote with a flourish, "Collin told me he loved me, right before he begged me to marry him."

Faith stopped, almost hesitant to subject her sister to such pain. But then Charity hadn't hesitated with her, had she? With renewed anger, she penned the final blow. "And if he still wants me, I'll gladly marry him, taking great pleasure in causing you as much pain as you've caused me."

Faith shivered. She had never done this before. It felt strange to strike out at her sister this way, to finally give full vent to all the hurt Charity had subjected her to. But her bitterness empowered her, a smiling insanity that spurred her on with each angry word spewed on the sheet.

With amazing calm, she folded the letter and set it aside. Walking to the bureau, she fingered the engagement ring she'd placed there the night before. It glimmered in the light as she held it, gleaming with broken promise. Wetness swam in her eyes, and she laid it on the dresser. She should write him a letter, but would not. Her silence would be the ultimate revenge. The thought made her satisfied and sick all at once.

Moving her hand to the other side of the bureau, she gently stroked the Bible that Mrs. Gerson had given her when she'd left Boston. A sad smile lined her lips as she touched its leather binding. It was cool to her touch—like her fervor for God. Fear prickled over her, causing a shiver despite the early morning warmth of the late-summer day. Hesitating, she started to pick it up, then put it back. She hadn't packed it on purpose. She wanted a clean break, from Mitch and from God, but found herself wrestling with the desire to take it. Shaking it off, she began to get ready. In every way, she must appear normal to her mother.

Her mother seemed relieved when Faith entered the kitchen dressed for work.

"Faith!" she cried and clutched her tightly. Faith returned her embrace, and Marcy's wavering sigh drifted against her ear. "You seem better this morning. Are you?"

She nodded and hugged her mother again. "Yes, Mother, I am. I'm so sorry about last night. Please forgive me. I love you, more than you'll ever know."

"I know you do. I love you too—very much. Are you hungry?" she asked with a smile.

"Not really. All I want to do is go into work and give my notice."

The smile faded on Marcy's face. "So, you're going through with it, then? You're going back to Boston?"

Faith squeezed her mother's hand. "I'm just going home a little early, that's all. It's almost September, and they've been saying the war is close to an end, maybe as soon as October or November. Just think, Mother, by Thanksgiving we could all be together again."

"Yes, God willing," Marcy answered quietly. "You'll talk to Mitch?"

Faith paused, then patted her mother's hand. "Yes, I'll talk to Mitch," she said, becoming as proficient a liar as her sister. "I'll tell him I need time away for a while, all right?"

Her mother nodded.

Faith glanced outside. "Grandmother up? I want to say good-bye."

Marcy looked at her oddly, and fear cramped in Faith's stomach. "Once I leave Ireland, I won't be seeing Grandmother and Mima again for a long time," she said quickly. She hunched her shoulders. "Just getting in hugs before I go."

Her mother stood at the window to watch as Faith embraced her grandmother in the garden, then returned to tiptoe into Mima's room.

"Are you planning to say good-bye to everyone?" Her mother's tone seemed measured.

Faith's eyes flickered to her face. "No, I'll see them tonight," she lied again. She was glad Steven and Katie had slept through the hug she'd given them before coming downstairs.

She hadn't been quite so lucky with Beth, who had rolled

over to peek through sleepy eyes. "Faith? Where are you going? You never kiss me when you go to work."

"I know, Beth, but today I just wanted to, okay? You go back to sleep now. And don't forget your big sister loves you."

Faith returned to the kitchen and to her mother, whose brow now crinkled above wary blue eyes. *Does she suspect anything?* Faith wondered. She pushed the thought aside. She was confident her rehearsed lies would deter her mother from acting on any qualms. After all, she had never lied to her before.

"I'll see you tonight, then?" her mother asked pointedly, and Faith silently cursed the blush that heated her cheeks.

"Of course you will, Mother," she said, not trusting herself to meet her gaze. She blew a kiss and bounded out the door. Her mother peered out the window as Faith traipsed past Bridget's garden into the street.

She was sure her mother never saw her rounding the neighbor's yard and collecting her valise from the bushes. She stole one final glimpse at the house, then tightened her grip on the bag, relieved her mother had never suspected a thing. It had become a game of deception, and by God—*or not*—one she would win.

He almost dropped the phone. "What did you say?" Mitch whispered hoarsely.

"I said, she's leaving," Marcy repeated, and his blood ran cold. "She's going to Boston—this weekend."

"What?" He could almost feel Marcy wince at the fear in his tone.

"I've never seen her like this, Mitch, full of rage at you and Charity and especially God."

His heart stopped for a moment before panic kicked in.

"Please, God, no," he whispered. "What did she say? How do you know?"

Marcy's voice trembled as she repeated the conversation. Mitch strained to listen through the sound of his own shallow breathing.

"I'm so afraid, Mitch," Marcy said, "afraid because she's said things I've never heard out of her mouth before. Awful things like God betrayed her, and that she no longer had faith in him or people."

He was too stunned to answer. It was a vicious nightmare! When would he wake up?

"And then I asked what I was supposed to tell you when she left, and she said something I never thought I would hear out of her mouth."

Mitch held his breath, his heart thudding in his chest. "What?" he whispered.

"She said, 'Tell him to go to the devil.'"

He groaned and closed his eyes. She hated him! How could it be that one awful moment in time could shatter his life so completely? He buried his face in his hands. When he finally spoke, his tone was bitter. "Well, she got her wish because that's where I've been the last twenty-four hours—sheer hell."

"She's on her way to talk to you now," Marcy said.

Mitch sat up in his chair. "What?"

"She left, not twenty minutes ago, to come in and give Michael her notice. She told me she would talk to you then."

A sick feeling cowered in his stomach. "Why would she do that?" he asked. "She called yesterday and gave Michael her notice."

"Oh, please, no . . ." Marcy whispered.

The air rushed from his lungs in a groan. "Check her room, her clothes . . ." His voice was a pained rasp.

Marcy must have dropped the phone and rushed to Faith's room. When she picked it up again, she was crying.

"She's gone, everything's gone, except the Bible Mrs. Gerson gave her! Her Bible! Oh, Mitch, she cherished that gift beyond measure. That tells me something's desperately wrong. The Faith I know would never do this. You've got to find her. Please, go to the shipyard and find her. Please, Mitch, don't let her go!"

He was breathing hard now. No, the Faith they both knew—or thought they knew—would never do this. But the Faith who'd been betrayed to the depth of her soul would, and the degree to which he must have wounded her cut him to the core.

"I'm leaving right now, Mrs. O'Connor." He hung up the phone, his heart hammering in his chest. He felt like a madman tearing out of the building. His hands shook as he stooped to rotate the crank of his car. *What would I do without her?* He got in and clutched the steering wheel, then hung his head and closed his eyes. "Oh, God," he prayed, "I need you. I need your strength and your wisdom. You brought her to me—please don't take her away."

A sense of peace settled as he shifted into gear. He sucked in a deep breath. That was the legacy she left him. She could leave and take his joy and his light, but she could never take the peace of God she had led him to. As he pulled out into the stream of traffic, the realization dawned like the pale light of a new day, and he gratefully allowed it to drive the fear from his soul.

No one ever told her anger kept you strong while you flouted God's will, then left you alone to cower in the face of fear when it was through with you. That was a lesson she would have to learn on her own as she shivered in the bleak bowels of a cold, gray freighter.

Faith stared at the restless waves, never seeing them for the restlessness thrashing in her mind. It had been almost a week since she had forged ahead with her plan, fueled and strengthened by the hurt and hate crowding her soul. And then the ship had set sail, and with it, any assurance she was doing the right thing. There wasn't a moment she didn't regret the lies and deceptions, the hate and the bitterness. Guilt and pain battered her brain like the threatening whitecaps that slammed daily against the hull of the ship. She was sickened, over her family and what she had done to them. All except Charity and Mitch. No, that anger still kindled white-hot. It made her glad she left Ireland, if only for them.

She thought about God, and guilt slithered in her gut. She knew enough of God to know she was cornered. There was no happiness apart from him. But she wasn't ready to make her peace. Not yet. The hurt was too deep, too raw. In time, she would, she knew. But for now, she would revel in the bitterness that swelled within, much like the swirling, savage waves of the sea.

She found herself thinking a great deal about Collin. There was little else to do as she kept to herself, seldom speaking to anyone on the ship. Periodically, she regretted her decision to leave her Bible behind. As angry as she was at God right now, the words from Mrs. Gerson's Bible had always had such a soothing effect on her. Like it or not, she missed her daily devotion more than she cared to admit. She refused to think about Mitch; it was still too painful. And so she focused on Collin—on where he might be, and if he ever thought of her.

She closed her eyes and visualized the last time he kissed her. Warmth immediately flooded her body. She had never allowed herself to think of those moments before, not only because of the torment over someone she could never have, but also because she believed it was wrong. Her faithfulness to God had been intensely devoted, even to the point of keeping her mind pure, and she had been completely diligent. Until now. Now, the anger searing within told her she didn't care. She would think what she liked, allowing her mind to dwell on the way he had kissed her and held her. The memory thrilled, shooting heat through her like electricity. Her feelings for him had never diminished, she realized, not in all the months she cared for Mitch. The thought no longer frightened her.

Suddenly, she stood straight at the railing as comprehension flooded her brain. *I'll marry him*, she decided, her heart throbbing within. She had never stopped loving him, after all, and if he still loved her, there would be nothing to stand in their way. God was no longer an issue. Fingers of fear suddenly snaked around her heart. Her body went slack as she exhaled in despair, her fantasy swirling away as the breath left her lungs.

She clenched her fists, anger resurging at this God who had betrayed her, then boxed her in so completely she could never leave. Yes, her faith in God had suffered a severe blow, but the knowledge that she would return to it grated on her. God had a way of ruining you for the world, and something told her she would never be happy until she was right with him again. The same something told her she would never be happy with Collin unless he felt the same way.

Faith sighed and pulled her shawl closer about her shoulders. She couldn't wait to be in Boston once again, to leave the painful past behind and go home. She thought of Mrs. Gerson, and a longing filled her soul. Faith knew she needed time to heal, and there was no better place to do so than in the presence of such a woman. Her broken heart was desperately sick. Hurt and bitterness had poisoned her, and she was confident Mrs. Gerson would know exactly what to do. She would, no doubt, call upon the Great Physician. And as angry as Faith was with the Good Doctor right now, she was more than well aware that when it came to her heart, his was a surgery that would leave no scars.

22

Patrick shivered on the firestep of the trench he'd been living in for over a month now. Rain pelted his back before falling into the rancid hole below. He glanced down at LaRue asleep in the funk hole they had scraped out of the side of the trench, then returned his gaze to the black no-man's-land ahead, strewn with barbwire that provided little, if any, separation from the Germans.

The German offensive had begun with a vengeance mid-July, and although it lasted only five days, the toll taken on the men defending the Marne River had been considerable indeed. Patrick took little comfort that the enemy had been driven back by early August. The price was high—dozens of his friends, hundreds from his own 30th Infantry Regiment and many thousands more from the 3rd Division, cut down as they defended the Marne River line in the effort to save Paris.

He heard LaRue moan and jumped down to check on him. His boots landed on the rotted wooden planking of the duckboard that did almost nothing to separate the men from the sewage and rats. He felt the heat of LaRue's forehead as he touched it, and knew the dysentery was sucking the life out of him. Patrick made up his mind to get him back to the billet.

He looked up at the soldier propped on the firestep next

to his and wondered if he was asleep. He smiled. Only Kapowsky could sleep standing up in the muck of a trench hole. He looked up at the lanky farm boy from Kansas whom everyone said could sleep on a picket fence. He prodded his boot. "Kapowsky!"

The farm boy roused, his eyelids heavy as he squinted down at Patrick.

"LaRue is really sick. He's been moaning all night, and this rain can't be good for him. I'm taking him back to the billet. Will you be okay here?"

Kapowsky nodded, returning his gaze ahead. He began dozing once again, surely dreaming of being astride his combine in a gleaming field of wheat.

It had been fairly quiet most of the night, except for the occasional artillery shells that lit up the sky over miles of trenches. He was blessed, Patrick realized. Rumor had it that as many as one-third of the soldiers killed on the Western Front met their demise in these trenches from the same shells that had been falling around him for the last month. Never was he more grateful for his faith than now, while in the bowels of these polluted trenches where death was all too frequent a visitor.

"LaRue!" he whispered, trying to stir his friend.

LaRue moaned and clutched at his stomach.

The stench of diarrhea filled Patrick's nostrils. "LaRue, I'm taking you back to the billet."

LaRue's eyelids flittered. He nodded weakly before doubling over into a cramp.

Patrick wondered how he would get him out of the trench, much less back to his bunk. He said a quick prayer and hoisted him up on the rear side of the firestep, where LaRue wavered precariously, weak as a kitten. With a moan, he fell back against Patrick, slamming him against the wall of the trench. Patrick cursed silently under his breath, a habit formed quickly in the company of men intimidated by war.

"LaRue, you've got to try! You can do it," Patrick said, his voice fierce as he leaned to pick him up in his arms. LaRue began to cry, and Patrick's jaw hardened. The tears of men had become all too common a sight in the trenches.

Clutching Patrick's arm, LaRue spoke with labored breath. "I won't make it, Patrick, I'm dying." He wheezed and doubled over again.

Patrick stared at LaRue's white face and felt him shivering in his arms. "No, you're not! You're going to make it."

LaRue's lips twitched. "Do something for me?" he whispered. He tugged at a chain on his neck that held a tiny silver cross hopelessly entangled with his dog tags.

"LaRue, what are you doing—don't!"

"Please . . . see that Evelyn gets this," he whispered. LaRue yanked at the cross with more strength than Patrick would have believed possible.

"Wait, LaRue, I'll get it." Patrick lifted the cross from his friend's neck. Clenching LaRue at the waist, he hauled him to his feet. He yelled for Kapowsky's help. The two managed to heave LaRue over the back of the trench. Patrick slapped Kapowsky on the back. "Thanks, Farm Boy. I won't be long."

Kapowsky nodded and returned to his post.

Patrick climbed up the back wall of the trench, where LaRue lay prostrate, and pulled him to his feet. With a heavy grunt, he hiked him over his shoulder. *LaRue is going to make it*, he thought to himself, *if I have to die trying*. Taking his next step, he saw the ground illuminate before him. Patrick felt something crease his head. He dropped to the rain-soaked ground, spilling them both into a sea of mud. He tried to get up, but a jolt of electricity scorched through him. His vision began to blur. He touched his hand to his head and felt a hole in his skull and the taste of blood warm in his mouth.

"Lord, help me . . ." he prayed. He could feel his energy ebbing away, and his hand strained for LaRue's. Another shaft of light lit up the night sky. It was brighter than anything he'd ever seen. He smiled into its luminance with an amazing peace. "I'm ready, Lord," Patrick whispered with unspeakable joy, as a blinding burst of light took his breath away.

Marcy sat up in the dark, her breathing shallow. Beads of perspiration dampened her forehead. She reached out to touch Katie, who was curled up in a ball, wedged between Bridget and her. They both shivered. Another nightmare, if not Katie's, then her own. Marcy squeezed her eyes shut to fight the tears, then placed her head on the pillow once again.

She lay there, ramrod straight, her body exhausted and her mind racing with anxious thoughts indifferent to her weariness. She wanted to spoon with Katie, but there was no room in the tiny bed. It was just as well. If she did, the longing for Patrick would be too great, the memories too painful. It would only remind her that almost a year had passed since he'd last lain beside her, gently spooning her while the warmth of his breath touched the back of her neck.

She got little sleep these days. Patrick was stationed on the Marne, where the German offensive was taking place in that battle-weary section of France. Marcy couldn't seem to shake this lingering uneasiness in her mind. It had begun the day Faith had left and grown steadily worse, finally invading her dreams on a regular basis. Even Katie, so happy in Ireland, had taken to more frequent bouts with nightmares, scurrying into Marcy's bed for comfort in the middle of the night.

Marcy gave up the quest for sleep and rose in the dark, padding quietly to where her housecoat lay on the chair. Wrapping it tightly around her, she headed downstairs to the kitchen, where she could read and pray and perhaps calm the frantic beating of her heart.

She wondered how Faith was doing in Boston, and the thought produced a twinge of hurt. She hadn't believed her daughter would leave. Never had one of her children spoken to her in such a manner that they weren't met with the wrath of her Irish temper. Yet she had remained almost silent throughout those last moments with Faith. Perhaps it was shock, Marcy reasoned. If it had been Charity, her eyes would have been flashing and the punishment swift. But Marcy had little experience with disciplining Faith. She seldom had to, so anxious had this daughter been to please her mother, so diligent to please her God.

Marcy bent over to add more peat to the fading fire. She worked until the warmth of its flames was steady and strong, filling the cozy kitchen with its welcome heat. She walked to the sink, filled the pot with water, and set it on the stove to boil for tea, then pulled a chair next to the fire. She grabbed the rosary off the mantel and held it in her lap, caressing the wooden beads as her thoughts drifted.

She knew Faith had arrived safely, for Mrs. Gerson had been kind enough to send a telegram telling her so. The day Faith left over a month ago, Marcy sent a telegram of her own, alerting Mrs. Gerson as to Faith's return and Marcy's deep concern for her emotional and spiritual well-being. Her message had been brief and void of details, but Marcy knew Christa would read between the lines. She would know exactly what to do with this wayward daughter of hers. The knowledge of this was one of the few comforts Marcy enjoyed.

Her daughter's departure in late August had changed everything. Marcy would never again remember the waning days of summer with fondness. Katie cried for days, on and off, almost retreating back into toddlerhood, so demanding was she of Marcy's attention. Steven seemed oblivious, as most young boys would be, but Marcy noticed that he, like the rest of them, was far more somber these days. Beth found solace in her world of books, and Charity seemed in a stupor, merely going through the motions of existence, so stunned was she at the viciousness of Faith's retaliation.

And Mitch. Marcy's fingers stilled on a wooden bead as she remembered how his voice had quavered when he had called hours later. He had checked the manifests of all freighters sailed, and although Faith's name had not been among them, she was gone nonetheless. Marcy had shivered at the news. Faith had probably given a false name, she realized, just another lie in her daughter's painful quest to flee. Mitch begged Marcy's absolution, telling her how sorry he was for the pain he caused, and his voice had broken several times during the discourse.

"Mrs. O'Connor," he said, his voice rough with emotion, "I hope you can forgive me for what I've done. There's no way I can make it up to you, I realize, but I want you to know I'm praying for all of you, especially Faith. I want you to understand if you need anything—moral support, money, help in any way—I would be crushed if you didn't call on me."

"Thank you, Mitch," she whispered, her voice as shaky as his. "I will, if I need to." He had not come around since, but she knew he wrestled with grief of his own and needed time to heal.

Marcy sighed. They all needed time to heal, she thought, rising at the wailing whistle of the teakettle. She poured herself a cup and absently bobbed the tea leaves up and down until the brew was dark and rich. Its fragrant steam drifted in the cool air. As she strained the leaves from the cup, she felt her uneasiness return, swirling through her like the cream in her tea. She hadn't heard from Patrick or Sean in over two months, and it worried her terribly, especially knowing both were in the heat of battle. She had, thank God, heard from Collin, in a letter from a Paris hospital informing them a piece of shrapnel had torn through his chest. Thankfully it was only a peripheral wound, though it had come within inches of taking his life. He would be good as new once it healed, he boasted, and hoped he would have the opportunity to return to the front before the fighting was done. Either Faith had thought better of her threats to write Collin about Charity or he had not yet received her letter, for he made no mention of it. It only spoke of his gratitude that his life had been spared by the hand of God.

Marcy sat down and held the steaming cup with both hands, allowing its heat to seep into her fingers. Its warmth did nothing, however, for the cold fingers of fear that clutched at her heart, and she wished she could rid herself of this strange sense of foreboding. Was it over Mima, she wondered? Her grandmother had taken a turn for the worse shortly after Faith had left. Although Marcy knew her grandmother's health had been steadily declining for a long time and had little to do with Faith's departure, the eerie coincidence bothered her all the same.

Marcy thought about the turn of events over the last year and wondered when she might ever again feel the joy for life she had once known. But as bad as things were, she knew in her heart they could be worse, and a shiver skipped down her spine as the uneasiness grew. She wouldn't think about that, she decided. She would, like Patrick had said so many times before, pray about it instead.

Carefully, she laid her cup at her feet and grasped the rosary in her hands. Prayer was what sustained her in her moments of need, always routing the grip of fear from her heart. God was her calm in the midst of this storm, this Prince of Peace, promising to keep her in perfect peace until the end. Closing her eyes, Marcy met with him there and let the warmth of his presence, like the warmth of the fire, chase the chill from her soul.

Charity couldn't stand it another moment, this abyss her sister had flung them all into. The house was like a morgue since she'd left over a month ago, and there seemed to be little joy available anywhere. It was bad enough Mother walked around as if in a daze most hours of the day, but Mima was getting progressively worse too, and Charity had never seen Bridget so depleted of her usual mirth and good humor.

Standing in her room in front of the mirror, Charity posed and held up the new dress she had just purchased from the store where she worked. It had taken three weeks to save up for it, but it was worth it. The pale blue frock went especially well with her coloring, and she was quite pleased how it matched her eyes exactly. She studied her reflection with approval. The dark circles plaguing her eyes since reading Faith's letter were finally gone now, as was the state of shock that had put a pall on her cheeks when she realized what her sister intended to do. A sharp intake of breath had fused to her throat when she had first read the letter, for she hadn't believed Faith capable of writing such hateful things. Then the words finally sank in, and the fear that pasted in her mouth kept her in turmoil for weeks.

But, she was feeling some better now, and had every intention of feeling better yet. Disrobing before the mirror, she surveyed her body in her chemise. Her breasts, though lush and full, lifted high, causing her creamy skin to mound softly above the neckline. She angled to the side with her hands on her hips, admiring the dark slash of cleavage. Dipping her head into a seductive pose, she peered out beneath sooty lashes and wondered how long it would take Mitch to fall in love with her. She was certainly more of a woman than her sister, at least to the eyes of a man of the world like Mitch Dennehy. And Charity already knew how he felt about that.

She smiled. His kiss had been as wonderful as Collin's, she thought for the hundredth time, and he'd certainly been putty in her hands! That is, until Faith arrived. Charity frowned in the mirror, then took a deep breath. But Faith was gone now, and Mitch was heartbroken, no doubt—a condition she hoped would make him more than susceptible to her charms.

Charity glanced at the clock on the nightstand and knew she had to hurry. It was almost 6:00 p.m., and Mitch usually left the office by 7:00. Things were always quieter then, he had told her mother once, which allowed him to get more work done. Charity slipped the blue dress over her shoulders and brushed her pale gold hair until it shimmered. She applied a touch of rouge to her lips and dabbed a bit of the color to her cheeks, then pinched them before heading downstairs.

"Mother, I'm going out," she said, entering the kitchen.

Marcy glanced up from the stove. "Charity, dinner will be ready in fifteen minutes; aren't you going to eat?"

Charity smiled one of the few smiles anyone had seen on her face in a long while. "I'll get something out."

"But, where are you going?"

"To Myrna's, then maybe out for supper."

Marcy gave her a weary smile. "I'm so glad you're taking an interest in your appearance once again, Charity. You look very pretty tonight. Will you be late?" Marcy asked.

Charity flashed a smile. "I certainly hope so!" she said

and grinned. She blew her mother a kiss and sailed out the door.

Mitch had taken to working later than usual these days. It helped to keep his mind busy, he noticed, and he took full advantage of the heavy load Michael doled out since Faith had left. He suspected Michael did it more out of concern than the pressing need to get the work done, but either way, Mitch was grateful. He liked pushing himself so hard that he would just fall into bed at night, too exhausted to realize how much he missed her.

He knew Michael was worried about him. For pity's sake, he was worried about himself and wondered when the sick feeling would finally go away. It had never taken this long to get over anyone. He frowned. But then, this wasn't just anyone. No, this was the woman who had captured his heart, the woman he had hoped to spend the rest of his life with. Mitch supposed the old timetables for getting on with one's life no longer applied.

He dropped his pencil on the desk, then leaned back in the chair and closed his eyes, his fingers massaging the fatigue from his face. He hoped he was tired enough to sleep tonight. He hated that more than anything—lying awake on his bed, staring at the ceiling, realizing she would never be there beside him.

He heard a sound at the door and reached to grab the wastebasket. "You're here a little early tonight, aren't you, Clara?" he asked, pushing the basket out from his desk.

"Early? I thought I was late."

Mitch looked up at Charity, and his mouth slacked open. Despite the element of surprise obviously playing to her advantage, he sensed fluster beneath the composure that masked her face. Even so, she draped herself regally against the door. He watched as she stepped into his office, striding as if she had just walked off the pages of a magazine. Her skin glowed, her eyes were luminous, and her body swayed in a haze of pale blue the exact shade of her eyes.

Mitch scowled. "I thought you were the cleaning lady. What the devil are you doing here?" He swore under his breath, then clamped his lips together. "Sorry. Tough habit to break."

Charity smiled. "Don't break it for me."

Mitch angled back in his chair and assessed her through hooded eyes. The blush on her cheeks deepened.

"So . . . why are you here?" he asked again, although he already knew the answer from the way she looked.

She smiled. "Look, Mitch, it's been a month since . . . well, since . . . look, I know you're hurting and . . . well, we're both hurting . . ."

It was the first time he ever heard her stammer, and it seemed to unnerve her completely.

"I mean, I just thought . . ." Her blue eyes pleaded. "Well, I just know I could use someone to talk to, and I thought that maybe . . . maybe you could too."

He studied her, never moving a muscle until he spoke. When he did, his voice was steeped with sarcasm. "That's what got us into trouble the last time."

"I know," she said, rubbing her arms with restless hands as she stared hard at the floor. "But I just thought you might, that's all. And I thought that maybe . . . well, maybe we could get a bite to eat."

He didn't say anything, and he could tell she was horribly uncomfortable, a condition he guessed was totally unfamiliar to her. He was tempted to finish her off.

As if reading his thoughts, her chin shot up, and arrogance peaked in her brow. "If you're not interested, Mitch, that's fine," she said coolly. "I just thought since we've so much in common . . ."

His laugh was harsh. "And what would that be?" he asked, pressing his hand to his eyes.

She paused before she spoke. "Well . . . we've both been wounded by my sister . . ."

His smile faded as he looked away. He closed his eyes to rub the back of his neck and then opened them once again, releasing a weary breath. "Sure, why not?" He heard her exhale slowly as he stood to put on his coat. "What are you hungry for?" he asked, immediately regretting the question.

A dangerous smile quirked at the corners of her full lips. This had the feel of trouble, he thought, but he shook it off. Hang it all, he could use a little trouble after all he'd been through. He rounded the desk and walked to the door.

"Whatever you like," she said, her silky voice suspended in the air. Her head tilted to the side while her full lips eased into a smile. He supposed she was making an offer he couldn't refuse. Too bad. There was a time he would've jumped at a chance like this. But that was before. Now he found himself saddled with a conscience and a boatload of heartache to boot. And between the two, he saw little chance for a meeting of the minds—or bodies—whatever the case may be.

Faith didn't have any idea why she'd been so frightened standing before Mrs. Gerson's door, suitcase in hand. But she'd been trembling, nonetheless, the day she arrived in Boston a month ago. Perhaps she worried what the old woman would think of her, a young woman once devoted to God, now so lukewarm and carrying far more baggage than a simple valise.

The door had opened, and Faith suddenly realized she needn't have worried. The joy in the old woman's face was unmistakable, as was the warmth in her voice as she welcomed her, a glimmer of tears in her vacant eyes. Faith's own eyes smarted with wetness as she picked up her valise. "Mrs. Gerson, would it be possible—"

"Of course, my dear!" Mrs. Gerson said, interrupting her before she could finish. "I'm thrilled to have you. I've been looking forward to it since I received your mother's telegram."

A stab of shame shot straight to Faith's heart at the mention of her mother. She was grateful Mrs. Gerson couldn't see the guilt on her face. "I'm glad Mother notified you. How is she?"

"Regretfully, I don't know, but I planned on sending a telegram the moment you arrived, safe and sound. Come now, let's get you settled in, and then we'll have tea."

The evening passed pleasantly enough with a lovely dinner and welcome conversation. Mrs. Gerson detailed all the news of the neighborhood and especially reports on Maisie and Briana. "I know I promised Maisie I would advise her of your arrival," Mrs. Gerson said with a twinkle in her eye, "but I'll call tomorrow. Tonight, I want you all to myself."

Faith followed into the parlor and took a seat, a familiar peace settling in her soul. She knew it was inevitable Mrs. Gerson would want to know why she was here without her family. For the first time in many days, she allowed herself to focus on the pain of Ireland. With an edge in her voice, she relayed the whole agonizing sequence, from her engagement to Mitch until the moment she found him in Charity's arms. Other than Mitch, no one but Mrs. Gerson knew more about the hurt Faith suffered through the years at the hand of her sister. Now, Faith found herself spilling all the sordid details of the bitterness that had imprisoned her since Mitch's betrayal. As good as it felt to have wounded them at the time, it felt even better now to speak it out in the open. She needed to rail against God without condemnation, baring her wounds to another human being who would listen in love. Mrs. Gerson was as patient as Faith had known she would be, and when she finally finished, the old woman was beaming.

"Why do you look so happy, Mrs. Gerson?" Faith asked, her voice tinged with the same bitterness she'd just espoused.

"Do you know what I see, Faith?" Mrs. Gerson asked, leaning forward in her chair.

"No," Faith responded curtly, "what do you see?"

Mrs. Gerson smiled a broad smile. "I see a golden opportunity, my dear."

Faith stared at the old woman, and for the first time in her life, a hint of irritation rankled. "And what would that be, Mrs. Gerson?" Faith asked, her tone clipped.

The old woman's smile remained unwavering. "Why, an opportunity to put God's Word to the test, of course! A golden opportunity, my dear." Mrs. Gerson hovered on the edge of her seat, her face aglow with the same excitement Faith had once known herself.

"You've always encountered problems with your sister Charity as long as I've known you, and you were always faithful to return love for the pain she inflicted. But this . . ." she said, stretching her hands out in front of her, "this, my dear, is the answer to your prayers. It's the way home, the resolution! You have an opportunity here to take the narrow path Jesus spoke about, and I have absolutely no doubt whatsoever, that you, Faith O'Connor, will choose life!"

Faith bristled, wondering if Mrs. Gerson had always spoken in riddles like this. What on earth was she rambling on about? "I'm afraid I don't understand your point."

Mrs. Gerson ignored her terse tone and smiled, picking up the Bible next to her chair. She held it aloft. Reluctantly, Faith reached for the book, surprised that her heart jumped as she touched its leather binding.

"Open it to Deuteronomy 30:15, please," Mrs. Gerson instructed.

Faith sat back in the chair and flipped through the pages of the book she'd read so often, up until a week ago. She found the passage and read it aloud.

"See, I have set before thee this day life and good, and death and evil; in that I command thee this day to love Jehovah thy God, to walk in his ways, and to keep his commandments and his statutes and his ordinances, that thou mayest live and multiply, and that Jehovah thy God may bless thee in the land whither thou goest in to possess it. But if thy heart turn away, and thou wilt not hear, but shalt be drawn away, and worship other gods, and serve them; I denounce unto you this day, that ye shall surely perish; ye shall not prolong your days in the land . . ."

Faith's voice trailed off, and Mrs. Gerson lifted her face, her eyes glowing. "Read on, Faith, the next paragraph, please."

Faith rolled her eyes and puffed out a sigh.

"I call heaven and earth to witness against you this day, that I have set before thee life and death, the blessing and the curse: therefore choose life, that thou mayest live, thou and thy seed . . ."

Faith couldn't go on. Her voice balked as she slapped the book closed. "These are just words, Mrs. Gerson. I don't even know what they mean."

The old woman bent forward, teetering on the edge of her chair, her eyes shimmering with joy. "It means, my dear, that every moment of our lives we have the opportunity to reap blessings from the hand of Almighty God. It means you have a choice in your future, Faith, that every decision you make shapes the course of your life, whether there will be joy or sorrow, blessing or curse. He's begging you, Faith—he begs each of us—to choose life! Choose his way, the way of forgiveness and prayer.

In the face of pain such as you've encountered, my dear, the choice is clear. You can choose to hate your sister and Mitch and hold on to your bitterness, or you can choose to forgive and be set free. If you choose hate, your heart will grow hard and cold as I suspect you've already seen, and you will be destroyed. God is very clear about that. But, if you choose life—his way and his precepts—you choose blessing, not only for your own life but for the life of your children after you."

Faith shook her head. "I can't forgive them; it's too hard."

Mrs. Gerson chuckled. "Skip up to verse 11, my dear."

Faith scowled as her fingers slapped through the pages once again. When she found the verse, she cleared her throat. "For this commandment which I command thee this day, it is not too hard for thee, neither is it far off. It is not in heaven, that thou shouldest say, Who shall go up for us to heaven, and bring it unto us, and make us to hear it, that we may do it? Neither is it beyond the sea, that thou shouldest say, Who shall go over the sea for us, and bring it unto us, and make us to hear it, that we may do it? But the word is very nigh unto thee, in thy mouth, and in thy heart, that thou mayest do it."

Mrs. Gerson's face was rapt with excitement, and Faith's eyes blinked wide. She slumped in the chair and pushed the hair from her face, the Bible splayed in her lap. Could it really be that easy to reap the blessings of God? With all of the hurt and hate within her, was it really within her reach to forgive? It was not an impossible thing to do—God was saying it right there in his Word. It was not too difficult or beyond her reach. No, his Word, which commanded her to forgive and love, could be in her mouth if she spoke it, and then in her heart to perform it. It was simply a decision, a choice, one that God himself begged her to make. And all because he wanted to bless her.

Faith closed her eyes; she had no power whatsoever over the flow of tears streaking her face. Suddenly, it all seemed perfectly clear, as if blinders had fallen from her eyes and shackles from her heart. Crumpling to her knees she sobbed before the Lord, her heart broken with grief at the path she had chosen. It had enticed her, taken her down before she ever realized, and only now was she able to see the folly of her ways. She felt the warmth of Mrs. Gerson's palm on her head, stroking like the hand of God on the prodigal child. Faith moaned and grabbed the old woman's hand, pressing it against her tearstained face. "I'm so sorry, Mrs. Gerson," she wept, her voice broken and rasped. "Please, God, forgive me and heal me."

She thought of Mitch, and pain seared her heart. She thought of Charity, and bitterness rose like bile in her throat. She shuddered. "No! I will forgive them, I will! Dear God, please help me to obey . . . to forgive. It's your will I choose, not my own."

She lay there in the old woman's arms until the trembling stopped and peace filled her soul. She felt as if she had returned from the brink of death, shivering while Mrs. Gerson held her. When she could finally speak, she lifted swollen eyes to peer into the face of the woman who had never failed her, not unlike their God. "Mrs. Gerson, will you pray for me? Will you pray I never turn on him again?"

Mrs. Gerson smiled and gently touched Faith's cheek as she stared straight ahead. "My dear Faith, I've never stopped," she whispered.

A smile trembled on Faith's lips. Slowly, she rested her head in the old woman's lap once again, quite forgiven . . . and quite ready for the peace that would follow.

Charity hadn't had this much fun since Collin. She studied the man across the table and decided if her sister ever spoiled her plan to become Mrs. Collin McGuire, she could be reasonably happy with someone as wonderful as Mitch Dennehy. Not that he entertained such thoughts, she suspected, judging from the dispassionate look on his face, but there were ways around his hesitation, she knew. And no one knew them better than Charity Katherine O'Connor. Smiling, she lifted the almost-empty glass of wine to her lips.

Mitch slid the bottle of wine out of her reach. "I think you've had enough," he remarked dryly, miffed he'd allowed her any at all.

Charity giggled. "It's my first, you know," she said with a grin, and he couldn't help but think he liked her this way, more the little girl than the vamp.

He reached for his wallet. "It's time to go home, young lady. Your mother will have my head."

Her eyes flitted closed. "I don't want to go home. I'm having way too much fun."

He signaled the waiter. "Hot coffee, please, and very strong." The waiter nodded and disappeared as Charity lounged against the booth. Tipsy as she was, he knew she was well aware of his gaze, and she made the most of it by stretching lazily, arms high above her head and seduction in her eyes. He shook his head and laughed.

A hint of fire sparked in her eyes as she opened them. She dropped her arms—and the act. "Why are you laughing?" she snapped.

His smile was patient. "Because you're such a little girl. You've got plenty of time for all of this, Charity. Why don't you just slow down?"

Her back squared, and for the first time, he saw the same Irish temper he'd seen in Faith. He grinned, despite the blistering look on her face.

"You didn't think I was a little girl when you kissed me," she said.

The smile froze on his lips. She thumped back against the booth, her arms rigidly crossed while the golden curls spilled down the front of that amazing blue dress.

His eyes smoldered as the waiter reappeared, setting the cups of coffee down. Mitch shoved a cup toward her, and the dark liquid sloshed into the saucer. "Drink it," he ordered, and she sulked as she grabbed the spoon to stir in the cream.

He brought his own cup to his lips and sipped while he watched her, then set it down again. He sloped forward to glare like a stern parent. "So help me, Charity, you tripped me up once; you can rest assured I'll do my level best to see it won't happen again. You are a handful, little girl, and one of these days it's going to get you into trouble way over your head."

Her eyes narrowed as she drank her coffee. "You know, Mitch, you can treat me like a child if you like, and you can even place yourself in the role of wise adult if it makes you feel any better. But the truth of the matter is, you wanted to kiss me. You know it, and I know it, and we're both well aware no child could have elicited that response."

Her smile was smug as his jaw slacked open. She picked up her cup to sip again, leveling her gaze. He snapped his mouth shut, and a muscle jerked in his cheek. He gulped his coffee and opened his wallet to pay the check, avoiding her eyes.

She took her time finishing, then stepped from behind the booth, never looking back as she calmly made her way toward the door. Mitch threw some money on the table and followed, completely aware of the stares she drew walking through the restaurant, shoulders back and head high. Outside, she waited for him with a frosty look on her face. "Will you give me a lift home?" she asked, her tone chilly.

He nodded and opened the door of the car, and she slipped in without so much as a thank-you. He pinched his lips together, afraid to risk any dialogue. She had a knack for turning things around on him, and he wasn't in the mood to give her the chance.

When he pulled up in front of Bridget's house, he left the engine running while he waited for her to get out, his jaw clamped tight. Despite the cool of the night, he was sweating. Not only because he'd sat in this same spot with Faith more times than he could remember, but because Charity made him downright nervous. In his book, she was only a kid of eighteen. Yet when it came to men, she was truly wise beyond her years, and he had already gone down that road one time too many. "Good night, Charity," he said, hoping the finality of his tone would tell her he wasn't interested.

"Good night, Mitch." She leaned over to kiss his lips. The shock of it caused his heart to stop as she balanced a hand on his leg.

He grabbed her wrist and jerked it back. "So help me, Charity—"

She lunged at him again, causing a surge of heat to roll over him. Blast it all, it wasn't fair, he moaned to himself. He pushed her away, his breathing too fast to suit him.

She fell hard against the seat, hair disheveled and defiance glowing in her eyes. "I know you're attracted to me, Mitch," she said, her voice tinged with anger and hurt.

He tunneled his hand through his hair and took a deep breath. "Whether I am or not is beside the point. You're too young, Charity."

"I'm only two years younger than Faith. Age didn't seem to be an issue with her."

Mitch sighed. "I know you don't want to hear this, but

I'm not looking for what you're offering. Before Faith, I would have gladly accommodated you. But not now. Your sister taught me something I never would have believed possible. True passion—the kind that really satisfies—isn't cheap. It doesn't manipulate and coax for a moment's pleasure. Believe it or not, it's tied to real love . . . and it always has God's blessing."

Tears welled in her eyes, and he sighed. He lifted her chin with his finger. "The truth is, Charity, yes, I am attracted to you. A man would have to be deaf, dumb, and blind not to be. But it's not enough. There's more out there than turning a head. And I'm really afraid if you don't find that out now, you're going to be one unhappy lady."

Charity sniffed and swiped a tear from her cheek. Mitch wiped another off with his hand. "Promise me you'll stop this. You're only going to end up getting hurt. Trust me, what you're selling, only the wrong guys will be buying."

For the first time, the facade appeared to be gone as she slumped in the seat, a sigh quivering from her lips. "I don't know how," she whispered. "This . . . comes so easily for me."

He nodded. "With your looks, I don't wonder. But you need to straighten up. Get yourself right with God. It'll do wonders in finding the love you're looking for."

Her brow wrinkled. She cocked her head and scrutinized him out of the corner of her eye. "If I did, would I have a chance with you?"

He laughed and shook his head. "We're not talking about me, Charity, we're talking about you. You just need to shape up. *And* get a little older."

He could see a smile forming on her lips. "I can do that," she whispered. She opened the door and slid out. After shutting the door behind her, she leaned in the window and grinned. "Once I go through that door, it's all over, you know. Sure you don't want to reconsider?"

He cleared his throat to keep from smiling. "Go to bed, little girl, and ask God to help you. I'll be watching."

"I'm counting on it," she said. Flouncing her hair over her shoulder, she disappeared into the house before he could even get out of gear.

23

Marcy caught herself humming, an unusual thing in itself these days. She seemed to have lost so much of her sparkle over the last year, but lately she had managed to rebound on Saturdays. Whether it was the fact she enjoyed knowing the children could sleep in and awaken to the hot breakfast she prepared, or whether it was the feeling that the war was coming to an end, she wasn't quite sure. But the lift was in her step, nonetheless, and when Saturdays rolled around, she was always grateful for the reprieve.

The end was near, she was certain. The newspapers tiptoed around it, and her neighbors spoke of it in hushed tones, almost afraid to speak too loud lest it not be true. But it was coming. She could feel it in her bones. Change—as sure as the autumn breeze silently whirling into a cool bluster—and Marcy couldn't wait. She was tired of the loneliness and the worry. She was tired of missing Patrick and Sean and Collin. And she was especially tired of her family scattered.

She glanced up at the clock as she kneaded the dough that would soon become popovers for her children's breakfast, and then pushed aside a strand of hair with her arm. Almost nine o'clock! She could hear footsteps above and knew Katie had wakened, no doubt refusing to let her grandmother sleep one moment longer. Marcy thought of how difficult it would be for her mother and Mima when she and her family left, as they all knew they would. They had shared laughter and love, tears and heartbreak for a year now, and Marcy worried how her family's departure might affect them.

The kitchen door flew open, and Katie came bounding in, blond hair streaming behind. She ran to clutch at Marcy's legs, nearly knocking her over. Steven was hot on her heels, a scowl on his face as he screeched to a stop in front of his mother. Marcy stared, her eyebrow arched in question. "Good morning," she said with a wry smile. "I think."

Steven apparently wasn't in agreement as he stood, arms crossed and a sour look on his face. "Mother, she's been at it again."

"What is it this time, Steven?" Marcy asked patiently, prying Katie from her legs.

"Five of my best marbles, including my aggie."

Marcy bent down to look into Katie's eyes, which were focused on the floor. "Katie, please tell me you didn't take Steven's marbles again! Katie?"

Katie peered up at Marcy. A pixie grin curled on her lips. "Okay, I didn't take 'em."

"She did, Mother, I found them in her dishes—in a bowl of milk!"

"Katie Rose!"

"My bear needs to eat, doesn't he? He needed cereal," she said, pouting.

"Young lady, first you lie and tell me you didn't take them—"

"You told me to, Mama! You said, 'Katie, please tell me you didn't take Steven's marbles.' So I did!"

Marcy groaned and picked Katie up in her arms. "A perfectly good Saturday morning, and you have to ruin it," she muttered, lugging Katie to the door.

"No, Mama, please, no . . ." Katie cried, cutting loose with a piercing scream.

Marcy attempted a smile at Steven. "Well, now, that should see to it that everyone's up for breakfast. Steven, bring the marbles to me, and I'll wash them for you, all right? Rest assured, Katie will be punished."

There were so many reasons she missed Patrick, she thought as she carried Katie kicking and screaming up the stairs, not the least of which was the deplorable chore of discipline. Katie had always been what Patrick lovingly referred to as a "handful." But the year of his absence had only made it worse, despite Marcy's best efforts at exercising control over their seven-year-old, strong-willed child. No, as far as Marcy was concerned—and Katie, apparently—Patrick could not return soon enough.

Katie was banished to her room for breakfast. The breakfast table would be a little less exciting today, but certainly more peaceful. Not necessarily a bad thing, Marcy decided. She made her rounds to waken the rest of the family, who, despite Katie's best efforts, were still sound asleep.

The doorbell rang as Marcy descended the steps, and she stopped midway. Perhaps it was Patricia looking for Elizabeth, she thought, making her way to the door. She pulled it open and was met by two soldiers who stood stone-faced, hats in hand. Marcy blinked, her hand paralyzed on the doorknob.

"Mrs. Patrick O'Connor?"

Marcy's gaze shifted to the soldier who had spoken, and she nodded slowly.

"May we come in, ma'am?" he asked.

She nodded again, never budging from the door. The soldiers glanced briefly at each other before the spokesman repeated the request.

"Ma'am, may we come inside, please?" he asked again, his voice gentle.

Marcy's hand clutched to her throat as fear fisted in her chest. "No!" she screamed. "What do you want?"

Her cry brought Charity to the landing. "Mother, what is it?" She sped down the steps, tying her robe tightly about her. She grabbed her mother's arm, but Marcy shook it off, glaring at the men.

"What do you want?" she said again.

The spokesman turned to Charity with a pleading look. "Miss, we have news of her husband. May we come in, please?"

"Of course," Charity said, her voice trembling as she pried Marcy's fingers from the door. Charity looped her arm around her mother's waist and led her to the parlor as if she were a child. The men followed silently while Bridget and the children huddled on the steps.

Charity looked up at Bridget. "Grandmother, these gentlemen have news about Father," she said calmly, and they exchanged a look of dread. "Can you take everyone into the kitchen and give them breakfast, please?" She spoke with an air of authority, and Bridget nodded, ushering Beth and Steven into the kitchen.

Marcy lowered to the couch, her eyes glazed as she stared at the floor. Charity took a seat beside her and clutched her arm around her mother's waist.

The soldier wasted no time. "Mrs. O'Connor, I regret to inform you that your husband, Private Patrick O'Connor of the 30th Infantry Regiment, 3rd Division, was killed in the line of duty—"

"Noooooooo!" The sound that issued from her lips was bloodcurdling as Marcy lunged at the soldier, her fists striking him in the chest before his arms immobilized her.

Charity reached for her mother, her eyes brimming with tears. "Mother, please . . ."

"He's lying . . . it's not true!" Marcy shrieked. "Patrick

wouldn't leave me . . . and God wouldn't do that!" Her body writhed in pain as she sank to the floor.

The soldier's face was etched in stone as he reached to pick her up. Silently, he placed her on the couch, and the two women collapsed in each other's arms. Sobs wracked their bodies.

The soldier knelt by the sofa, his voice filled with compassion. "Ma'am," he began again, "your husband died saving another soldier. He was a hero, ma'am."

Marcy gripped the sofa, her small frame convulsing.

Charity lifted her chin and blinked back the tears. "When?" she whispered.

"September 30. Your father was killed instantly by an enemy artillery shell."

"Faith's birthday," Charity whispered listlessly. "Where?" she asked, her voice cracking.

"Along the Marne River, ma'am, right outside of Paris."

Through her weeping, Marcy heard Charity choke back a sob. "Where is my father's body?" she whispered.

The soldier stood up, as if at attention.

"Ma'am, Private O'Connor was buried with military honors at the Aisen-Marne Cemetery, not far from Paris."

A violent tremor shuddered through Marcy's body. Holding onto her daughter, she attempted to rise, quivering as she stood. "Sir, we need to be alone now . . ."

The second soldier stepped forward, and for the first time, Marcy noticed the box in his hands, which he now held forward. "Ma'am, these are your husband's personal effects."

Marcy's eyes fixed on the box that was all she had left of the man she loved. Taking a step forward, she held her hands out and grasped it in her arms as a low, aching moan left her lips. The room darkened, as if the sun had suddenly left the sky on this bright, October morn, and her vision began to blur, from tears, she thought. But as the room began to spin and the blood left her brain, Marcy felt herself letting go—not the box, which she clenched tightly in her hands—but her consciousness, which demanded escape as she slowly slumped to the floor.

It was as if she were walking in a fog or a dream, so surreal were the next few moments for Charity. She saw the men to the door and returned to where her mother lay limp on the sofa. She heard Katie chattering in the kitchen, but nothing else, and realized her grandmother must have rescued her sister from her punishment. Her mother stirred, and Charity braced herself for the torment that would follow. All at once, her mother's eyes opened, and she groped at her daughter. Her sobs rose again to fill the empty parlor with the sound of her anguish.

Charity laid her head against her mother's and stroked her hair as tears streamed her own face. She didn't want to think about it now. She couldn't. Her father was dead, and she had never let him know how very much she loved him. How much she wanted to please him, to be "his girl." Charity closed her eyes, the pain in her heart choking her with grief. No, she thought to herself. Her mother needed her to be strong, not weak. She touched her mother's face. "You need to eat," she whispered, "and we need to tell the others."

Marcy nodded, and Charity braced her, and the two went arm in arm into the kitchen. Never had there been a blacker day. It passed, and then the night, but never the pain. It seemed to grow with each successive moment, and Charity felt as if they all had died. In the days that followed, when she wasn't weeping in her room, her mother would roam aimlessly through the silent house, listless as she tended duties more from habit than thought. Her grandmother did her best to uplift them all, futile as it was.

It was Charity who took on the task of notifying Sean and Faith, and of course, Collin. Her messages were brief and sparse on detail, so unusual for her, but she couldn't bring herself to say more. She grew increasingly concerned about her mother as she watched her spiral into a black hole of depression. Always an early riser, her mother now took to sleeping much later, forcing her grandmother, at times, to try and rouse her in the early afternoon so she would not be up half the night with her thoughts.

By the end of the first week following the news of Patrick's death, Charity was sick with worry. Her mother wouldn't eat and was wasting away to nothing, her face pale and her eyes lifeless. Her grandmother was distraught, as well, and both she and Charity were at a loss as to what to say or do.

As they sat in the kitchen one morning, her mother suddenly appeared at the door, dark circles under her eyes and a vacant stare that had become all too familiar. "Mother, you're up! Can I get you some coffee?" Charity asked. Marcy nodded, and Charity jumped up to pour a cup. She handed it to her.

Marcy closed her eyes and sipped it slowly. When she opened them again, the faraway look was steeled with determination. "Mother, Charity . . . I know you've been worried about me, and I'm sorry. I know I haven't been myself, but then I wonder if I will ever be again." She took a deep breath and another sip of coffee. Tears welled in her eyes. "Your father . . . Patrick . . . was the world to me. I still can't believe he's gone." The wetness began to spill, and she quickly rubbed it away. "But he is," she breathed, "and we all must go on. I've decided to sell the house in Boston." Marcy looked at Bridget. "Mother, if you don't mind, I'd like to stay with you indefinitely, at least till my head is clearer. Then, I can find a house of my own here in Ireland."

Bridget grabbed her hand. "Marcy, stay as long as you like. I love you; you know that."

Marcy nodded. "Charity, I need you to call Mitch. Tell him I need to see him."

Charity opened her mouth, her heart fluttering in surprise. *Mitch!* In the agony of Patrick's death, he hadn't entered her mind, and the thought shocked her. As she thought of him now, a flood of peace rushed in. "Of course, Mother. I'll call him on Monday, unless you have his home number."

"No, Monday's fine, dear. Mitch was kind enough to offer his help after Faith left, and I never believed I would need it, but I do. I've decided to go to Boston and settle things there. I'll bring Faith home, then maybe we can get some closure, and in time, get on with our lives."

Marcy reached for Charity's hand. "Charity, when the war is over, I don't expect you to stay, you know. I'm sure Collin will want to live in Boston."

Charity caught her breath. "There's no telling what Collin will want to do, Mother," she whispered. "I don't even know if he still cares for me."

Marcy's smile was faint. "He'd be a fool not to," she said, and Charity remembered Mitch had said the very same thing.

Marcy finished her coffee and stood up. She leaned on the chair and gave them a weary look. "It's time I go to my room and spend time with Faith's Bible. Perhaps that's why the Lord allowed her to leave it. It always was such a source of comfort to her, and I've found it's done the same for me. Besides, it wouldn't do to neglect the best friend I have right now, would it?" She sighed. "I opened it this morning to John 14:18, and do you know what it said?"

Charity and Bridget shook their heads.

"It said, 'I will not leave you desolate.'" Marcy straightened her shoulders and pushed the hair from her face. "I'm going to hold him to that," she said.

"I don't care what O'Reilly says, the Fraser story stays on page one." Mitch scowled at Aiden McCrae and snatched the phone from its cradle. "Dennehy, here."

"Mitch? It's Charity. I'm so sorry to disturb you, but we need your help."

He paused. "What kind of help?"

"My mother would like to talk to you. You see, my f-father was . . . well, he was . . . killed." Her voice broke.

Mitch stiffened. He dismissed Aiden with an abrupt wave and dropped back in the chair. He shielded his eyes with his hand. "Charity . . . I'm so sorry."

"I know, Mitch. Mother asked me to call. She said that you once offered help if she ever needed it. It seems she wants to go back to Boston to . . . take care of things."

"Absolutely. I can come tonight, right after work."

"For dinner, then."

"No, I don't want to impose." He shifted in the chair, kneading the deep furrows above the bridge of his nose.

"We insist. Would 6:30 be all right? Or does it need to be later?"

"No, no, 6:30 is fine. I'll be there."

"We'll see you then. Thank you, Mitch."

He replaced the receiver and slumped back in the chair, staring ahead into nothing. He had never met Patrick O'Connor, but he had no doubt he would have liked him. Faith had been crazy about her father. Always wanted to marry a man just like him, she would say with that gleam in her eye, then tease that she always got what she wanted.

He rubbed his eyes and stood up. He suspected Marcy needed money for the passage. He sighed. Well, this was the sign he was looking for. He'd been praying for God to either take Faith out of his heart or give him the nerve to go after her. If Marcy was going to Boston by herself, Mitch had his answer. There was no way he could let her go alone, and for the first time in over a month, a surge of hope rushed through him.

Michael wasn't going to like this, but that was too bad. He had three weeks of vacation, and now was as good a time as any. Jamie would just have to fill in. Mitch walked to the door and suddenly realized that within weeks, he would be seeing Faith again. The thought sent his pulse racing. He took a deep breath, then followed it with a quick prayer. *Lord, please don't let her hate me.*

He hesitated. No, he was doing this for Marcy, not himself. He swallowed hard. *No*, he was doing it for himself, and would have done it eventually anyway if she hadn't made it so easy for him. Either way, the woman he loved was at the end of the line. And quite frankly, one reason was as good as the next.

Coming home again was like working all day in shoes that pinched your feet and a corset that cinched your waist—suddenly you slipped into a chenille robe and goose-down slippers, and it felt good.

Faith hadn't wasted too much time moping or missing Mitch, although it wouldn't have been difficult to do. Since she made her peace with God, she found she also made her peace with Mitch, and the anger stepped aside to let the longing have a shot at her. She wasn't sure what she would have done without Maisie and her job at the *Herald*; both worked in tandem to keep her from sinking into a depression. The only moments that really took her down were the nights she lay in Mrs. Gerson's guest room, wondering what woman Mitch was seeing at the moment.

All along she'd known he was a man of the world, which simply meant he had weathered his fair share of heartbreaks, she supposed, and given more than a few of his own. No doubt, he was back at it by now, buying a round of drinks at Brody's or taking a lady friend to their favorite spot at Duffy's. Faith tried to think of something else. The thought of another woman sitting in her booth was a little too hard to take, especially now that the anger was nowhere in sight.

She thought about Charity and wondered if she ever felt any remorse over her actions. Faith had no doubt her sister had masterminded the whole seduction. She was a beautiful woman, after all, a point on which Faith needed no reminding. And Mitch was a man. A man who up to a year prior had fed his appetites as regularly as her mother fed Blarney. As much as she didn't want to admit it, a part of her understood why Mitch had fallen prey.

A soft sigh feathered her lips, and Faith wondered if she would ever marry. It seemed whenever she fell in love, something derailed it, and she contemplated devoting her life to God at the St. Stephen's Convent. But only for a moment, and then thoughts of Mitch would come racing through her mind, trampling the religious vocation faster than the clip of her heart.

"So, have you even worked today?" Maisie asked, rudely interrupting Faith's daydream. "I mean, I've walked by three different times, and all I've seen is you mooning into space. Let me feel those keys—I'll bet they're cold!" She poked at Faith's Underwood.

Faith pretended to scowl. "You can be such a pain, you know that, Maisie? How did we ever become friends?"

Maisie's brows lifted a full half inch. "Don't you remember? Miss Hayword figured you needed to learn from the brightest, most attractive typist in the pool!"

Faith smirked and looked at her watch. "Thank goodness it's five o'clock." She bent to grab her purse. "Honestly, for some reason, this has been the hardest day to concentrate.

I swear, if had to type one more obituary, I would have screamed."

"So that's why you kept drifting off into dreamland, eh? I thought it might be because of a certain editor at the *Times*."

Faith delivered a withering look as she put the cover on her typewriter. "You know, I didn't realize how good I had it back in Ireland with no one to drive me crazy."

Maisie feigned surprise. "Oh, don't you remember? You had Mitch!" She exposed a toothy grin, and Faith finally laughed. There was nothing else to do. Maisie could bottom-line it better than anyone she knew and pull a smile out of you as she did it.

"Okay, okay, I miss him—horribly! Ohhhh! Where is the anger when you need it?" she cried as she draped the back of her wrist dramatically against her forehead.

"At least you're finally admitting it. Honestly, Faith, how could you expect me to believe you hated him after all the lovesick letters you wrote? I mean, really, credit me with some intelligence, will you?"

Faith's smile softened. "I know. I was pretty angry when I arrived in Boston, and yes, I will confess I now see things differently. But only because Mrs. Gerson helped me see the error of my ways."

"So, what are you going to do about it?"

"I'm not sure. What if he's in love with someone else by now?"

Maisie rolled her eyes and groaned. "If even a tenth of what you wrote in your letters is true, the man is so crazy in love, he should be committed. You need to write him."

"I want to, but . . ."

"But what?" Maisie asked. She folded her arms.

Faith slumped back in her chair, lost in a bleak stare. Her throat bobbed with emotion. "There's a part of me that's scared."

"About what?" Maisie sat down in the empty desk next to her, her brows knitted in a frown.

Faith released a heavy breath and glanced up. "I miss Mitch and I still care about him, I do, but I think I'm scared to trust him again."

Maisie put a hand on Faith's arm. "That's understandable, Faith—he hurt you. But you also left without giving him a chance to explain, a chance to make it right. If Mitch Dennehy is even half the man you said he is, you owe him that chance . . . and yourself."

Faith bit her lip, and Maisie's cheeks huffed with an impatient sigh. "Honestly, Faith, if I didn't love you so much, I'd boot you from here to Ireland just to shake you up. Goodness, how did you ever manage without me? You love the man; he loves you. He made a mistake—give him a chance to make it right. How hard is that to understand?"

Faith mulled over Maisie's words, then broke into a grin. "Okay, I will! Oh, by the way, you're supposed to come to dinner tonight. Mrs. Gerson asked me to invite you."

Maisie arched a brow. "Oh, really? And when exactly were you planning on telling me? After dessert?"

Faith laughed and gave her a hug. "I'm sorry, my mind has been somewhere else, I suppose. I'm moving back into our house tomorrow, so I've been preoccupied with that."

"*And* Mitch."

A foolish grin tickled Faith's lips. "*And* Mitch," she repeated.

"Oh. Didn't notice," Maisie said with a yawn.

Faith gave her a wry smile. "That's why Mrs. Gerson is making such a fuss about dinner tonight. It's my farewell. So, can you come?"

"Are you kidding? Pass up one of Mrs. Gerson's home-cooked meals? I think not," Maisie said with a note of indignation. She leaned forward to flick Faith on the head, and the two giggled all the way to the door.

When they arrived at Mrs. Gerson's, the house was dark. Maisie's brows rumpled in a frown. "I thought you said she was fixing dinner? Are you sure it's tonight?"

"I'm sure," Faith said quietly. Her fingers felt thick as she fumbled with the spare key to unlock the door.

"Mrs. Gerson?"

The dining room was empty, eclipsed in shadows from a single light in the foyer. Its table was void of any signs of a dinner, and Faith stopped to listen. Shards of fear prickled her skin.

"I don't understand . . ." Maisie began.

Faith waved her quiet. "Mrs. Gerson?" She waited for an answer, her heart thumping in her chest. Her mouth opened to cry out again when she heard the response, frail and broken, from the gloom of the parlor.

"In here, Faith."

The room was as black as pitch, and Faith blinked to adjust her eyes, moving toward a form sitting on the edge of the sofa, stiff and straight in the shadows. "Mrs. Gerson, are you all right?" she asked, her voice cloaked in fear.

The old woman's head slowly moved back and forth. A faint mewing sound came from her lips. And then Faith saw it—a piece of paper floating in her hand. In slow motion, Faith reached to take it. The feel of it was fragile and light to her fingers, but its heaviness crushed her lungs.

"It's a telegram . . . from your sister. I had the delivery boy read it to me. Your father . . ." Mrs. Gerson couldn't go on.

Everything in the room seized to a stop. "What?" she whispered, and for the first time in her life she saw Mrs. Gerson weep.

"Your father . . . he . . . he was killed . . ." Mrs. Gerson said, breaking on a sob.

The breath left Faith's lungs. Fear coiled within her and wrenched a moan from her lips. Maisie rushed to her side, but Faith slapped her away, hovering over Mrs. Gerson, her fists clenched at her sides. "It's not true! God wouldn't let it happen, Mrs. Gerson—you've taught me that. 'No weapon that is formed against thee shall prosper,' that's what you said! You quoted it, Mrs. Gerson . . . *from the Bible*!"

Weeping, the old woman rose to embrace her, but Faith pushed her aside. She fled to the light of the foyer, the telegram fluttering in her hand. She blinked to focus through the blur of tears and then cried out in anguish. "Maisie!" she screamed. "Read it . . . I can't see!"

Maisie took the paper from her hand. Fear bobbed in her throat as she scanned it.

"Read it!" Faith screamed again.

Maisie flinched. "Father killed in action in France. Stop. Mother and Mitch arriving by weekend. Stop. Please tell Faith. Stop. Charity."

The room started to spin, and there was a drone in her brain, but Faith ignored it. Her legs weakened as she staggered to the sofa where Mrs. Gerson sat hunched and weeping. Her eyes burned, and she squeezed them shut. Hot tears scalded her face. Mrs. Gerson reached to touch her, and this time she didn't fight.

Never had she come this close to wanting to die. How could she go on in a world without her father? He was the strength of the family, of her life as she knew it, other than God, and Faith could not fathom life without him. They had managed in Ireland only because they had been waiting, waiting for their once-happy lives to begin again. The war was to be only a brief pause in their otherwise blissful existence, not an end to it all. God had promised, hadn't he?

She thought of her mother, and anguish filled her soul.

"Oh, God," she cried. "You said you would never leave us nor forsake us. Where are you?"

Mrs. Gerson rose and put her hand on her head, and Faith felt her body go limp as the old woman prayed. Somewhere in the recesses of her mind, she heard Maisie reading, her words a distant murmuring in her brain . . .

"The Lord is my shepherd; I shall not want. He maketh me to lie down in green pastures: he leadeth me beside the still waters. He restoreth my soul: he leadeth me in the paths of righteousness for his name's sake. Yea, though I walk through the valley of the shadow of death, I will fear no evil: for thou art with me . . ."

A whimpering sob choked from Faith's throat, and her limbs felt like boulders as she rose from the couch. Mrs. Gerson reached to steady her arm, and Faith grasped the old woman's hand. "I need to go . . . go to my room . . ." she whispered.

Mrs. Gerson nodded, and Faith inched forward, teetering on her feet.

"I'll walk you up," Maisie said.

Faith stared as if she didn't understand her words. "I have to go up," she repeated in a lifeless tone. Maisie hooked an arm around her waist and led her upstairs.

She had no recollection of Maisie walking her to the room, nor did she remember getting undressed and into bed. The only memory lodged in her brain was the chilling sound of Maisie's voice as she read the telegram; the shock of it reverberated in her mind as she lay staring at the ceiling. The pain buzzed in her brain and ripped at her heart until she thought she would lose her mind. "Oh, God," she cried, "I can't get through this . . . I can't! I've lost my father . . ."

I am . . . a father to the fatherless . . .

She jerked up in the dark and groped for the light. Mrs. Gerson's guest-room Bible rested on the nightstand, and she gripped it with the same ferocity as the pain gripping her. She flung it open, her fingers trembling down the page until she found it.

"His name is the Lord—and rejoice before him. A father to the fatherless, a defender of widows, is God in his holy dwelling."

With a pitiful moan, she fell onto the open book, and her desolate sob pierced the solitude of her room. "Oh, God, no . . . please no . . ." she wailed as she thought of her father, so young and so strong. Images of him holding her mother, wrestling with Katie, stroking Beth's cheek, and playing chess with Sean—all swam before her in a kaleidoscope of tears. She saw his teasing smile as they drove to work and remembered the warmth of his embrace whenever her heart had been broken. All the love he had given, all the joy he brought to the family who all but worshiped him, all gone . . . gone.

Suddenly, she thought of Marcy and knew that whatever grief she felt as a daughter, it paled in the face of her mother's. Theirs was a love Faith had seldom seen in her lifetime, the kind that inspired and instilled hope. Patrick O'Connor had not just been a father and a husband, he had been a life force in the O'Connor family. Some might say, in time, they would get over it, and in an attempt to comfort, say that the best was yet to come. But Faith knew in her heart that the best had come and gone, snuffed out on a field in France, taking with him any hope of regaining the joy they had once known.

She had no idea of the time or how many hours she had lain prostrate on her bed. She hadn't expected to sleep, but the shock had taken its toll. As the haze of the full moon rose in the sky and filled the darkness of the room with its eerie light, Faith slipped into a restless slumber. But not before whispering a prayer for strength. She had to be strong, strong for her mother—requiring, she knew, a strength far beyond human will. Exhaustion finally loosed the grip of pain from her mind and sent her fading into the night, her lips moving with a promise, silent and salted with tears. *He healeth the broken in heart, and bindeth up their wounds.* A final breath shuddered through her, stealing her certainty of faith. He was, after all, Jehovah-Rapha—the God who binds wounds no matter how deep the gash or boundless the bleeding.

Mitch stole a glimpse at Marcy out of the corner of his eye and smiled. She perched on the edge of the seat and peered out the taxi window, hands all but welded to the door, poised as if she would spring out the moment it stopped. Mitch shook his head. She was a woman in her forties, and yet she exuded this little-girl quality he'd seen so many times in Faith, and even Charity. Now he knew where they'd gotten it.

He was grateful he had come along. It had been good for her, the trip over. They had spent a great deal of time talking, and crying too, on Marcy's part, of course. He had been the perfect sounding board, not close enough for her to worry that her sorrow would bring him down, yet far enough away from being a stranger. They even found time to laugh, over stories he'd tell of Faith's unbelievable stubbornness, and she with tales of the same in her husband.

Marcy's love for Patrick had been fierce, and as he listened to her, he doubted it would ever wane. In his life, he'd seen marriages that had been good, but this—this was the stuff Faith had so often spoken of, an intangible bond of love stronger than anything she had ever seen. She had been bent on having it for herself. It was what drove her, along with her love for God, to run the race set before her, and to wait until she had it, holy and pure in the grasp of her hand.

"Look, Mitch!" Marcy cried as they rounded the corner.

"That's it—our home! Driver, right here is fine." The taxi came to a halt long after she opened the door.

Mitch laughed and pulled out his wallet. Marcy reeled to face him. "I intend to pay for every cent," she vowed, "from the ship to the taxi, I will reimburse you, Mitch, rest assured."

Mitch handed the cabbie his fare and gave Marcy a threatening look. "So help me, Mrs. O'Connor, if you mention paying me back one more time, I'm turning around and going home."

Marcy vaulted from the cab and smiled. "Oh, I don't think so. I have a feeling you'll be quite enamored with Boston. Or at least, a certain Bostonian."

Mitch grinned. "Now I know where your daughters get it from!" he teased, and he heard her laugh—one of the first since the ship had sailed into the harbor. "Are we going to your home?" he asked, hoisting the luggage in both hands.

"No . . . no, renters live in it now, I'm afraid . . ." Her voice withered as she stood before the home where she and Patrick had made their life.

Mitch sensed an instant heaviness in her manner. But then, that was the way it was, she had said—overwhelming grief punctuated by moments of peace that quickly faded whenever she thought of Patrick. And how could she help but think of him now as she looked at the home where he had loved her and fathered her children and promised he would never leave her . . .

"I just wanted to see it again, that's all," she whispered. "We'll go to Mrs. Gerson's, my neighbor who lives three houses down." Marcy swiped at the tears on her face, and a heavy sigh shuddered from her lips. "I'm so very tired of crying," she said. "How one woman can cry so many tears is beyond me. But then again, how one woman could have been blessed with such a love astounds me even more. And now it's gone . . ."

Mitch watched as one of the sudden mood swings he'd become so familiar with took its toll, and his heart ached for her. He gently touched her arm. "Which way?" he asked.

"That way," she whispered and linked her arm with his.

They walked, Mitch's heart hammering in his chest at the thought of seeing Faith again. She would be home, he supposed; it was Saturday, after all. But then again, she might be out, and a twinge cramped in his chest. Maybe she had met someone. Maybe she was still angry and would treat him coldly. Maybe she wouldn't speak to him at all. He took a deep breath. No, she wasn't like that. She would, he knew, treat him with the utmost courtesy. His lips compressed into a tight line. But confound it, it wasn't courtesy he wanted, and he found his stomach tightening as they climbed the steps to the house.

He rang the bell and thought he could feel Marcy shivering, or maybe it was him. And then the door opened, and he saw her, auburn hair spilling over her shoulders and green eyes glistening with tears. He swallowed hard as he stared and knew he never wanted to be without her again. She fell into her mother's arms, and the two of them wept, their fingers knuckled white as they clung. For the first few moments, she never even noticed he was there.

All at once, Marcy pulled away and wiped her face with her sleeve. "Goodness, I almost forgot," she said with a shaky laugh. "Mitch brought me, Faith. I hope you don't mind."

For the first time in over a month and a half, their eyes met. His heart stopped. "Hello, Faith," he whispered.

She smiled—the most perfect smile he had ever seen— and his heart took off again.

"Hello, Mitch."

She embraced him, and he could smell the familiar scent of her hair. He pulled away. "I'm so very sorry about your father," he said quietly. "I wish I could have met him." He hesitated. "I've missed you." He hadn't planned on saying it like that, but his lips betrayed him.

"Me too," she whispered, and his heart soared.

She turned to her mother and linked her arm to take her inside. Mitch stooped to pick up their luggage. She glanced back. "You can leave it on the porch, Mitch. Mrs. Gerson is anxious to see Mother, and she really wants to meet you. But after that, we're going home."

Marcy stopped. "Home?" she whispered.

Faith smiled. "I gave the renters notice right after I started back at the *Herald*. They moved out a week ago Friday. And, I'll have you know, I've been cleaning every day since."

Marcy threw her arms around Faith's neck and started to cry, prompting a fresh round of tears from her daughter as well.

Mitch sighed and reached in his pocket for a handkerchief. He pushed it into Marcy's hand. "Are you people going to stand out here crying on the porch, or do I get to meet this incredible woman I've heard so much about?"

Faith wiped her eyes with her sleeve and laughed. His brows rose in humor as he held the door. She brushed passed him, and the old familiar warmth surged through him once again. He had been a fool, he decided for the hundredth time. Closing the door behind, he made up his mind to never let it happen again.

24

It was their first meal in their home in a year, and the taste of it was bittersweet. The moment Marcy stepped foot over the threshold, a solemnity settled over her, and at times, Faith felt as if she and Mitch were alone. Of course, it helped to have Mrs. Gerson there, now recovered from her own shock at Patrick's death. She seemed reenergized with her faith and chattered about anything she hoped would take their minds off the pain they were feeling. She enjoyed Mitch, it was obvious, but then who didn't, Faith wondered as she watched the two of them discuss Scripture. She had forgotten how handsome he was. Even her recent daydreams had not done him justice, and her heart picked up pace as she sipped her tea.

As the evening wore on, Marcy rose from the table, her face drawn and her body exhausted. "I think it's time for me to retire."

Mitch started to get up.

"No, Mitch, you stay. You and Faith have a lot to talk about. I'm tired and could do with a good night's sleep."

Mrs. Gerson rose. "I couldn't agree more. Mitch, could I trouble you to walk me home?" she asked, and he obliged by jumping up and taking her arm.

"Christa, how I can ever thank you for all you've done, for all your prayers . . ."

Mrs. Gerson smiled and patted Marcy's hand. "How can you thank me for something that has given me so much joy? It is I who needs to thank you for the gift of your family in my life. I am blessed to have such good neighbors."

Marcy hugged her and then squeezed Mitch's arm. "Thanks, Mitch, for seeing Christa home . . . and for everything." Tears reappeared.

Mitch nodded and cleared his throat as he escorted Mrs. Gerson to the door. "My pleasure, Mrs. O'Connor," he said gruffly.

Marcy headed for the stairs, then turned, somewhat tentative. "Faith . . . would you mind very much sleeping with me tonight?"

Faith smiled. "I planned to, Mother, whether you liked it or not." She moved to her mother's side and hugged her.

"Good night, Faith. I love you," she whispered and turned to slowly mount the stairs.

Faith watched her mother head up, then returned to the dining room to clear the table. She paused, dishes in hand, a sudden thought blinking in her mind. *She would be alone with Mitch.* The realization made her lightheaded as she carried the dishes to the kitchen. She was finishing up when the creak of the kitchen door set her stomach aflutter. Whirling to face him, her mouth parched to cotton at the sight of him. His blue eyes probed, and she swallowed hard before she was able to smile.

"That was fast," she managed, drying her hands on a towel.

"Not fast enough," he whispered, taking a step toward her. "About six weeks too late."

Her stomach performed a somersault, and she stared at the floor, rubbing her arms.

"Are you cold?" he asked. Another step forward.

"A little," she lied, painfully aware of the warmth he generated.

He stood before her and placed his hands on her shoulders. "We need to talk."

She nodded, too afraid to look in his eyes.

"But . . . first things first." He lifted her chin with his fingers and gently stroked her cheek before carefully leaning to brush his lips against hers. It was a quiet kiss, his hands lightly cupping her face as if she were the most fragile thing in the world. "I love you, Faith. And I've missed you . . ."

"I've missed you too, Mitch," she whispered.

He kissed her again, then lifted her in his arms. He carried her into the parlor, then set her on the couch and sat beside her, his touch gentle on her arm. "Faith, I was sick when I heard about your father. I'm so sorry."

The mention of Patrick brought a rush of tears to her eyes. "I know. It's been pretty devastating for us all. The pain . . . it's . . . well, it's just so very hard to get past." She stared at him intently. "I'm glad you're here, Mitch, I really am. I need you right now. I think I'm going to need you for a long time."

He folded her into his arms and closed his eyes. "I think we need each other," he whispered, "and I'm hoping and praying it will be for a very long time."

He held her for several moments, then pulled away to reach into his coat pocket. He palmed the ring she had once worn. "This belongs to you," he said. "I'm asking you to take it back, Faith. There's not another woman alive who could wear it."

She touched it slowly, fingers trembling and vision blurred with tears.

He gently closed her fingers over the ring and covered her hand with his. His eyes reflected a rare humility. "Faith, whether or not you decide to wear this, it belongs to you.

I don't blame you if you don't put it back on your finger. What I did was"—he glanced away, the muscles working in his throat—"despicable, unforgivable, and yet . . ." He looked up again, a glimmer of hope in his eyes, "I'm asking for forgiveness. Asking for you to give me another chance . . . to prove that you can trust me."

She stared at his hands locked over hers, and drew in a shaky breath. "I want to, Mitch, but I'm scared."

He lifted her hand and kissed it, his eyes earnest. "I know, Faith. Me too. Scared to death that I'm going to lose you."

She looked up then. "Trust is such a fragile thing. I didn't realize that before. Mine for you was so strong, so invincible. But now . . ."

He gripped her close, his voice steeped in remorse. "As God as my witness, I will never hurt you like that again, I swear. Please, Faith, trust me . . . just one more time."

She pulled away and looked at the ring in her hand. Her eyes welled with water, and a single tear trailed her cheek as she slowly slipped it on her finger. "I forgive you, Mitch," she whispered, "but I need you to forgive me too."

He lifted her chin with his finger. "Why would I need to forgive you?"

She sniffed. "The way I treated you when I left, how I treated everyone . . ."

He rested his face against her hair. "I won't lie to you, Faith, it hurt. You all but cut my heart out by leaving like you did." He pulled back and lifted her face with his hands. "But I deserved it. I love you so much, Faith, and yet, I let a moment of lust sever what we had. I don't know which has been more painful—knowing the pain I caused or you leaving."

She sighed and dropped back on the couch, her hand extended as she gazed at the ring on her finger. "I was pretty angry when I left," she mused. "I went to a place

I've never been before, so much hurt and hate inside, I thought I would die. I wanted to cause you as much pain as you caused me."

"Good job," he said, his tone droll. He became solemn as he took her hand in his. "I was so wrong in what I did. Although I never planned it or sought it out, it happened, and I can't pretend in any way I was innocent." He sighed and rested against the back of the couch, one hand in hers as he rubbed his eyes with the other. "I'd suspected for some time that Charity . . . well, that she was attracted to me, but I thought it was harmless enough." He ducked his head in shame. "I never dreamed it would come to that. She was so distraught, and I was only trying to comfort her . . ."

Faith couldn't resist a thin smile. "Pretty intense comfort," she whispered. It was the first time she ever saw him blush scarlet.

"I know. It's just that, well, it'd been so long . . ."

It was Faith's turn to blush. She lifted her chin. "A condition I hope to correct soon enough."

He glanced at her with a sharp intake of breath. "When?" he whispered.

"As soon as Mother and I settle things here. I don't want to wait any longer."

"Me either," he said, his voice husky with emotion. "I'm lonely for my wife."

Faith gently kissed him, the warmth returning in a rush. He returned her kiss with a heated one of his own before nudging her away. He stood up.

"It's late and we better get you to bed," he said. A grin creased his lips. "There are limits to my willpower, you know."

She rose to her feet with mischief in her eyes. "Thank goodness," she exclaimed. "A little help in the restraint department—I like that."

"Don't get used to it," he teased. "It's definitely short-term. I'm just biding my time until the gold band's in place. When it is, there'll be no mercy."

Faith's eyes twinkled as she gave him a smirk. "Likewise," she said.

Mitch didn't want it to end. His two weeks in Boston were dwindling fast, and the thought of returning to Ireland without her chilled him to the bone like an icy gust on a winter day. Their home was on the market, but there was no telling how long it would take to sell, and Faith insisted Marcy return with Mitch while she herself put their life in Boston to rest.

It helped having him there, he knew, because both Marcy and Faith repeatedly told him so, and he could see the relief in their eyes when he made them laugh. Somehow, with him there, they didn't seem to notice the pain as much when they spoke of Patrick, which they did often throughout the course of their many conversations. Mitch bitterly regretted never having met him, this man so loved by the women who had profoundly affected his own life. It was, perhaps, the greatest regret he had during the time he spent with them in their mourning.

The days flew by, as he'd known they would, and there was a degree of guilt over enjoying it so while they were engulfed in their grief. But the moments of laughter had been frequent enough, what with Mrs. Gerson's visits, and those of Maisie and Briana. Mitch smiled now as he thought of the shocked look on Maisie's face when she had met him.

"Oh, my goodness," she had cried, the spray of freckles becoming more noticeable as her face paled. "It's just not fair! He's gorgeous!"

Mitch laughed, embarrassed at her candor, while Faith

took possession of his arm. "Back off, Tanner, he's spoken for."

Maisie rolled her eyes. "Mmm, they're all spoken for when it comes to you," she teased, and Mitch's eyebrow angled in question.

"Oh, really?" he said with a smile, shards of jealousy prickling his tone.

"I don't know what she's talking about," Faith said with a grin, and Mitch doubted it.

The evenings had been filled with wonderful meals, sometimes at Mrs. Gerson's, sometimes at Marcy's, but always served up with lots of conversation and laughter. The days were spent running errands and helping Marcy pack while Faith was at work.

And then the day he'd dreaded finally arrived. Tomorrow they would leave for Ireland—he and Marcy—and the thought of leaving Faith behind rolled his gut like a bout with the flu. She had, at least, agreed to take the day off so they could be together, but it was small consolation for the agony he felt.

She came down for breakfast, her eyes tired and a bit sunken, and he suspected she hadn't slept any more than he had. "Good morning," she said, obviously attempting to sound as bright as she could. She gave her mother a peck on the cheek as Marcy and Mitch sat at the kitchen table with their coffee. Standing behind him, she wrapped her arms around his shoulders and kissed the top of his head. "Good morning, Mr. Dennehy," she whispered. She turned and walked to the counter in search of coffee.

He looked up, his eyes tender. "Did you get any sleep?"

She scrunched her shoulders and poured herself a cup. "Sleep," she announced, "is not foremost on my mind right now."

He smiled. "Yeah, I didn't either."

"How about you, Mother?" Faith asked as she sat with them at the table.

Marcy sighed. "Oh, well enough, I suppose. But I wish we were all back in Ireland."

Faith reached to put her hand over her mother's. "We'll all be there before you know it. And now that the war is almost over, Sean will be home too, and hopefully he'll decide to stay with us in Ireland. We'll finally be together again."

Mitch could see the tears welling in Marcy's eyes and quickly sought a diversion. "Faith, what's the scuttlebutt at the *Herald* regarding the armistice?" He leaned back in his chair while he sipped his coffee.

"Well, everybody's been pretty much holding their breath since early October when the Germans and Austrians contacted President Wilson about an armistice. But nobody trusts them, of course, and you'll find as many that don't think the war's over as those who do. But honestly, Mitch, I can feel it in my bones. It's coming. By the grace of God, the armistice is coming, and we'll finally be able to get on with our lives." Faith stirred the cream in her cup. "I wonder how Mima's doing?" she said, changing the subject.

Marcy looked up in surprise, a look of apology on her face. "Oh my goodness," she cried, "I can't believe I forgot to tell you! I just received a letter from Mother yesterday. She must have written it right after we left, and Christa just received it." She jumped up to retrieve it from the counter and handed it to Faith, who laid it on the table and smoothed out the folded sheets.

"Sean and Collin are both doing fine and quite anxious to come home, I understand. Mother told them our plans to relocate to Ireland, so I suppose both of them will head there first. At least, I certainly hope Collin will. I know Sean will, of course, but there's no telling what's going to happen with Collin and Charity." Her tone was worried once again.

Mitch stiffened at the mention of Collin's name. He glanced at Faith. The mere utterance of his name had affected her as well, sending a faint blush into her cheeks. He frowned.

"Mother, they do know about . . ." Faith couldn't go on, and Marcy nodded, rising to refill her coffee. She kept her back to them.

"Yes, of course, dear. Charity notified them the first week." She returned to the table, her eyes moist as she poured them another cup, then managed a shaky smile as she put the pot back on the stove. "Well, I've got a few more things to pack. You two better get going and enjoy your day." She headed toward the door.

Faith looked up, concern creasing her brow. "Mother, why don't you come with us? It'll do you good, and I won't have to worry about you being here alone."

"Nonsense," she said. "You two need some time together, and so do I. I want to be—no, I need to be here—alone." She turned and left the room too quickly.

Faith sighed. "I suppose she's right. But I can't help but ache for her."

"I ache for all of us," he said quietly.

"I can't believe it! Look, we've gone and gotten you all gloomy too. That's got to change. All I need to do is grab my jacket and we can be off. Are you ready?"

He didn't blink as he stared hard at the table, his jaw angled tight. Faith bent to smile into his eyes. "Hey, Dennehy . . . what's wrong? In a few short weeks, I'll be back in your life, the same old thorn in your side."

He looked up but didn't smile. "Where does Collin stand?"

Her eyelids flickered. "I don't know. You'll have to ask Charity."

"I'm asking you," he whispered.

Her face went pale, and she sat down, avoiding his eyes. "What do you mean?" she asked, and he was pretty sure she knew exactly what he meant.

"Do you still have feelings for him?" He could barely form the words. His stomach curled into a knot when he heard her catch her breath. She took too long to answer, and Mitch stood up, looming over her as she sat at the table, her eyes fixed on the cup in her hands.

Without notice, he reached to yank her up, gripping her in his arms. Her coffee teetered and sloshed in the saucer from the force of his action. His eyes burned into hers. "I don't care if you do," he breathed. "You belong to me, not him. I hope and pray he marries that sister of yours— Boston can have 'em!" His tone was harsh.

She touched his cheek. "Mitch, please don't worry," she whispered. "The ring on my finger belongs to you, and so do I."

He stared for a long moment, then crushed her tightly against his chest, his face buried in her hair. Suddenly, he hefted her high in his arms until her feet dangled in the air. Bent on staking his claim, he kissed her soundly before finally setting her down with a thud.

She jumped back, eyes and mouth rounded in surprise. "What was that for?"

"That's for even thinking of him," he muttered as he carried their coffee cups to the sink. He walked to the door and held it for her, his eyes menacing. "Don't do it again," he ordered and followed her out the door.

It was fun showing Mitch this city she loved, but melancholy at the same time. She showed him Boston Harbor, site of the famous Boston Tea Party where a band of angry patriots had disguised themselves as Indians to dump English tea into the harbor. They masterminded one of the most important events leading up to the American Revolution, she explained. Mitch seemed completely absorbed, both with the history lesson and with her.

"I like the way you Americans think," he teased with a note of respect, as only an Irishman could. They walked along the wharf, hand in hand, while she pointed out sights, both historical and personal. From Paul Revere's house to the Bunker Hill Monument, she worked at being the perfect tour guide, and she hated for the day to end.

The sun was sinking fast into the dusky skyline when Mitch glanced at his watch. "Your mother said dinner is at six; we better head back." His tone was laced with disappointment.

She nodded, and he put his arm around her and hailed a taxi. Only one more night, she thought solemnly when the taxi pulled up in front of her house. Mitch helped her out of the cab before turning to pay the driver. It was dark now, and Faith tugged her jacket tighter to ward off the chill from the air—or maybe from the thought that tomorrow he'd be gone. Either way, she still had tonight, and she clutched his arm tightly as they climbed the steps. Mitch opened the door, and she stepped inside.

"Mother, we're home!" she cried.

"In the kitchen," Marcy called.

Mitch sniffed the air while helping Faith with her jacket. "Boy, am I starved."

"You're always starved," she teased and grabbed his hand to pull him into the kitchen.

Marcy seemed relaxed working at the sink, rinsing the vegetables she was preparing. She had the fire crackling, and the kitchen was warm and cozy, filled with the aroma of fresh-baked apple cobbler.

"Mother, we're famished, and it smells so wonderful!" Faith made a beeline for Marcy and wrapped her arms around her from behind.

Marcy laughed and turned, her hand stroking Faith's ruddy cheek. "Goodness, you're like ice!" she exclaimed and then grinned. "But I think I've got something that will warm you up." Stretching her hand, she directed Faith's gaze across the room.

Faith turned, and the blood in her face coursed to her toes like a thundering waterfall. There stood Collin McGuire casually leaning against the counter as he had so often done, legs crossed and stretched out before him. But this time he wore a uniform as he relaxed, arms folded across his chest. His body was leaner and harder, his handsome face tan and weathered. But the gray eyes were as mesmerizing as ever. And as soon as they saw her face, the deadly smile went to work.

"Hello, Faith," he drawled. He stood up slowly. A twinkle lit his eyes. "You can breathe now."

"Collin . . ." Her voice drifted out on a soft gasp, and her tongue felt pasted to the roof of her mouth.

Collin walked over to Mitch, who stood beside her with shock glazing his eyes. Collin extended his hand and smiled sheepishly. "You must be Mitch. Congratulations on snagging this one. She'll give you a run for your money, but you won't be sorry."

Mitch hesitated, then gave him a wooden handshake, quickly withdrawing to latch a protective arm over Faith's shoulder.

"Collin showed up early this afternoon," Marcy said, her voice breathless with excitement. "We've had a wonderful visit. He's almost completely recovered now."

Mitch peered at Collin, his eyes narrowing just the slightest bit. "You were wounded?"

Collin nodded and grinned, tapping his chest over his heart. He lifted his hand to measure a quarter inch of air with his index finger and thumb. "Yeah, a piece of shrapnel came this close to putting a harp in my hand. But

somebody up there decided I had payback to do, I guess."
He grinned at Faith.

She swallowed hard and attempted a smile. "I'm . . . so
glad to see you, Collin, really I am. You just shocked me,
that's all."

His eyes softened. "I know," he said gently, then turned
his attention to Marcy. "Your mother almost fainted dead
out."

Marcy laughed and put a hand to her chest. "Honestly,
Faith, a feather could have knocked me over when I opened
that door and saw him standing there. What a wonderful
farewell evening to Boston." She wiped her eye with the
corner of her apron. "Somehow, having you here, Collin,
well . . . it almost feels like Patrick's here too."

Collin nodded, and Faith saw the grief in his eyes. She
took a deep breath and turned to her mother. "Well! What
can I do? Set the table?"

"No, Collin's already handled that." She pulled the roast
from the oven. "Why don't you two run over and collect
Christa, and when you get back, we should be pretty close
to eating."

"Great!" Faith breathed, then flashed a quick smile in
Collin's direction. She turned and clutched Mitch's arm.
"Ready, Mitch?"

He nodded, his eyes locked on hers. She pushed through
the kitchen door, and he followed, hesitating long enough
to turn and look at Collin.

Faith grabbed her coat from the rack in the foyer and
prayed it was too dim for Mitch to see the shock in her
face.

Mitch secured her arm in his, but even in the dark, he
could sense her tension. His lips flattened into a hard line.
Blast that pretty boy, he thought to himself. *Too bad the shrap-*

nel missed. He sucked in a harsh breath and then exhaled. "Sorry about that," he whispered to God.

Faith looked up. "What, Mitch?"

"Nothing," he said, and then uttered a silent prayer that he was right.

Although Marcy had packed away her best china, her prized candlesticks still remained to grace the table. Their soft light painted a warm glow in the room where Collin joined them for their final dinner. Mrs. Gerson resided at the head of the table with Marcy to her side while Mitch sat close to Faith, his arm grafted to her shoulder.

Collin was determined to fight the melancholy he was feeling. He stretched back in the chair and sipped hot coffee as he entertained them with colorful war stories that didn't resemble war at all.

He noticed that Faith seemed uneasy, but as Marcy poured the wine that warmed them all, she slowly began to relax, her tension giving way to easy laughter as Collin regaled them with his misadventures in France.

"What have you decided with Charity?" Faith suddenly asked, as if waiting until the opportune time to broach the subject. Her eyes focused on her mother's homemade cobbler as she carved out a mouth-sized piece with her fork.

Collin looked up from his plate and smiled faintly. "I'm not sure," he said, stabbing at his own dessert. "Things are different now."

Marcy fumbled her coffee as she set it down. "Collin, you can't be serious! What could possibly be different? Charity loves you."

Collin attempted a reassuring smile. "I'm not the same man she fell in love with, Mrs. O'Connor."

His serious tone caused Faith to hesitate, her fork poised midair. "How so, Collin?"

He sighed. "Things change, Faith. Your father once told

me war has a way of illuminating the face of God. He was right."

The fork dropped from her hand and clattered to the plate. Cheeks blooming bright red, she picked it up and took a deep breath. "What do you mean?" she asked.

Collin stared straight into her eyes, feeling the heat of Mitch's glare. "I mean that your prayers worked. I gave my life to God. He got me through this foul war, and from now on, it's me and him."

A spasm twitched in his gut as he watched her face drain to the color of Marcy's ivory tablecloth, and for a brief moment, he thought she was going to faint. No, it doesn't matter, he thought; it's too late. She may have a twinge of regret, possibly, but any regret she might have would be quickly doused by this Mitch character, who hovered over her like a fog on a rainy day.

Marcy's face registered alarm at the prospect of Collin never being part of the family. "Collin, please, talk to her! You owe her that much. She loves you."

He nodded and gave Marcy a gentle smile. "I will, Mrs. O'Connor. There's no place I'd rather be than in your family." He quickly deflected the emotion he felt by reaching for his wine glass and emptying it.

Marcy smiled and stood. "Well, as much as I hate for this evening to end, I have a kitchen full of dishes to do. And Mitch and I have a busy day tomorrow."

Collin rose and pushed in his chair. "Dinner was wonderful, Mrs. O'Connor."

She held his face in her hands. "Collin, it's done me a world of good to see you again. Nothing makes me feel better than knowing you'll be here to look after Faith when we leave."

Collin resisted the urge to smile when Mitch's face blanched white. He saw him tighten his grip on Faith's arm. "I'm sorry, Mrs. O'Connor, but I'm leaving Boston myself tomorrow," he said, noting that Mitch's grip suddenly relaxed once again.

"Where are you going?" Faith asked, her eyes rounded like a toddler caught by surprise.

He looked at her, his heart melting in his chest. "To New York," he said quietly. "A good friend from the army lives there. He's still in France because he wasn't lucky enough to get shot." Collin grinned before becoming serious again. "But it's just a matter of days before the armistice now, and he'll be out soon. He and I have talked about going into business together—the printing business," he emphasized with a faint smile. "So, I thought I'd head up there and settle in, you know, just to see how it fits." He flashed a teasing grin. "You'd like him, Faith. He was the one who preached to me day and night until I turned to God just to shut him up. His name is Brady. I hope I can introduce you someday."

A lump shifted in her throat. "I'd like that, Collin."

He picked up his plate. "Come on, Mrs. O'Connor. What do you say you and I knock out these dishes? I did have kitchen duty once or twice in the army, you know."

Faith jumped up. "No, Mother, I'll do the dishes. You cooked this wonderful meal, and now you've got to get into bed."

Marcy opened her mouth to protest, but Faith cut her off. "No argument, I'm doing dishes, period. Go to bed." Ignoring the hesitant look on her mother's face, Faith rounded the table to collect plates and utensils.

Marcy sighed. "All right, no argument. I will admit that I am tired. Thanks, Faith. I can always count on you." She put her arms around her daughter's neck and gave her a hug, then turned to Mrs. Gerson. "Christa, I guess this is good-bye. I wish I knew when I would see you again."

Mrs. Gerson rose from the table and gave Marcy a tight hug. "Soon enough, my dear, soon enough." She dabbed her handkerchief at the wetness in her eyes and sighed. "Mitch, could I trouble you to walk me home?"

Collin didn't miss the panic in Mitch's face before he answered in a gracious tone. "Absolutely, Mrs. Gerson." He stood and took her arm, glancing first at Faith, then briefly at Collin. A frown puckered his brow. Collin cleared his throat and pushed the chairs in around the table.

"I'll be by on Sunday, Mrs. Gerson," Faith said, dishes stacked high in her arms.

"Looking forward to it, my dear, as always. Good night."

"Good night, Mrs. Gerson," Collin called, battling a grin as Mitch shot a scorching look.

Marcy closed the door and yawned, a limp hand over her mouth. "Oh goodness, maybe I'll actually sleep tonight." She gave Faith a hug. "Good night, Faith. Don't stay up too late. We've got a long day tomorrow."

Faith nodded and kissed her mother's cheek. Marcy turned to Collin. "Promise me, Collin, when the war is over, you'll talk to Charity. Losing you would be like losing a son."

Collin grinned to diffuse the moisture in his eyes. "You won't be rid of me so easily, Mrs. O'Connor. I feel exactly the same way. And I promise I will talk to Charity."

She patted his cheek. "Good boy—just like one of my own. God bless you, Collin," she whispered, then headed up the steps.

Collin turned to see Faith watching him. She quickly looked away and focused on her stack of dishes as she headed to the kitchen. He followed with more dishes in hand and carried them to the sink. He reached for a dish towel, slung it over his shoulder, and casually leaned against the counter, arms crossed. His eyes followed her every move.

She filled the sink with soap and water before she

glanced up, catching his gaze. A soft tint of color fanned her cheeks.

He grinned. "Mitch seems a bit overprotective—he knows about us, doesn't he?"

She bit her lip. The pastel in her cheeks blossomed to flame.

He shook his head and laughed. "I thought so. Did you see the look on his face when Mrs. Gerson asked him to walk her home?"

She suddenly giggled and nodded.

Collin grabbed the dish towel from his shoulder. "Okay, Little Bit, are you going to start washing, or am I gonna have to flick you with this towel?"

She gave him a smirk. "Why do I have to wash?"

"Because I'm bigger than you . . . and meaner." He snapped the towel hard in the air, making a loud pop.

She chuckled and rolled her sleeves, then piled the dishes into the water.

"By the way, congratulations."

She shot him a quick glance before returning her focus to the pot in her hands. "Thanks, Collin. He's a good man."

His gut twisted. "Wouldn't expect otherwise. When's the big day?"

Faith took a deep breath and pushed a strand of hair from her eyes. "The plan is for me to finish things here as quickly as possible, then head back to Ireland. Once I return, we plan to be married as soon as possible."

"Smart guy. It's tough to wait—especially with a girl like you."

She kept her gaze straight ahead, but he didn't miss the quiver in her cheek. She handed him a dripping pot, and he proceeded to dry, his thoughts reflective. "I'm happy for you, Faith. You got just what you wanted. I've been praying you would."

She looked up in surprise. "You have?" she asked, wet hands dripping on the floor.

He laughed and gently steered them back over the sink. "You're dripping." He continued to dry the pot. "Of course I have. It's the least I could do after all you did for me."

She faced him again, hands dribbling as before. He arched an eyebrow. Distracted, she impatiently wiped her wet hands on her dress and peered up at him. "What have I done for you?"

He set the pot on the counter and smiled. "You prayed your heart out for me."

"How do you know that?" she whispered.

He reached over to push a stray curl from her eyes. "Because I know you, and I wouldn't be here today, alive and a changed man, if you hadn't. So you see, I owe you."

She drooped against the counter as if the wind had been sucked out of her.

He laughed. "Don't tell me you're surprised. Isn't that what you've been praying for?"

She nodded.

"Well, it worked. Not soon enough for us," he said, his tone light but his heart heavy, "but effective, nonetheless."

Her eyelids fluttered ever so slightly, and he noticed her nails pinched white on the counter. Her lips parted, giving vent to shallow breaths.

His jaw clamped tight. It wasn't fair! Here she was a breath away, his heart's desire, and now she belonged to somebody else.

Abruptly, Collin flung the towel on the counter and stepped in front of her, his eyes burning. "You know, he's going to walk through that door any minute now, and you and I will never be alone again. Come on, Faith, what do you say—do I get to kiss the bride?"

The breath seized in Faith's lungs, and old, familiar feelings surged before he even laid a hand on her. Her heart pounded at a pace she hadn't felt since the last time he had touched her, and she wondered how that could possibly be after all this time. *No*, she thought to herself, *I can't let this happen!*

She started to protest when his mouth met hers, warm and sweet as he kissed her, and the heat that coursed made her dizzy in his arms. His kiss remained gentle and lingering, so unlike his kisses of the past, and she found herself returning it with a vehemence that shocked them both. He drew back, lips parted in surprise, and in the catch of his breath, the gray eyes heated like molten lava. With a low groan, his mouth took hers once again, evoking a soft moan from her lips. She could feel his breath warm against her skin, and a jolt of heat seared unlike anything she had ever felt, except with him. It was as if they'd never been apart, like he had never left at all, and in her heart, she knew he hadn't. A rush of emotion flooded, and before she realized, words were tumbling from her lips.

"Oh Collin . . ." she breathed, and she wanted to say she loved him, that she had always loved him, but the words choked thick in her throat. She thought of Mitch, and an aching filled her soul at the pain she would cause if he found them like this. She had to stop. But she needn't have worried.

In the next second, Collin wrenched away, his eyes filled with longing. He stepped back and breathed in deeply, shoving the hair in his eyes away from his face. His lips puffed, expelling another loud breath, and then the trademark smile returned with a vengeance. "Yep, we still got it," he whispered, exhaling again while his fingers threaded his hair.

Her mouth slacked open. "You stopped!"

He eyed her, his brow slanted in surprise. "Give me a little credit, will you? A guy has to learn a lot of restraint living in a trench."

"Why did you?"

His eyes sobered. "Because I shouldn't have done it in the first place. You're engaged to someone else," he said quietly. "And because you were right."

She pushed the hair from her face and smoothed out her dress, hands trembling and tears puddling in her eyes. "About what?"

"About genuine love. You once told me all I cared about was my desire for the moment. You were right, as much as I hated you at the time for saying it. You said you wanted genuine love—like the kind between your mother and father." Collin smiled and shook his head. "Unfortunately, it took twenty-three years and the hell of war to understand what you meant, but I finally do. Genuine love is just another name for doing it God's way—a relationship between two people brought together by him and devoted to him. You knew that all along, Faith. You're a lucky woman. I just found that out, and I'm afraid my luck ran out before I did."

He gently stroked her cheek, blotting a tear with his finger. "Look, I didn't mean to make you cry. I just wanted you to know you've had a profound impact on my life, and I'm grateful. Because, you see, Faith, just knowing you has made me a better man."

Wetness shimmered to the brim of her eyes and spilled. He reached for the towel and tossed it. It landed on her shoulder. She laughed and took it, dabbing her eyes.

"Tell me," he said, his gaze never leaving hers, "does he realize he's the luckiest man in the world? And I wonder . . . does he know I'd kill to trade places with him?"

The door swung wide, and Mitch entered the kitchen, appearing considerably relieved at the secure distance between the two. Faith stood with a limp towel dangling from her hands while Collin leaned against the counter.

"What, is he making you do all the work?" Mitch asked.

Faith managed a wobbly smile. "He made me wash," she said, sounding a lot like she was squabbling with Charity.

Collin grinned. "What are you talking about? I would have had these dishes done by now. You've done nothing but stall."

"I've got an idea," Mitch said. "Why don't I help Faith finish up? You must be tired, Collin. I know I am, and we both have to leave in the morning."

Collin looked at Mitch out of the corner of his eye and laughed. "Okay, you don't have to spell it out for me; I get the picture. I am tired." He stretched before turning his attention to Faith. "It was great seeing you again, Faith." He glanced at Mitch. "Nice meeting you too, Mitch. Do you mind if I give her a hug?"

Mitch shook his head.

Collin walked to where Faith stood and put his hands on her shoulders. "Have a great life, Faith," he whispered, then kissed her gently on the cheek.

Her heart was beating erratically. He scooped her up in a hug and clung for a few seconds with his face buried in her hair. A lump shifted in her throat. *I might never see him again*, she thought, and an awful ache stabbed within. He let go and stepped back. He walked to the door and pushed his palm against it, then glanced at Mitch. "I hope you know how lucky you are."

Mitch's lips pressed into a tight smile. "I do."

Collin nodded. His arm tensed as he pushed against the door. Over his shoulder, he flashed a final smile. "Here's to a happy ending," he quipped. And then he was gone.

Mitch shook his head and moved to her side. "That

guy's something else," he remarked dryly. "I think Charity has her work cut out for her." He took her in his arms and held her close. "It made me crazy knowing he was alone with you." He took a deep breath. "He didn't make a pass, did he?"

She didn't answer, and he stiffened. "Never mind," he said. "I don't want to know. As long as you still care for me."

She shivered and leaned against him. "I do," she whispered, and it seemed to satisfy him.

"Let's get you to bed," he said. "Tomorrow's going to be a tough one."

She looked up, her eyelids weighted with fatigue. "Mitch? Will you hold me for a while?"

He smiled. "All night, if I have to." He picked her up in his arms and carried her into the parlor. He set her down on the sofa and leaned back, tucking her against his chest with his arms safely around her. She laid her head against him and closed her eyes. Whether she was just spent from the events of the day or emotionally drained, she wasn't quite sure. The only thing she was sure of at the moment was that thoughts of Collin McGuire were heavy on her mind, and the soundness of sleep was her only escape.

25

Suddenly he wasn't so tired anymore. It wasn't like he was
going to sleep anyway, he thought as he made his way to
Brannigan's. He had a suspicion that insomnia—like the
sick feeling in his gut—was going to be around for a while.
Collin pulled his jacket tighter, bracing himself against the
chill of the November night, but he was pretty sure the
coldness he felt had nothing to do with the weather.

He couldn't get her out of his mind, a condition that
had plagued him the entire year. Now that he knew for a
certainty he would never have her, it festered and throbbed
inside of him like the piece of shrapnel that ripped through
his chest. That had missed his heart by mere inches; this
had hit it dead on, and at the moment, he wasn't all that
certain he would survive.

Never had he been more grateful for Jackson, who had
begged him to stop by for a drink, even though at the time
he had no intention of obliging him. It had been a while
since he'd seen the inside of a bar, or even wanted to. But
tonight, well, tonight called for desperate measures for
desperate men. And he was—a man desperate to forget
he just lost his best shot at happiness.

Collin blew on his hands as he entered Brannigan's, his
body chilled and his fingers near frozen. He spotted Jackson
at the bar and headed his way, aware of the attention he

drew as a man in uniform. He slid onto the stool next to his friend, who was doing his best to make time with a pretty young thing who eyed Jackson through wary eyes.

Collin grinned and waved at Lucas for a beer, then leaned to whisper in Jackson's ear. "Have you even managed to get lucky one night since I've been gone, old buddy?"

Jackson jumped up and wrestled him around the neck. "Well, I'll be doggone!" he shouted, giving Collin a bear hug. "Our doughboy hero is back. Got a feeling the ladies will be saying their prayers tonight!" He slapped Collin on the back. "So, how was the front? You teach them Germans what for?"

"I did and got wounded for the cause," he said as he shook Lucas's hand.

"Well, aren't you a sight for sore eyes, now." Lucas laughed. He coasted a foaming mug of beer across the bar to him. "And in uniform too. Same old Collin—show no mercy to the ladies. So, ya back for good now?"

Collin took a swig of his beer. "Afraid so. A piece of shrapnel sent me home early. But don't expect me to boost your profits any, Lucas. I'm off to New York in the morning."

"Not too early, I hope," Lucas said with a grin. "That's going to break a few hearts, mine included." Lucas cocked his head, giving Collin a wicked smile. "Those Germans didn't hurt nothin' valuable, now did they?"

Collin grinned. "You think I'm a fool? I laid low."

Lucas laughed and made his way to the other end of the bar. Collin turned to Jackson. "Missed you, ol' buddy. How the devil did you manage to weasel out of the war anyway?"

Jackson chuckled. "Don't ya know? My eyesight's downright awful. Why else ya think you always got the pretty girls and me the ugly ones? I just couldn't see!"

Collin laughed and took another sip of his beer. "I

wondered why," he said, leaning back on the stool while taking stock of the action in the pub.

"So, what's up with you, Collin? Hear tell you're planning on going into business with an army buddy in New York. What the blazes for?"

Collin sighed and turned to face the bar. He circled the mug with his hands, his fingers twirling it on the counter.

"It seemed like a good idea at the time," he said, staring straight ahead. "The plan was to come back to Boston, and if things didn't work out like I hoped, well, then I would move on." He stopped twisting and took a drink.

"And things haven't worked out? You're not marrying Charity?"

"Nope, things didn't work out." Collin hung his head and looked at Jackson out of the corner of his eyes. "And I don't know about Charity yet."

"What? What do you mean you don't know about Charity yet?" Jackson frowned. "I thought you said things didn't work out."

Collin rotated his neck, then rubbed his eyes with his hand. "They didn't. I came back for the sister, but it seems she's happily engaged."

Jackson's eyes almost bugged out of his head. "You wanted the holy-roller sister? What, are you crazy? You sure that shrapnel didn't hit your brain instead? Or, you just planning to convert?"

Collin grinned again. "Yes, no, and yes," he said, laughing at the confusion puckering on Jackson's face. "Yes, I'm crazy—about her. No, the shrapnel did not hit my brain, and yes, I not only planned to convert, I have."

"What?" Jackson looked like he'd just been on a twenty-four-hour drunk, ready to keel over.

Collin chuckled. "I guess you could say the worst thing

in the world happened to a man who likes drinking too much and women even better. I found God."

Jackson blinked and stared, then whacked Collin on the back, hooting and hollering. "Boy, I've missed you! You had me going there for a minute!"

"I'm not joking, Jackson," Collin said, his tone as calm as the drunk passed out at the end of the bar. He finished half of his beer and pushed the mug away.

Jackson's wide-eyed gaze flittered from the half-empty mug to Collin's face. "You're serious!" He shoved the mug back toward Collin. "And you're wasting half a beer?"

Collin laughed and pushed it away again. "Jackson, I don't want any more. I can't stay that long. I just wanted to see you before I go."

"What's this mean, Collin? Ya can't have a beer with a friend? What, God won't like it?"

"I just did," Collin said.

"What about your mother?" Jackson asked in a desperate voice. "You go off to war, and now you're gonna leave again? How does that square with God?"

"Pretty well, actually," Collin said. "My mother has a beau, Jackson. Seems she got pretty depressed when I left for the war and started going back to church. Found herself a really good man who loves her. I'll be back for the wedding next spring."

Jackson shook his head and gulped another drink. "You got it all figured out now, don't you? I'm sorry, but I just don't get it. You—of all people—a fanatic! Why? You have it all. The looks, the brains, the women!"

"Let's just say I was looking for something more—more than this." Collin's voice was quiet, and his eyes sobered. "And I found it, Jackson, or it found me. Oh, I'll admit, it doesn't sound as exciting as drinking you under the table, or as much fun as getting lucky with a pretty woman, I guess, but in a strange way it is. I used to do all those things because of this awful loneliness inside. I couldn't shake it, Jackson, you know that. You saw me down enough times to understand the demons that had me by the throat. But now, now I'm not so lonely anymore, and there's a part of me that's . . . well, at peace. Corny as it may sound, I'm never alone—God is always with me. Don't get me wrong, I still like a beer with a good friend, but I'm not driven to it anymore. I don't have to prove to myself, or to a woman or to the world, that Collin McGuire is worth something. I just know I am—because of *him*."

Jackson gaped with his mouth dangling open, and Collin couldn't help but grin.

"Does that mean you're swearing off women?" Jackson asked, his voice hushed as if he had just spoken blasphemy.

"No, just waiting for the right one." Collin stood and grabbed his jacket. His grin faded. "Problem is, she's marrying someone else."

For the first time, Jackson seemed to comprehend, and he grabbed his arm. "I'm really sorry, Collin. I guess I should have figured you had a thing for her all along. She's the only woman I ever saw who could send you over the edge. That should have been my first clue." Jackson's eyes suddenly perked up. He wagged Collin's arm in excitement. "Hey, maybe God could fix it for you. You know, since you and he are pretty thick right now?"

Collin chuckled. He was going to miss Jackson something fierce. "That would be one miraculous answer to prayer, Jackson my man, but I'm not holding my breath."

"What about Charity?" Jackson asked.

Collin sighed and put on his coat. "I don't know," he said, his voice still. "I think she would have trouble understanding this new facet of my personality, and I'm not really sure I even want to try. As much as I love that family and want to be part of it, I think it might be wrong for me to marry Charity. And it would kill me to see Faith with someone else. Don't know that I could stomach it, unless God took her out of my heart." Collin buttoned his coat and slapped Jackson on the back. "Which," he said with a smile, "is exactly what I'm counting on. You take care, ol' buddy."

Collin turned, and Jackson hooked his arm before he could go. "Blast it all, Collin, what's the world coming to if a guy like you turns to God?"

Collin grinned like the Collin of old. "A better place, old buddy, a better place." Cuffing Jackson on the back one last time, Collin bowed and strode out the door, breathing deeply to fill his lungs before finally heading for home.

"It's natural to be nervous," her mother was saying, but Faith wasn't so sure. She had never imagined her wedding day like this. She couldn't seem to shake the uneasiness. The music played, a soft ethereal melody floating through the air along with a heavy mist that swirled, compelling her toward a final destiny. Everything seemed so beautiful, so perfect, and yet she was anxious. The nervousness remained until she saw her father smile, with her mother close by his side. The feeling of peace their love always produced settled on her like the mist in the air. I'm ready, *she thought, and entered the sanctuary. She saw him then, more handsome than she remembered, and her heart raced like the wind. He took her hand as they stood before God and man.*

"Do you take this man?"

"I do," she whispered and felt his lips on hers, warm and unwavering. "I love you . . ." she said, and meant it with all her heart.

"Collin, wait!"

He turned in the dark to see a young woman hurrying toward him, her tawny hair whipping in the wind as she ran. She stopped before him, smiling nervously, cheeks flushed and eyes bright as she briskly rubbed her arms to ward off the chill of the night. "What's your hurry?" she breathed. "I seem to remember you owe me a dance."

Collin smiled as her eyes met his, and there was no mistaking the invitation being issued. His heart picked up pace, more out of habit than desire, and his mouth went dry. Swallowing hard, he kept his tone light. "I do at that, Shannon, but I'm afraid it will have to keep a while. I'm leaving in the morning, and I best be getting home to bed."

She rested her hand on his arm, and the smile on her lips broke into a grin. She gazed up at him from under silky lashes. "Even better."

He could feel the old, familiar heat begin to burn before he gently pushed her back, his heart thudding in his chest. He hadn't been with a woman since the night he had fallen to his knees in the moonlight and given his heart to God. Hadn't wanted to, hadn't needed to. His mind was made up. He was through living for his own desires. Now he was living for God's, a commitment on which his heart and his head were in total agreement. But right now, with Shannon only a breath away—so soft, so sweet, so willing—well, suddenly his body wasn't so sure. Despite the coolness of the night, he could feel the sweat beading at the back of his neck.

"As tempting as that is, Shannon, I really need to go home—to sleep."

Unwilling to take no for an answer, she casually slid her hands down the sides of his waist. "Come on, Collin, it'll be fun," she whispered, "for old time's sake?"

Electricity jolted through him before he grabbed her hands and pushed them away. The muscles tensed in his face. "Shannon, no!"

She staggered back in apparent shock. "But, why? You've never objected before . . ."

Shame flushed in his face. "I know, and I owe you an apology for all the times I took advantage of you. I hope you can forgive me."

She blinked. "What do you mean, Collin? I wanted it as much as you."

His face gentled as he looked in her eyes. "No, you just wanted to be loved as much as I did. Unfortunately, neither of us knew we were going about it in the wrong way. You're too good for that, Shannon, too special."

Her cheeks flamed with embarrassment. "Yeah, right, Collin. I'm special, all right. That's why you're turning me away."

He folded her hand in his, his voice barely a whisper. "You are—very special. Maybe not to the men you've been giving yourself to, but to someone who loves you with a passion you never dreamed possible."

She took a step back. "Who?"

"God loves you, Shannon, and he has a plan for your life."

He heard her gasp as her eyes opened wide. "What? You, Collin? You're preaching God?"

A sheepish smile creased his lips, and he combed his fingers through his hair. "Yeah, it is pretty crazy, isn't it? But he bailed me out on a field in France, and I can tell ya the life that passed before my eyes was anything but pretty. I realized the huge void I was trying to fill with women and booze could only be filled by him. We're a team now, and I'm at peace for the first time in my life." He tilted his head and grinned. "You should try it."

She rubbed her arms. "Goodness, Collin, I wouldn't know where to start . . ."

He laughed and slung an arm around her shoulder. "How about starting with a cup of coffee at my house? It's not too late, and I have a feeling my mother will have a pot brewed and waiting. What do you say—great coffee and a new life—I guarantee it's a deal you can't refuse."

She smiled and took his arm. Her eyes sparkled. "So I'm going home with you after all, am I now? There'll be talk, you know."

Collin laughed and squeezed her shoulder, steering her down the street. "And it's only the beginning, Shannon darlin', only the beginning."

She twitched, and it woke him. His eyes were heavy with sleep as he slumped on the couch, arms wound around her while she slept on his chest. Mitch had no idea what time it was, but he knew it was late. How long had they slept? She twitched again and then moaned, and he stroked her hair, resting his face against it. He knew he should wake her, or at least carry her to her room, but he couldn't. There were so few moments left. And so, he remained still, listening to the sound of her soft breathing. Occasionally she would flinch so hard it would jolt him. *She's dreaming*, he thought, and his arms held her closer. He could hear her mumble, and he bent his head to listen, catching a gentle laugh.

"I do," she whispered, and Mitch smiled. "I love you, Collin, I do," she said, and his blood ran cold. She jerked once more and moaned before finally resting once again, totally unaware she had just inflicted more pain than he had ever known in his life. A sick feeling settled in his stomach. It had always been there, he knew, in the back of his mind, this gnawing fear she still cared for Collin, but he had refused to face it. He had been convinced, as she had been, that once they were married, Collin's hold on her would be broken. But the nausea in his gut told him he was wrong. Collin would always be there—in the family and in her heart. The reality all but paralyzed him.

He laid his head back and stared in the dark, his breathing

shallow while his brain wrestled with what to do. He couldn't live with knowing she loved another man. And he wasn't sure he could live without her. Mitch held her tighter and closed his eyes. "God help me," he whispered. And letting the pain go until tomorrow, he drifted off into what little rest was left in a night he wanted to forget.

Collin shut the door and locked it quietly, then turned to sling his coat on the hook. Rubbing his face, he yawned and glanced at the clock on the windowsill—1:30 a.m. He still had a chance for a decent night's sleep, he thought as he carried the dirty coffee cups from the table to the sink.

The evening certainly hadn't gone as he'd hoped—he lost the only woman he had ever really loved—yet somehow God had brought good from it, nonetheless, as promised. His lips tilted into a tired smile as he washed and dried the dishes, then placed them in the cupboard.

All things work together for good to them that love God . . .

Faith had quoted that once, he remembered, and the thought of her suddenly twisted his heart like a fist of iron. He turned out the light and headed to his room, choosing to think about the "good" God had brought instead. Shannon had given her life to God tonight, right there in the kitchen of the very man who had often made love to her in a bedroom down the hall, unbeknownst to his mother. Collin shivered inside at the flagrant arrogance and rebellion he had once shown to the God who loved him. A sharp stab of grief pierced his heart. How could he have been so blind, so hard, so very cold? His parents hadn't raised him that way; certainly his father, so kind and loving, had given him a better example to follow.

Collin closed the bathroom door and leaned over the basin to splash cold water on his face. He stared in the mirror for a moment, then leaned heavily against the sink, eyes tightly closed. God help him, how he had loved his father! He had wanted nothing more than to be just like him—a caring human being who was gentle and kind, a defender of the weak. Those were the true marks of a man, his father would tell him. Collin had longed to be that kind of man. And so he had learned to use his abundance of charm to make others feel special, loved, like his father had so often done for him.

Collin sighed, looked into the mirror once again, then proceeded to brush his teeth. Somewhere along the way it had all changed. Memories of his mother picking at his father—a barb here, a cut there—came back to him in a rush of sadness. She'd been raised to enjoy the finer things in life, and no matter how hard his father worked, it had never been enough. She had seen his gentleness as a weakness, his kindness as a flaw, and before his young eyes, Collin watched as she slowly sucked the life out of the marriage—and the man himself.

A malaise descended upon his spirit like the web of a spider, and Collin suddenly recognized the bitterness that had grown in him toward his mother, a bitterness that hardened and solidified upon the death of his father. It was that bitterness—that sin—that turned him away from God. Collin stared at his reflection in the mirror, his eyes rimmed with wetness at just how far he had strayed from his father's hand, and God's.

"Forgive me, Lord, for the bitterness I've held toward my mother all these years. I love her, and I choose to forgive her. Please give her happiness."

Turning out the light, Collin made his way down the dark hall, past his mother's room, only to stop at the faint sound of her voice edged with sleep.

"Collin?"

"Mother, why are you still awake? The coffee keeping you up?" He moved into the room and hunched beside her bed.

Her hand reached up to touch his cheek. "You walked Shannon home?"

He nodded and gently brushed the hair from her eyes. She smiled in the dark. "She's nice, Collin. I think things will go well for her now. She's lucky to have you as a friend."

Collin felt the sting of tears in his eyes. His laugh was harsh. "Tonight, yes—in the past, no, I don't think so. But, she is on her way now, Mother, and that's what matters."

"You are too, aren't you, Collin? You're finally back on track, well on your way to being the kind of man your father wanted you to be, I think." Katherine McGuire squeezed her son's hand. Tears glinted in her eyes. "I'm so very proud of you, Collin. Your father would be too."

A lump sealed his throat as he leaned to put his arms around his mother. Tears blurred his eyes, and without the slightest embarrassment, he clutched her tightly, an overwhelming rush of love welling his heart. "Mother, I hope you can forgive me for all the grief I've caused, and for all the bitterness I've held against you. I love you. I've always loved you."

Katherine McGuire's body quivered with a sob as she gripped her son in her arms. "I know, son. And I love you too. More than you'll ever know. And I loved your father . . ." Her voice broke as she clung to him. "I never fully appreciated what a good man he was until it was too late. Will you forgive me for that, Collin?"

Collin pulled away to smile into his mother's face. He reached out a hand to stroke her hair. "I already have. And if I'm not mistaken, I'd say we're both well on our way." He kissed her cheek and stood, then pulled the covers tightly to her chin. "Good night, Mother. Sleep well."

"Good night, Collin, you too. Sweet dreams."

His smile was thin as he made his way to his room.

Sweet dreams had been noticeably absent from his life for well over a year now, he thought dryly. He unbuttoned his shirt and tossed it on the chair, then did the same with his trousers. After climbing into bed, he stretched out on the cool sheets, arms behind his head as he stared at the ceiling. All at once, thoughts of Faith's fiery kiss invaded his thoughts, and a slash of heat shot through him along with a flicker of pain.

"No!" he said out loud, the sound of his voice shrill to his own ears. "She doesn't belong to me, God; please take her out of my mind." He turned on his side and squeezed his eyes shut, but it was no use. He saw her again, laughing, teasing, her eyes searching his as they talked in the kitchen, and a desperate longing filled his soul. He couldn't forget the look on her face. She had been stunned at the change in him, almost a look of alarm . . .

He sat up abruptly. A flash of heat soaked him, causing sweat to trickle his neck. He found himself falling to his knees beside the bed, hands grasped tightly in prayer. His muscles, layered with sweat, strained in the dark. "Oh, God, you're the desire of my heart now, not her. Help me to let her go. All the longing and passion I have for her, take it and use it for you. Use me, God, any way you want. Just take me where you want me to go."

Slowly he rose from the floor and tumbled back into bed, all energy depleted. He closed his eyes again and saw her face, but this time peace filled his soul. He loved her. Loved her with the spiritual intensity she had always longed for, an intensity she had introduced him to, an intensity sanctioned by God. Love like that just didn't vanish with the utterance of a prayer. It took time to heal, time to redirect. And so he would use it instead—the beautiful power of it to do God's bidding. He would pray. Every thought of her would become a prayer, a blessing on her head. He would return to her, through the depth of his love, the good she had brought to him. And he knew to the core of his being that in the process of blessing the one he could never have, he would find his way to peace.

Marcy opened her eyes to the final shaft of sunlight she would ever see streaming through her bedroom window, a blinding reminder of just how dark her life had become. She squinted to block it out and turned in the bed, her arm falling upon the emptiness beside her. She sat up, eyes wide, looking for her daughter, and wondered if she had risen early because she couldn't sleep. That was more her pattern than Faith's, but Faith was, after all, the one being left behind. Perhaps the loneliness had begun to set in.

Marcy rose from the bed and grabbed her robe. Wrapping it tightly around her, she tiptoed down the stairs into the parlor that was now filled with morning. She stopped at the door. There they lay, the two of them, sound asleep on the couch. Mitch sat, his arms draped over Faith while she rested, her legs curled on the sofa and her head in his lap. Marcy blinked. How in the world could anyone sleep like that, she wondered, and then smiled when she realized there would have been a time she would have taken them to task for such an incident.

She gently shook Mitch's shoulder, and the blue eyes opened, filled with fatigue. She smiled. "Good morning. I trust you slept well?" she asked, and he seemed embarrassed as he shifted on the sofa. Marcy put her hand on his shoulder. "No, it's all right. Are you ready for coffee now, or do you need to go up and get a few more hours of decent sleep? We've got the time, you know—ship doesn't sail until late this afternoon."

Mitch blinked, then rubbed his eyes and yawned. "No, I wouldn't sleep." He put his hand on Faith's head and stroked her hair while Marcy watched. "Faith," he whispered, "we fell asleep on the couch. I think you better get up."

Faith stirred, her eyes lidded with confusion. "What?" she asked, then bolted upright when she saw Marcy.

Marcy smiled. "It's all right, Faith; I understand how you could have fallen asleep. I'm just worried the sleep you did manage to get wasn't as restful as it might have been. Do you need to go up and get into bed?"

Faith shook her head and groped at her hair to pull it away from her face. "No . . . no, I'll be fine. I can always sleep in tomorrow. We've got too much to do."

Marcy patted her cheek. "You'll feel better when you freshen up," she said, heading for the kitchen, "*and* get a good hot cup of coffee inside of you." She disappeared through the door.

Faith hesitated before turning to Mitch. "Good morning," she whispered, rubbing her arms to hide her awkwardness. "Goodness, I guess we've spent our first night together. I hope I didn't drool on you."

"No," he said quietly.

She squinted a bit. "Are you all right?" Her hand reached to touch his cheek. "You look . . . drained. But then I guess you would. I hogged the couch, didn't I?"

"Completely," he said with a faint smile.

She laughed. "I'll do better, I promise." His smile faded enough to catch her eye. "What?" she persisted, her brows crinkled in concern.

He stared with sober eyes, and his voice held no mirth. "Are we doing the right thing?"

She felt her face go pale. "What?" she asked again.

He stood and stretched, his eyes brooding. "Getting married. Is it what you want?" He watched her carefully, as if measuring her response—the way she looked at him, the color in her face, her tone.

She suddenly felt chilled and buffed her arms with her palms. "Of course it is, Mitch. Why would you ask that? As a matter of fact, I just dreamed of our wedding last night."

"I figured you were dreaming of a wedding," he said. "You said 'I do.'"

"Well, then, look at that. I can't even be without you in my dreams. What more proof do you need than that?" she asked with a laugh.

"More, I'm afraid."

Her heart stopped. "What are you talking about?"

He closed his eyes and rubbed the bridge of his nose. "It's not my name you said, Faith."

The oxygen swirled still in her lungs. "What?"

His eyes snapped open, and his pupils dilated in anger. "It wasn't our wedding."

"That's not true! You were there. We were married!"

"All I heard was his name. You said, 'I love you, Collin, I do.'"

She recoiled as if he slapped her. "No! That didn't happen." Closing her eyes, she put her hand to her head and tried to think, to remember. She thought of Collin, of how she felt when he held her, kissed her, and a sick feeling buzzed inside. Her eyes flew open. "I love you!" she cried. She reached for him, but he stepped back.

"Do you love him too?"

Her heart thudded, and her gaze dropped to the floor. "I don't know," she whispered.

He grabbed her then, his fingers gouging her shoulders. "You do know—you're lying to me! Tell me the truth. Do you still love him?"

She jerked away, wet fury stinging her eyes. "Yes!" she screamed, and his face calcified to stone. He spun around. She clutched his arm. "Mitch, don't do this. I want to marry you!"

He turned, his blue eyes glazed with ice. "Perhaps we better sleep on it."

Her temper flashed. "I just did, and I want to marry *you*. I won't lie to you, Mitch, ever again when it comes to Collin. No, I'm not over him yet—I realized that fully last night. But the fact of the matter is he's leaving, and in a very short time I am too. There's nothing more for me here. I want to go home—home to Ireland and to you."

"And if he marries Charity? How am I supposed to cope with that? Knowing he's part of our lives forever, part of you forever . . ."

She put a hand to her throat, the taste of fear weighting her tongue. "Collin wouldn't want to live in Ireland, I'm sure, if he even marries Charity. We still don't know that for sure."

A spasm jerked in his jaw. "No," he whispered, "all we do know for sure is that you love him . . . and that he loves you."

She gasped at the sound of his words and dropped to the sofa, her hand shielding her eyes. "He doesn't love me . . ."

"The devil he doesn't! Do you think I'm blind? The way he looks at you makes me sick. But even that didn't matter until I saw how you looked at him. It tears my heart out, Faith, and I'm not sure I can handle it."

She started to cry. "So, what do we do?"

"I don't know. Maybe we need to give it a rest for a while. God knows we could use some time apart to pray about it."

She nodded and wiped the tears from her eyes, then stood to face him. "I love you, Mitch," she whispered.

His mouth tightened in a hard line. "I know. As much as you can with another man in your heart. But I won't share you, Faith, not with any man."

She nodded again and took a deep breath. She pried the

ring from her finger and held it out with a quivering hand. "Keep it for me, will you?" He stared at it for a moment, then took it and dropped it in his pocket.

She pushed the hair from her eyes and tried to smile. "Goodness, no wonder you want to postpone the engagement," she said, attempting to be light, "I must look frightful! I better go freshen up." Without a backward glance, she fled the room, fighting a fresh blur of tears as she ascended the stairs.

The morning was strained, but then Marcy wasn't surprised. Why should any of them be happy, she thought. They were all being torn—she from the life she'd known, Mitch from the woman he loved, and Faith from everything she held dear. It was not a day to remember; it was a day to forget, and for Marcy, the memory of it could not pass soon enough.

She fixed them breakfast, although none of them really ate; each picked at their plate as if their thoughts and appetites were somewhere else. Marcy sensed tension between Faith and Mitch but attributed it to sheer anxiety at their pending separation. They would be together again soon enough, she mused, and the thought warmed her. Unlike she and Patrick, she suddenly remembered, and the warmth was pushed aside, as always, by the cold grip of reality.

The plan for the day was simple enough. Mitch and she would assist Faith in packing up as much of the house as they could. They would leave only a few things for Faith until the house could be sold and their lives in Boston put to rest. Faith might even move in with Mrs. Gerson for a while, Marcy thought, although she suspected her daughter would stay until the bitter end. Her daughter's heart was tenacious in its clinging to the things and people she loved, and Marcy knew she loved this house, or at least the life it once held for her.

"Why don't you two start here and pack up as much as you can? I'll head upstairs and finish the bedrooms," Marcy said.

"We'll make short work of it, Mrs. O'Connor," Mitch assured her, and Marcy gave him a tired smile before leaving the kitchen.

Mitch rose to his feet with a sour feeling in his stomach. Faith looked up. "Is that all right with you?"

"I'm not fragile, Faith," he said with a hard stare. "I won't break if we're alone in the same room together."

She bit her lip. "I know. I just meant—"

"I know what you meant," he said curtly. He moved to the counter to commence packing.

They worked quietly side by side, wrapping dishes in newspaper before packing them away into boxes and crates throughout the room. There was a mundane ease to the task, which helped for the moment to quell the uneasiness he felt. Eventually, they began to talk about things that didn't hurt as much—her job at the *Herald*, Mrs. Gerson, Maisie and some person named Danny whom Maisie was seeing.

It didn't take long for the laughter to surface, and Mitch sensed his anger fading, a development that only caused him alarm. He needed the anger to stay strong. If he lost it, there was no telling what he would do. And he couldn't afford to relent, not on this. When the sound of her laughter would soften his heart, he would remember Collin. Then the edge would return, keeping his feelings safely pinned beneath the heat of his anger. He could do this, he thought. He would get through this day and on that ship with his anger intact, where he could put a little distance between them—distance to think, distance to pray, and distance to get on with his life if he had to.

Marcy silently made her way from bedroom to bedroom, packing away the few things still left after days of dismantling each of her family's rooms. She moved slowly, her face void of any expression as she methodically went about the business of storing their lives into crate after crate. All of the rooms were mostly barren by now, except for Sean and Steven's, where Mitch had stayed, and her own, of course, where she and Faith had slept, when sleep came. More often than not, it evaded them altogether.

Marcy stood in the hall and stared at the only room left to pack. For a moment, she couldn't move, or wouldn't, so unwilling was she to face her final moments in the room she had shared with Patrick. The door was closed, and a part of her wanted it to remain that way. Opening it would only subject her to further pain, and yet, she knew that this would be her moment of closure, her final good-bye to the man whose love was still more real than his death.

Straightening her shoulders, she walked to the door and pushed it open. She caught her breath, totally unprepared for the grief that gripped her heart. She stood there, hand propped against the side of the door as her legs weakened and tears sprang to her eyes. The sunlight filled the room with its glorious light—the same light where she had awakened for over twenty-one years next to the man who had been the light of her life. The room had been stripped except for the bed and a few items on the bureau, but Marcy looked at the bare walls and stark furnishings and saw only the years of joy she had known.

She moved to the bureau and raised her hand to trace the outline of the pitcher and glass sitting next to her perfume and toiletries. Her thoughts wandered to the night Patrick had come home from Brannigan's, liquor on his breath and perfume on his clothes. She smiled, recalling how he'd tiptoed into the room and gargled with her perfumed water before sneaking into bed. She had been so wounded, and he had been so tender . . .

Her eyes squeezed shut, sending hot tears streaming down her face. *No*, she thought to herself, *I won't think about that now*. She turned to strip the bed and stopped, taking his pillow in hand as she stood transfixed. Slowly, painfully, she wrapped her arms around it and closed her eyes, breathing in the scent of him with his musk soap and hint of pipe tobacco, and her heart ached for his touch. She looked at the bed where he had held her and loved her and given her his children. She collapsed on it, and a choked cry escaped her lips. Clutching his pillow in her arms, she rolled into a fetal position and wept, her anguish rebounding once again.

"Oh, God," she cried through broken sobs, "I can't live without him! Everywhere I go, I see his face and hear his voice. Why did you allow this? Why? Why did you take him?"

"Marcy . . ." She heard the voice of God more clearly and audibly than she had ever heard it before. She listened intently, a strange warmth flooding her soul.

"Marcy," it said again, and her heart froze. "He kept me alive for this moment."

The room grew hazy white around the edges as she looked up. She screamed, and her eyes blurred with wetness as she stared. Frantically, she blinked the tears away, and when she looked again, he was still there, standing in the doorway. She screamed again and he laughed. Then she did, and within two great strides, her husband was holding her in his arms, hoisting her from the bed.

"Oh, Patrick!" She wept as she seized him, unwilling to let go, even to look into his face. She could feel his lips in her hair, on her neck, and she cried harder until he picked her up and placed her back on the bed. He crawled in beside her and clutched her tightly.

"How?" she cried, her fingers digging into his back. She felt the movement of his laughter against her cheek as she pressed hard against his chest. "They said you were dead!"

He pulled back to take her face in his hands.

"Not dead," he said with a faint smile. "Wounded. Enough to be unconscious awhile."

"A coma?" she asked, her hand tenderly exploring his face.

Patrick nodded and rubbed the back of his head. "A piece of shrapnel put a pretty good dent in my skull, but I made it."

"But they said you were buried in France—with military honors. How could they make such a mistake?"

His smile faded. "They buried my friend, Thomas LaRue. They thought it was me."

"Was he the friend you tried to save, or did he save you?"

"How did you know that?"

Marcy gently touched the back of his head and shivered. She stroked his cheek again to make sure he was real. "The soldiers who notified us . . . they said you died trying to save a friend. They said you were a hero."

Patrick's eyes were somber. "Some hero. I got myself wounded and LaRue killed trying to get him back to the barracks. He was sick, and I was afraid he would die."

Marcy reached to brush her lips against his, and he kissed her back, jerking her to him with a force that sent a wave of heat pulsing through her.

She pulled away, breathless. "But, Patrick, how could they make such an awful mistake?"

"LaRue said he was dying, but I refused to believe it. He wanted me to make sure his wife got the cross he wore, but it was tangled with his dog tags. I argued with him, but he insisted. To appease him, I put it around my neck, fully intending to return it once I got him to the billet. But we never made it. I felt something hit my head, and I could tell I was blanking out. I grabbed his chain from my neck and put it on his arm before passing out. Only, it wasn't his chain; it was mine. LaRue died, and they thought it was me."

Marcy stared, her eyes and mouth gaping as tears puddled her cheek. She put her hand to her lips. "Oh, Patrick, I wanted to die, I missed you so much."

He buried his face in her hair, and his voice brimmed with emotion as he held her close. "I know, Marcy, I'm so sorry. I notified your mother before I was to ship out, and that's when I discovered you'd gone to Boston. I came directly here."

"They know you're alive?" she cried, and he nodded. "Thank God!" she whispered and then suddenly sat upright on the bed. "Why didn't they send me a telegram? Why didn't you?"

He gazed up at her, his lips suddenly solemn. "I'm sorry, Marcy, but a cold telegram would have arrived only days prior, and I . . . I wanted to see—no, I had to see—your face . . . when you found out. I had to."

Her lips parted in shock. She slapped him on the chest. "Patrick O'Connor," she screamed, "how dare you put me through such torture!"

He grinned and traced his finger on her arm. "Forgive me, Marcy. But like I said—God kept me alive for this moment—the moment I could touch you again, love you again . . ."

She caught her breath. He smiled, his eyes never leaving hers as he leaned to kiss her. The minute their lips touched, he pulled her to him, his hands hot as they caressed her body.

"Oh, Patrick, there's no way I can tell you how much I missed you," she whispered.

All at once, he pulled away. Standing up, he quietly walked to the door while Marcy sat up in surprise. She watched as he closed it, her heart beating wildly. He was thinner, but muscular, she thought, and a lump bobbed in her throat when she heard the lock click. Turning around, he slowly walked to the bed with a grin on his face. "Try," he whispered.

Her cheeks burned as heat jolted through her. Easing back on the bed, she tossed a strand of hair over her shoulder and returned his grin with a saucy one of her own. "Thought you'd never ask, soldier."

His laugh was decadent as he sank beside her, pulling her to him with an urgency that made her dizzy. "Oh, Patrick, I love you so much," she breathed. Her pulse pounded as his lips traveled her neck and shoulders. Her hands couldn't get enough of touching him, and he responded by kissing her hard on the mouth, passion raging through them like wildfire.

"It was thoughts of you, Marcy, that kept me sane," he whispered in her ear, "and thoughts of *this* that drove me crazy." He laughed and rolled on his back, his eyes wicked with desire. In one abrupt motion, he pulled her to him and kissed her, enflaming the fire within until it was out of control.

Never in all her twenty-one years had Faith known such gratitude as this, sitting across from her father and mother in a disrupted kitchen, laughing and crying as they sipped endless cups of coffee. Her father looked leaner and harder, perhaps his face more lined from the weathered look of a soldier too long in the trenches, but handsome as ever. He sat lounging in the chair, his arm draped over her mother's shoulder. Marcy's eyes glowed as she snuggled near, leaning against his chest as if she couldn't quite get close enough. Indeed, she couldn't. She had her husband back from the dead, and Faith suspected she wouldn't let him too far out of range anytime soon.

Faith would never forget the moment he entered the kitchen. She and Mitch had been talking about something Maisie had said when the door swung open. She had assumed it was her mother and continued wrapping newspaper around the plate she'd been holding. "Are you done already?" she had asked, her back to the door. And then she heard him laugh.

"More than done," he said.

The plate in her hand crashed to the floor. She whirled around, and her hand flew to her mouth as a faint cry issued forth. In the next moment, she was bolting across the room, flinging herself into his arms. Patrick scooped her up off the floor and gave her a ferocious hug. "Oh, I've missed my girl!" he said with a throaty laugh.

She clutched his neck, sobbing in his arms. "Daddy, oh Daddy . . ."

Patrick smiled and put her back down. "Look at you! You've gone and grown up on me."

"They said you were dead . . ."

"And you believed them?" he scoffed. "Where's your faith, young lady?" He stroked the tears from her cheek. "I'll tell you all about it soon enough. But for now, where's your mother?" His eyes scanned the kitchen and rested on Mitch.

Faith blushed. "Oh, Father, this is Mitch. I wrote you about him; he's my . . . well, we were . . . engaged."

Patrick's eyebrow arched in surprise. "Were?"

Mitch held out his hand to Patrick, a grin on his face. "It's a real pleasure to meet you, Mr. O'Connor. Faith has talked so much about you, I feel like we've already met."

"Good to meet you too, Mitch, but I hope you'll excuse

me if I cut this short for now." His eyes twinkled. "You see, I have an important message for my wife. Where is she?"

"In her bedroom," Faith said with a giggle. "Uh, excuse me . . . *your* bedroom," she corrected, prompting a wink from her father before he left the kitchen.

The excitement coursed through Faith's body as she thought about what her mother's reaction would be. Within seconds she heard a scream, and then another, and she grinned at Mitch, her hands over her heart. "I tell you Mitch, theirs is the most romantic relationship I've ever seen."

Mitch smiled faintly.

"Ours was too," she whispered, her voice shy. He flinched and turned away to grab another plate. She sighed. So that was how he wanted it, she thought sadly, reaching for a dish to wrap. "What time does your ship pull out again?" she asked, changing the subject.

Mitch looked at his watch briefly, then returned his attention to wrapping one of Marcy's huge salad bowls. "Five," he said, his tone flat.

"What time is it now?"

"Noon." He never missed a beat putting the newspaper-wrapped bowl into a crate. He grabbed another.

Faith eyed him, somewhat annoyed. "Is this what the next few hours are going to be like? Because if they are, I'd just as soon you leave now."

He slowly turned, his blue eyes glinting like quartz. "I'll leave when I'm good and ready."

Heat flooded her cheeks. "Michael was right. You are pigheaded."

"Words spoken by the master," he remarked dryly. *Stay angry*, he told himself. She spun around with her hands clenched on her hips. "I wouldn't marry you if you got down on your knees and begged."

Mitch glanced at her out of the corner of his eye. "Well, we both know that's not going to happen. If memory serves, I believe I'm the one who called the engagement off."

He watched the fuse lick its way to the dynamite. Her green eyes sparked with anger, and her lips pressed white. She turned and kicked an empty crate.

Mitch felt his resolve thawing. He fought a smile twitching at the corners of his lips. "Your temper is going to get you into trouble one of these days."

Her chin lashed up in defiance. "Well, you won't have to worry about that, now will you? I never would have said yes if I'd known what a bully you were."

"You knew," he said curtly, then turned to face her full on. "And trust me—I never would have asked had I'd known how much grief you'd be."

Blood surged into her cheeks. She slapped at a wild strand of hair in her eyes and then struggled to compose herself. Her eyes iced to cool. "Forgive me for ruining your life," she whispered. "Now, if you'll excuse me, there's packing I can do upstairs." She turned.

He swore out loud and strode toward her, eyes blazing and jaw clenched tight. He reached for her arm and spun her around. "I don't want to fight with you."

"You could have fooled me."

He took a deep breath and loosened his grip. Instantly, his anger faded to hurt. "Go home with me," he whispered, his tone suddenly pleading. "Your mother won't be sailing now; you can use her ticket. Faith, I love you . . ." He released his hold, then slammed his palm against the wall. "I wish I didn't, but I do."

She blinked, her anger melting away. Everything had happened so quickly, it hadn't occurred that her mother would stay . . . that they would all stay. Only moments ago, Boston had been dead to her and Ireland the home she longed for. Suddenly, in the time it took for her father to walk through that door, it all changed again, and the shock of it chilled her. Mitch seemed to be watching her closely, his breathing suspended as he awaited her answer.

"Oh. I hadn't realized . . . yes, of course Mother will stay . . ." she whispered.

He took her face in his hands. "Come with me," he said, bending to kiss her. Her pulse stirred, and then without warning, she thought of Collin. An awful ache severed her response.

"Come with me," he repeated, and she shivered in his arms when she realized she couldn't. All at once, in the time it took for the breath to rise and fall in her chest, she knew—knew that her life was here, here with her parents, in Boston. To begin again, after a painful delay, the life she had known and loved. And, she thought to herself with trembling, a life with Collin, if he would still have her.

Mitch searched her face, and what he saw must have spelled his doom. He dropped his hands to his sides.

"I can't," she whispered.

"I didn't think so." He slowly walked to the table and sagged into the chair, as if in a stupor. "But you know how stubborn we newsmen can be." He attempted a faint smile, then looked up. The smile faded. "It's over, isn't it, Faith?"

Her knees buckled at the weight of his words, and she gripped the wall to steady herself.

"I thought so," he said quietly. "The moment I saw that pretty-boy soldier standing in your kitchen, I had a hunch I was history."

She slacked against the wall, hand over her mouth.

He jumped up and walked to her side and folded her in his arms. His head rested on hers as she wept against his chest. He stroked her hair. "I'm going to be fine, you know. And so are you. We both know God's in control of our lives. This is his doing, not ours. Apparently he has something even better in mind for both of us."

Faith looked up through swollen eyes. "I do love you, Mitch."

"I know you do. What's not to love?" he asked, a shaky smile on his lips. "But, we both know it's Collin who has the corner on your heart."

He grabbed her chin with his hand. "So help me, if that fool doesn't appreciate what he has, I'll take him down, I swear I will. Nothing would give me more pleasure . . . except having you. If it doesn't work out, I want you on the first ship to Ireland. Understood?"

She nodded while her eyes pooled with tears once again. He wiped the wetness from her face and shook his head. "As God as my witness, never have I seen more tears in my entire life until I met you and your family. Tell me, please, that the O'Connor men aren't like this." He gave her a hug, then released her again. He picked up a wrapped dish from a crate and waved it in the air. "We've wasted enough time. Start unpacking."

For the first time that day, Faith sensed that the tension between them had finally eased, and the finality of their decision left them with a strange peace.

Eventually, Patrick and Marcy arrived in the kitchen, their faces aglow with the same love and tenderness that had mesmerized Faith her whole life. Mother and daughter took one look at each other, and the tears bubbled in unison. Patrick grinned at Mitch.

"Oh, Faith, isn't God wonderful?" her mother breathed. She touched her daughter's cheek. "I have my Patrick back, and you have your father! Who would have thought after all we went through that we would have our lives back again?" She wiped her eyes with her sleeve. "How about some lunch?"

Her father grinned again. "Well, I don't know about

Mitch, but this homecoming has helped me work up quite an appetite." His comment sent a soft blush into his wife's cheeks, and he laughed out loud. "Have I told you, Marceline, just how much I love you?"

"You have," she quipped with a twinkle in her eye, "but you're a year behind, I'm afraid, and you've got some making up to do."

"Well, I do," he stated. "And that goes for my girl, as well." He turned to Mitch. "Honestly, Mitch, do I or do I not have some of the most beautiful women in my life?"

Mitch smiled. "You're a lucky man, Mr. O'Connor."

Patrick shook his head and stretched back in his chair. "Oh no, my boy. I'm afraid luck has nothing to do with it, whatsoever. It's called 'blessed,' and I most definitely am."

26

They devoured egg salad and toast as if it were one of Marcy's Christmas feasts, then finished off the cobbler from the night before. When it was gone, they talked over coffee fresh brewed by Marcy as Patrick recounted his year in France for them.

For Patrick, it was therapeutic to laugh in this kitchen once again where so many good memories sheltered him from the horrors of war. He sipped his coffee, thoroughly enjoying Mitch as they chatted about the newspaper business and Michael Reardon.

All at once, Patrick set his cup down and turned his attention to Marcy. "So! Collin's home, is he now? How did he look?"

Mitch bounded up to get more coffee and brought the pot over, his eyes avoiding Faith's. "Anybody need a refill?" he asked.

Patrick nodded and held out his cup. "Thanks, Mitch." He took a sip. "Is he completely recovered from the chest wound?"

"He seems to be," Marcy said. "And he looks wonderful. A little thinner, perhaps—like you, my love, but handsome as ever."

"Good," he exclaimed. "Goodness knows I missed that boy. Truth be told, Mitch, he's like one of my own." Suddenly

Patrick bolted upright with a surge of adrenaline. "Faith, darlin', ring him up on the phone, will you? Tell him to come over, but don't say why."

Faith's head jerked up. Her eyes blinked wide. "I . . . I think he's gone," she stammered.

"She's right," Marcy chimed in. "Collin said he was leaving for New York this morning."

"New York!" Patrick cried. "What's in New York, for pity's sake?"

"A friend he wants to start a business with," Marcy said.

Patrick squinted, ridging his brow. "What about Charity?"

Marcy sighed. "Collin feels the war may have changed him too much to suit her—"

"Changed? What the devil is he talking about? The war's changed us all, but it doesn't change who you love."

Mitch shifted in his chair and cleared his throat, gulping the rest of his coffee. Faith fixated on a blob of uneaten egg salad on her plate while absently pushing it with her fork. She sighed and picked up her cup.

Marcy patted Patrick's hand. "It seems Collin has had an encounter with God, Patrick, and it's changed him. We talked for hours, and I didn't know this, but apparently before the war his belief in God was pretty minimal. I think we would have been alarmed had we known how much. But this friend of his, Brady—the one he hopes to go into business with—opened his eyes to the reality of God, and honestly, Patrick, he's like a different man. He reminds me of you, my love. But I am concerned he's not the man Charity fell in love with, and equally concerned she's not the woman he's looking to love."

Patrick's gaze flitted to Faith, and comprehension suddenly flooded his brain. So this was the reason her engagement to Mitch was off. He looked at his daughter, who sipped her coffee with an air of dejection, and then at Mitch, whose fingers idly twiddled the empty cup in his hands. Patrick sighed. He certainly would be glad when his daughters were all safely married. Their love lives took more shots at his emotional well-being than the Germans. Patrick was ready for a truce.

He turned his attention to Mitch. "I want to thank you for bringing Marcy home. I fully intend to reimburse you for the fare." Patrick's hold on Marcy tightened. "But obviously, she won't be going back."

Mitch nodded, a faint smile on his lips. "I figured as much, Mr. O'Connor. And no reimbursement is necessary. Your family has given me a lot of joy." He turned to Faith and reached to take her hand in his. "I need to be going," he whispered. "It's almost four o'clock, and my cab will be here in a few moments."

A faint gasp parted from his daughter's lips, and Patrick winced when a fresh wave of tears welled in her eyes.

Mitch smiled down at her. "Don't. You're going to get dehydrated." She jumped up to loop her arms around his neck. He closed his eyes, aware of a sick feeling in his gut.

"Mitch, I'm so sorry."

"Me too." He stroked her chin with his finger. Turning to Marcy, he held out his hand.

She stood and pushed it aside. "How dare you insult me with a handshake, Mitch Dennehy!" She threw her arms around him. "You're family."

"Thanks, Mrs. O'Connor. You have no idea how I wish I were." He extended his hand to Patrick. "A handshake okay with you, Mr. O'Connor?"

Patrick grinned and pumped his hand. "They're a weepy lot, aren't they, Mitch?"

Mitch laughed. "I'd say you have more waterworks on

your hands than the city water supply. Do they ever stop crying?"

Patrick shook his head. "Not even when they're happy."

Mitch reached into his pocket and pulled out his handkerchief. "Here, you need this more than I do," he said to Faith.

A horn sounded, and Mitch sighed. "Ireland calls." He turned to go.

"Mitch!" Faith ran to embrace him.

"You remember what I said," he whispered. "Ireland's there for you, if you ever need it."

She nodded and clenched his handkerchief to her mouth to stifle a sob.

Mitch didn't trust himself to look back as he walked to the door and pushed it open, but when he was on the other side, the breath left his lungs with a sharp pain.

He hated Collin McGuire, almost as much as he loved Faith, and he wondered if God could possibly honor a prayer for their relationship to fail. Probably not, he mused to himself. Although he was known for bucking most authority, Mitch knew in his gut this was one time, like it or not, he would have to submit. Like Faith had often said—it had to be God's way, not his. And Mitch had a sinking feeling when it came to Faith O'Connor, he didn't have a prayer.

Faith stood there sobbing, and her father pulled her into his arms while her mother hovered. "I'm so sorry, Faith," she whispered, stroking her daughter's hair. "I had no idea you and Mitch had called off your engagement. But things will work out, you'll see."

Faith wiped her eyes with Mitch's handkerchief. "I know, Mother. It's just so hard. Mitch is a wonderful man. It's difficult to let him go."

Patrick sat down and pulled Faith onto his lap like he'd done hundreds of times when she was a child, his arms wound around her as she rested her head against his chest.

Her mother sank into the chair beside them. "Why did you?" she asked.

Faith sniffed. "I couldn't bear the thought of leaving you and Father. With Father gone, it was easy to think about living in Ireland with all of us there. But now, I don't think I could stand to be there without you."

Patrick rubbed Faith's arms and glanced up at his wife. "It wouldn't have anything to do with Collin McGuire, would it?"

Faith stiffened.

Her mother blinked in surprise. "Why do you say that, Patrick?"

Patrick lifted Faith's head off his chest and held her chin with his hand. "Because you know, Marcy, she's always been in love with him. The only thing that ever really stopped her before was the fact Collin didn't believe in God."

Faith sat up abruptly, her eyes wide. "How did you know that?"

Patrick smiled. "He told me. Right after he told me he loved you."

Faith froze and Marcy gasped. "What? When did he tell you that?" Marcy demanded.

Patrick's look was tender. "A few weeks before he left. I wanted to tell you, Marcy, but if you'll remember, you were a bit emotional, and I didn't want to add to it."

She nodded slowly, then touched Faith's arm. "Do you love Collin?"

Faith looked at her without answering.

"Faith! Do you love him?"

She took a deep breath. "Yes, Mother, I do. I've always

loved him. I guess I've never stopped, even with Mitch, and Mitch knew it. That's why he broke the engagement."

"Well, then, if you love him, and he loves you—call him!"

"But I'm not really sure he still loves me," she said, her voice wavering, "although he did kiss me when Mitch took Mrs. Gerson home last night. But even so, I'm not sure . . ."

"Yes, you are," Patrick said firmly, "or you would have never let Mitch walk out that door. Call him!"

"Well, he never said it directly . . ."

Patrick pushed her off his lap. "Call him—now!"

Faith chewed her lip. "He's gone, I just know it." Her hand shook as she cranked the phone. Patrick and Marcy watched as she clutched the receiver. She spoke briefly to the operator, then fell silent, continuing to work her lip as she waited. "Yes, hello . . . Mrs. McGuire? This is Faith O'Connor. Yes . . ." She paused for a moment, then laughed. "Yes, he did. It was wonderful seeing him again. And I understand congratulations are in order? Collin tells us you're to be married."

Her mother and father exchanged looks as Faith paused again, a tight smile on her face. "Yes, well, that's why I'm calling, as a matter of fact. You see, the most amazing thing has happened—my father is alive, and he's home, and I wanted to surprise Collin."

Patrick pulled Marcy on his lap while Faith nodded silently, the smile fading from her lips. "Yes, of course, please tell him when you hear from him. And good luck to you, Mrs. McGuire." She replaced the receiver slowly and turned to her parents, tears brimming.

Her father eyed her sternly. "Don't start with that again, young lady; I can't take much more of your heartbreak. Just come over here and tell us what she said."

Sniffing back the tears, Faith sat and took a deep breath.

"He's gone; he left this morning. She doesn't know where to reach him, but he promised to call when he was settled in New York." She looked up at her parents. "It could be weeks before we hear from him," she whispered.

Marcy stood and wrapped her arms around Faith's neck. "He'll call," she insisted, then kissed her daughter's head. "You've waited this long; you can wait a few weeks more. Besides, at the moment, that's not our biggest problem."

Marcy raised a brow at Patrick, and he moaned, slapping a hand to his forehead. "I completely forgot about Charity."

"Oh no . . . so did I!" Faith groaned.

"I suppose we all have," her mother murmured, slumping into the chair.

"Sweet heaven above, why do you girls have to be so blasted complicated?" Patrick said.

"It's going to work out, Patrick," Marcy insisted, a note of confidence in her voice. "I don't know how or when, but God will work it out; I'm sure of it."

"Not without heartbreak, I'm afraid," Patrick replied.

Marcy looked at her husband pointedly. "Well, at least heartbreak doesn't kill you. I should be proof of that after what you've put me through the last few months."

Patrick grinned. "I plan to make it all up to you."

"I plan to let you," she countered, then reached for her daughter's hand. "We need to pray about this, I think. And while we're at it, I think Mitch could use a few prayers, as well. I really hate to lose that boy. He would have been such an asset to the family."

"If Charity has her way, he still might be," Faith muttered.

Patrick looked confused. "What?"

Faith and Marcy glanced at each other. "It's a long story, Patrick," Marcy said. "Are you sure you're up to it?"

Patrick joined hands with his wife and daughter. "I've

got nothing but time, my love," he said with a twinkle in his eye. "Although I'm not sure that even the shock of war has prepared me to hear it." And bowing his head, he led his family in prayer.

It was almost the perfect Thanksgiving, Faith thought, looking around the room filled with most of the people she loved. The war was over, and Sean had traveled from France to Ireland to bring Beth, Steven, Katie, and Blarney home. They just arrived the day before, sending the previously quiet O'Connor household into the blessed state of pre-war pandemonium.

Patrick was upset because Charity opted to stay with her grandmother for a while, but both Marcy and Faith were grateful. Marcy, because at least Bridget and Mima wouldn't lose their loved ones all at once, and because Charity would be there if anything happened to Mima.

Unfortunately, Faith's reasons were not as noble. She didn't look forward to confronting her sister again if Collin decided he loved her rather than Charity. But then, for all Faith knew, Collin could have written her sister and the two of them could be finalizing plans for their future even now.

Faith found herself pushing thoughts of Collin with Charity from her mind, as she often had to do since he'd left. He hadn't contacted his mother within the three weeks following Faith's call, but then Mrs. McGuire hadn't really expected him to, she said. She had given him a number where she could be reached over Thanksgiving, seeming to think she would hear from him then. And she took great pains to assure Faith that, when he did call, she would be sure to give him the good news about her father.

He was probably speaking to his mother right now from New York, she thought with a surge of hope, perhaps even calling yet this evening to talk to Patrick. Faith released a quiet sigh and looked around the table. Her father carved the turkey while Sean entertained them with stories of his adventures overseas. All the while, Katie did her best to swipe a few pieces of turkey when her father wasn't looking, giggling and slipping them under the table to Blarney. Faith couldn't help but smile at the sight of Blarney's tail, only partially visible as it swished back and forth, bunching Marcy's tablecloth and swatting at Beth.

Beth didn't seem to notice. She sat, gaze fixed on her father and brother, mesmerized by their tales of France, obviously breathless at the idea of such a romantic place. Steven, too, seemed enthralled with their stories, more for the war than the romance, and the looks he gave his father and brother were almost worshipful. Mrs. Gerson and her father chatted while her mother and she carted heaping bowls to the dining room table, which once again shimmered with candlelight and china.

When Patrick finished carving, he laid the knife aside and bowed his head. The others followed suit. "Heavenly Father, where would we be without you?" he whispered, a slight tremor in his voice. "You said you would never leave us nor forsake us, and you are faithful. We bow before you with such profound gratitude for your continued blessings. Please shine your light and your blessing upon our loved ones in Ireland—and in New York—and bless this bounty before us, and the hands that prepared it. Amen."

Faith felt warm as she sipped the wine her mother had poured and smiled as her father pulled the wishbone with Katie. She had wishes of her own tonight, she reflected, and wondered what Collin was doing. Did he even think about her anymore, or had he quickly pushed her from his thoughts, as she seemed to do with thoughts of him with Charity?

As evening wore on, Faith felt a heaviness settling, or maybe she was just tired. She looked at the clock, and her heart sank—nine o'clock—probably too late for him to call. Faith sighed. She would have to wait another day, if not longer. The thought depleted her.

"You look tired, Faith," her mother remarked with a knowing look. "Why don't you go on up to bed? Beth and Sean can help with what dishes are left."

"No, I'll help, Mother."

Marcy shook her head. "You've been helping all day. I could have never finished without you. I want you to go to bed and get some rest. Who knows what tomorrow will bring?"

"All right, Mother." Faith stood and bent to give her father a hug. "Good night, Daddy."

"I love my girl," he whispered back.

Circling the table, Faith hugged everyone, ending with Mrs. Gerson.

The old woman squeezed her hand. "Tell me, Faith, do you delight yourself in the Lord?"

"Goodness knows I've tried, Mrs. Gerson," Faith answered, a bit puzzled at the question.

"Then you have nothing to worry about, my dear. Your heart's desire is his promise."

"Thank you," Faith said quietly. "See you Saturday night?"

"I'm looking forward to it, my dear, as always. Good night."

Her mother followed her into the hall and watched as she climbed the stairs. "Faith?"

Faith turned.

"Mrs. Gerson's right, you know. You have nothing to worry about."

She managed a smile. "I pray you're right, Mother."

Once in her room, she didn't even turn on the light, but undressed in the dark and slipped her nightgown over her head. She brushed her teeth in the bathroom, then crawled into bed, her thoughts drifting, as always these days, to thoughts of Collin. She closed her eyes and saw his face, handsome and lean, those probing gray eyes and that ready smile, and a familiar warmth seeped into her bones. She sighed. Just once, she'd like to experience the flood of that warmth with God's full approval. It would be wonderful, she knew. Collin was, bar none, the most exciting man she had ever met, and it felt good—and so natural—to be thinking of him this way.

Faith opened her eyes and stared at the shaft of moonlight that split the room. He was out there, somewhere in New York, completely unaware she loved him and wanted him. Totally oblivious to the fact that, after all the times he had sought her love, she was finally ready to give it. He was, after all, her heart's desire. Had been from the start. Faith couldn't help but wonder if she was the desire of his too. *Oh, Lord, let it be!*

Closing her eyes, she felt the last of her energy drain from her body into the bed. With the prayer still warm on her lips and thoughts of Collin still warm in her mind, sleep lighted like the softest of butterflies, bringing with it new hope for tomorrow.

It was pure, breathless magic. Gliding on Katie's swings, Faith grinned at her sister Hope. The two sailed side by side into the heavens. They pumped in perfect harmony, breeze lashing their hair and toes skimming the sky. Higher and higher they flew, their bodies taut with exhilaration. Their laughter floated upon the wind as they thrust themselves into the blue, eyes open wide. Faith's heart, like her body, was soaring with joy. Never had she felt so free, so peaceful . . .

"Higher, Hope, higher!" she said, and Hope smiled back, aiming for the sky with all her might. God's love embraced them both, and a sensation of pure joy washed over her, sending goose bumps

throughout her body. "I love you, God," Faith whispered, and the delight of her soul was only him . . .

Faith opened her eyes and blinked. Moonlight flooded the room like the light of day. She sat up and peered at the clock—3:20 a.m. Lying back down, she thought of the dream that had awakened her, and a smile rested on her lips. Nothing, she decided, felt as wonderful as the love of God in your life. She breathed in deeply and then out again, her heart filled with a quiet joy. She could almost feel God's love—and Hope's—enveloping her there in the moonlit room, and tears sprang to her eyes. It was a graced moment, she was sure, one of those rare times when she felt the love of God to the core of her being. There in the dark, she spoke her gratitude to him, and her heart and emotions soared.

"No matter what happens, God," she whispered, "I know you love me and are with me always. I will worship you all the days of my life." Stretching, she sighed and closed her eyes, drowsiness settling once again.

And then she heard it. She sat upright and strained to listen, her heart hammering in her chest. It came again—the faint clink of something against the glass. Bolting from the bed, she ran to the window, her eyes searching the yard for what she hoped to see. But Marcy's garden was still, like the night, and Faith felt the peace of the prior moment shatter within. With a sick feeling in her stomach, she returned to bed, heaviness lodged in her heart. *You're a fool, Faith O'Connor*, something said in her mind. She shivered, struggling to regain the peace that had been hers only moments before.

Then she heard it again. This time she saw him, standing in the moonlight with that maddening smile, gazing up into her window. Her hand pressed hard against the frigid pane while her heart raced wildly. "Collin!" she whispered, feeling as if she might faint. Barely stopping to don slippers and housecoat, she tore down the stairs into the kitchen, ignoring Blarney as he trotted close on her heels. "Stay, Blarney," she whispered. Her breathing was heavy as she wrestled with the door. Flinging it wide, she stepped into the night, not even feeling the icy air that rushed against her. She clutched her housecoat and ran to the edge of the porch, a child on a treasure hunt, her eyes scanning the yard. "Collin!" she whispered.

Suddenly his strong arms encircled her waist. Turning, she stared up at him, her eyes glowing. She saw the curve of his smile in the moonlight, and warmth fanned through her like a warm breeze.

"My mother told me you called. Took me forever to get here," he said, picking her up in his arms and twirling her high in the air. His husky laugh vibrated in her ears. "I never thought I'd hear anything so wonderful as when she told me your father was alive. Sweet heaven above, I just want to run up there right now and wake him up." He put her down again. "Sorry, you must be cold." He started to take off his coat.

"No, Collin, let's just sit on the porch and share it."

He pulled her close, tucking her inside his jacket. Plopping into the swing, he bundled her in his strong arms. "You know, it would probably make a whole lot more sense if we went inside," he said with a chuckle. His breath escaped into the cold air like drifting puffs of smoke.

She shook her head. "Maybe in a minute or two. It's such a beautiful night, I'd just like to shiver out here for a while. Besides, knowing our past history, I have every confidence you can keep me warm." Faith chewed on her lip, suddenly shy.

He gave her a funny look. "I don't mind," he said nonchalantly, "but I sure don't think Mitch would like it."

Faith stared up at the moon. "Mitch doesn't have a whole lot to say about it."

His body tensed. He leaned forward. "He doesn't?"

Faith shook her head and held out her left hand.

Collin stared hard at her ring finger. He gripped her by the shoulders. "What happened?"

She took a deep breath and looked into his eyes, never even feeling the cold. "He said he wouldn't share me with another man."

Collin blinked. All at once, the dangerous smile traveled his lips, and her body flooded with a familiar surge of heat. His gray eyes narrowed. "What other man?"

"I think you know," she said. "I think you've always known."

She heard him laugh, husky and low, before he pulled her close. His face was just inches from her own, and his gray eyes were smoldering. "What are you saying?" he breathed.

Her pulse took off at the fire in his eyes. A lump bobbed in her throat. "I'm saying I love you and I want you."

She heard his breath catch, and then his mouth pressed hard against hers. She moaned and melted into his embrace, kissing him with all the passion she had saved just for him. "I love you, Collin McGuire—I've always loved you."

His breath was warm on her neck as he clutched her with a low groan. "Oh, Faith, I've waited so long!" He held her face in his hands, and then his mouth wandered wildly from her lips to her throat. Her hair spilled over his arms as he wrenched her against him. "Thank you, God," he whispered before kissing her again.

Breathless, she kissed him back. "Oh, Collin, I've wanted you for my own since the day Margaret Mary pushed me against that school-yard fence."

He suddenly pulled back to study her in the moonlight, his labored breathing billowing soft in the night. "More than you wanted Mitch?"

She nodded, answering him with a lunge, her mouth seeking his once again. She heard his low chuckle as he gripped her tighter, then his heavy sigh when he pushed her away. "Good. I want him out of your mind completely, understood? From the very beginning, Faith O'Connor, you were meant for me."

Faith nodded and threw her arms around his neck to kiss him once again. Exhaling slowly, he gently pried her arms away. "I don't know how in the world I'm going to keep my hands off you till the wedding, but I'm determined to do it."

She felt warm and heady, as if she'd had too many sips of wine. A low, throaty laugh rolled from her lips. "And what if I'm not?"

His smile was wicked. He traced his finger from her lips down to rest in the little hollow at the base of her neck, just above the nightgown that peeked through her robe. A sobering tremor of heat shot through her, causing her to gasp. She hurled his hand away.

He laughed. "Something tells me you will. But if not, you'll be to blame because I intend to do this the right way. His way, not ours, remember? We've got the rest of our lives to make love." He grinned in the dark. "And believe me, we will."

Heat shot to her cheeks, and he laughed again, tugging her back in the swing to sit beside him. He kissed her gently this time, then slowly released her, holding her hand while leaning back in the swing. Wetness shimmered in his eyes. "He did it," he whispered. "I never dreamed it was possible, that it could ever really happen. First, he gives me his love and forgiveness . . . and then he gives me you." His voice choked with emotion. "I never knew the love I needed was in him, Faith. Not until you. And now . . . now he's blessed me with the desire of my heart, and

I will never be the same." He wrapped his arms around her and buried his face in her neck.

"Me too," she whispered, tears streaming her cheeks. For several moments, they sat on the swing in sweet silence, resting in each other's arms. Faith tucked her head against his shoulder while a profound gratitude filled her soul. All at once, she sat up, her eyes rounded as she swiped at the tears on her face. "What about Charity?"

She saw the rise and fall of his chest, his warm sigh swirling into the frosty air. "We've corresponded, and it seems we both want different things."

"I don't understand that, Collin."

"Yeah, well, apparently somebody else caught her eye . . ."

Faith blinked. "Goodness, that was fast."

"Not really. It seems she's been smitten for a while, whoever he is."

Faith scrunched her nose. Bridget hadn't mentioned Charity having a new beau. And Charity never seemed even remotely interested in anyone else . . . Faith suddenly sucked in a breath.

Collin slanted a brow. "What?"

"Mitch!" she whispered, pressing her lips tight.

The smile faded from Collin's lips. "Do you care?"

Faith blushed. "Well, no, of course not. But honestly, Collin, I was engaged to the man—naturally it shocks me."

His arms clenched at the small of her back. "Well, no offense intended," he whispered with an edge of jealousy in his tone, "but Mitch can go to the devil."

She stroked his cheek. "Mitch is a good man, Collin," she said quietly. "If you knew him, you'd like him. And I care about him, I do. But he's not the man I've carried in my heart all these years, and he's not the man I'm going to marry."

Collin swallowed hard, then kissed her in a rush, his fingers twined in her hair.

She returned his kiss with a gentle one of her own, then sighed and rested her face against his soft flannel shirt. "You don't have feelings for Charity?" she asked, her tone hesitant.

"Not when I'm crazy in love with somebody else."

Her lips softened into a little-girl grin. "Who?" she breathed, wanting to hear him say it.

He lifted her chin. "I think you know. I think you've always known."

Without notice, he suddenly stood and plucked her from the swing, backing her against the wall with a gleam in his eye. "Faith O'Connor," he said with authority, "I'm going to court you—court you like you've never been courted before. And I'm going to make you fall madly in love with me."

"Too late," she quipped. "I already am."

The grin stretched across his lips as he grabbed her hand to pull her toward the door. "Oh no, Little Bit," he said in a hush. "We're not even close."